Time Traveler

1492

SEARCHING FOR TREASURED ANCIENT MANUSCRIPTS

ROBERT D. OBERST

GLOBAL FUTURE PRESS

Third Edition, June 2025

For permission requests or other information contact

Global Future Press

RobOberst@SBCGlobal.net

ISBN: 978-1-7366271-8-1, 978-1736627129, eBook: 978-1736627136

Dedication

T his book is dedicated to Frank Elliott and Hy Sockel, PhD., two highly intelligent, lifelong friends who helped me along my writing journey and recently passed.

Acknowledgements

I greatly appreciate my wife, Pat and dear friends, Col. Daryl Kelly Ph.D. and Carolyn Kelly's editing of this book and to all those who provided helpful feedback on *Time Traveler 1491*.

Contents

Recap of Time Traveler 1491

TRANSPORTED BACK TO THE 15TH CENTURY, RAND JOINS THE GLOBAL REVOLUTION

When venture capitalists stole his lucrative app, Rand sought solace on a backpacking expedition to the bottom of the Grand Canyon, where he slipped and was swept into the turbulent rapids. Nearly drowned, battered and bruised, he took refuge in a hidden cave, where a mysterious galvanic force overcame him. Barely able to move, he woke in the bed of a beautiful maiden who nursed him back to health in Ireland in 1491. While recovering, her father, Michael McCarron, Ireland's first printer, taught him the revolutionary profession that, similar to the Web five centuries later, was transforming the world. Becoming embroiled in castle politics but unskilled in their weapons, Rand had one advantage—a downloaded copy of Wikipedia on his iPhone, which he must access judiciously before its battery died.

After their London agent died, since about half of their sales and new titles came from there, Michael sent Rand to London to check on the operation and hire a new man to replace him. While traveling to London in the fall of 1491 on his grand adventure, Rand Roberts would remain oblivious to all that would transpire back in Bunkillarny. To him, the quaint, picturesque, seaside Irish village with its spectacular castle, glorious cathedral, and enchanting people had become home and family, a home he would remember fondly and yearn for during the inevitable travails on what would become an epic journey.

Bunkillarny also held the cave with the mysterious portal he hoped to enter to transport him back to San Francisco in the 2020s. He had finally become somewhat accustomed to 15th-century living and all its inconveniences—the frustratingly slow transportation; freezing, smoky, dim, candlelit rooms that required constant fire-stoking to emit a semblance of heat; manure-laden, muddy streets in an era with no TV, Internet or cell coverage. In some ways, he thought that this life was superior to one ensconced in impersonal digital technology that he was addicted to for at least fourteen hours a day. In an undefinable way, he somehow felt more himself, more authentic, but knew this was not where he belonged, and he greatly missed all those devices, his friends and his family.*

While away, he would not know of beloved King Edward's assassination back in Bunkillarny. During the annual fall hunt, after the king shot a five-point buck with his crossbow, his horse slipped on the icy fall leaves, throwing Edward to the cliff's edge. Instead of helping him, seeking revenge for being punished for his disgusting, sexual-predatory behavior, General Reginald Van Cleve III pushed the king off the 200-foot precipice. Dastardly Lord Boston was the only witness to the despicable act, who, in exchange for his silence, would become the chief minister of the shire.

Nor would Rand know of the tumultuous battle of Nealland, where Reginald betrayed the lawful heir to the throne, King Edward's oldest son, Prince John. Before he had been crowned, Reginald and Boston spread vicious rumors about Prince John, saying that the lying womanizer was unfit for the throne. John had married the King of Nealland's daughter, where he was given a large estate as a dowry. Reginald should have supported John when he and the Neallanders were attacked by the largest kingdom in northern Ireland, ruled by the O'Donnell clan. Instead, he had conspired with the O'Donnells and had his army outflank the overwhelmed Nealland forces, compelling them to surrender.

Pursued by Reginald and his knights, John rode hard to Nealland's port, barely escaping Reginald's musket fire. He rowed furiously out into the bay, climbed aboard the royal sloop and sailed to Scotland, from whence he planned to travel to London, where he would plead his case to King Henry VII to restore his throne. With John gone, the younger son, whom Reginald had supported, Prince Patrick, would become the heir to the throne.

Since fighting to help King Henry secure the contentious English throne during the 30-year-long War of the Roses, Reginald knew that throughout Europe matters of succession were often clouded and that force was the only way to ensure the desired outcome. Since he did not have a legitimate claim, he knew he could not immediately seize the throne himself, that is, until he found a way to dispose of Patrick.

Nor would Rand know of young Prince Patrick's consequent ascension to the throne or of Reginald and Boston's devious plot to control the shy, adolescent king and surreptitiously rule Bunkillarny. They set up Reginald as Patrick's regent, he in command of Bunkillarny's army, and Boston in control of its finances, who together would, in effect, rule the shire. With the weapons and tribute they acquired from the devious war and the funds they would skim from their oppressive taxes, the two would become the wealthiest men in Bunkillarny and perhaps the richest in all of Ireland. With his expanded army, Reginald planned to subjugate or imprison those who opposed him, then conquer other helpless lands. They would also move to control the McCarron press, which might publish articles shining light upon their misdeeds, to one that would promote their spurious propaganda.

Under their oppressive rule, previously cheerful and prosperous Bunkillarny descended into a dystopic malaise, where drunken soldiers roamed the streets, fought and whored, and young maidens dared not venture out into the dark night for fear of being harassed or worse. Rand's beloved Princess Marie, his savior Queen Catherine, and the one he owed his life to, Gwendolyn, would have to deal with Reginald's unquenchable sexual desires. Before he departed, Rand had saved Marie from being raped by Reginald, who, being enraged, challenged the unskilled Rand to a duel, where he immediately dominated Rand and, piercing his neck, would have slayed him if not for Queen Catherine's intercession.

Still ingrained in a 21st-century mindset, Rand would naturally expect news bulletins, texts or phone calls over his iPhone informing him of the events transpiring back in Bunkillarny. The lack of such information provided an unrealistic calmness of mind, for if he knew of all of this, he would have surely returned to Bunkillarny to rescue those who had saved his life and he cared so much for.

15th Century London

At the end of the 15th century, the population of London was the size of a small American city—between 50,000 and 100,000. Cover picture by Samuel Scott.

ONE

London

When I left Bunkillarny for London, the dense, dripping fog that shrouded the ship's riggings, decks and dock soon obscured my friends, especially the fetching Gwendolyn, her kiss still tingling on my lips, delightfully numbing my brain. Out of sight of the port, all was white—the sea, the sky, the land—all erased by the hand of fog. Still, I could smell the salty sea air, hear the wind flapping the sails, the sea sloshing against the clapboards of the ship's bow, and clanging metal against the wooden masts. I could feel the unfamiliar pitching of the ship, something that disturbed my sense of balance and made my stomach queasy.

Without the faintest idea which direction we were heading, I hoped the nefarious-looking, black-bearded Captain Black knew where we were going and would not crash into some rocky shoal or another blinded ship, but I guessed that was why one of the crew periodically rang the ship's brass bell, its clanging piercing the mysterious, soupy fog like the shrill call of a distant gull. Similar to nervousness on my first airplane flight, and despite my dread, all I could do was put my trust in this captain on this, my first voyage on a 15th-century sailing vessel. Captain Black was a short, stocky, swarthy, commanding man with a thick black beard, black hair and a salt-worn, ruddy, red complexion, who I hoped was not a pirate, for he sure looked the part.

With my complaining stomach finally settled, by midmorning, the fog cleared, and by afternoon, we sailed under a clear blue sky, skimming along the brilliantly blue sea, frothy wave peaks glistening in the sunlight. As my mood brightened, I spied Scotland in the distance, and when we rounded the rocky northern corner of Ireland, as the booms creaked into position, the flapping sails filled with a burst of wind, powering our voyage southward. Surely there could be no more than fifteen miles between Ireland and the coast of Scotland poking out above the Irish Sea. Captain Black had said we would be off the coast of England in a mere couple of days. I could disembark there, but even though it would be a shorter route, in a wagon at a mere 20 to 25 miles a day, it would take substantially longer to reach my destination. We would, instead, sail around the British Isle to the east coast, then up the Thames until we arrived in London.

The caravel was a pretty boat. Her gently sloping bow and stern castle were the prominent features of the vessel that carried both a mainmast and a mizzenmast, which were lateen-rigged with a massive triangular sail.

Like Doctor Jekyll and Mister Hyde, Captain Black's gruff manner changed dramatically at dinner that night with the first and second mates and Mr. McDonald, a wool merchant and my cabin mate. On the deck, the captain was demanding, harsh and vulgar with his crew, but in his cabin, he was a gracious, well-read and surprisingly refined host—an elegant rogue, as it were. When they were both younger, he had sailed with my boss, Michael McCarron, saying that Michael, making up for lost time in the seminary, was quite the ladies' man. The captain had even sailed with the Portuguese explorers down the African coast and, since they were the most advanced shipbuilders in the world, had purchased the sturdy, state-of-the-art caravel from them. At dinner, the captain regaled us with stories of his various voyages and adventures around the known world, including his battles with fearsome pirates.

Surprised by how good the food was, I commented, "This casserole is delicious and not like any of the dishes I had in Ireland."

"Yes, I hired François in Paris. Many of me crew left after one or two sailins, and I thought that if I had a good chef who cooks flavorsome meals, they would stay longer, especially since our British grub be so bland and our previous cook was so bad. And then there was his food poisoning that occurred more than once. It has worked out even better than I 'spected, for although some of the worst swabs leaves after one trip, most of me loyal crew has been with me for years. I pay François well and gives 'im a generous allowance for his vittles. He is passionate about his meals, acquiring local spices and fresh ingredients and tasty recipes from every port we docks at from Turkey, throughout the Mediterranean to the north coast of Africa, Spain and even the Nordic regions."

My room was tiny, with a two-foot-wide door I had to duck under and slide through and two small drawers under the bed for both of us. Earlier, Mr. McDonald had commandeered the lower berth, so I was relegated to the top cubby of the ornately crafted, dark-wooden bunk that was six inches too short for my long legs. Since it was also very narrow, the only position I could find was one with my body in a fetal position, my knees sticking a half-foot over the side.

I could hear raindrops pattering on the deck above, growing ever more fervent until the downpour became a deluge. Driven by the howling wind, the waves began growing, the caravel climbing and falling, pitching and rolling. Despite the insecurity of the small room teetering like a funhouse ride, tired from the long day, I soon fell into a fitful slumber.

I heard Princess Marie yelling and ran to her cabin, where I saw Reginald on top of her between her bare white legs, her dress pushed above her waist, his hand muffling her cries for help. Where and when did they board the ship? Am I dreaming?

I had thought they were still back in Bunkillarny at the hunt. Grabbing him from the shoulder, I spun him around and, before he could respond, slugged him squarely in his square jaw. In an instant, he sprung to his feet and unsheathed his deadly sword, Megan, which had slayed dozens of hapless souls. He resembled a young, blond Brad Pitt with a countenance hardened by war and killings. His face beet-red, his skilled, muscular, lean body tensing, swishing his sword Megan wildly in the air, he was enraged.

We began sword fighting, me aggressively wanting to destroy him for terrifying my beloved Marie. I unleashed a series of mighty blows, causing him to back up to the cabin wall. Whether striking from the left, the right, from above or below, with the slightest twisting of his wrist, he thwarted my feeble incursions. Then he began laughing, a terrible mocking laugh that frightened me to my core, for I knew what a formidable swordsman he was. He began toying with me, backing me up, letting me advance, continuously smiling through his perfect white teeth, glaring at me with his shark-like blue eyes as if I were a petulant, powerless child needing to be punished, like a cat playing with a mouse. He stabbed my right thigh, then my left calf, and I began to limp but fueled by adrenaline, I kept fighting on. When he slashed my right forearm, I could no longer grasp the sword and switched it to the left, which he also penetrated with Megan's point, the injured artery gushing red blood with every heartbeat. I felt like a cattle carcass being butchered piece by piece.

"Rand, Rand," he taunted. "You are such a pitiful swordsman. I don't think I have ever faced a less worthy opponent. I would like to say this was enjoyable, but you are so pathetic. Fencing with you is a waste of my time, and I have unfinished business with the lovely Marie whom I must devote my attention to. It was very rude of you to interrupt our passions. For that insult, you shall forfeit your life."

I looked to Marie, whose ashen face was frozen in terror. She couldn't move. Anger welled up in me, and I mounted one final attack, in which he flicked my sword out of my hand, tripped me, brought Megan's tip to my throat, smiled insanely at Marie, then, raising his hand high, brought the blade swiftly down and sliced my neck, severing my head, the vision of Marie still projected on my fading brain.

"Wake up, lad, wake up!" McDonald pleaded, shocking me out of my nightmare. "You must have had a terrible dream. You be thrashing all about; I thought you would fall off the bed."

Shaken in a cold sweat, I realized I was, thankfully, still alive. The nightmare was obviously a reliving of when I tried to rescue Marie from being raped by Reginald in the castle. Reginald wanted to possess Princess Marie, the most beautiful woman in all of Ireland. During the ball following the games, we surreptitiously left the party and, on the castle's ramparts overlooking the romantic, moonlit, glowing festivities below, we passionately kissed for what seemed like eternity. Then a group of young, noble partiers appeared, and she ignored me, which I guess I understood since her reputation was at stake.

I was such a pathetic swordsman against the best in all Bunkillarny, perhaps the best in Ireland, who had won the dueling competitions at the massive biannual Bunkillarny Games. He had toyed with me, embarrassed me in front of my lovely Marie and was about to slay me, which he would have surely done had it not been for Queen Catherine's intercession at the last second.

Previously, I had done well, winning or placing in four events: throwing the spear the farthest and second closest to the target, finishing second in the 1200-meter run and first in the putting of the stone. As a decathlete, I had competed in these events on the track team in college and had the advantage of modern training methods. Interesting how these war-like skills of throwing a spear, running, and tossing a heavy cannonball date back to the ancient Greek Olympics 2,800 years ago and would still exist into the third millennium.

With everyone treating me like I was a hero, I became full of myself until Reginald punctured my ego. He mastered me, made me look ridiculous, and there was nothing I could do about it. I thought I had moved on, that it was over, but evidently, I was still haunted by the memory. Perhaps I had PTSD, but hoped I would not have another nightmare like that one again. It was so, so real—too real.

Still disturbed, I could not sleep. The waves became fiercer, and now I wrestled with my stomach, wishing I had not eaten so much of François's wonderful dinner. Thinking about François's food did not help my churning stomach, me hoping that time would settle it down, but it soon became evident that was not going to happen, and my gut felt like a boiling volcano about to erupt. I ran out of the room, down the teeter-tottering narrow corridor, up the steep steps, across the deck to the merciful railing. My stomach spasming, I threw up, then threw up again and once more. Afterwards, my head cool, I felt so much better. Relieved, I looked out at the dark, hilly sea just as a sheet of rain washed over me.

The waves seemed to be cresting at fifteen feet. I saw Jack, the first mate, manning the wheel, and since I was already drenched in cold water, I climbed up the slanted, slippery deck to where he stood. He looked surprisingly calm and collected, so I asked him, "Are you worried about this storm and the high waves?"

"No, not at awl. This be a little run-about that don' bother our Christine at awl." After guiding Christine up one massive wave, turning slightly to the left and down the other side to minimize the impact upon the ship, he turned towards me and, smiling, added, "This be great fun.

Gives me something to do on the night watch. Much better than fighting the sleeps all by meself."

His attitude eased my fears. Then I thought steering the ship was like guiding my sportscar around the steep curves of multicolored Appalachian foothills or above the splashing, thundering surf along the Pacific Coast Highway—what fun that was.*

The next morning, we passed the Isle of Man and then entered the open Irish Sea. I didn't spend much time in my crowded, dark cabin but rather enjoyed being up on the deck looking out over the water, breathing in the fresh sea air, watching the crew man the fluffy, white sails. At times, the sea was choppy and the day cool, so I wore my thick woolen sweater Daisy, the McCarrons' delightful, somewhat ditzy maid, had knitted for me. On a clear day with a bright sun beating down on the wooden deck, it became toasty—the smell of salty seawater and baking wood stirred by the gentle breeze, the ship slowly pitching up, then gradually down, the shifting breeze causing the sails to flap crisply, and the ship's brass bell to tingle.

During the long voyage, I had plenty of time to think and gain perspective on all that had happened to me. I still did not know how it ensued, but somehow, I ended up here in the 15th century, a fact I had reluctantly accepted. When I was transported here, due to the trauma, my body felt like scrambled eggs, every bone, every muscle shooting pain to my brain. I had been unconscious for days and was near death. If it were not for sweet Gwendolyn finding me in the woods near that cave and nursing me back to health, I surely would have perished. I owe her my life.

I thought back to how all this had happened. As the chief designer and project manager for a startup in Silicon Valley, I had been slaving over a brilliant app for three years. I had inspired my team of over a dozen developers, artists and writers with promises of stock that Steve, the CEO, authorized. They had worked relentlessly for up to a hundred hours a week to construct the app, which was an instant success, garnering hundreds of thousands of downloads daily. Then Steve laid all of us off and sold the brilliant app to a Fortune 50 tech company, pocketing hundreds of millions of dollars, then flying to Saint Bart's on a private jet with a voluptuous California blond. I felt awful about his deceit and desperately wanted to make it up to my team.

I was extremely depressed, not only for myself but for what the greedy bastards had done to my team, and spent weeks cloistered in my apartment overlooking the scenic San Francisco Bay, singing that "Dock of the Bay" song to myself over and over.

My college friends, sensing the deep emotional hole I had fallen into, insisted that I join them on a backpacking expedition to the bottom of the Grand Canyon. With two billion years of geological history, the canyon was magnificent, and we had so much fun traveling down through the differently colored geologic eras and rekindling our bond.

At the bottom of the spectacular canyon, while seeking solace in a remote gorge, mesmerized by the thundering rapids, I slipped off a high cliff into the rapids and, after being battered, bruised and knocked out, found shelter in a hidden cave. Following a strange light that I thought might lead me back to my friends, I encountered a flowing river of lava whose perpendicular galvanic force, like an electric generator whose spinning magnets create electricity, somehow stretched me like toffee. I felt as if I was on an acid-induced trip where my senses deserted me one by one, and my life passed backwards like frames on a 3-D IMAX movie going ever faster. When I woke, I struggled to make my way out of the cave, eventually fainting in an unfamiliar woods. Evidently, I had been out for days until I saw the beautiful face of an angelic strawberry blond with alabaster skin punctuated by a few becoming freckles.

I thought I had been rescued and taken to the canyon's north rim to some kind of recreation village similar to Williamsburg to convalesce. The houses looked like they were from a medieval Christmas village, and there were no cars, only horses and carts, and the people wore ancient garb, while talking in a strange accent. The only explanation I could fathom was that my friends were playing an elaborate joke on me—a very cruel joke. Over my difficult month-long recovery, when my attractive nurse asked where I was from, I told her I came from the bottom of the Grand Canyon in Arizona and had an apartment in San Francisco overlooking the beautiful bay, neither of which she slyly admitted to ever hearing of.

After arguing with the feisty, Irish-tempered maiden for days, trying to get her to admit the ruse, I read the date on the Bunkillarny Reader—July 8, 1491—and finally had to accept what had happened to me.

Her father, Michael McCarron, who had sailed around much of the known world because of my Spanish-sounding whereabouts, thought I was from Spain. At first, due to my strange accent, the scandalous undergarments she found me in (my shorts, t-shirt and bedeviled Indians, Yahoo cap), and the way I talked about another world, Gwendolyn thought I was crazy and seemed to think I had some strange secret that I was hiding, which I was, for I knew no one would ever believe that I came from the new world over five centuries into the future.

Stranded in time with nowhere to go, to pay them back for saving my life, I volunteered to help in the print shop; that is, until I figured out a way to return through the portal back to the 21st century. While there, I learned how to set type and operate the revolutionary Gutenberg press—the main means of mass communication over the next 400 years—the most transformative communication technology in a half-millennium. I learned not just how to handle the machine but all the steps leading up to the printing process of the magnificent bound books, constructed to last for centuries—steps that were remarkably similar to my work designing and laying out webpages. My web pages dwelled in a virtual world, whereas these magnificent tomes had substance and were tangible—part of the physical world.

When I tried to build my muscles back by walking through the village, the town folk looked at me as if I was from another planet. Eventually, Michael insisted that I join him at the pub frequented by the merchants. There, he introduced me to his friends, who looked at me strangely until he told a story explaining my unusual appearance in the village. He said that I was a Spanish merchant who had been robbed and beaten by highway brigands, who stole all my merchandise, my horse, wagon and clothes, leaving me to die. He pointed to the bump on my head and rolled up my sleeves to reveal the scars on my arms to emphasize the beating. Then he said that because of my concussion, I had lost my memory, and that was why I sounded so strange and could not remember my prior life. "It were like he had a stroke, like old man Quinn, and lost some o' his faculties, like dear ole Ruddy Quinn, bless his heart."

Since they thought of me as a merchant like themselves, over a few rounds of beer and song they came to accept me. It's interesting how people seek explanations for strange things they don't understand, and once there is a feasible solution, they accept it and move on. Since his explanation helped explain my oddities and I desperately wanted to fit into my new, unfamiliar world, I didn't contradict him.

By now, I had gotten used to this time and place, but it had taken a mighty effort, constantly trying to fit in, watching what I said so as not to reveal my identity or seem insane. In my time, due to the Internet, social media, movies and TV, the world had become much more homogenized. Still, in this time when few people traveled more than a few miles in a lifetime, the cultural differences were magnified. Even people from Dublin or the southern coast of Ireland seemed like foreigners to Bunkillarnians. Eventually, these naturally friendly people accepted me like any foreigner who tried to fit in.

During my convalescence, I heard the amazing story of Michael's life, his adventures sailing around Europe, and how he became the first printer in Ireland, the second printer in all the British Isles. Through him, I beheld, then read, the first priceless books ever printed in English. If I could find my way back to my own time, I would buy these ancient titles and take them back with me, where I could sell them for a fortune. I did not want to do this just to be wealthy—what good does that do—but wanted the world to see and experience what magnificent works of art these unblemished original documents represented. It was not just the words but the artistry of the fonts, the graphics and fine leather bindings, carried over from the previous period of laborious transcription, but still during a time when books were treasured works of art to be passed on from generation to generation. Sure, there were a few remnants of these remarkable works that survived over the centuries, but nothing like these mint-condition originals.

In a karmic sense, my time-traveling would somehow make up for our app being stolen. With the funds from the book sales, I would get my team back together, give them shares in the new venture, and build the next app I had planned several years ago without the VCs and Steve—an innovation far beyond what they stole from us, something highly valuable that the world would love that might even be worth billions.

I came to know the citizens of Bunkillarny, a delightful, colorful group of characters who, although they shunned me at first, became my friends. I would miss them on my trip to London and long to see them again.

Screens had dominated my previous burned-out life—up to sixteen hours a day, seven days a week. Periodically, I had wanted to divorce myself from these and become more human again, for although they gave you much, they seemed to take away a portion of your humanity. In the sense of being careful what you ask for, I obtained my wish, which I regretted for a time but now had largely adjusted to. Considering the lack of modern conveniences, it is difficult to surmise, but my life now seemed fuller. I still have my iPhone loaded with Wikipedia that allows me to see into the future—a power I must be careful how I apply, for I do not want to alter the course of history, and, anyway, I won't be able to charge my battery for hundreds of years.

I enjoyed competing in the biannual Bunkillarny games, where I had won the heart of the elusive Princess Marie, Queen Catherine's niece from France, the most beautiful woman I had ever beheld in any century. It seemed that every knight and noble in the shire was in love with her. Marie was the one who insisted I compete at the Bunkillarny Games, and due to my prowess at the events, she seemed to fall in love with me. But as a royal, I was afraid she might reject me, for I was but a lowly printer. Perhaps if I became a partner of the king in the print shop, my prospects would improve. After all, Michael's wife was a noble, and Marie, like King Edward, loved books.

I was headed for London now, carrying a letter of introduction from Michael to William Caxton, the first English printer. I could not wait to meet such a famous personage and hoped to acquire those first famous English books, such as The Canterbury Tales and the History of Troy, and have mister Caxton sign these.

Once I hired a new agent there and got our business back on track, Michael and King Edward had promised to make me a junior partner. I did not know if I believed in fate, but somehow, I felt that this was where I was supposed to be for a while during this remarkable time at the center of the transformation of humankind from a medieval, meager, feudal existence to a more intellectual, free-thinking, expansive realm when the Renaissance bloomed and the Enlightenment commenced. I did not know what adventures lay ahead of me, but I was psyched, confident and looked forward to them.*

In another couple of days, we sailed past the southwestern corner of England. There, I felt as if we were sailing along the forearm of Cape Cod as we passed the familiar-sounding towns of Falmouth, Truro and Plymouth—where those American villages would someday acquire their names. Eventually, on a clear day, we sailed by the brilliantly-lit White Cliffs of Dover, where we could see Calais and northern France perhaps fifteen or twenty miles away.

Proceeding up the Thames under a gorgeous, velvety purple sky, we saw picturesque pastoral scenes of fields tended by peasants working in ant-like precision. On a previous trip, 500 years from now, something I still could not fathom, I remembered flying in a jet over the Thames into Heathrow and seeing mile after mile of factories, residential streets, and shopping centers that would someday occupy these rich, alluvial, 15th-century farmlands. Picturing 21st-century London in my head against this 15th-century London boggled my mind. How could I possibly be here at this time? It wasn't easy, but I had finally become accustomed to this period, and rather than potentially sticking out like a sore thumb, constantly conscious of myself, I carefully chose my speech and idioms to fit this time so I wouldn't be detected.

I felt like a stranger in a strange land or a traveler whose plane goes down in the middle of the Amazon, unable to speak the language or understand the native customs, afraid I might make a colossal social error that would tip my hand and be discovered. Even though I spoke English, as did my friends in Ireland and the sailors on the ship, the variations were so vastly different, not like the differences between Cockney, Australian, Scottish or that formal English accent I loved. Sometimes, I just couldn't understand them. At times, I felt so alone, so out of place, and so longed to be home in San Francisco in my own time, in my own apartment overlooking that beautiful bay. I wanted to tell someone who I really was and gain their insights regarding my predicament but knew I could not. Each day I picked myself up and started over again, gradually adjusting to my remarkable situation, and each day things got just a little bit easier.

Suddenly, we were in medieval London, a city stripped of all its urban sprawl that, judging by its size, resembled Canton, Ohio with a population of perhaps 75,000 to 100,000. With most of the buildings on the right bank, very little development occupied the southern shore of the famous river. I was pleased to see that some of the familiar sites were already there, such as the formidable Tower of London. With numerous church and cathedral spires reaching for the sky, I thought this must be a highly religious city. A wall built over 1,000 years ago by the Romans still surrounded the city where most of the buildings resided. Beyond the wall there were fields, no doubt harvested to feed hungry Londoners. I wondered how long it would be before those would be consumed by the city's amoebic sprawl.

After seven days cooped up in a tiny, shared cabin, when the lines were finally secured to the dock, I could not contain my excitement. I hastily packed and readied myself to disembark onto the busy, churning, noisy wharf below. As I climbed down the gangplank, since my legs were used to the constant seesawing of the waves, I had to adjust to the stability of land. At the landing, I vigorously shook the captain's hand, saying how much I enjoyed his hospitality and his stories. He replied, "Michael wod o' had me hide if I'd not taken good care o' you, me lad."

I shook Mr. McDonald's hand, too, wishing him success in selling his cargo of Irish wool while my crate of books was lifted off the sturdy caravel. I checked to make sure I had the address just as a grimy, thin, older-looking chap with missing teeth approached and asked, "Do ya needs a ride somewheres, me lord?"

Not sure of him, I asked how much it would cost to go to my location, to which he gave me what I thought was a reasonable price of a penny and responded, "I knows that place well, even knows the widow Jones who lives thar. What a shame it were, her 'usband passing an awl."

Stephen retrieved a cart to carry the crate and my bag and took these to his wagon pulled by two weary-looking, hunchbacked gray mares. Thrilled to be on land once again, I told him I would pay him an extra penny if he drove me around the town, for I found 15th-century London intriguing and wanted to see how much would change over the next half-millennium. He enthusiastically responded that he would.

When I had previously stayed in London, because it was so sprawling, expansive and crowded, I never got a good feel for the city. This new London, or rather this old London, would be much easier to comprehend. As we rolled along the streets, I saw three- or four-story quaint

Tudor-style houses and shops crowded together that extended all the way to the dirt streets—pedestrians, horses, and carts all mixing in a seemingly random fashion. The houses were mostly wooden, some still with thatched roofs, plastered upper floors, having exposed wooden beams like Tudors.

It seemed as if they were trying to crowd as many people and businesses as possible within the old city's Roman walls, and I wondered if it was still vulnerable to attacks, or perhaps it was just a vestige of the past centuries when such attacks were common. With no sidewalks, pedestrians stayed to the side, leaving most of the street available for horses and carts. Many of the houses' upper floors overhung the street, leaving little space on the crowded alleys off the main roads. With so much manure and waste from the horses (and unfortunately the humans too), it took quite a while for my nose to adjust to the smell. The fragrant smell of burning wood wafting from the chimneys helped cover up the stench. Oblivious to my presence, the people went about their daily business, filling the air with a cacophony of sounds.

Obviously proud of his town, Stephen pointed out the various sites, taking me first to London Bridge. It was nothing like what I had imagined. As we approached, I could see that the bridge perched upon about 20 piers jutting out far into the water. When we came closer, I could see that sitting atop the bridge were scores of buildings up to four stories high. In my 21st-century mind, I thought about how magnificent the views of the river and city would be from those buildings—how expensive such housing would be in modern-day London. We entered the bridge, but nearly all of the space was occupied by shops with houses above, leaving a narrow passageway of only seven or eight feet in either direction, overflowing with horses, carts and pedestrians narrowly missing each other, moving in random concert. In some places, there were walkways and buildings that extended over the street, such that I felt as if we were driving through a long tunnel. Along the way, I must have seen an overwhelming 150 quaint shops of all kinds, many of which were haberdasheries. Stephen pointed out those he thought were the best, saying, "The rents 'elps pays for the bridge, they do."

Near the middle was the church of Saint Thomas. Stephen told me that Henry II erected it in the 12th century after he recanted for killing Sir Thomas Beckett, the Archbishop of Canterbury. There was a drawbridge near the center of the bridge, where we had to wait as a two-masted schooner sailed by. While we waited, he pointed out the public privy in case I needed to stop. It smelled bad, and I could hear it emptying into the river, so I passed.

After we crossed the 900-foot bridge, we turned around in Southwark and headed back. At the Southwark gate, we saw a gruesome display of three bloody severed heads, Stephen saying, "The traitors were executed las' week, they was. I saw it, I did. They gots what they deserved, they did."

I was horrified by the stomach-churning sight of rotting, bloody heads covered in buzzing flies. Repulsed by the ugly yet riveting sight, I had to force myself to turn my head and look forward, literally raising my arm and pushing my head forward with my hand. As we rolled over the clacking planks of the great bridge, I asked Stephen, "What had they done to deserve such a fate?"

"Well, they be nobles aligned with Yorkshire, who fought agin Henery at Bostwick Field, they did. After prevailing, Henery could ha' taken their lands, but graciously granted clemency to all them who foughts under the white rose. But these three plotted agin him, began raising an army and wanted to overthrows Henery when he captured them, he did. There still be rebellion in the land, which is why Henery has ta constantly be on guard, as it were."

Heading down the center of town along broad Fleet Street, I could see that the city was so much smaller now—no more than seven or eight city blocks wide. There seemed to be a church or cathedral on every block, with several under construction, masons, busy at their trade, noisily hammering away at the stones, using ropes and pulleys to yank the massive blocks up and into place. I thought that Londoners must be very religious to have so many places of worship. Considering the monasteries outside of town, Stephen the carter said, "The church owns more than 'af the land in and round London, they does."

We soon arrived at the glorious Westminster Abbey, which, at Stephen's insistence, I had to walk through. I was in awe of how tall and grand it was and how much light streamed through the abundant windows on this brilliant day. I would have liked to tour more of the cathedral and see those who had been entombed since the 13th century, but I felt I should not keep my driver waiting. I knew that many more royals, nobles, scientists and writers would be buried there over the coming centuries, such as Queen Elizabeth I and her stepsister Mary Queen of Scots, as well as Newton, Darwin and Dickens. Stephen then drove by Windsor Palace, saying, "King Henery's thar now, he is."

By attending a medieval feast back in San Francisco, I knew that Henry VIII was only a child now, so Stephen must be referring to his father, so I said, "That's Henry the VII, isn't it?"

"Of course," chuckling to himself, "who don knows that." Then catching himself and not wanting to offend me, he offered, "But I guesses with your strange accent and you not bein' from here 'bouts, you might not knows that."

I remembered that Henry VIII would soon repossess much of the church's lands, which, seeing all of their prime real estate, I guess I might understand.

Reveling in his role as city guide, Stephen added, "Other than the church, much of London be run by the guilds." Then he began telling me about all of them, being sure not to offend any by omitting one. "There's the grocers, the rappers, the fishmongers, the goldsmiths, and the skinners. Then let me see, there's the merchants, the tailors, the haberdashers, the salters, and the ironmongers. Oh, and then there's the vintners and the clock workers, there is." I did not know what all of these guilds meant, but I found their prominence in the city interesting and vital to the city's growing economy for even now, there was an emerging middle class that the guilds were facilitating. I wondered if having guilds in the 21st century might make sense.*

By then, it was late afternoon, and I felt it was time to get to the agent's house, where I would check on our business and start searching for a new agent. Because this was where about half of our sales were, without an agent to represent our interests throughout England, Michael's profits would be decimated and he would have to lay off one of our two apprentices or perhaps myself.

The Jones house turned out to be only a couple blocks away. The three-story Tudor building stood in a row of similar townhouses with a simple, small, red-painted wooden sign over the window announcing BOOK SELLERS. I gave Stephen an extra penny, a 50% tip, which he was thrilled by, telling him how much I appreciated his tour. I walked through the door and saw a few shelves of books for sale. It was evidently an early version of a bookstore. A lady in her thirties, with dark hair and spectacles, who looked like she could be a librarian stacking books, asked if she could help me. I said, "I am not here to buy anything, ma'am. Michael McCarron, John's longtime friend and business partner, has sent me. My name is Rand Roberts."

She smiled, responding, "Oh yes, Michael sent me a letter saying you would be coming, but he did no say when you might be arrivin'. I'm runnin' the shop since my dear John left us and until you finds an agent. I be Colleen, Colleen Jones. Pleased ta meet you, Mister Roberts. I hope you had a pleasant journey."

"I did. Captain Black was an interesting fellow."

"Oh yes, I know him, and he is quite an interesting character, as you say. The captain would supply us with books ta sell from Michael, and John would give him the money from the sales and books he had acquired for Michael to print. Although you wud na know it at first, he is actually very intelligent and has a warm heart."

Somehow, I had expected an older, dour woman—my image of a widow, I guess, but Colleen, despite the apparent pain painted on her face, was fairly attractive. "I am very sorry to hear of the loss of your husband, Missus Jones."

"Thank you. It has been very difficult raising five children since then. Are you hungry?" Since I hadn't eaten anything since breakfast on the ship, I told her I was famished.

She led me back to the kitchen, where I met her four towheaded children ranging in age from perhaps four to eleven—Andrew, Joan, Patricia and Albert. "The oldest, Harry, who's twelve, be working at the spinners to earn some money for the family. Albert will soon work at a spinning wheel too, spinning the wool into balls of yarn, he will."

With strands of hair flying out of her bun, their mother looked frazzled, as anyone would be trying to care for five children and a shop by herself. There were no schools to help care for the kids, but she told me, "Patricia is a big 'elp in caring of the younger ones." They were all cute but looked a little disheveled. With sad faces, I could tell they dearly missed their dad. They looked up at me through adorable puppy-dog eyes with a mixture of awe and fear.

After dinner, we sat down in a small living room behind the shop in front of the blazing fire. Waiting for her to sit down, I sat in the other one of the two comfortable chairs. Three small stools were stacked on top of each other, upon which the three older children sat while the younger two sprawled on the floor. I remembered from 21st-century London how small the rooms were compared to a typical American family room, but this was even smaller. There was barely enough room for all of us, but even though it was small, it was a cozy, warm space for the entire family. The two older boys put the side table between them and began playing chess, while Patricia read a story to Joanie, her face looking up fondly at her big sister with little Andrew gazing contentedly into the fire. Their cherub-like faces lit by the warm glow of the fire looked like a scene from a Hallmark Christmas card. Even though I had spent little time with them, I could tell this was a close-knit, loving family. Without being told, the children had helped make and deliver the meal, set the table and cleaned up. There was no sign of bickering.

I always thought it was interesting how some families who had little and lived close to each other seemed much richer, in a spiritual sense, than some wealthy, troubled families living in McMansions who rarely interacted with each other. The dark maple walls had a delightful tinge of red highlighted by the flickering flames, which lit the objects and those in the room facing the fire, while the other sides were darkened in the shadows.

I asked Colleen if I could tell the children a story, to which she consented. When I asked them if they would like to hear a story, they immediately responded that they would and gathered around me on the floor. I decided to tell them the story of Snow White, at least what I remembered.

After she put the children to bed, Colleen said, "I wish I could offer ye some wine." Then she remembered she had some sherry that John had acquired on a trip to Spain—"A rare treat not yet widely available here in London. John was always bringing back interesting souvenirs from his travels. Have ye er tasted it before? Let me open up the boutel. We were saving it for a special occasion, which I think having a visitor all the way from me Ireland would certainly merit."

The delectable sherry seemed to finally relax her, temporarily washing away the stress from having to raise five children and run a business at the same time.

Colleen Jones, with penetrating blue eyes, a bright, toothsome, reluctant smile, a perfectly symmetrical face with high cheekbones, a petite nose and brown hair, told me, "I came from Bunkillarny before I traveled to London with Michael, where I met me 'usband, John, and we fell instantly in love. We were soon married and had Harry within the year. Back in Ireland, Michael had taught me ta read, which I became fascinated with and the new printin' profession. After me father died, Michael, me mother's beloved cousin, became like a da ta me."

According to Colleen, "John ha' apprenticed under Mr. William Caxton, where he met Michael. William had another agent, so John 'elped Michael sell the books he printed 'ere in England to the growing number of readers. He wanted to outshine Caxton's agent, which is why John and Michael prospered 'ere. Due to John's efforts, Michael's sales in England soared both to the merchants and to the clergy. Michael introduced us to each other and our fascination with readin' and printin' became the basis of our relationship, as it were.

"John also performed a valuable service for Michael by acquiring works to print not only from England but from France too. Most of these were in Latin but there be an expanding number of works in our native tongue. He had hoped to go to the Italian peninsula because that was where the seat of the church were, and there was a vast supply of Latin books he hoped to tap into, to have translated and printed in English by Michael. Michael be a great translator and editor, he is. He be most as good as William Caxton. You know Mister Caxton be the first to print books in English. Before him there were none. Other than the wealthy, no one could afford to have books scribed by hand. I feel we are part of something important—helping more people to become educated and spreading of the knowledge."

I realized, as the center of the burgeoning renaissance, there would be many captivating new books for our print shop to tap into, translate and sell from Florence, Venice, Rome and throughout Italy. As if she was relieved to finally have someone to talk to about our mutual business, Colleen's thoughts poured out, as if she had been storing these up, and being able to finally release them granted her a measure of relief.

"John even helped Michael in the southern sections of Ireland, particularly acquiring works from the monasteries surrounding Dublin. During the Middle Ages, due to all the plagues and wars, he said many of the best works from the Roman Empire were thought to be lost, but John found some of those treasures in the monasteries that had been faithfully copied and preserved o'r the centuries.

"Before John died, I had spent me time teaching the young ones how to read, and other lessons too. Now me oldest boys will have to work to support the family. I had hoped they would apprentice in the printing business and continue in their father's footsteps, but I realize that without John to bring them along and a formal education, it's not going to happen."

It was getting late, the fire was dying out, and she looked exhausted. "I keeps the ledgers and will run through these with ye in the morning." She gathered the coals together so they would last the night, then guided me up the stairs with a candle to a bedroom.

As she gathered her dresses from the hooks, I realized this was her and John's bedroom and said, "I would not want to take your bed. I can sleep in the living room on the floor."

"I can sleep in the girls' bed." Proudly she added, "Including the attic where the boys sleeps, we have three bedrooms. Many a family sleeps in the same room; we are blessed. But with John gone, I will have to give up me house soon," she said with a crackling voice, firm chin and a worried look, while holding back tears.

The next morning after breakfast, we sat down with the ledgers. I could see that she was very intelligent and had done an excellent job keeping the books. Her writing was perfect and neat, and her integrity was unimpeachable. In addition, she seemed to be the one who had the business acumen and understood well how it worked. After deducting the agent commission, Michael would make a substantial profit of 20 pounds.

He had instructed me to double the commission John had earned on his sales throughout England, Scotland and Wales and give it to his widow. When I told her that, she began to cry. A burden had been lifted from her, at least for now. "O Michael! Dear Michael, this means so much to me. What a kindness. Please thank him for me!" Then she grabbed my hands and impetuously kissed me on the cheek.

That afternoon we visited several of the merchants whom John worked with to disseminate Michael's books I had brought in the crate throughout London. They kept copies of the books in their various retail establishments to sell, for which they received a handsome portion of the proceeds. They all expressed sorrow at John's loss and said what a fine man he was. They seemed to know Colleen well and asked if there was anything they could do to help.

She told me John also had many contacts at Windsor Castle and in the various churches throughout Britain, where he also sold our books. The town of Windsor housed all the nobles, the bureaucrats, and the wealthy who would likely read. The shop, whether intentionally or not, occupied space near its primary market in the suburb of Windsor, not far from the center of this tiny predecessor of mighty London.

TWO

Bunkillarny

Haunted by his memory, Queen Catherine was still recovering from the loss of her husband, King Edward, whom she loved more than life itself. On most days, she didn't think she could carry on, and on rainy, cool mornings like the one on which he perished, she was so, so deeply depressed. The stunningly beautiful French queen with porcelain-white skin, deep-purple eyes bordering a long regal nose leading to high cheekbones above thick, ruby-red lips, all framed by cascading dark hair, looked gaunt. Her internal force of personality that enchanted all she met had been punctured and deflated. Previously, she had a model's figure and bearing, but now her head hung low, and she bordered on the anorexic. Why did he leave her alone? Why did he have to go hunting? Why did he have to slip and fall off that abysmal cliff? Unable to sleep nights, roaming the halls aimlessly, she found it difficult to get out of bed each morn and often slept till noon. The only thing that kept her from ending the pain was her three children.

As if it were a lightning bolt, the news of Donegal's "victory" hit the regal Queen squarely in her already depleted heart.

Previously, Donegal, the largest kingdom along the north coast of Ireland, had massed its forces on Nealland's border, the other large kingdom along the north coast adjacent to Bunkillarny. For decades, Bunkillarny had wisely stayed out of their periodic border skirmishes. Prince John, King Edward's oldest surviving son and the legitimate heir to the Bunkillarny throne, had married the Nealland king's daughter and, as a dowry, was given a substantial estate to rule, along with the rank of a colonel in Nealland's army.

She expected that General Reginald Van Cleve III, commanding the Bunkillarny army, would join Prince John's forces and that the outnumbered O'Donnells would back off rather than fighting a war where many men on both sides would perish or be maimed for life. Even though he had advocated for Prince Patrick in the council meeting, she could not comprehend that Reginald supported the O'Donnells. After all, John was Edward's oldest surviving son, the heir apparent to the Bunkillarny throne. Many of the nobles were also in a state of shock and worried about the future of their beloved shire.

Queen Catherine felt she was in an awkward position. She loved her stepson, Prince John, and thought he possessed many of the qualities of his departed father. But Patrick was her beloved son and he would be king, and with John nowhere to be found and possibly dead, there was no other alternative. She would be regent, and she could not undermine her son's reign.*

Reginald had justified his betrayal by casting aspersions upon John, saying that he was unfit for the office, that he was saving the kingdom from John's debauchery. He had learned from the many battles he fought that successions were often blurry, and regardless of the claims, he who had the most effective military force usually prevailed. Other than the officers, during the fog of war, the men they commanded fought where they were told to fight and did not know they were fighting Neallanders until after the battle.

General Reginald had drafted all able-bodied Bunkillarny men over fifteen, many relishing the call to arms and glory and to serve with such a renowned leader. Unbeknownst to anyone other than Reginald's senior knights and a few of the lords, Reginald had surreptitiously made a pact with King Rory of Donegal to support them against Nealland. Because of his treachery, he and Rory won the day-long battle and divided up the spoils. Reginald wanted to take half of Nealland, but King Rory, adhering to the rules of chivalry, would not cause further harm to Nealland. Besides, he had acquired the borderlands the two kingdoms had fought over for centuries, which was all he really wanted. He had never wanted the hassle of ruling Nealland and had great respect for his cousin, Nealland's King Albert.

Immediately after the war ended, Reginald wasted no time consolidating his power, sending his senior knights, commanding a contingent of soldiers, to each of the nobles' castles. There, they informed the lords of the results of the battle and that philandering, immoral Prince John had likely died in the battle or fled like the coward he was, thereby abdicating his throne. Of course, the persistent rumors that devious Lord Boston had spawned regarding John's abysmal character were utter lies. John was one of the noblest, kindest, Christian lords in all of Ireland, whose serfs loved him for how well he treated them, but the spurious rumors wormed their way into the psyche of Bunkillarny.

Many of the nobles were surprised at the outcome of the battle and that the Bunkillarny troops, many of whom they supplied, had been misused, but reluctantly realized that "might makes right," a fact underscored by the soldiers at their door. The officers, according to the laws of the land, demanded they swear allegiance to Prince (soon to be King) Patrick. Reginald thought about claiming the throne himself, but knew he had no legitimate claim to it and that the royal council, the people and even much of his army would not support him, at least not now. Besides, King Henry VII in England, who was also the presumptive ruler of Ireland, would certainly not support such a power grab. He would bide his time until Patrick could be removed—one way or another.

All the lords, with the exception of Lord O'Flannery and Lord Brogan, capitulated. Lords O'Flannery and Brogan had been King Edward's two best friends and closest advisors. Even though Lord O'Flannery was Prince Patrick's godfather, he could not condone Reginald's actions. When the advisory council convened, the vote was nine to three for Patrick to assume the throne with Michael McCarron, the printer, royal tutor, counselor and partner of the king, being the other nay.*

After King Edward died, Reginald spared no effort in appearing to care for the lost king's family, especially Patrick, to whom he was a hero. When Reginald finally came to see the queen, who was dressed in black and wearing a veil, he said with a sullen, sorrowful face, "Oh, my dear Queen, I am so sorry for what has befallen you. I too loved Edward—like a, a brother. Please let me know if there is anything more I can do for you or your lovely children. While you are in mourning for dear King Edward, something I suspect will consume at least half a year, I propose that I handle the bothersome responsibilities of managing the shire, and guiding young Patrick until he is able to assume the full role. We will be joint regents. You will see to his motherly needs. I shall see to his duties as king."

She responded, "Reginald, I appreciate your offer and all you have done for our family, but I am quite capable of managing my son and the shire. After all, I was by the king's side and am better acquainted with the affairs of state than anyone. Before I married Edward, I was a member of the French court, where I learned the intricacies of monarchical politics."

"I have spoken with Patrick, and joint regency is what the king wishes. My dear lady, as the general of Bunkillarny's army, considering what has befallen you, I am afraid you do not have the stamina for such a demanding role. I would prefer that you be involved, for it would lend credibility to Patrick's reign and help the kingdom move forward, but as would be expected of any noblewoman such as yourself, you seem consumed with grief. You should not concern yourself with such matters that only a man can handle. I assure you I am fully able to assume the entire role myself. Bunkillarny needs a strong hand now, for we face threats from within and from without to Patrick's reign. Being so young, he is very vulnerable. We do not wish to end up like Britain, where the throne was supposed to initially go to an adolescent heir, where we battled for thirty years. As you know, I fought with Henry to secure his throne, but it was a very ugly and very bloody affair. So many men died or were maimed and so many of their homes, crops and towns were laid to waste. We need to exhibit strength to avoid such an outcome."

Without the support of the nobles, with Nealland defeated, with Reginald in charge of the army and Donegal aligned with Reginald, she realized she had little choice—she had to support her son and agreed to Reginald's demands to be co-regents. She was uncertain of Reginald's motives, but he had been truly kind to her and her children, plus Patrick adored him. He was a warrior and had some rough edges, which even her husband possessed until he matured. She was unclear regarding Reginald's character. Was he still the man who tried to rape her niece, or had he turned a new leaf and, as advised by Edward, become more chivalrous?

She would keep an eye on him. At least she would be a check on him, and her young son would, after all, have the final say.

Having lost her husband and losing the desired heir apparent, Catherine retreated to her mourning, wearing black and spending her days caring for her children and her household. She was depressed, ate her meals with the children, lost much weight, looked gaunt and was rarely seen in public or at court.*

Prince Patrick had admired Reginald for some time and was glad to have him guiding him as co-regent. After all, he was the one who won the dueling competition, won the jousting competition, won all those glorious battles for the kingdom and England and had slain so many vile enemies. Similar to any boy in any era, he worshiped his hero. His departed father was kind and treated him well but was so involved in running the kingdom, he had little time for his younger son other than infrequently talking to him about building his character. Even though Edward had been a brilliant general and fearsome, skilled warrior when he was younger, that all had happened before Patrick was born and was not something Patrick knew much about. Reginald had spent time with him, showing him how to sword fight, shoot a bow and even ride a horse with a small lance. Rather than spending endless hours with his tutors or his younger siblings, these were naturally the type of activities a young teenage royal wanted to pursue in the late 15th century.

The shy, blond, blue-eyed teenager with a firm, dimpled jaw resembled his father, except he was shorter than average and had a slight build. After his oldest half-brother Edward died in the recent plague, he had hoped his other half-brother from Edward's first wife, John, would assume the crown and had little interest in it himself—something that he had never considered happening. Still, he reluctantly felt he had to live up to the expectations of his mother and father for in less than three years, when he turned eighteen, he would be thrust into the role—something he dreaded and something that kept him up nights.

During the royal coronation ceremony, he would have rather been anywhere else other than the center of attention at the cathedral, where at any minute, his knees shuddering, he felt he might pass out. At the end of the ceremony, he struggled mightily to deliver his oft-rehearsed vow pledging allegiance to Bunkillarny, its people, the king of England and God the Father, God the Son and the Holy Ghost.

That night there was a royal banquet in the expansive hall where Reginald gave a well-received, rousing speech. In it, he reenacted the heroic battle against the O'Neals, warned they might try to get revenge, and that all had to be vigilant and aware of anyone from Nealland, for they might be up to some dastardly deed. Reginald promised to shepherd the newly crowned king and to ensure that the shire continued the long road of prosperity that Edward had begun—"We will all be better off and richer than ever. 'Twill be a time of peace, prosperity and glory!"

Having to force herself for her son's sake, the queen mother attended the ceremony. Everyone in the kingdom loved her dearly and if they had any doubts, the reassuring sight of her presence calmed their fears regarding her bashful young son. She hoped Reginald would live up to what he had promised in his speech but had her doubts.

THREE

The First Printer

After Michael had told me about William Caxton, I wanted to visit the pioneer who printed those first books in the English language, which would be worth millions in the 21st century. From what Colleen had told me, the demand had greatly expanded, no doubt due to Caxton's efforts. Sure, there had been hand-copied versions of books for centuries, but these were very tedious to produce and therefore very expensive—something that only the wealthiest nobles or merchants could afford. Now that they were more affordable, more people could read, thereby providing more information, knowledge and opportunities for the British people.

Michael had given me a letter of introduction to Caxton, a separate personal letter from Michael to William, and books we had printed that Michael was proud to present to William, his mentor.

The next day, I visited William Caxton's print shop in Westminster. It was much larger than ours, and much busier than I anticipated, with the mechanical sounds of presses creaking away. There must've been nearly a couple dozen men working at the now familiar tasks—setting the type, inking the form and pulling the devil's tail, while others bound the pages together. I saw dozens of pages hanging up to dry, smelled the familiar odor of oil-based ink and heard the familiar 'pluck' sound as the presses kissed the page into being. When I asked a young, red-haired apprentice where Mr. Caxton might be, without saying a word, looking befuddled, he disappeared into an office and reappeared with another man, who, looking suspiciously at me, asked abruptly in a gruff tone, "What do ye want?"

"My name is Rand Roberts. I would like to see Mr. William Caxton, please."

Forcefully, in an accent I could barely understand, he said, "'es na 'ere."

"Where is he?"

"E's na 'ere, go away! We are fery bussy."

I had come so far and was greatly disappointed that I would not be able to see him. Then I explained, "I am an admirer of his and would like to speak to him, please. Michael McCarron has sent me all the way from Ireland, and I have some of our books to present to Mr. Caxton and, oh, I have a letter of introduction," which I took out of my pocket and handed to him.

His face softened and his mood gradually brightened as he read the letter. He apologized, "I am sorry, lad. Mr. Caxton ha been sick and he only comes to the shop a couble times a week now. Do you verks fer Michael?"

"Why, yes, I do. I guess you'd say I am his right-hand man."

Extending his hand, in an English accent punctuated with German overtones he said, "Sorry. I be running the shop in 'is absence by me-self and am wery busy. I verked with Michael vhen he vere 'ere and ve becomes good friends, ve did. Seeing ya is from Michael and has these things fer him, I think Bill vod vants ta see ye. I will take ye ta is 'ouse. O, me name be Vynkyn, Vynkyn de Vorde."

"Pleased to meet you. Considering what you do, it seems appropriate that your last name is Worde."

"Yes, I guesses it was me destiny to be a printer. Please ta meet ya too, Rand. Actually, I changed me name.

"I be born in the Alsace, which 'as a mix o' the Germans and the Frenchers. Originally me name be Jan Van Vynkyn, which sounded too Germanic for a printer in London ta be successful, 'specially considerin' the large number o' printers in the German provinces. We wanted ta distinguish our shop as purely English so I changed me name here."

While walking on the way to Bill's house, Wynkyn said, "You 'as a strange accent and speak strange words too, where ye be from?"

Referring to my oft-used response, first used by Michael to explain my oddities to himself and others, which seemed to work, I replied, "It's a long story, but after being robbed and beaten to within an inch of my life, my speech sounded different than others."

I noticed that accents changed from shire to shire in Ireland and even here in England from town to town. Why, even in our shire some of the country folk only spoke Gaelic or a difficult-to-understand mixture of Gaelic and English. Even in my time, back in the 21st century, when viewing some English shows on PBS where the characters had heavy accents, I had to turn on the subtitles, but finally, my ear was becoming better tuned to the variations here and I thought, considering the vast differences in this time, my odd-sounding accent would be more acceptable.

Wynkyn looked at me strangely, as if he did not quite believe me. We walked onward, somewhat uncomfortably.

The house was only a couple of short blocks away and when Wynkyn knocked on the door, a servant appeared, Wynkyn saying, "'ello, Mary, is Bill up to seeing a fisitor? It's someone I thinks he vould vant ta meets."

"Today is a good day. Come in, I will check on 'im, Wynkyn."

She led us into a bedroom, where William looked grayish and gaunt, obviously affected by a serious malady like cancer, or as they called it, the consumption. The room had that smell of someone who had been sick for some time. And William had that look of someone who would not last long—a look my sister had before she died young of cancer.

When I introduced myself and gave him the letter of introduction from Michael, he perked up, smiled, and said, "You be from me good friend Michael, the best apprentice I ever 'ad." Then, looking at Wynkyn, he added, "Next to Wynkyn, tha is."

I gave him the letter and books from Michael, which seemed to please him greatly. I added, "Michael has told me much about you and we both hold you in the highest esteem. I am amazed at what you have been able to accomplish as a printer, and how you have produced so many significant works in English. Your legacy will last for centuries and no doubt it will have a profound effect upon the future generations of Britons. Someday, due to your spreading of knowledge, English may conquer the world, not only the known world but much of the rest of the world yet to be discovered." I was somewhat surprised by all I said, but was overwhelmed by meeting this famous, transformative man and nervously could not stop.

"Thank you, me lad, I appreciate your elegant words."

Mary brought us some port and we spent the rest of our time discussing the works he had produced and the innovations he had made. I realized that his goal was to reproduce great literature and, as a result, foster the rapid spread of knowledge. I was so pleased to meet the man who had done so much to advance the profession and become the catalyst of English literature—the prime mover.

Bill remembered Michael well, saying, "We still correspond with each other regarding our latest works and I am most happy to have this recent letter from him. Our shop now supports three presses with a large group of apprentices and journeymen. In my soul, I truly believe as more people learn to read and as the cost of books continues to fall, our profession will change the world." We also talked about some of the old Roman works they were currently reproducing. Then Mary came in and said he was getting tired and it was time for us to leave soon. I grasped his shaking hand in both of mine, looked at him in his fading blue eyes and told him how much it meant to me to meet him, whereupon his eyes lit up, shining a light on the genius behind them.

He told me, "Give my fondest regards to Michael. Tell him I care deeply for him and know he will carry on our proud mission in life. Also, tell him I'm glad he had settled down and had stopped chasing the skirts," after which we all laughed.

Even though I thought we should leave, Mr. Caxton continued, "Michael wrote me periodically regarding his beautiful wife, who loved books as much as he and his three lovely daughters. I was sorry to hear she died. I could tell how much he loved her and how much he missed her. Oh, and that Gwendolyn sounds like a corker, beautiful to behold, intelligent, well-read, and a woman who helps him with his business. Michael even said because she is so lovely, he taught her how to use a sword to defend herself. She will make some lucky man a spectacular wife; that is, if he can tame the spirited lass."

"She is, indeed, an amazing woman." Even though I didn't realize it at first, I now understood that it was very rare for a woman these days to be so involved in business.

When I shook his hand, he pulled me close and whispered in my ear, "You do not seem to be from this time, but from the future, lad. Do something amazing with the knowledge that only you possess."

I was shocked. From the little I said, how could he know my secret? Could it be the insights of a dying man, who sees things that those of us who are encased in our daily routines cannot perceive? Is it possible that he too is a time traveler and recognized another time traveler, for he was so far ahead of his time? Similarly, was Gutenberg a time traveler? How could one man have accomplished so much that led to the revolution in European civilization, the equivalent of founding the Internet, the World Wide Web, Google and Facebook?

I left with tears in my eyes. Wynkyn, looking somewhat verklempt, said, "He is a force of nature, and none of us thought he would last as long as he has. I am very glad ye cud see 'im. I cud sees 'ow much it meant to 'im."

"I felt privileged to meet such a great man. Thank you!*"

That night Wynkyn and I had dinner at a quaint pub and, over a few rounds of ale, talked enthusiastically about our mutual profession until the wee hours. Wynkyn was shorter than the average height with a large forehead that fit his fierce intelligence, large piercing eyes bracketing a short nose, and thick, well-spoken lips. His countenance fit his passion for printing and its commercial possibilities, for he desired to take the profession from the realm of early adopters, such as the royalty, nobles and clergy who had been the only ones able to afford transcribed books that Mr. Caxton had initially sold to, to the next strata of society by penetrating the growing market of merchants, guildsmen and the middle class who had been learning how to read—a 20th-century marketing concept.

In the darkened, candlelit pub, the attractive waitress in a low-cut dress brought us our beef and bread and another round of ale when Wynkyn pulled his chair closer, rested his elbows on the rickety table and looked at me straight in my eyes with a penetrating stare. "Vere did ye say ye be from, Rand? It don' make sense that you vuld not have some memory o' thar."

He was an extremely intelligent man and I knew my standard amnesia story that had worked for others wasn't working with him. Caught off guard, I responded, "I think I'm from Spain but can't recall exactly where." I know that he spoke excellent German, Latin, French and English, and some Italian, but I hoped he didn't know Spanish, for although

I had some Spanish in high school and college, I was very rusty. When I was transported to this time, due to the heat, my skin had become extremely dark, the darkest I had ever been in my life, so I thought I might pass as a Spaniard. I immediately filled my mouth with a big chunk of beef, hoping that my explanation satisfied him and he, too would begin eating. After chewing, attempting to change the subject, I launched into a discussion of printing and thankfully he dug into his food.

As comrades, we talked about a myriad of topics: the presses, type fonts, colored ink, graphic blocks, and the various works we had produced. Then, we discussed the state and future of English literature, French literature, ancient texts from the Greeks and Romans, and how much the royals supported their work. I asked why he left Alsace to come to England.

He replied, "There vere so many printers in the Germanic provinces, some cities having five or more, I realized it vud be difficult ta compete, which is vhy I cames ere ta London, where there be only da one."

Then I said, "I saw that you pad the form with paper to hold the lines in place."

"Yes, ve do, but sometimes the lines on the page are a little off and are vavy, vhich is why we have a journeyman check each form and adjust it to be as straight as possible." Then I described how we used bars for spacing between columns.

"We filled in dents on each of the type to fix the type in place on a bar, thereby limiting having to pack it with discarded paper, which produces a nearly flawless line and saves a step or two."

"Oh, that be a brilliant idea!"

I also told him about my felt roller I had invented that made distributing the ink on the type so much easier and more even than the goose-leather mushrooms. With these changes we had substantially increased our productivity, printing more pages every hour. He greatly appreciated the ideas and promised to give me a guided tour of the shop the next day, showing how they had also advanced the art.

Then I remembered I had a question for him. "Where do you get your paper from?"

"Ve'fe been getting it from Holland."

I interjected, "We've been getting it from there too, but sometimes the shipments don't arrive on time, and we've had to slow down our press. So lately, we order a huge supply to keep on hand, but it's very expensive."

Wynkyn said, "Yes, 'tis. Lately, we svitched to a mill up in Hertford that just started makin' paper last year."

"How's the quality of the paper?"

"Vell, at first it was na goot, so ve still be getting most of it from Holland. It 'ad a lot of brown spots in it and easily tore. But his quality 'tis much better now, and we expects to get most of ours there soon."

"What's his name? I would like to see if he could supply us too."

"He be Tate in Hertford. Tis about twenty miles from here, about a day's ride. Vould be good if you used 'im too, because ve vant ta keep 'im in business. Even though his prices be a bit higher, it's still cheaper than shippin' all the vay from Holland."

Wynkyn said, "I'd likes to expand our books even more. Most of our works has gone ta priests, the upper crust, the royals and the members of 'enry's court. Of course, theys the ones that sponsored us and got us to vheres ve are today. Ve've just started to print up books that is meant fer the tradesmen and merchants. More and more people is coming ta read. I'd like ta print books fer them too. Ve can print more of 'em and thereby lower the price fer each book, vhich will lead ta even more people a-readin. Do ye see vhat I mean?"

"Yes, I do, Wynkyn. Once you do the translation, editing and set up a form, it's as easy to print a thousand books as a hundred. It's a brilliant strategy."

"Thank yeuw, Master Rand," he said with a wry smile.

Since other than Michael there was no one else to have such a discussion with, I greatly enjoyed our time together, as I could tell Wynkyn did too. In a sense, we were competitors but as so often happens in a fresh, new profession, we were allies pioneering the state of the art, anxious to learn from each other and compare notes. There was just so much to print.

I didn't, however, tell him about how we had pioneered etchings. With his doubts about my whereabouts, I was uncomfortable telling him about something from the future. Besides, it would give us a significant strategic advantage, for it wouldn't be until the 16th century that anyone else would use etchings. I found the process on my iPhone and worked with Michael's artistic, fun-loving daughter, Megan, to perfect the process. Printers were currently using print blocks to add graphics to books, but these were time-consuming to produce, error-prone and looked less than optimal.

Before, Megan would draw the artwork out, and then Ryan, John the blacksmith's son, would carve the graphic into a block of wood to be filled with ink and printed on each page. The etchings were easier to produce, with much finer detail that looked substantially better. The difference was like that between a 6th-grader's artwork and that of a professional artist, or a 100 dot-per-inch picture versus a 1200 DPI picture, or a low-definition movie versus one in high-def. I also was worried that if I told him about this major advancement in printing, it would spread like wildfire and somehow interfere with history.

At one point, I imagined him in the 21st century, thinking that with his attention to detail, genius-level intelligence and business acumen, he could easily become a billionaire tech entrepreneur. In my own time, I had met a few men like him. Those I had met rose to the top of our profession, men similar to Gates and Jobs, Bezos and Zuckerberg.

After the pub owner pushed us out the door, stumbling and slurring my words a bit, I said how much I enjoyed his company and remembered, "I would like to purchase some of your books."

He said, "Given the gifts you gave Bill and that you verks vith Michael, I will give ye whatever ye likes."

Not wanting to wake the children, I sneaked into Colleen's house. Curious about Wynkyn, I grabbed my iPhone, turned it on for the first time in weeks and looked him up. Of course, there was no internet, but before I left for the Grand Canyon, I downloaded a compressed Wikipedia version onto my phone. I knew we would have some intellectual discussions in the canyon and planned to use my phone to reference tidbits of facts or argue my point and amaze my friends. I milked it as long as I could until they finally saw the phone light's reflection and figured out what I was doing. After earlier telling them how I wanted to get away from all the tech in the remoteness of the Grand Canyon, Jenny and Betty were not pleased. Now, due to my practical joke, I had access to much of the world's knowledge from the 21st century in the 15th century—something that could potentially be extremely valuable, at least as long as the battery held out.

On Wikipedia, I saw that Bill would indeed soon die and that Wynkyn de Worde would take over the print shop, producing another 600-plus books. Wikipedia continued:

England's first typographer, de Worde is generally credited for moving English printing away from its late-medieval beginnings and toward a "modern" model of functioning. Caxton had depended on noble patrons to sustain his enterprise; while de Worde enjoyed the support of patrons too (principally Margaret Beaufort, mother of King Henry VII), he shifted his emphasis to the creation of relatively inexpensive books for a commercial audience and the beginnings of a mass market. De Worde also printed volumes ranging from romantic novels to poetry and from children's books to volumes on household practice and animal husbandry. Using woodcuts, 500 of Wynkyn's editions had illustrations.

He moved his firm from Caxton's location in Westminster to London and was the first printer to set up a site on Fleet Street (1500), which for centuries became synonymous with printing. He was also the first person to build a bookstall in St. Paul's Churchyard, which soon became a centre of the book trade in London.

De Worde was the first to use italic type (1528) and Hebrew and Arabic characters (1524) in English books; and his 1495 version of Polychronicon by Ranulf Higdon was the first English work to use movable type to print music. (https://en.wikipedia.org/wiki/Wynkyn_de_Worde)

WOW!! What an impressive guy, someone I also felt privileged to meet. He and Bill were indeed the founders of the British press—the pioneers of printing in the British Isles and, indeed, the English-speaking world.

On Wikipedia, I also saw that Caxton had coined 1,300 English words—again, WOW! Using my 21st-century vocabulary, people were constantly asking me what I meant, which I thought was a problem with my unusual accent, but I now realized it was also because the English language was still evolving and many of the words I used did not yet exist, some likely invented by Caxton that had not even reached Ireland yet. Subconsciously, though, I adapted to their much smaller vocabulary, and those in Bunkillarny who initially didn't know what to make of me or thought I was "crazy" eventually accepted me, many becoming my friends in the close-knit town.

By the time I was done, I saw that my phone had only 65% of its battery left, and even if I had a charger, there would be no electricity to charge it—no London Electric for hundreds of years. I rarely used the phone and had previously turned off the WiFi and put it into airplane mode, then turned off all the background processes, lowered the brightness, turned on the battery saver and did some things only a skilled app developer would know how to do. I did not know when it would come in handy, but I wanted to save the battery as much as possible. Unlike my previous life, where it was on all the time, I would rarely turn it on—only where access to its invaluable knowledge was crucial.

I settled into bed and quickly entered the twilight zone between being awake and asleep when my shocking discussion with Mr. Caxton burst into my mind. How could he have possibly known I was from the future if he, himself, was not from the future? After reading about him and Wynkyn on my iPhone, I realized how far they had advanced publishing and English literature, much faster than could have been expected, unless, perhaps, they too were from the future. The thought struck me—what if other major innovators such as Gates or Jobs or Musk, who vastly altered the course of civilization, were also from the future? In the time-travel novels that I read, to varying degrees, the protagonists were careful not to alter the future, for it might have devastating consequences. But what if time travel was a normal way of advancing civilization??? After all, due to printing technology, there was no other time in history, except perhaps around the year 2000, when civilization advanced so rapidly. Hmmm!

I hadn't thought much about the hieroglyphs that I saw in both caves when I was somehow transported through time and space. At first, I thought these might have been from some ancient Indian tribe that occupied the Southwest and lived in the cave. But they were much more elaborate than any Indians had created and far beyond the Egyptian hieroglyphs I had seen on my backpacking trip to the pyramids. Could it be possible that these were from some advanced civilization that landed on Earth and intended the portals in the caves to transport people from the future to the past to advance human civilization? Sounds fantastical.

What if I was supposed to be here and didn't have to worry about altering the future? But I really didn't want to be here. I wanted to be back in my own time.

Before I left for London, I had Gwendolyn lead me to the area where she found me passed out. There, I rediscovered that hidden, mysterious cave. I left her at the tiny entrance, telling her that the cave was unsafe and to stay there as I squirmed through the small opening into the massive cavern, hoping to be transported back to my time. As I wound through the maze-like cave, I began to feel the same tingling sensation I had first felt in the original cave at the bottom of the Grand Canyon and saw the same type of multicolored lights. Hearing her call for me after she had surreptitiously entered the dangerous cave, I had to whisk her out so she wouldn't potentially be transported to an unfamiliar time or die in the process. So, it seemed that it might still work. My mind was boggled and being extremely tired from the long day and too much ale, I suddenly slipped into slumber.

The next day I woke up to a throbbing headache and promised not to drink that much ale again. I so, so wanted some coffee or Coke or tea or even a hot chocolate, but alas, none of these existed in England yet. Earlier, back in Bunkillarny, I had assumed Daisy, the McCarrons' maid, could brew me some tea, the national drink of Britain, but she had no idea why I was asking to drink the letter 'T' (another one of my faux pas that I constantly tried to cover up, telling her I must be confused, grabbing my head in a pained expression, eliciting her compassionate understanding).

I wished I could run to get my circulation flowing but knew no one did such an outrageous thing these days, for it would look very odd. People did so much physical labor they really didn't need any extra exertion—at least twelve hours a day, six days a week for both men and the women who took care of their numerous children and demanding home without any modern appliances. Instead, I worked through my normal periodic exercise routine of 50 pushups, 25 burpees and a mixture of Tai Chi, yoga and stretching, after which I felt a little better. I took a long, brisk walk through brightly lit, unusually warm Westminster to get some fresh air and clear my head when my thoughts from last night regarding time travel and what Mr. Caxton had said seeped back into my mind. I had been worried about using my phone to introduce future technologies over the last couple months, such as printing innovations, etchings, indoor plumbing (which Daisy loved), indoor toilets that everyone in our shop loved, and an advanced heating system to warm ourselves during those freezing Bunkillarny nights.

Could there be other time travelers such as myself and perhaps like Caxton who brought advanced technologies from the future to the past? As a systems guy, I had previously wondered about evolutionary technology. Most people thought technology moved too fast and that it was hard to keep up with, but I thought it moved too slowly and wondered why it took so long. After all, the television was invented in the 1920s, but it took until the 1950s before it really took off. The Internet was invented in 1969, but it wasn't until the mid-1990s, 25 years later, that it boomed. And the microchip was invented in 1959, but it wasn't until 1981 that we had the first IBM PC—some 22 years later. It seemed that many of the technologies of, say, the 2040s would be there in the 2020s in an elemental form, it just took someone to see the possibilities and put it all together. I didn't think of technology as developing from a starting point forward but rather like solving a puzzle—uncovering what was meant to be. When I designed a system, I started at the desired endpoint and worked forward to the beginning, then built it from there, discovering its true nature.

The app I designed was based on these principles, which would fulfill a vital societal need. It was something that hadn't been uncovered yet and was just waiting for someone to develop it. I had started working on the concept before I joined Steve and had invested my previous windfall on it, but due to a lack of funding, I had not been able to get it off the ground. I used an iterative technique to flush out the physical and software design and had hoped to fully develop it with my team and convince Steve and the VCs to fund it with our profits.

The application would revolutionize society by redesigning the way we process goods. It would reduce energy and handling costs for consumers and producers, resulting in lower prices. It would vastly reduce plastics in our landfills, PCBs in our water and carbon emissions in our air. All the technology, such as robotics and AI, was available in the 21st century, but without substantial financing I had thought it would be too large an undertaking. After all, eventually, it could be as large as Amazon.com, but would be four times faster while taking up a quarter of the space of a typical automated warehouse. It would be a radical improvement compared to the aging online delivery paradigm.

Perhaps this was why I was here—to take the priceless books forward in time, to sell them for tens of millions and use the money to fund this revolutionary concept.

Traveling gives you a new perspective, and after traveling back in time, seeing how much our civilization advanced over the next 500 years, and after meeting Mr. Caxton and seeing what one man can do, I had a new perspective and renewed motivation. That is if I could find my way back to the 21st century.

As my thoughts rambled on, I had passed through London, wandering along the Thames enjoying the scenery when, after encountering the Tower of London, I had reached the eastern border of the Roman wall. Having walked a little over two miles encompassing all of 15th-century London, I thought it was time to head back. Because London was so much smaller now, I could have run from one end of the city to the other in about fifteen minutes.*

Hungry and desperately thirsty from the long, brisk walk, I felt the need to find a tavern or pothouse to quench my thirst. The water these days could be contaminated, which had led to repeated bouts of typhoid and plague, so I would look for an alehouse that had weak beer, but I realized that I had not seen any place to eat or drink on the journey thus far; therefore, I walked a block north, away from the Thames, where I hoped to find an ordinary or a pub. There were no street signs, but I took the first left off the main road heading west towards Westminster on a much narrower street, no bigger than an alleyway, with the second floors hanging over the narrow, dirty, smelly lane. Thick, dark clouds welled up to the west and what had been a brilliantly lit, warm day rapidly cooled, dramatically dimming the passageway even more as the winter solstice approached when the sun hung low above the horizon.

I had heard from Stephen that the various guilds occupied separate sections of the prosperous city. However, this was certainly not one that the goldsmiths controlled, for it seemed dilapidated, resembling a scene from a Dickens novel, inhabited only by the poor and downtrodden. Tiles were missing from the roofs, wattle had fallen from the walls, revealing timbers and ugly, weathered twigs that hung out at odd angles, and due to a lack of paint, the walls themselves looked worn, torn and splintered with a layer of soot coating every surface. The people I passed looked bedraggled, unwashed, and had that hopeless look in their eyes set deep within their life-worn faces.

Whenever I had visited a new city, I enjoyed walking the streets, getting to know the area and people-watching. However, in cities such as DC, San Francisco and New York, one block could be affluent, whereas the next could be a slum. Therefore, you had to be careful where you ventured. Despite my building thirst, I thought I should reverse my course and head back towards the river.

Just as I turned, I saw two rough-looking characters bearing down on me. One was short, stocky and muscular with a barrel chest, scraggly peppered beard, greasy, unkempt black hair and a ruddy, red face. The other looked like his brother, who was a bit taller with a thick neck and a scar across his left cheek. I always wanted to avoid conflict and immediately spun around, heading the other way, when the first brother called out, saying, "'Ello, govnir." I ignored him, hoping the situation would fade away, and began quickening my pace when, ahead, I saw two more unsavory characters standing in the middle of the lane, blocking my egress. One was lanky and tall, at least for the period, at perhaps 5'10", with shabby, torn clothes. With a scraggly beard, he had a crazy look in his eyes and a mouse-like face that twitched like, well, a nervous mouse. The other seemed as though he didn't fit, for he was younger, somewhat handsome and better dressed. Both squinted, frowned, straightened up, puffed up their chests and looked menacing. I could feel my blood pressure rising, the vein in my neck thumping. I had a hollow feeling in my chest and felt faint. As they closed, I thought I would hit the young, less fearsome-looking one with a block and run as fast as I could, when from behind the first short, stocky one, who seemed to be their leader, growled, "You don' look likes ye belongs 'ere, govnir, arr ye lost?"

Colleen had told me that what people wore was prescribed by law according to class, so evidently, I stood out. "You don't seem very friendly, govnir." The fight-or-flight response was boiling and all I really wanted to do was have this incident end, for I didn't have much experience fighting. I had always been one of the taller kids in school and had rarely experienced or seen much bullying, let alone fights. I was more likely to break up a fight.

By this time, they were within a few feet. In a very stern, low voice, their leader asked, "You be red or blue?"

Confused, my voice cracking, I replied, "I don't know what you're talking about."

With a raised eyebrow, as if I was stupid, he added, "Would ye be for the red rose or the white rose?" I guessed this referred to the War of the Roses, which I knew little about. If I chose the right rose, I surmised I would be spared, but if I chose the wrong rose, I would likely be beaten or worse, so I asked, "Which rose you be for?"

"We be fer the red rose, o' course and 'Enry who we foughts fer. We comes from York, home of the white roses, and be farmers until the lord kicked us out and replaced us with sheep cause they didn't needs many shepherds and could make more money from the wool. Now them lords and those damned merchant adventurers who sells the wool are wealthy havn' fine houses, fetching wives, meat at every meal and as much wine as they can drinks, while we ha' noting."

"I'm sorry to hear that. Thank you for your service," which I immediately regretted saying since it seemed to anger them more.

"You not be from these parts. Ye ha' the look of a Westminsterian and don' belong here, do ye?" he said firmly. "We don' like westsiders, do we, lads?" While shaking their heads grimly, in seemingly prescribed unison, they all growled like wolves—"GRERRRRR!"

Hoping to de-escalate the situation, I replied, "No, I do not belong here. Sorry. I will leave immediately."

"Ye sound like ye be a Scot."

"No, I came from Ireland."

"Thas even worse, then ye be a foreigner trying to steal ar jobs."

"Surely you could find work with one of the guilds; they all seem to be looking for help."

"We don' want to be working with piss, tanning hides or sitting at a loom all day making cloth from the wool of the sheep that replaced us. We be farmers who works outdoors with ar 'ands in the soll. Men who fought for ar country should no be penned up in a dark dingy workshop fourteen hours a day." With each sentence, he and his men seemed to grow madder.

The four of them started advancing slowly, blocking my escape on the constricted street. I was scared, very scared, but I had to somehow defend myself. I wished I was one of those superheroes like Bruce Lee or Charlize Theron who could readily dispatch a dozen bad guys. They always seemed to take them on one by one, but these guys were all coming at me at once. Even though I had never taken a karate class and hadn't been in a fight since second grade, I assumed a karate stance, alternately facing each of my gruff-looking opponents circling me like hungry wolves sizing me up. The second brother had a stick similar to a nightstick with which he was beating his hand as he circled. I couldn't just wait to be pummeled, so I took a three-point stance and charged the tall, thin, crazy-looking one. I hit him hard in the stomach, and he bounced off my shoulder, flying four feet, doubling over on the ground. Just as I thought I might escape, the young one jumped on my back, grabbing my neck, and the others tackled me before I could run five hampered steps. I fended off a blow with the nightstick, hitting the taller brother squarely in the jaw, sending him reeling backwards. My adrenaline surging in the melee, I entered the zone where time slows to a crawl and, thanks to my long arms and legs, was able to give as many blows as I received. However, whenever I knocked one down or forced him back, unlike in the movies, they kept coming relentlessly back at me. Then the crazy one came at me with a knife, and that made me so furious I morphed into hyper mode, grabbing his hand and breaking it, causing the knife to fall to the ground. I didn't feel most of their blows and wanted to laugh at them, but when the shorter brother hit me hard in my side, I doubled over in extreme pain. Then, the other three climbed on my back and forced me to the ground, where they relentlessly kicked and punched me. I felt detached as if I was watching myself being beaten, as if it wasn't really me. Part of me was deathly afraid and wanted to roll up into a ball until the steam of their attack lost momentum. With all my strength, I rose up like a wounded water buffalo flicking lions off its back, picking up and throwing the young one up against a wall. For a moment, they stood in awe, and I thought I might run away until the club hit me in the back of my neck and, seeing multicolored, flickering stars, I blacked out...

A waterfall of rain cascading off the roof hit me in the face, suddenly snapping me back to reality. I tried to pull myself to my feet, but every movement caused such pain. I was soaked to the bone but had to get out of this dreadful part of town, so, gritting my teeth, groaning and grunting, I rolled over, pushed my left arm off the muddy, puddled road, got up to one knee and slowly, very slowly, experiencing shocks of pain, rose to my feet. Taking inventory of my injuries, my shins hurt, my right knee hurt, my buttocks and back and shoulders hurt, and since I had taken several blows to the face, my entire face felt like a balloon being inflated by the swelling. The worst pain pulsated from my right ribcage, which I feared might be cracked.

The yet-to-be-invented pocket I had Daisy sew into my coat was ripped, and my money pouch was gone, but, gratefully, so were the muggers. I wished I could have just given the money to them without all that pugilism, but the angry, desperate men wanted more than money, they wanted revenge for how their lives had turned out, and somehow, I was retribution for the grievances they suffered. Each hobbled step hurt, but I had to get back home —a slow, fraught process that would take much longer than the joyous journey here. Step by anguished step, under a pelting, cold rain, I proceeded westward under the cover of darkness.

After what seemed like an eternity, I eventually arrived home. Colleen, gasping in disbelief, was horrified by the sight of me. Having reached my goal, I could not take another step without her supporting me and collapsed into the living room chair, where she tended my wounds—the right eye already turning black and blue, the cauliflower ear, the bloody nose and the blood-caked cut on my cheek. She helped me up the stairs to the bedroom and, keeping her eyes closed, pulled off my soaked coat, pants and shirt, then told the children not to disturb me. She didn't want them to be horrified by the sight of me. After returning from the apothecary, she applied a mysterious ointment to my bumps and bruises distributed throughout my body and determined that my ribs had not been cracked but merely bruised. And since I could not move without causing them to scream in pain, she wrapped them as the apothecary had instructed. She then gave me some willow bark to chew on, and although I hurt, feeling immensely relieved to be home, unable to move, I slept like a petrified log.

Up until this time, I felt like a naïve, time-traveling, archaeological tourist enjoying my 15th-century tour of post-medieval London. Now I realized how dangerous this time and place could be, vowing to be more careful in the future and to limit my excursions to the safer regions.

FOUR

Back in Bunkillarny

The deceitful, spindly, pale Lord Coldwell Boston IV, who had been cooped up in a cubbyhole under the main staircase along with a few other scribes and bookkeepers keeping King Edward's books, had long desired more power for himself and resented the king. Unlike his father, the previous king, King Edward actually checked his accounts regularly, such that Boston could skim very little off the top, something Boston felt was his due because without his scrupulous accounting, the kingdom would falter financially. After all, it was he who ensured that everyone paid their taxes and he who kept track of what they owed. It was he who prevented overspending on lavish extravagances. It was he who ensured payment for the kingdom's mercenary troops and that their expeditions were profitable. It was he who ensured that the businesses and lands that the king owned, such as the McCarron print shop, made money and that the king received his share. Considering the valuable service he provided, so what if he took a percent or two (or sometimes five or ten) for himself.

He was glad that Reginald had assassinated King Edward because he had heard Edward was about to fire him and exile him or, worse, cut his head off. Fortunately, Reginald did not know of Edward's plans for Boston; therefore, in return for his silence regarding Edward's demise, Boston could extract his new position from Reginald. After all, Boston was the only one who witnessed the heinous deed, and if the nobles knew this, Reginald would have his head cut off.

Boston's devious mind devised an ingenious plan to increase both his and Reginald's power—a plan that would ensure their control of the kingdom and make them two of the wealthiest and most powerful men in all of Ireland. Reginald was a formidable man of action who lived in the moment, but not one who could formulate a plan for the future. He disclosed his seven-point plan to Reginald, a plan that they both vowed not to disclose to another living soul.

As agreed, Reginald installed devious Boston as the chief minister, to whom all bureaucratic offices would report. From each office holder, Boston would demand consideration and kickbacks amounting to perhaps 10% to 20% of their pay—an "oversight tax," as he called it, for his role in hiring and supervising them, which he would share with Reginald. King Edward would never have allowed this, but naïve Patrick would have no idea of.

Reginald had nationalized the troops for the war. Previously, each lord had their own forces composed of men from their districts. If the shire were in danger, the king would call upon them to serve until the danger had passed, when they would return to their lords and most would return to their "day jobs" as farmers, merchants, artisans, etc. The king maintained his own professional standing army, which could handle most of the threats both domestic and foreign. Citing possible attacks from those dastardly Neallanders, Reginald continued the nationalization of the troops. In reality, the Neallanders had given up their weapons and wealth, which made an attack impossible, but Reginald needed them as pawns to keep his army intact—a tactic of casting aspersions on others that autocrats back to the time of the Greeks and Romans employed throughout history to hold onto and enrich their power.

Reginald set up guard posts at each road along the western border with Nealland. In consultation with Boston, he called upon his most loyal senior knight, Hugh of Aberdeen, to disguise himself and, using a bomb, blow up one of the posts. The dastardly deed came off as planned, killing three men. Since Hugh also handled the investigation, nobody knew of the treachery, which Reginald saw as necessary casualties of war. Blaming the unscrupulous Neallanders for the bombing, saying they might overwhelm Bunkillarny at any time, he used this as an excuse to keep the army under his control and effectively usurp the lords' power to resist him. His real motive was to conquer defenseless Nealland and other hapless shires after things had settled down.

Then he ginned up rumors about the Neallanders, saying they were dirty, poor, unchristian barbarians, ate unsanitary food, and slept with pigs. Of course, in nearly every respect, they were practically the same as those who lived in Bunkillarny, but Reginald was following a "Machiavellian" guidebook, where you cast another group as the evil one to blame for all your woes. If the price of crops goes down—blame the Neallanders for flooding the market; if your taxes go up—blame the Neallanders for needing to keep the army intact, etc. Previously Bunkillarny readily traded with neighboring Nealland and had friendly relationships with them for decades. It took time, but Reginald and Boston could see how the constant aspersions cast against Neallanders bore fruit as the citizenry gradually fell for their lies and reverberated them.

To fund the kingdom's army, with Boston overseeing the collections, Reginald doubled the taxes. Previously the citizens of Bunkillarny paid their taxes willingly and on time because they felt the peace and prosperity King Edward provided were well worth their contributions. The doubled taxes, ostensibly to fund the war, the army and all the new required armaments, were not well received and Boston called upon troops to enforce the collections. Hence, the citizenry was harassed and sometimes severely beaten or imprisoned if they could not pay, while some struggled to feed their families. With more of their earnings going to taxes, they had less to spend with each other and Bunkillarny's economy began a downward spiral. Since Boston controlled all the accounting, he and Reginald took their percentage off the top to fund their vastly improving lifestyle—something they felt was required to enhance their prominent positions.

Because of the nationalization, with so many troops now housed on the castle's grounds, the streets were flooded with soldiers. Two new taverns opened to cater to their thirst, and the town had its first brothel. Having been accosted before, decent young ladies knew to stay off the streets after dusk. In the past, the shop owners had rarely seen soldiers in town—something King Edward restricted.

The bishop complained to Reginald about the brothel and the immoral women now inhabiting the town from other parts of Ireland and nearby Scotland. Reginald replied, "What do you expect these men to do when they are away from their wives and girlfriends? As a celibate, you do not understand men's needs. If there were no way to meet those needs, the pure women of the town would be in peril. The brothel is there to protect their virginity, so they might marry good husbands."

Ending a successful fledgling program, Reginald banned Edward's education plan for the children of the merchants and some peasants, leaving such education to the parents—"As God intended." He did not want them getting any new ideas that might induce them to try to better themselves and vacate the fields.

Reginald toured each of the towns and villages in the shire, gathering the inhabitants together in the center of town. Wearing Henry's silver cross, which he won for meritorious service to the King of England, that he held high, he recounted the glorious victory at Nealland and his own heroic deeds defending Patrick against John, the philanderer. Even though it was far from the truth, he referred to John as the philanderer multiple times during the speech so that it would sink in.

The way he told the story, slaying a score of Neallanders, made it seem like he single-handedly won the day. He told them of the bomb, how devious the Neallanders were, cautioning them to be on the lookout for them. He explained that because Neallanders could not be trusted, the army had been nationalized to protect them. He called attention to their local heroes on the display platform with him.

He told them how he had improved the management of the shire and how well the shire was faring—even better than under Edward. Shills were planted in the audience to stimulate cheering. Throughout his speeches, which became better with each delivery, he learned to pause after each statement when they all cheered. At the end, he told them that he would convene the games next spring rather than after the normal two years, which brought out the loudest cheers! And that he, who had won the last three games, would, despite his all-consuming duties, compete again—more cheers! Because of his prowess winning the sword and jousting competitions, and his victories in the wars in England and the south of Ireland, like Caesar, the people lauded Reginald as their hero. They blamed Boston for the taxes, not Reginald, and were thrilled to see their hero in their hamlet.

Reginald and Boston moved to remove the three "disloyal" council members who had voted against them when they supported John instead of Patrick for the throne: "Lord Brogan, Lord O'Flannery and that intellectual printer, Michael McCarron." Reginald had Patrick, unknowingly, sign their choices for the council, replacing the three with three of Reginald's most loyal senior knights, including Hugh—something Edward, eschewing having military men on the council, would never have approved. Adoring Reginald, trusting him completely, wanting to please the father figure who finally paid attention to him, teenage Patrick signed whatever Reginald put in front of him with little explanation or having read it. Reginald would preside over the council, with Lord Boston performing the roles of vice chair, treasurer and secretary.

When word of this realignment reached Queen Mother Catherine, she queried her son, who, like any petulant teenager, shrugged his shoulders. She demanded that before he sign any further orders, she would review these first. She told him that it was her duty as regent to do so. She vacillated between wanting to take a larger role and yet needing to mourn. Still devastated by her husband's untimely death, weakened and despondent from her anorexia and depression, the mourning won out, and she retreated to her cloistered, subdued life. Patrick, realizing how pained his mother was, came to rely more and more upon Reginald for counsel.*

During the first council meeting under the new king, who was not even present, O'Flannery, Brogan and McCarron were thanked for their long service to the king and shire and released from their duties. Outraged, the three longtime comrades and veterans, who had fought together in previous wars, rode to the print shop to discuss the matter.

In the backyard overlooking the gurgling Bunkillarny River, Lord O'Flannery started the discussion among the three concerned citizens, saying, "Since Reginald and Boston took over a couple of months ago, they moved quickly to cement their power. Boston had been libeling the legitimate heir, Prince John, and Reginald betrayed him. They have doubled the taxes, conscripted our men of arms, and by doing so, pulled our workers from our fields and shops."

Michael next spoke, "And look what has happened to our town. Not a night goes by that I do not see a drunken soldier on the streets or hear of a fight spilling out of one of the new taverns. I will not let Gwendolyn go out. And then there are those whores in the center of town, a block from the holy cathedral. It's an affront to us all.

"When the brothel first opened, Gwendolyn went down to the docks to fetch some fresh fish for dinner. As she told it ta me, there be a beautiful sunset o'er the bay that night that she lingered to behold rather than gettin' back home before nightfall as I had cautioned her.

"The sky came alive with streaks of crimson, highlighted by bedazzling golds, vivid, translucent violets and radiant shades of turquoise. Mesmerized, Gwendolyn lingered after the brilliant sun had settled into the swilly and watched the spectacular show until the end when it suddenly became pitch dark. She remembered her da had told her not to be out so late and, fearful of what might transpire, her senses were on high alert when, from behind the bushes, two soldiers suddenly blocked her path, one in front and one behind, who grabbed her around her waist and started kissing her neck. The other, the fat one, who smelled of sweat and stale ale, looked at her with perverse lust in his eyes, came closer, grabbed her by the shoulders, pulled her towards him, puckered his lips and was about to kiss her. She kneed him in the groin, which caused him to bend over crying out in pain, raised her arm backwards, hooked her hand and scratched the eye of the other, then ran away. They chased her, but the fat one could not keep up. The thin one reversed course when he saw O'Leary, responding to her cries for help, come to her rescue, swinging his massive butcher cleaver wildly in the air, which she grabbed and threatened the abuser with. O'Leary had to hold her back as the thin one ran for his life.

"When she returned to the print shop, her face was red as a beet and she was beyond fury, a-grabbin' me sword and wantin' to hunt the bastards down till I wrestled it from her."

Finding it difficult to contain his mounting anger, Brogan broke in, "Reginald and Boston know we would oppose what they are a-doin', which is why they removed us from the council. And poor Patrick, he is a good lad who is being co-opted by a man with vile intentions. Who knows what he will do next? With his lust for gold and power, he might use his army to invade one of the lesser kingdoms to the south or even the larger Nealland.

"For years, King Edward and his father before him and his grandfather before that refused to side with either Donegal or Nealland, staying neutral, realizing that if they did choose one side or ta other, they would tip the balance of power and forever be the enemy of the loser. The two mighty kingdoms to the west were always squabbling like a married couple, but nothing serious ever came o' it. As you be a-knowin', I blame him for the jousting death of my son Thomas, my poor, heroic knight who had such a bright future, the apple o' his mother's eye. I want to strangle him for that and for his betrayal of Bonnie Prince John."

O'Flannery injected, "But what can we do? We are powerless without our men and no seat at the old oak table."

Michael responded, "We could test the waters to see if other lords feel the way we do. After all, when we first voted, five of them supported John's ascension to the throne. We should feel out those who are most likely upset with the current regime. We could start with three: Lord Connelly, Lord McGlinchey and Lord Harold. Each one of us could talk to one. I could also feel out the shop owners and merchants, I know most of them are upset with the taxes and debauchery."

They decided who would talk to whom.

McGlinchey and Harold were sympathetic, suggesting two more lords who might join them in ousting Reginald—that is, if the circumstances were right.

Unbeknownst to them, Boston promised Connelly a new position in return for swearing loyalty to Reginald rather than to King Patrick. He subsequently told Reginald about the three lords plotting against him.*

Upon hearing a relentless booming knock at the door, Michael sleepily rose out of bed, incessantly yawning. Thinking it was likely some drunken soldier, he grabbed his saber, the one he acquired as a sailor, and made his way to the door. The knocking was so loud it also woke the apprentices, who lived in a room above the print shop, and Gwendolyn, who made their way to the entryway.

When he opened the door, he was surprised to see Reginald, who, looking forward to this enjoyable task, had a smirk on his face. Four formidable knights stood behind him.

"Michael McCarron, in the name of the King of Bunkillarny, I hereby arrest you for plotting against the king!"

"Reginald, surely this is some kind of jest. I love Patrick. Have known him since he was a bairn, when I bounced him on me knee."

Abruptly ending the discussion, Reginald said, "Men, take him." As two of them approached, Michael raised his saber, ready to defend himself, which was not an idle threat, for, unbeknownst to Reginald, he was an expert swordsman who had slain pirates more bloodthirsty than these men.

Gwendolyn, fearing her father would be killed, stepped in front of him, facing the five men with swords drawn. Reginald was ready for his sword, Megan, to taste blood. With fear in her eyes, she said, "Father, stop! I am sure this is some kind of mistake that will soon be rectified. Patrick would not want this to 'appen." Then, turning to Reginald, she said, "Please at least let me get him some clothes. He is in his bedclothes and there be a chill in the air this night."

Reginald, seeing her in her nightgown accented by the candle she used to light the way, taking her in from head to toe, seeing her curvaceous body, long reddish-blond hair and beautiful, symmetrical face, leering at her lasciviously, said, "Go get them quickly, Gwen," then beheld her as she scurried away.

Reginald's men tied Michael's hands and roughly threw him into a cart like a sack of gourds, where he banged his head and began bleeding. At the castle, they tossed him into a dirty, dark, dank cell that smelled of old sweat, excrement and the slimy, blackish-green mold clinging to the walls. There, Michael saw that Lords Brogan and O'Flannery had also been imprisoned. At one corner of the small room lay a bed of straw too small for all three of them and a wooden bucket as their toilet. With no window, the only light they had emanated from one lonely candle that would soon burn out.

Concerned for her father's welfare, seeing how ruthless Reginald could be, thinking he might be beaten, flogged, or, worse, killed, Gwendolyn felt alone and wished Rand were there to help her figure this out, for he would surely know what to do. He should have been able to hire a publisher's agent by now. When, oh when, would he return from London? Each day, she longed to see him at the door of the shop, and each night, she felt disappointment. It seemed like such a long time since he left the Bunkillarny dock with Captain Black on that foggy morn when she couldn't help but kiss him on the lips. It had been over three months; he should be back by now. She needed him. Her father needed him. Showing his prowess, he had done so well at the biannual

Bunkillarny games, and he had even stood up to Reginald to save the honor of Marie, that princess with whom all the men at court seemed to be infatuated.

When she first cared for him, she thought he was so weird, but he seemed to have some quirky vision of the future and would somehow know what to do.*

Still dressed in black, Queen Catherine, who remained cloistered, continued mourning for her departed husband. She was incensed when she finally heard the news of her three friends' imprisonment. Angrily she marched down the hall to Reginald's spacious rooms—the rooms that had been Patrick's until he became king.

"Reginald, is it true that Lords Brogan, O'Flannery and McCarron have been arrested?"

In a matter-of-fact, dismissive tone, he replied, "Yes, they were plotting against King Patrick, so as is to duty to my king, I arrested them."

"That's ridiculous!"

"We heard from a reputable source that they were discussing installing John. That's sedition. As you well know, they were the only ones on the council who voted against your son Patrick's assumption to the throne, and they could not accept the decision of the council."

"They were three of Edward's most trusted advisors, and each knew Patrick well. Lord O'Flannery is, after all, Patrick's godfather, Michael his tutor. They would never do anything to harm Patrick, or me or Bunkillarny. I insist they be released immediately."

"Perhaps, Lady Catherine, we can work something out. You are still a very desirable woman, and although it is still a little soon, you will need a husband to protect you and guide you and your children. It would be so much simpler if, rather than bickering with each other, we were to wed—for Patrick's sake, of course, not now, but in a few months after your mourning period has expired. We can keep our intentions a secret until then."

She knew he wanted to access her assets in France to add to his coffers, and as Patrick's stepfather, as a man, he would have even more influence over him and be one step closer to the throne. It was, after all, a man's world, in which women had few possessions or power.

"Am I not an attractive man? There is certainly no one more formidable as a protector than I. You are such a fine queen, someone who is adored by your subjects. Think of all the good you could do for them and the shire. I could see that you continue to live the royal life that you have become accustomed to."

Disgusted, Catherine replied, "I would never marry you!"

"But we would make such a fine pair, and if you are worried about me bothering you every night, I promise I will not do that. Once we have a male heir or two, I will divert myself with my mistresses."

"If you do not release the lords, I will go to my son Patrick and have him sign an order to do so."

"Don't upset yourself. I was only planning to teach them a lesson. I will release them soon enough, but we will keep an eye on them. For the king's protection, that is. Return to your mourning and let my generous offer fill your heart."*

Sir Hugh of Aberdeen, a tall, handsome, large man with massive arms, a barrel chest, a square face and cleft chin, approached the jailer in the dark, dingy, leaky bowels of the castle, asking for the keys. When the sound of metal inserting into the lock and the turning click reached the ears of the three friends, they were in a catatonic state. By now, in near total darkness and isolation, they had no idea whether it was day or night, let alone what day of the week it was or how long they had been imprisoned.

Hugh told them they would be released on the condition that they did not ferment any more insurgencies against the king and his regents, General Reginald and Queen Catherine. If they did, they would be imprisoned for much longer or, more likely, hanged.

When the three principled men hobbled out into the light, the sun blinded them. Their muscles and bones were slight and, without exercise, difficult to command. Their unkempt beards, sallow, anemic, dirty faces, rumpled, torn, unwashed clothes, and rancid odor elicited the impression that they were three beggars. In a window above the gate, Reginald and Boston enjoyed the sight of the three humiliated men, laughing at what they had brought them to. Catherine met them, covered them with clean, warm robes, and hugged each, while apologizing for what had befallen them. She had arranged for carts, driven by their own men, to take them home, the sight of whom comforted the disoriented lords. John, the blacksmith who drove the cart for Michael, had to hold back tears when he saw his friend.

During Michael's imprisonment, Gwendolyn published an article in the Bunkillarny Reader detailing his arrest in the middle of the night on trumped-up charges. By now the Reader had acquired an audience not only in the town but also in the other large hamlets throughout the shire, and it was part of the new apprentice Tommy's duty to ride out and deliver the broadsides to them.

Upon his return, Michael wrote subtle articles about how the "new administration" was not living up to the ideals of King Edward. This was new territory because there were no true newspapers anywhere in Europe, let alone on the edge of the civilized world in Ireland, and the concept of journalism did not yet exist, let alone freedom of the press. As with Caxton in London, the first press in the British Isles would be beholden to the crown. Indeed, King Edward had owned half of Michael's press. So, he trod lightly, careful not to cast aspersions upon King Patrick. Each week in his "editorials," Michael went a little further with his criticisms about the conditions in the shire, the brothel, the continued conscription of the troops, in effect testing the waters. It wasn't likely that Reginald read the Reader, but someone might get word to him, so he had to be careful about what he said. The lack of retribution encouraged him to push further.

On his tour of the shire, Reginald held one of his meetings in Ballyangle, demanding that Lord O'Flannery, along with a couple of O'Flannery's "heroic" knights from the victorious battle of Nealland, be on the wooden stand with him—the same stand that traveled from town to town. This was part of the conditions for Lord O'Flannery's release from prison. Although he detested the role, implying that he supported Reginald, he did not look like he relished being next to his oppressor.

After the speech, while they were deconstructing the stand to take to the next hamlet, one of the knights in Reginald's entourage saw a young man hand some kind of paper to a burgher for a farthing.

The knight grabbed one of Tommy's papers and read an article claiming that it was necessary to release the soldiers from the army so they could tend to their fields during the planting season. His first instinct was to tear it up, but instead, he took it to Reginald, who, upon reading it, went into an uncontrollable rage, grabbing Megan and wreaking havoc on a nearby vegetable cart to the horror of its owner. He had just given a splendid speech, which everyone loved and adored him for, and then they would read this slop, which undermined the good work he had done. How could such a dastardly thing happen to him? He had the knight track down the petrified apprentice and burn all of his papers.

Forgetting about the tour, he and his knights stormed back to Bunkillarny, where he broke down the print shop door, demanding to see Michael immediately. Seamus sheepishly went to retrieve Michael, who, hearing Reginald raging, walked slowly, seeming cool and collected. Not wanting to have him ogle her again, Gwendolyn stayed in the kitchen with an anxious Daisy, the maid, but kept an ear to the door, listening, in case she had to intercede to save her father's life again.

"What is this rubbish printed about my army? I have never read your little page, but did not think these dastardly things could be used to undermine my authority. The thin thing doesn't even weigh an ounce. I am the general of the army and a regent and the richest man in the shire. Surely, you do not think you could get away with this. I will shut you down. No, I will burn you down. Hugh, get a torch and start burning this place to the ground and smash this damn press to pieces." Then he grabbed Megan, swiftly sliced through the paper holder, and then slashed through the table that held the type, mighty blow after enraged, mighty blow, effectively putting the press out of commission.

Hugh lit a torch from the fireplace and said, "If you wants to save yourselves, you had all better git out o' here. Where would you like me to start, General?"

Reginald grabbed the large container of ink, spilling it on the press, tables, type and floor, saying, "Over here by the ink, which appears to be made o' oil. The whole place will go up quickly then."

Having heard the ruckus next door, John the blacksmith and his three sons grabbed pistols they had fashioned and were ready to shoot Reginald and his men if they dared to set the torch to the oil-based ink. Michael had seen them and realized though they might win the battle, their lives would be in jeopardy, so he remained calm and sought a peaceful solution.

Gwendolyn ran from the kitchen and was about to plead for the life of the shop when trying mightily to remain calm, Michael said, "I am not sure you want to do that, General Van Cleve. I do not know if you know this, but the crown owns half of this shop, and half of the profits go to the king. If you destroy our press and our shop, you would be destroying the king's property, which is a serious crime, for which you would surely lose your positions."

Reginald faced a tough decision. He dearly wanted to set the whole place ablaze, effectively destroying Michael. Still, he knew he would face serious consequences, which he thought he and Boston could somehow finagle a way to overcome, but it would diminish all they had accomplished thus far. His face still engorged red in rage, still seething, breathing deeply, he tried to calm himself. Then he had Megan chop through the composing table, causing thousands of carefully corralled type to spray, bounce and slide over the entire room. Venting his anger helped. Gwendolyn and the apprentices were terrified. Michael had seen such anger in his earlier battles with the pirates and, reaching into his battle-tested emotional reserves, contained his temper, because he knew he had won the war and this was just a minor skirmish.

Finally gaining his composure, Reginald found an angle he relished. "So this is the king's property. Then you should not be printing seditious rumors about the king."

"I have never said a negative word about Patrick. I am his loyal subject. Indeed, I wrote about what a wonderful ceremony his coronation was."

"But you do undermine his administration and his duly appointed regent who represents the king. Therefore, you should not print anything that undermines the king, his regents, the queen, myself, or his ministers, such as Lord Boston. Hugh tells me that this disgusting rubbish appears every Thursday. From now on, he will read and approve the final version before you print it. If you print anything else that undermines our regime, we will shut you down. Do you understand? Do you understand?!"

Considering that the life of his press, of which the Reader was such a small part, and that Gwendolyn and all who worked at the press depended upon its revenue, Michael had no other alternative. He merely nodded in a controlled, knowing way.

Hugh scanned the shop, now in tatters, and grabbing the copies of the Reader, threw these into the fireplace, where they quickly ignited in a boom and burst of multicolored flames—greens, blues, reds and oranges.

When they exited the shop, Reginald told Hugh to take the men and round up all the copies of the Reader in the town, regardless of who possessed them. Then he had another stroke of genius and strolled back into the shop as if he were just a casual shopper perusing the books, where he saw the desirable Gwendolyn in the arms of her treacherous father.

When he spoke, their faces turned towards him. "Oh, by the way, McCarron, since this is the king's print shop, from time to time, the king will have you print items on his behalf." Then, thinking along this line further, "The first thing you shall print is my schedule of appearances. And, yes, also a summary of what I have said at each. Lord Boston will write these and give these to Hugh, which you will print. One other thing you can do is print an announcement for each of my upcoming speeches, which I will have nailed to the storefronts of the towns before I appear. Yes, this will be good. [smiling broadly with a smirk as the exclamation mark!] Thank you, Michael!"

Reginald strolled out as if he didn't have a care in the world. In a stroke of genius, he had silenced a potentially dangerous printing press, then perceived how it would help cement his reign and the love of his people. He could not wait to tell Boston his brilliant idea. Boston would love it. And, with his command of the language, would write who knows how many beautiful articles aggrandizing their successes and belittling their foes. He was entirely pleased with himself. Who would ever think a little piece of paper that could be torn to pieces or instantly vanish in a flame could be so powerful? Who would have ever thought that that little press, not much bigger than a wine press, could be more powerful than a trebuchet or a cannon? My, my, my!

When Reginald left the shop, he pushed past the large, formidable, glaring John, who, with his two pistols held behind his back, could have easily slain Reginald with his strong, bare hands used to hammer iron into shape.

Relieved that his shop had been spared and that nobody was hurt, Michael looked at the shambles and broken press and sighed. It would take months to order parts from Germany, during which time the shop would be out of business, struggling to survive. The four smithies came in, observed the damage, helped with the cleanup, and said with their carpentry and metal-working skills, they could rebuild the press, which they accomplished in two weeks.*

Reginald and Boston moved to consolidate their power. The two were proud of all they had accomplished—they had exiled Prince John, crowned a powerless child, taken over the shire's administration, doubled the taxes, nationalized the army, jailed dissenters, united the kingdom against Nealland, sidelined a despondent queen, and vastly increased their wealth and standing. In addition, with his speeches, Reginald was gaining a cult-like following with his subjects throughout the shire. The peasants resented the increased taxes but blamed this on the lords who subjugated them and Boston and his tax collectors. To them, Reginald, the one who excelled at the games, the one who won all those heralded battles, was a hero. He had co-opted all but two of the lords, who dared not to oppose him for fear of being imprisoned or worse or were given higher positions so that they would support him. Besides, the lords realized too late that he had become more popular than they were with their people, and that he was highly effective at cutting them down and bullying them if they spoke out against them. One lord supposedly died of food poisoning and three, including Lords Brogan and O'Flannery, had been imprisoned. He had belittled a couple of lords at his rallies, which the populous seemed to love—something Edward would never consider doing. If he had a problem with the behavior of a particular lord, he would talk to him privately rather than embarrass him in front of his peasants, for doing so would tear the social fabric.

Reginald, a persuasive liar, was coming to enjoy the speeches—becoming addicted to their adulation as much as to all his power—he truly loved his life. Plus, because of his powerful position and classic Nordic good looks, women could not resist him. He had his way with any fetching wench or noble lady he desired, even if she happened to be married—the right of droit du seigneur. The tour around the shire provided him the opportunity to see and bed the prettiest and most well-endowed women he desired. As quickly as he conquered them, he discarded them, thinking how wonderful it must have been for them to be pleasured and brought to ecstasy by him.

After days spent hunting for boar, deer and elk, Reginald hosted bawdy parties at the "king's" hunting lodge, where he and his knights partied deep into the night with women of questionable character. He also took over the "king's" seaside chateau with a spectacular view of the bay below, a long beach and pier with a large yacht attached. A multitude of servants maintained these facilities and catered to his every whim. Life was good!

On the other hand, Boston didn't care much for the outdoors, hunting or partying, but was constructing a massive chateau adjacent to the king's as a status symbol befitting his station. He enjoyed gourmet meals prepared by the queen's French chefs and fine French wines from the castle's extensive wine cellar. Boston greatly relished his position, lording it over the various nobles and managers who ran the kingdom, many of whom had previously looked down on him and now owed their livelihood to him. They knew he could fire them instantly, so they had to do whatever ridiculous or unsavory task he told them to do, and he enjoyed belittling them. To reinforce his control, periodically, he would fire one. So what if there were no other such positions. So what if they and their family might starve. That was not his concern. Life was rough. It was not just the strong who, like Reginald, could defeat others, but also the clever and cunning men, such as himself, who rose like cream to the top. Such men ruled the others who were meant to serve them. Plus, when he appointed a new person to the vacated job, he would get his kickback. And more than anything, he enjoyed counting his money and seeing his wealth pile up. Life was good!

At the next council meeting, with Reginald's three knights replacing the three dissenting voters, the pair expected the meeting to be a rubber-stamp of their successful actions, further expanding their domination of the kingdom.

Lord Harold asked, "Should not the Queen Regent be here?"

Boston said, "She is still mourning, and we would not want to disturb her with such matters. She is, after all, but a woman, tending to her children."

The lords were, however, not as malleable as the two plotters expected. Their taxes had doubled, but their income came from the crops their serfs grew and the herds their serfs shepherded on their lands.

Lord McGlinchey took the floor. "You have nationalized our men-of-arms, but we need these men in the field. They are farmers or store owners, or are the knights who oversee our serfs. Spring is coming, and if the fields are not plowed and seeds are not planted soon, we will not have crops in the fall to harvest. Without the crops, we will have no funds to pay your outrageous taxes. We need them back in their fields immediately."

Reginald looked at him as if he were shooting daggers, wanting Megan to kiss his neck, but tried mightily to appear in control in front of the lords. As a man-of-arms, he had never cared much about farming or herding and relied on cruel overseers to manage his estate. His lack of care showed, for his district was the poorest in the shire, his lands the least productive, and his serfs the most abused. The lords knew of his mismanagement and wondered how he could aspire to manage the kingdom but looked forward to when Patrick would take over in a few years—if they could hold on that long.

Lord Harold added, "Other than the one incident, there has been no legitimate threat from Nealland. They have been disarmed and depleted. It is planting season for them, too, and they will be tending their fields. There is no need for all of our men to remain on duty. Those attached to the castle can handle any minor incursions, and if Nealland threatens us, our men can be called back."

As these two talked, Boston looked around the table and, seeing the supportive expressions on the others' faces, sensed they did not have the votes to carry the day. Typically, he had a sour expression dominated by a long nose too big for his long, narrow face to support. When he spoke, though, his face came alive, and he had a deep, commanding voice and elocution that garnered attention.

"Well, noble lords, we certainly understand your just concerns. I am sure we can reach a solution that will meet your legitimate needs and still provide protection for King Patrick's reign and our glorious kingdom. We have recently heard that Prince John is abroad plotting to retake Bunkillarny and make us vassals of Nealland, something I am sure you would not want to submit to." (He was proud he had instantly made this up.)

"Here is what I propose. If General Reginald thinks we can accommodate it, your men will be allowed to return for the planting season and then, in a month or two, return to Bunkillarny. Those men who are not needed for the planting or those knights who do not oversee them will remain here. Certainly, after their glorious victory, the men deserve a respite to be with their families in their own homes."

McGlinchey—"That sounds reasonable, Boston, but what about the harvest in the fall?"

"Depending upon the threats we face from John and Nealland, we plan to release the men then too."

The devious Boston's motion carried.

Feeling blindsided, afterward, in private, Reginald angrily scolded Boston, who explained that they really did not have a choice. "If we do not have the harvest, we will not have the taxes to fund the army or increase our fortunes, let alone feed them. If we went to our bashful king to overrule the council, his meddling mother would likely interfere. You will soon have your army back, refreshed and ready for battle. Besides," rubbing his hands together and smirking, "we will not have to pay the troops over the planting season, which means more funds for ourselves."*

Reginald visited John the blacksmith and demanded that he spend half his time producing arms—saying it was his patriotic duty to do so and that he would be handsomely rewarded. After the battle, he acquired a portion of the Neallanders' armaments, but the O'Donnells collected the vast majority. Boston would arrange for a kickback, listing the weapons as costing 10% more, which he and Reginald would split for their troubles. If anyone asked, it was a procurement and transportation fee.

In the meantime, Reginald traveled to meet with his ally, King Rory. For the previous meeting, he had sailed on a sloop to the castle, but this time he traveled through Nealland, accompanied by a dozen knights, in case there was any trouble along the way, which he expected and looked forward to, for he loved to fight.

The journey unfurled very differently, though. Neallanders were little different than Bunkillarnians. They were generally genial people who tended to their fields or shops and had few political concerns. In fact, they thought he and his party were Nealland knights heading back to the castle and treated them well along the road and at the inns where they ate and slept. Evidently, they did not know that he was the one who betrayed them, and he did not want himself or his men to dispute that assumption.

Reginald saw that Nealland was a rich land, richer than his own lands, and better managed, and that its people seemed happier than his lowly serfs. He actually enjoyed the trip and thought how easy it would be to conquer them and how richly he would be rewarded.

As allies, Reginald and his men were graciously welcomed at O'Donnell castle. During a banquet that night, Reginald, sitting beside Rory, disclosed his proposal.

"Esteemed King Rory, we have been informed that Prince John of Nealland is in England, plotting to return with armaments and an army to rearm the O'Neals [something Boston had also fabricated and written about in the Reader]. There are those in Bunkillarny who still support him. To thwart such divisive efforts, I propose we unite again and occupy Nealland. We will split it into two parts: I will rule the portion east of the Celtic Bay, while you rule the larger portion to the west. Since we have degraded their forces, they will be easy to conquer, and John will not be able to gain a foothold when he returns. But we must do this soon.

"I have just traveled through their lands and have seen how rich they are. The peasants will little know or care who rules them, and once the lords have been subjugated and King Albert and all his heirs, including John's wife, are disposed of before she can provide an heir, they will fall in line. But we must hurry. 'Twill be as easy as picking ripened fruit off a quince tree."

FIVE

Regicide

Reginald's favorite mistress, Brianha, was a slinky, enticing seductress with long black hair, porcelain white skin, broad cheeks, full, enticing red lips, mesmerizing green eyes, and a voluptuous figure; she knew how to use this to her advantage. She was said to have powers over men, and some considered her a witch or a sorceress, but like most men, he could not resist her charms. Brianha's origins were uncertain. Some say she was expelled from Scotland for sorcery; others say she originally came from Egypt and was a direct descendant of Queen Cleopatra. She had been the mistress of a Nealland lord until Reginald splayed him on the battlefield. Then, through seduction, she found a way to attach herself to Reginald, who housed her in a room in the castle so that she could "tend to the sick" with her various potions, for which she charged a hefty fee.

When asked about poisons, she said she knew of several made from natural plants and snake venoms, some of which were practically undetectable, especially if administered over time. Reginald did not tell her who he wanted to kill, not that she cared, but he had her mix up some for him. He planned to administer it periodically to King Patrick, who still looked up to him.

After practicing dueling with a broadsword with Patrick, the weight of which he could not have handled before, Reginald sat down and poured ale into a glass where he had put a couple of drops of Brianha's poison. Patrick was thrilled to be drinking with his idol, who told him of his victory against the pigs to the south and how he had slain each of a dozen men, highlighting the gore and how much an O'Callaghan prince suffered when he tortured him. Patrick was not comfortable with the torture, but if Reginald did it, it must be for a good reason. Reginald said, "Your Highness, we should do this regularly, perhaps every other day, get together, practice, work up a sweat, then have a glass, and I can teach you the strategy of war."

"Oh yes Sir Reginald. I would enjoy that very much. I will make sure that my tutors are aware of my new schedule. Lately, I have been reading about the strategies the Roman generals utilized."

The two met nearly every day, practicing with their swords, talking about the strategies of war. Reginald was impressed with Patrick's book learning and actually learned some things from him that he might apply in his next conquest. At first, he did not think the potion was working and berated Brehana, who, in her sultry, French-accented voice, told him to up the dosage just a little (four drops versus three) and give it some time. After a week of dropping the increased dosage into the ale, Patrick began to tire sooner and his wielding of the broadsword became challenging to command. At one point, he dropped the weapon, which clanged upon reaching the stone floor; Patrick apologized for his clumsiness, unsure why he was having so much trouble.

Reginald truly liked the boy and had doubts about gradually poisoning him, but had long ago learned from his abusive father that he had to be strong and that other's lives should be of no concern to him as long as he increased his power and wealth. As his father explained, "The world be a brutal place, and life is short, only the strong and the ruthless prosper—those willing to do whatever it takes to remain in power. Regardless of how distasteful they may be, only those who take advantage of opportunities rise higher."

"But what about the teachings of the church and Christ, father?"

"The church and priests help us to keep the others in line, which works to our benefit. You must appear to be a believer and to be religious when it suits you, but do not let all that influence your true motives required to reach your goals."

"But if you do these things, you will not go to heaven. You will go to hell."

His father hit him across the mouth then said, "That's what indulgences are for. You buy an indulgence from the church, which forgives all your sins and guarantees your place in heaven. Just to be safe, I buy one anytime I do something particularly heinous. Oh, and that reminds me of something else. It is important to appear noble and charitable. Give to the church or charity periodically when such an act will boost your standing. And be sure that everyone knows what you have done. For instance, I gave a small amount to the widow Mary O'Brian after her husband, one of my most popular knights, died in the war. It was only a few shillings, and I did not do so for other similar widows, but everybody thought I was generous. Sometimes, when a tragedy occurs and everyone is paying attention to it, I promise to help out, then later, when the fervor subsides, I happen to forget about it."*

Every time Hugh came to Michael with a new account of the glorious war to the south or an article aggrandizing the new regime, Boston had written, he cringed. Hugh was there at least twice a week proofing the Reader, meddling in the shop as if he owned it. Michael looked forward to when he would leave, but despite their animosity, they developed a necessary cordial, business-like relationship.

Daisy could not stand Hugh because he was always in her kitchen, tasting what she was cooking, pilfering food, belittling her like a servant, which she was, but everybody else in the shop treated her like a member of the family. After he ate nearly half of her delicious stew, Hugh's face swelled up and had bumps that grew rapidly larger. The doctor came, applied some ointment to his face, and he had to lie down for half a day before the swelling subsided. She, therefore, found out that he was allergic to onions, so most of the meals she made from then on happened to have onions, but Hugh still managed to eat everything else.

The unjustified war revealed Reginald's true nature. Since his blood-lust, ego and greed would not be quenched, he wanted to conquer other defenseless inland clans, growing his army with conscripts from these lands to apply to the next. He knew of at least five of the lords who were wary of him but would not dare oppose him—he was just too powerful now, and it was easier to go along, for if they did not, they knew he would find a way to have them killed and confiscate their lands, leaving their heirs penniless.

Reginald had already accused his neighbor Lord Buckingham of treason for criticizing the war and, therefore, not supporting King Patrick's reign. He had him hastily tried, convicted, and beheaded with his head displayed at Bunkillarny Square as a warning to anyone who opposed him. Then, he annexed his lands and expelled his family, who had been there for 300 years. Since Buckingham's castle was much larger than his own, that was long in need of repairs, and had a beautiful view of the bay, he appropriated it.

While Reginald was away at the war, Michael had renewed his relationship with the queen, who, although she thought of Edward multiple times a day, was moving past her mourning and depression. He also was able to converse with Patrick, who had missed him and was impressed by Patrick's growing intelligence, kind heart, physical development and honorable nature, but who seemed to be somewhat lethargic at times.

It would be less than two years until he would be independent of his regents, but Michael was unsure the kingdom could wait that long. He was also unsure Reginald would voluntarily relinquish his power. Reginald controlled the army, while that dishonorable, slimy Boston controlled everything else. Michael counseled the queen on what he perceived as dangers to her and her son from the power-hungry duo.

He had to do something, but Hugh was always there and consistently edited the Reader. Finally, he decided to print a surreptitious piece that described what Reginald and Boston were up to. To avoid any suspicion, he would set it up and print himself late at night after the apprentices had gone home or were asleep and when Hugh would not be around. The circulation would be small—only to those he could absolutely trust, such as his father-in-law, Lord O'Flannery, and Lords Brogan, Harold and McGlinchy. He would also give copies to some of the merchants he trusted, such as John, who hated the taxes, the brothel, all the fights, and being afraid to let their daughters out at night. Their sons had to go off to Reginald's feckless wars, and some had tragically died or were maimed for life. He had never heard of anyone producing such a document, but he had to do something and hoped that telling the truth might somehow help. The title at the top of the one-sided broadside said, "THE TRUTH".

Despite her instincts and Michael's warnings, Queen Catherine was having second thoughts. Reginald had been kind to her; her son adored him; he had treated her well and had not bothered her. Besides, he was a good-looking, viral man and, similar to her husband, an attractive warrior. For her children's sake, she thought she should consider his proposal. There really were no eligible men of suitable age, nobility or character in the land. All the lords were too old and their sons too young. She could not stand or trust slimy Boston, though, and he and Reginald seemed to be conspiring together.

The wars bothered her, but Reginald had explained that the O'Callaghan's, sensing that the king was so young and that Bunkillarny would be ripe for the picking, were amassing an army on their border to attack soon. Reginald attacked them first in order to save Patrick, her children, and the throne, for as he explained, "If they won, their first act would be to execute the possible heirs to the throne— in other words, her children. Even though the excuse was fabricated, she took him at his word. She thought that perhaps he had matured and reformed himself and had finally become more chivalrous.

She was very worried about her son, though. He had been so strong and alert, but each day, he seemed more and more lethargic. She was concerned that he had one of the mysterious maladies that regularly plagued the kingdom and, in the past, killed nearly half the population, including Patrick's older half-brother, Edward II, Prince John's brother, who had been the heir apparent until he died.

After a couple of weeks, Patrick became too weak to continue with the sword practices, which oddly presented Reginald with a problem. If he were not there, Reginald would not be able to administer the regular dose of poison. And, it would not take much more poison for him to die.

As Patrick became sicker, Reginald had second thoughts, for he truly liked the lad and did not want to see him perish. He consulted with Boston, who said, "My dear Reginald, I am sure you have witnessed the death of many of your warriors, whom you loved, but you knew that that is one of the hazards of leading men—an unfortunate necessity to reach your just goals. So it is with Patrick, whom I also like. But we both know you would be a much better king than this naive adolescent child. He wants to be a soldier and, similar to any soldier, must be prepared to die for a greater cause and for the glory of Bunkillarny. It is not just about Bunkillarny either, for what we are doing is building an empire."

Reginald thought there was one way he might be able to spare Patrick's life—if he could convince Catharine to marry him. There was no more suitable queen than her, plus, as her husband, he would gain control of her generous income from Normandy. She was still a beautiful woman, and he had lusted after her for a long time, even when King Edward was in the picture. He would be able to manipulate Patrick and, as her husband, would have the final say on such matters.

Later, like his father, perhaps Patrick would die on the battlefield or in a hunting accident. Most people did not live much beyond thirty anyway. Besides, by then, he would be so powerful that none would oppose him, and he would make himself king. With Patrick out of the way, the son he would have from Catherine would rule after his death—what a magnificent bloodline he would have—a line that could carry on for generations and perhaps conquer all of Ireland. He would make sure his son would be as skilled a warrior and as ruthless as he was, just as he was taught by his father, who would be so proud of their bloodline.*

As Reginald approached Catherine's chamber, he found himself surprisingly nervous, as if he were going into battle. If she accepted his proposal, he would, in essence, be the king. He felt asking her was the noble thing to do, for it would save her son's life. His knock on the door was greeted with a sweet voice, "Come in."

"How is Patrick faring? I am very concerned about the young lad, who is like a son to me,"

"He seems to be doing better, thank you."

Reginald, who realized that without the regular dose of poison, Patrick would recover, exclaimed, "That's good to know. I miss our regular dueling sessions. Perhaps we can still meet and discuss things over a pint."

"The doctor thinks the ale may have somehow affected him negatively."

"But, drinking water causes more ills than ale."

"That is why he insisted we get pure spring water from the Bunkhill spring on the side of the mountain above the castle."

Reginald gave Catherine the large bouquet of roses he had hidden behind his back, then said, "Catherine, have you thought about my proposal?"

"Yes, Reginald, I have, and I consider it a generous offer, but I cannot make a final decision until Patrick recovers."

Reginald realized that if Patrick recovered and she refused his proposal, he would lose his kingdom. But if he did not administer more poison, Patrick would recover. More demonstrably he said, "My dear Catherine, I have given you much time. I need a decision immediately, your life and that of Patrick's depends on it."

She suddenly realized that Reginald had something to do with her son's condition and, in the commanding voice of a queen, replied, "I cannot decide at this time. Please leave!"

Rejected, Reginald flew into an uncontrollable rage, "You bitch, how dare you, I have given you more than enough time. You will never find anybody better suited than me in this kingdom. I don't need you, and I don't need Patrick. The lords and the people are for me and not for you."

She attempted to flee the room when he hastily grabbed her arm and hit her with his right fist and then his left open hand. She fell to the ground in a lump, both cheeks stinging and red, her lip bleeding. Then he came down upon her and tore off her dress. She yelled," STOP! Get off me, you devil!"

Patrick heard his mother's cries and ran into the room with sword drawn, where he saw Reginald about to rape his mom. He hesitated for a second when he realized his hero was evil and said, "Stop this immediately, I command you!"

Reginald looked over his shoulder and saw the lad with a sword. He turned, jumped up, and unsheathed Megan. Now, he was even more enraged. No one could dare stop him from having his pleasures.

He lit into Patrick with a flurry, Patrick stumbling backward under the constant barrage of clanging swords, saying, "When we were dueling, I was merely toying with you, child. I will show you what war really is, you silly little boy." He relentlessly worked him into a corner, flipped his sword away, and had Megan's point at his chest, ready to commit another regicide as he had done to his father.

Aghast, Catherine ran to Reginald and grabbed his shoulder, pleading," I will marry you; I will marry you. Let my son go! Please, please let him go!"

Finally, having what he wanted—the beautiful Catherine and the keys to the kingdom, quickly gaining composure, with his chest swollen, head held high, Reginald said, "I am pleased you have come to your senses. You will soon enjoy bedding with me. Patrick, I did not mean what I said. You are a fine lad, someone I care much for. Even the best of friends have occasional spats. We will make arrangements to have the wedding next week." Then he went to Brianha's room to release his passion roughly. Afterward, he told her how well their plans had gone.

This was the first time that Brianha had learned who was being poisoned, and although she had long ago learned how to manipulate her emotions, she was shocked that he was in the process of killing the young boy, the king.

She had meticulously built a relationship with Reginald. If there was such a thing as love, she thought she might even love him, but now he was going to marry the imperial Catherine. Catherine was the opposite of everything she was—entitled, rich without having to work for it, haughty, and she looked down her nose at Brianha. They did not get along. Indeed, they despised each other.

"Where does this leave me, Reginald?"

"You will still be my number one. You are very useful to me. We will have to keep our relationship a secret, though, and I may not visit you for a few months while I bed Catherine, but after that, after she is pregnant, we can resume where we left off. Don't worry, you will be well cared for until then." He threw her a few coins as he left her room, something she found insulting but quickly scooped up.*

Immediately afterward, Catherine gathered Patrick and her other two children, a sack of gold coins from a hidden space behind a stone in the wall. She told her lady's maid to wake the four loyal royal guards she knew she could depend upon and meet in her chambers. Meanwhile, she woke up her children and told them to fill a sack with clothes and join her. Then she put on her rings, necklaces, and bracelets and placed the rest of her jewelry into her bag, which a guard carried. She knew she could not take the numerous pieces of luggage she traveled with because there was no time to pack; she did not want to attract attention, and they needed to hurry.

Fearing Reginald might descend upon them at any moment, the black carriage, surrounded by the guards on horseback, quickly rode through the moonless night through town to the wharf. She ascended to the gangplank of the royal sloop and woke the bewildered captain, telling him, "Captain O'Boyle, gather your crew and cast off. We need to sail immediately."

"But, me laddy, I 'av only three o' me crew on board and twill take time to roust the rest who be in town w' their wives."

"We have no time, raise the sail and cast off immediately. That is an order"

"Yes, yer ladyship."

As the crew went about their preparations, each minute that ticked by tightened the screws of their nerves like a guitar string being tightened, its pitch rising until it was at the breaking point. She tried to appear calm for her children, but they sensed her fear, which enveloped them.

Reginald and a dozen of his troops descended upon the wharf. Catherine's four courageous guards held them off with their pistols and swords as long as they could, one after another going down under the relentless assault.

The last man was able to cast off the last line just as the wind mercifully filled the sails. As the ship pulled away from the dock, two of Reginald's men fell off the cascading gangplank, and another boarded, ordering the captain to take down the sails. Enraged, Patrick approached him with his sword drawn, and after the assailant laughed, in five strokes, Patrick readily slayed him, to the surprise of his mother and cheers of his siblings. Reginald realized that his time spent with Patrick teaching him had, unfortunately, set him free. As they sailed away, Catherine told her children to hug the deck to avoid the rain of pistol fire that hit a sailor tending a. Reginald yelled curses after them.

With only a couple of men manning the sails, Catherine ordered her children to help pull the ropes, which she also relentlessly did herself, glad to be out of the grasp of her fearsome enemy and glad to be away from the minutes of the castle. They had all learned to sail on small sailboats around their summer chateau off Craggy Point. With the wind whipping through her hair, she felt free for the first time since her husband's death. The captain could not believe his eyes when he saw the king and all his family helping to sail the ship. Soon, the fresh salt, scented breeze carried them out into the Irish Sea, where they headed for refuge in Scotland.

Concerned that Reginald might be pursuing them in a confiscated ship, Catharine and her children spent a fitful night on deck, serving as deckhands. By the time the morning sun rose off the windward coast of Scotland, they settled into a small fishing village, where Captain O'Boyle hired several hands. Since it would take over a week to sail to London, Catherine decided to head for Glasgow instead—only a day away, where she hoped to find refuge with Marie.

Catherine remembered from her visit during the funeral that her niece, Princess Marie, stayed with Lord and Lady McIntyre. Therefore, they took a cart to their mansion, where although Marie had proceeded on to London, Lady McIntyre, upon hearing of their travails, insisted the downtrodden, exhausted-looking royal family stay with them. The McIntyres were wonderful caring hosts who treated the children like their own grandchildren, even introducing King Patrick to one of their redheaded, tall, fair, fetching young nieces, who stole his heart.

While in Glasgow, Catherine inquired about Prince John, who, although he had been there, had left Glasgow over a month ago. Fearing that he might be assassinated, John had not disclosed his intended route or destination.

After a fortnight and hiring a full crew, under Captain Smith, Catherine and her bairns sailed for London, where she hoped to find Marie and plead her case to King Henry to intercede on her son's behalf.*

Back in Bunkillarny, exhausted by the long night's activities and not having slept, Reginald met with scheming Boston just before dawn, telling Boston about how their plans had unraveled. Boston devised a cover-up as if nothing unusual had happened.

"HISS! Tell me about what occurred last night."

After Reginald recounted the story, sleazy Boston said, "Well, let's see. So, Patrick was sick and in danger of perishing. Catherine decided to sail to the South of France for his health when a group of O'Callaghan's or Neallanders, your choice, pursued them to the port and ruthlessly attacked them, brutally killing all her guards.

You did kill all the guards, didn't you?"

"Yes, Megan slit the last one's throat on the dock, and we dumped them all in the sea."

Duplicitous Boston continued with the devilish plot, "Then you came to the rescue, saved Catherine and Patrick, and as they had previously planned, they sailed safely away."

"But what will we say if Catherine and Patrick come back?"

"She will likely go to London to petition the king. So, we need to send some of your most loyal soldiers, who will be disguised, to spy on them and kill the entire family. We can blame the murders on Prince John's forces, who murdered them so he could claim the throne without interference and merge Bunkillarny with Nealland."

"Even her younger children?"

"Yes, it is not something I relish doing either, but it must be done for the glory of Bunkillarny. If we only killed Patrick, the younger boy would be next in line for the throne. Sadly, he must be dispatched too. We will need to convene a council meeting immediately to tell the lords what happened and how heroic you were, but we will spread rumors before then, and, oh yes, I will write a story for the Bunkillarny Reader for Hugh to have printed. Since you are the regent and the general of the army, they will have no choice other than to crown you king, well, acting king, until Patrick returns—of course—ha, ha, hiss. By the time they realize he is not returning, with all the heirs dead, you will be king. This whole mess will work in our favor."

"There is another matter we must tend to, though. You need to stop whoring around and select a wife. Don't worry; you can still have two or three mistresses, as most kings such as Henry do, but you can never visit the brothel again. You would not want your seed spawning a bastard from there that would jeopardize the succession. The people and the nobles need to see that you are serious, have settled down, and will provide a suitable heir. A regal queen will cement your rule. Plus, once you have a son, your rule will be secure. The history of Europe is full of failed dynasties that could not provide a male heir."

The two discussed possible candidates from the nobility, but most were too old, too young, too skinny, or too ugly for Reginald to consider. Then, the memory of Gwendolyn in her nightgown came to him. "Gwendolyn McCarron shall be my queen."

"Yes," conniving Boston replied, "She's perfect. She's the grand-daughter of a lord; she's beautiful and smart, too. And as I have seen from the accounts, their print shop produces quite a bit of revenue, which will make a suitable dowry for a queen."*

Following Rand's departure and Seamus' promotion to a journey-man, he decided that with his increased wages, it was time to ask Michael for Gwendolyn's hand. Michael did not want to discourage the young lad he had quartered and taught for the last half-dozen years, so he told Seamus he would leave the decision up to Gwendolyn. Seamus had wanted her for a long time, and after she kindly rejected his offer, feeling dejected, he felt as if the dream he longed for was over and his life had ended.

Instead of Hugh, Reginald brought this week's article that Boston had written regarding the queen's turbulent departure to the print shop, where he engaged Gwendolyn in innocent conversation. She was deathly afraid of him but did not want to insult him because he might arrest her father again or burn the print shop to the ground as he had pre-viously threatened to do, so she went along with him. As he left, he invited her and her father to the castle for dinner, saying, "I want to improve relationships with the print shop, which I now realize is an important member of the Bunkillarny community that Michael and you too, Gwendolyn, have done such a marvelous job building."

In the stately dining room, with servants at their elbows, elegant silverware, and china on a fine linen tablecloth displaying perfect, well-mannered behavior, Reginald entertained them. Gwendolyn was impressed by the trappings, his performance, and a little tipsy from all the "finest wine in all of Ireland" he had plied her with—her drinking it because she had at first been so nervous being there. Similar to many women he had bedded, Reginald felt that with his charm and extensive knowledge of women, he had her in the palm of his hand, and she would soon marry him. Michael, not trusting his motives, cautioned her to be careful. Reginald dropped by the print shop a couple of other times to see how she was doing, thinking in two or three weeks after a suitable courtship period, she would agree to marry him.

Following Queen Catherine's untimely departure, not trusting Boston's account, Michael worked on an article for the Truth. In it, he questioned Catherine's sudden departure. After visiting the castle and interviewing those closest to her, he discovered that she only took one of her maids, did not take her luggage, and had not told any of her ladies-in-waiting of her plans. Typically, such a royal trip would involve packing trunks for days and an accompaniment of servants to tend them. Besides, Michael had visited Catherine and Patrick two days earlier when Patrick was recovering. He suspected that Reginald and his sorceress, Brianha, had something to do with Patrick's decline and the royal family's sudden departure, but he had no proof.

After the print shop closed, Michael sat at the composing desk, placing the letters into the printer's form. Then, he placed the form in the platen and printed copies of the article he planned to distribute to his undercover friends. From his room, Seamus could hear the rhythmic printer at work. When he finished printing the copies, unable to keep his eyes open and nodding off from a long day, instead of breaking down the form, Michael placed it in his office, planning to restore the letters to their cubbies in the composing desk early the next morning. He just needed a couple of hours of sleep, and he would be fine.

In the middle of the night, Seamus slipped into Michael's office where he read the form backward, which he was now somewhat skilled at doing, but he could not fully comprehend what it said. Realizing what Michael might be doing, he grabbed the form, inked it just a little, carefully placed it into the printer, then pulled the devil's tail as quietly as possible, printing it on a single piece of paper. Then he returned the form to the office, carefully placing it exactly where he had found it.

Feeling rejected by Gwendolyn and Michael, he thought about getting the seditious paper to Reginald. He felt badly about implicating Michael though, who had done so much for him and was like a father. But, if he turned the paper over, Michael would be arrested, and Seamus would oversee the shop. Then Gwendolyn would have to pay attention to him and would surely marry him. He debated what he should do, but his obsession with the lovely Gwendolyn drove him into the hands of Reginald, who gave him a pound for the single sheet of paper—blood money that, when he returned to the shop, made him feel dirty, as if he were Judas.

When Reginald and Boston read the missive, they both went into a rage, and Reginald stormed out of the castle to arrest Michael. With

Gwendolyn pulling on his leg as the guards dragged him off, Reginald had Michael's hands and legs tied and thrown into the cart. Reginald returned to the shop and told Gwendolyn, "This is a very serious offense, one that will hang your father in my court. If, however, you were my wife, I could grant clemency. Think about it, Gwen, but there won't be much time—a fortnight is all you shall have, at most. Oh, and during that time, think about your poor, disgraced father rotting in jail."

With her father facing a possible death sentence, Gwendolyn spent the rest of her day crying in her room, wishing that Rand was there to help. Seamus looked guilty, and she instinctively felt she could no longer trust him. Seamus tried to take over the operation of the print shop, but she told him in no uncertain terms that she was in charge. He would be responsible for the press, but there was much more than just printing that she would oversee—business aspects he had no idea of. Seamus thought it was just about the printing and had no idea of the effort required to acquire the titles, translate, edit, distribute, and account for it all in the ledgers. He did not even know where the most vital supplies, the ink and paper, came from.

She thought, where was Rand? Surely, he should be back by now. I need him to help run the shop and save me da. I pray he hasn't perished. Dear God, protect Rand and bring him safely back to me!

SIX

The Agent

My main goal in coming to London was to hire a new agent, but there was no Internet, no Indeed, no Monster.com, no LinkedIn, Zip Recruiter nor Career Builder, or any of the myriad of job search sites yet; not even a newspaper that might have job listings. With no contacts in London, how would I find a suitable agent? Back in the 21st century, or more appropriately, I guess, forward in the 21st century, even though I would be bombarded with hundreds of resumes, finding a good software engineer could take weeks. If Wynkyn and Bill Caxton, who was intimately involved with the printing profession in London, could not find a suitable agent, how could I? My potential partnership with Michael and King Edward, and, therefore, my relationship with Marie, depended upon me finding that darned agent.

I walked to a nearby pub to noodle it over. I brought a quill pen, ink, and a couple of sheets of paper with me. I do not know if anyone else did this, but when I had a particularly bothersome problem or had to do some planning, I found sitting at a coffee shop, which did not exist yet, or a bar away from home and work a good place to work through a conundrum to gain perspective and hopefully an innovative solution. Of course, that was in the 21st century, when people at a bar were absorbed in their cell phones or the TVs behind the bar, watching some sports show or a news channel. Even though individuals surrounded me, I oddly found solitude there. Besides, the food and drinks were readily accessible, delivered promptly with a minimum of interference or solicitude. And, since my usual meals consisted of fast food, pizza, or lean cuisines, some bar food was probably more nutritious.

I was not sure how this would work in the 15th century, but I thought I would give it a shot. After I ordered a pint from the bartender and set to writing, those sitting at the bar by themselves or conversing, seeing me working on something, left me alone, just as they had done in my time, just what I wanted. In the back of the bar, I even noticed a man reading a book and another reading what looked to be important legal papers by candlelight as if they were at a Starbucks.

While I had toured Westminster with Stephen, he mentioned that this was where all the bureaucrats and lawyers lived in the more prestigious section of town, where the housing was much more substantial. According to him, Westminster was a separate town but was beginning to be absorbed into London. Perhaps I could find someone near here who could become our agent. But how would I insert myself into their society, and how long would that take? Even if I found someone, would they work out? Soon, I would be back in Ireland and unable to check on them to see how they were progressing. I couldn't even call them, and there was no formal mail system, and Zoom was centuries away. If they did not work out, our business might fail, for there wasn't that large a demand in Ireland alone. Plus, how would we find future titles to print?

Although I wished I had my gel pen, frequently dipping my quill in the ink was something I was finally growing accustomed to. The quill pen was a decent invention. The tip was cut at an angle, and when you pressed it into the well, through capillary action, ink was drawn up into the quill so you could write a small sentence before reloading. My quill feather came from a goose, which was evidently the best. Colleen used a crow feather for the books because it produced a smaller line. When the tip became damaged, similar to a pencil, I would cut it off with the scissors of my Swiss Army Knife to produce a new tip. I scrawled out the possibilities. Considering I would spend more time thinking than writing, by now, I had developed a rhythm. The golden holder and inkwell Queen Catharine gave me aided the writing process. Still, it could be messy, but I had fewer spills now. At the top, I wrote:

Where would I find an agent?

1. *Place Help Wanted sign in shop window - readers come to the shop*

for books. Perhaps one would want the position.

2. *Talk to the merchants who stock our books. They might know someone, could spread the word.*

3. *Move to Westminster Hotel, where you might find someone. (I am not sure how well this would work, as it might take time and be expensive.)*

4. *Hang out at in Westminster pubs, where readers live.* (I could tell by the political buzz here that pubs were popular among the intelligentsia.)

The next day, I placed a help wanted sign in the shop window and visited the merchants asking each of them if they knew of a suitable agent, and asking them to spread the word that we were looking for someone.

I asked Colleen, "What pubs do the members of Parliament and the bureaucrats frequent?"

When I asked that question, she seemed upset and without saying a word, just walked out of the room, which was not like her. I thought it might be because I somehow reminded her of John.

When she returned a bit later, her eyes looked like she had been crying. In a slightly choked-up but fervent voice, she replied, "The members of Parliament tend to go to the Hamstead Inn right across from Parliament. And many of the bureaucrats go to the Bull and Bear public house mostly. John used to visit both occasionally to drum up business."

I inquired, "Colleen, are you all right?"

Straightening up, with a smile and several nods of her head, she said, "Yes, Rand, I'm fine."

I knew she wasn't.

I thought the MPs would be good contacts because the Lords were well-educated and likely had libraries that indicated an interest in acquiring books and, therefore, might know of a likely agent. Over the next three weeks, I alternated between the two pubs, arriving early when I was sure to get a seat at the bar, and was successful in striking up conversations with several members of parliament and administrative officials. Some of the discourse was interesting, and I learned much about the politics of England, but I could not find anyone who was interested in being an agent or knew of anyone who would want such a position. I did generate more interest in our books, though. Some of those I talked to promised to stop by our little shop to buy a particular book I mentioned.

One fellow I met, Wilbert Robbins, a heavy set, jolly, red-faced, talkative, member of parliament, said in a huffy voice, "I think it be a fine thing you lookin' fer such an agent and all. Printing is an up-and-coming profession. I have a couple of dozen books meself, and I encourage me children to educate themselves, but by 'Enry, I cannot think of one who would want such an endeavor. It does not involve governing, there is no guild, and it's not really like being a merchant that sells everyday things is it. Sorry sir."

I had offered to move back to a hotel and give Colleen back her bedroom, but she insisted I stay. She was so thankful for the extra commission and now she felt better sleeping with her daughters in their bed versus sleeping in her and John's bed alone where she was constantly haunted by memories of him.

It dawned on me that once I found an agent, she might not have a source of income. She did not disclose this, but I could sense she was concerned about how she would provide for her five children. I insisted upon contributing to the household expenses, "By staying here versus staying at a hotel, I am saving Michael a substantial amount of money. Plus, I greatly enjoy being with you and your marvelous family versus being with strangers in a hotel. I insist." She reluctantly agreed.

I thought that she could still keep the books and the shop, which should provide a bit of revenue but that would depend on the agent, who might prefer to house it all himself. But maybe I could make that part of the deal.

After three weeks, other than a couple of dead-end leads, I had not found anyone interested in the position. A couple of young fellows applied for it, but as is so often the case, they were not a good match. One was too bashful to be a good salesman and the other, the son of a wealthy MP in the House of Lords, who read all the time, was completely scatterbrained.

I was tired of checking with the merchants and going to the pubs and did not think I could drink another drop of ale. I thought that perhaps I could be the agent, but I was no salesman, and it was not something I wanted to do or would be good at. I was very discouraged and thought of returning to Ireland and admitting to Michael and King Edward that I had failed. London had become cold and with the nearly constant rain or fog, a dreary, dim place to live—the weather matching my discouraged, depressed mood.

On a rare warm, sunny, late fall day, I bought a sausage at a butcher shop, a loaf of bread at the baker's, and some butter and cheese at a dairy. I cut the loaf in half and made myself a sandwich–something that probably would not exist for another couple hundred years. Enjoying my independence from the time, I walked out of one of the substantial London gates and sat down on the grass on a hill in a nearby field that had recently been sickled and sat on the fluffy, cut-grass-scented hay. I could see peasants in the distance cutting more hay, hearing their rhythmic, swishing strokes, feeling glad to be out of the crowded, noisy, smelly city, where I ate my sandwich in the serenity of sweet-smelling hay, at peace. Amazingly, I had walked less than a mile to be out in this lovely countryside.

The fall leaves at the edges of the fields were brightly illuminated in various shades of orange, reds, purples, yellows and golds and the air had that delightful smell of fall–crisp, clean, and earthy. I thought about my dilemma, occasionally looking at the inspiring scene painted across an exquisite canvas, munching on my delicious sandwich.

After lunch, while walking through the fields, down a delightful, sun-drenched, tan lane, an idea came to me. What if Colleen became the agent? She obviously loved books, knew the business, and had a long-term relationship with the various merchants who wanted to help her. I had hired many women and found that they performed as well or better than their male counterparts. Even though IT was a male dominated profession, I could not perceive the difference between the sexes' abilities. This oddly worked in my favor because even in the 21st century, other employers tended to have that subtle, obscure prejudice of preferring males, thereby allowing me to acquire better-talented females.

Still, it was the end of the 15th century, and this was a male-dominated society with few jobs for women or widows other than as spinners, barmaids, or in the oldest profession. I was not sure Colleen would be accepted in the agent's role, and that would not be good for Michael's business. Thinking about all the prejudice and discrimination she would encounter, I was also not sure she would even want to undertake such an ordeal. Perhaps I should not even ask her. Walking further down the enchanting, cottonwood tree-shrouded lane whose yellow leaves rustled in the breeze, I thought it should be her choice.

I went back to the shop and discussed the idea with Colleen. She was ecstatic, and suddenly, her sullen, beaten-down countenance lit up with the glow of enthusiasm. "But would the merchants ever accept me, a woman?" she stammered.

I cautioned her that I was not sure they would accept her—that we would have to convince them. "They did say they would do anything to help you out, though, didn't they?"

I knew that such a change would be challenging to accept and that it would be an extreme change for the time. I asked her who the main merchant was, and she replied, "Charles Foresight." *

A neighbor agreed to watch the kids. When we met Charles at his shop, Colleen seemed transformed. She wore her best blue-velvet outfit, radiating confidence and a nervous competence. Indeed, with those enticing blue eyes and honest, character-laden face, she was a surprisingly attractive woman. Charles was impressed by Colleen and wanted to help but was reluctant to deal with a woman. "Sorry me dear, it is something that the guilds just don' do."

Forcefully, Colleen said, "Charlie, you know well there is no printers' guild, or agents' guild, or booksellers' guild for that matter. It's a new profession with no such rules. Eventually, there may be more stores for books, but we rely on you to have our books in yer shop, we do."

I reminded him that he had said he wanted to help her and her five lovely children! "How else would they live? All they want is to work. All they want is a chance to survive."

Feeling sorry and understanding of her plight, he relented somewhat but said, "I won' be the only merchant who works with a woman, they'd have me hide, they wud."

"We will introduce the idea to the other merchants," I said.

The following week, we rented one of their guild halls and invited the merchants. We purchased a keg of ale and a case of wine. As they consumed their second glasses while locked in noisy discussions after banging loudly on the table with my shoe, I asked them to sit down and introduced the idea. They looked shocked and I knew then convincing them would not be an easy task.

"From what you have told me, evidently, John was a remarkable man and a splendid agent. I am not sure that you knew how much Colleen helped run their business. It was she who kept the ledgers. She kept the inventory, organized and sold the books at their shop. It was she who provided you with a constant supply of books, from which you made a substantial profit. It was she who read every book and constantly provided ideas to John to make the business thrive. I am sure as business-men yourselves; you know how difficult it is to perform all these various tasks."

"Colleen will speak to you now."

Colleen, who looked even more resplendent, spoke, "I promise I will continue ta meets your needs for books, guaranteeing that you will not be experiencin' any interruptions or problems. The business is called McCarron Printing, and you will not just be working with me, but with the business. I mean, don' yer wifes and children help with yer businesses anyway. Rand here, along with Mister Michael McCarron Esquire, would oversee me. If I do not fulfill your needs, you will no longer 'ave to do business wi' us, but that would be a shame since you would be missin' the substantial profits you have made on the books ye sells in yer shops, and as ye have seen more and more people are reading needing more and more books. With Christmas a comin' and some of the Lords likely to buy books fer their wives and bairn, I be sure you wo' not want to disappoint them now, wud ye? Plus, those who be a buyin the books wud ner see me. I'll arrange to ha' one o' me lads bring 'em to you. But, I will be the one meeting with you in your office if you like to take your orders and show you all new, wonderous books that your customers will love."

After fending off several questions like an experienced fencer, they unanimously agreed to try the concept "for three months"—a trial period as it were.

I lifted my glass and proposed a toast, "To McCarron Printing, may we all prosper!" They all joined me, smiled and proceeded to get drunk, paying more than a little attention to their charming, new business partner, who skillfully fended off their amorous advances without harming their egos.

We both realized that Michael had to approve the arrangement, so I wrote a letter to him explaining the situation. According to my copy of Wikipedia, there would be no formal mail system in England for another century or more. Still, Colleen agreed to send Harry to the docks every day until he found a captain sailing to Bunkillarny who would promise to deliver the letter for a steep fee. Since another woman, Michael's daughter Gwendolyn performed a major role in running the print shop, I felt he would acquiesce. Besides, he had given me the authority to hire an agent, and I could not imagine anyone better than Colleen.

I wish I could have used my cell phone to call him, text him, or even email him. Instead, it might take weeks for him to receive the letter and for me to receive his reply. *

I felt different in this place at this time—like, in a way, I had become a different person—somewhat like I felt when I was backpacking. As someone previously immersed in technology, backpacking in the wilderness, away from my myriad of electronic devices, provided welcome relief. I had felt continuously more intertwined with these devices as if, similar to a limb, they had grown onto my body, like a benign tumor. Working such long hours constantly on my iPhone, PC or tablet, holding meetings through Zoom, seeking relief on my widescreen TV, or Xbox or 3-D glasses, listening to my tunes on my earbuds, catching up with my friends through social media, I felt as if I was John Wick in the Matrix—as if I was more in a digital world than the real world. Although an adjustment, similar to diving into a pool of cool water, my forced escapes from that digital world always made me feel surprisingly more human.

The tech gives so much but takes something unidentifiable away from you. Backpacking restored my soul. After backpacking, I would come back to the digital world, the world of instant communications restored. I enjoyed getting back to it as much as getting away from it. Back here in the late 15th century, though, I oddly felt consistently less fragmented and more focused. Even though I had none of the modern conveniences, I actually felt more like myself than I had in years—like when I was a teenager before the iPhone was invented.

It was difficult getting used to this time of glacial communications, though. Missing the digital world so much that night alone in my room,

I had to turn on my phone and listen to a few of my favorite tunes. I looked longingly at my social media icons, wishing I could see what my friends were up to, and then I turned the phone off. The battery was now less than 50%.

Harry would help Colleen deliver the heavy books and learn the business that he would someday manage. Colleen would hire a live-in-maid to care for the children, but an important part of the agent's role would be unfulfilled—acquiring new books to print and publish. From a nearby clothier shop, she purchased a smart-looking black outfit she had her eye on to go with her new role. At first, she felt that such an expenditure would be frivolous until I convinced her it was an investment in herself and her business.*

The sounds of a dozen concussing, clamoring, clanging bells woke me from a deep sleep. Colleen poked her head in and urged me to hurry and get ready for mass. With a church on nearly every block, the whole town seemed to be heading to services. I would have liked to stay in bed, but unless I appeared to be a heathen, that was not an option; besides, how would she explain my reticence to the children, who had no option but to attend church services. The typically frenetic pace of commerce slowed to a trickle as people in their Sunday best filled the streets and queued up at the various churches.

Since it was only a few blocks away, we headed to Westminster Abbey because Colleen wanted me to experience mass in the glorious cathedral. The children's faces were scrubbed clean, and they resembled little angels at the Latin mass. I had been an altar boy, so I understood the ancient service well, but I had never experienced it in such a magnificent setting. I could not help gazing up at the glorious cathedral's tall ceilings, flying buttresses, intricate woodwork, and stained-glass windows. It had such a spacious, regal feel to it. I thought about all of the coronations and royal weddings that would transpire here: those of King Henry VIII and his six wives, his daughter Queen Elizabeth I when the British Empires started to take shape, Queen Victoria, who reigned over the largest empire in the 19th century, upon which the sun never set, and Queen Elizabeth II and Philip—the longest reigning monarch, and most recently King Charles III, her son.*

The crate I brought from Bunkillarny contained the original man-uscripts we had printed from the monastery outside the Roman-built wall encasing ancient London. On Monday, we went to the monastery to return their treasured manuscripts along with the copies John had promised. With so many churches, monasteries, and cathedrals in London and throughout England, reproductions of key books became a large portion of our print shop's business. John, a fervent Christian, had done a splendid job cementing relationships with the church officials. Plus, the English churches' facilities had a high demand for the works the Irish monks had preserved that could now be sold at a much more reasonable price while still providing us a substantial profit. Along with the five copies promised to the monastery and the original manuscript, we brought along a small cask of prized sherry that John had acquired on his trip to Spain.

Colleen had made arrangements with Stephen to carry us to the monastery. I was pleased to see my friendly tour guide that morning. It was essential to the business that Colleen be able to continue the relationships John had begun—something that could be difficult to maintain in a male-dominated church and society. A monk led us down a long, cool, quiet corridor to the Abbott's office—a large, comfortable, oak-laden, ornate room where we met Abbott Phillip—a short, balding man with a round face, engaging smile and warm, caring, deep-blue eyes.

He expressed his sincere regrets at John's death, for which he had presided over the funeral services, and reminisced about how much he enjoyed discussing literature and philosophy with him. We presented the cask to Phillip, and even though it was Monday morning, he insisted that we sample the fine sherry, something that he sipped with delight and a glint in his eyes, lifting his glass and saying, "To John."

We responded in kind, "To John."

Then, we broached the controversial subject of having Colleen assume John's role. He said he would gladly accept Colleen but worried about other church officials throughout England being as understanding as he, "Sorry, but they are not enlightened and would find it difficult to deal with an unaccompanied woman, my dear."

"I will be going back to Ireland shortly," I said. "Is there someone else who might accompany you, Colleen?"

"Harry, but he is too young. No, I cannot think of anyone."

Phillip offered a potential solution. "Whenever Colleen visits a church facility, Brother Martin, who is the monastery's chief librarian, a man of extensive knowledge and broad interests, could accompany her. He is the one who will be in charge of the marvelous books you delivered and the one who would have transcribed the text by hand if not for you doing such a marvelous job printing them. He would enjoy such excursions." We enthusiastically agreed to the plan.

That afternoon, we rode to the offices of the Archbishop of Canterbury in a sudden driving, cold rain. Fortunately, we had brought sheepskin tunics with hoods to shelter us from the rain for the cart had no covering. Stephan pulled up to a building adjacent to Westminster Abbey, shrouded in a stirring, gray mist, the spires no longer visible. We slogged through nearly an inch of mud to the entrance, where we stomped our feet to remove as much of the mud as possible, our footfalls echoing throughout the hall.

The archbishop was the Roman Catholic Church's highest-ranking official in all of England—considering the overarching power of the church, someone who was nearly as powerful as the King. As Colleen mentioned, the church controlled vast tracts of land, including nearly half of London, as witnessed by the number of churches in the small city. They also had vast wealth, and the archbishop crowned the King.

The Catholic Church's power and influence extended throughout Europe, including the selection of the Holy Roman Emperor. Indeed, it was more powerful than any King—the Pope lording over all the Kings. Even the kings had to abide by the church's laws and the rulings of the Pope. According to the "Devine Right of Kings," kings derived their authority directly from God and, therefore, could not be accountable to earthly authorities for their actions. God had chosen a particular family to rule, and the birth of a child within that family meant that God wanted that person to rule. Subjects should submit themselves to the king because it was God's will. Since the kings owed their positions to God, they should submit to his representative on earth—the Pope.

John did not know the archbishop, but he had established a relationship with a major official in the church, Monsignor Albert, who reported directly to the archbishop. After our splendid meeting with Phillip, I looked forward to this one but unlike Abbott Phillip, the Monsignor did not seem the least bit warm or friendly. He was an older man with a long, protruding nose and thin lips, set in a permanent scowl accented by deep-set wrinkles that belied years of frowning. We presented him with their manuscripts and copies. Among other duties, he was in charge of the abbey's library and its acquisitions. Although he expressed sorrow over John's death, when we broached the subject of Colleen carrying on after him, he said, "Sorry, my dear, but I absolutely would not consider working with a woman." Without his approval, our access to church documents throughout Britain would be restricted, and our business would suffer greatly.

I said, "We would like to continue our mutually beneficial arrangement and that Colleen was merely a representative for myself and the McCarron Publishing Company." He refused to relent and seemed disturbed by our mere presence.

I leafed through one of the reproductions from the samples I had brought, showing him how we applied block printing to enhance the text, to no avail. Then I showed him how we had pioneered etchings, which I was sure would wow him—nothing. I agreed to give him ten copies versus the usual five, which he could distribute to churches of his choosing throughout England and a share of the profits. He callously rejected the offer!

Feeling dejected, we hastily retreated to the door. Colleen grabbed my arm and turned me around, then looked the Monsignor straight in his eyes, and, smiling broadly, said, "Your eminence, I realize I am but a mere woman trying to feed me five children and provide a roof over their heads, but I have played a major role in me 'usband's busness. I have read every book we acquired from you and produced several Latin to English translations meself. The picture that Rand just showed you was based on a sketch I drew. I kept all the ledgers for our agency and can tell you to the penny our account balances."

He seemed to be softening just a bit. Well at least he had not kicked us out yet. She asked, "Do you know Friar Martin?"

Albert responded, "We are good friends, and we frequently speak about our common interests in liturgical literature."

"Father Martin will accompany me on our visits to cathedrals and monasteries within the realm and will advise me on the worth of various works." She confidently continued, "We will visit many such holy properties, providing them with the benefits of printing. Just think of all the time our dear Catholic monks would save copying texts. Just think of all the books that could be printed to spread the word of God. It would be such a shame if we could not provide such blessings to you, too."

And with that, the Monsignor agreed to the arrangement, ensuring that the percentage of sales was part of the deal. Colleen smiled broadly, shook his hand, and he was smitten. Then he did something I did not think possible—he smiled.

Afterward, we stopped at the Hampstead Inn and toasted Colleen's sterling success. It did not fit the time, but I raised my hand and, urging her to do the same, smacked hers, thereby teaching her how to high-five. She smiled—such a delightful smile.

As we supped on roast beef, cheddar cheese, bread and ale, Colleen spoke about Spain, "John said that he was about to acquire some amazing historical manuscripts thought to be lost forever. He said that these were beyond anything he had acquired before and that they were priceless."

I asked what they were, to which she replied, "I don' know exactly, but I think they be rare manuscripts from Rome and Greece, perhaps on Greek philosophy, Greek mathematicians such as Euclid, Greek and Roman plays—works that may not exist anywhere else in the world—works that may have been lost in the wars throughout Europe—works that may have been lost when the library at Alexandria in Egypt burned to the ground. John felt it was his calling to duplicate these manuscripts as insurance against their thoughts being lost forever and to translate them into English so that all mankind could obtain the benefits of such irreplaceable knowledge. Who knows what magical insights these may possess?"

"I knows Michael has worked to duplicate and preserve books from the Irish monasteries that after the dark ages, many thought were lost forever, but these go back even farther, back two-thousand years or more. When John described 'em his face was illuminated, saying that these treasures contain precious ideas and thoughts that man may never discover again—far beyond anything we are capable of imagining today. It was like he had beheld the holy grail it were."

I had hoped to return to Bunkillarny and be with Marie again, but I felt that as Michael's agent, I had to complete John's work. Intrigued by what I heard, I agreed to sail to Spain. I wrote a second letter to

Michael explaining my mission to complete the process John had commenced—to acquire treasures in Spain for the print shop and to do my bit to expand the world's knowledge. We had not been able to send the first letter yet, so Harry added this one to the first in a pouch.

I could not really fathom if it was true, but perhaps this is why I was here at this particular time in history—my purpose, my calling. Maybe I will find a lost manuscript in Spain from one of the famous philosophers, such as Aristotle's Politics or Plato's Republic. I thought about all those toiling in academia to add to our accumulated knowledge and earn their PhDs and how such a venture would substantially add to that knowledge. And I thought about how my Marie, who loved books, would be so impressed by such monumental acquisitions.

I walked down to the wharf to see if any of the ships were heading to Spain. There I saw the familiar caravel, Christine, just back from another trip. Captain Black was as happy to see me as I was him, saying that he had a cargo to go to Liverpool. After that he planned a trip to Spain in a couple of weeks and said that if I joined him as a passenger, he would reserve the larger cabin at a special rate. On the previous voyage, it had been provided to Lord Carrington, who we picked up en route to Dublin. Whether it was because he was seasick or he just looked down on us and did not want to associate with us, we rarely saw him. His butler delivered his food to the cabin.

Since I would not be returning to Bunkillarny soon, and it had been so long since I was there, I thought Marie might be in London by now. I walked to the Castle and inquired regarding her, but she had not been there. I reread her loving letter for the fifth time and longed for her, after which I thought I should forget the Spanish trip and sail back to Bunkillarny or Dublin or wherever and make my way back to her even if I had to walk all the way, for people walked long distances these days.

I could do it, but if I did so, I would not be doing what is best for the print shop. I always thought that as an employee, whenever you faced a difficult decision, it was your responsibility to do what was best and ethical for the business. Some people got wrapped up in politics and their own personal desires, but I felt this simple platitude made life much simpler. I usually avoided controversy and was eventually rewarded. Besides, if I ignored the opportunity, Michael might not promote me, and as a simple printer, I would not be able to ask Marie, a princess, to marry me. *

While waiting for Captain Black to return for our voyage to Spain, in the intervening weeks, I waited for a letter from Michael, toured London, hiked through the countryside, ran when I would not call attention to myself and played with the children, who I came to greatly enjoy.

Since this would be the first Christmas without their husband and father, thinking it would be a rough time for them, I wanted to do something special for Colleen and her family. John's parents had died, as had his only brother. His only sister had died at six. The average life expectancy now was about 35. Colleen's parents had died, and the rest of the family lived in Ireland, so they had no relatives in England. I asked Colleen how they normally celebrated Christmas.

"Christmas Eve is a day of fasting and abstinence. The four weeks of Advent are also days of abstinence when only the elderly, laborers and children are allowed to eat more than one meal a day. Since food is scarce during the winter months, tis a way to ensure supplies will last while also preparing ourselves for Christ's birth."

She was only eating one meal a day. I had assumed she had eaten breakfast before we woke, but I had not realized that she did not eat breakfast, and since I was usually the last one up, I usually did not eat breakfast either. Then, I thought she did not eat lunch because she was not hungry. Sometimes, I am so dense.

"You must think I am a pagan," I exclaimed.

"No, I just assumed that wherever you came from this was not your custom."

"Is there anything else you do for Christmas?"

"For Christmas Eve, we canna have meat. We have oyster stew, which I will prepare for the children to keep up our tradition. Then, on Christmas day, we goes to church to celebrate Christ's birth, and I make a mincemeat pie. Some people work on Christmas, but John did not."

"Did you and John have presents for the children or decorate the house?"

"No, don' know of anyone who do."

I had assumed they had a Dicken's-like Christmas, something I was looking forward to, but that evidently would not occur for centuries.

Christmas festivities were evidently just not that big a deal yet. Then I remembered that Christmas wasn't celebrated until Victoria married Prince Albert, who brought customs such as Christmas trees to the Isle in the 19th century.

I was still determined to make this day special for the children, though. Well, I had to admit, for myself too, since it was such a big celebration for my family that I missed so much.

While walking along the streets a couple of days before Christmas, careful not to walk into the seedier side of town, it was cold and gray with feathery flakes falling and melting on the dark-brown dirt streets. I found a ball in a shop window. I would give this to Harry. I turned down an obscure, narrow lane I had never seen before, where I finally discovered a quaint Geppetto-like toy shop. There, I found a spinning top for Albert, who seemed fascinated with such things, and a flute for Patricia, who was always singing.

Leaning into a stiff wind, as the snow fell at a progressively faster pace and began rapidly accumulating, it seemed I searched all of London for presents for the remaining two children. Obtaining a headache for my efforts, I had to find just the right gift for them. Finally, I headed for London Bridge, which with scores of shops crowded onto both sides of the bridge, resembled a modern-day mall, which prevented the now sideways, wind-blown snow from penetrating the cavernous street. The shops served as a barrier to the wind and since many of the buildings overhung the street with a festive atmosphere, it did seem like a mall during Christmas. There, I purchased a doll for adorable little Joanie and a hobby horse for headstrong Andrew.

On Christmas Eve morn, feeling like the redeemed Scrooge after he caught the spirit, I went to the butcher shop. I asked for a turkey, but he said, "I ner herd o such a bird." It was probably something only found in the Americas. So, I acquired a large goose from him. Since there was no wrapping paper, I also acquired some of his butcher paper to wrap the gifts. When I asked him about London Christmas traditions, he said, "Somes 'as yule logs, they does. Is a solstice tradition leftover from the Vikings, it is. You burn the log o'r the twelve days of Christmas."

That afternoon, I grabbed Albert and Harry and a long tree saw John had in the shed. We got Stephen to drive us and went off into the woods south of the river to cut ourselves a large log. Stephen said, "You knows ye ca-na cut down a live tree. Twil ner burn. Ye needs to find a fallen tree trunk ta saw. And this saw is dull let me file it down a bit fer ye."

We found such a tree, took turns at the saw, and the four of us dragged it onto the cart. Then, when we returned, we placed it in the fireplace to dry out overnight. Realizing such a large log would never burn, I cut slits on the top with John's ax, where I would place twigs, branches and bits of wax to get it started.

That night, when I went to bed, I felt the most homesick I had been. I looked out the tiny window, where the snow was falling harder and starting to accumulate. I could see the reflection of the snowflakes from the street lamps that cast an orange glow and blue shadows over the pure white snow. I missed my time, my friends, and my large family who would gather in a celebratory mood and I missed Christmas decorations, Christmas trees and turkey, dressing and all the trimmings. I missed Marie too and wondered if I would ever see her again. I so longed to spend Christmas with her, and I reread her letter once again, hoping she still felt the same.

The next crisp, cold morning we ventured out of our cold beds to attend Christmas Mass, where the priest talked of Christ's life. Even though the streets were void of decorations, after fasting for the four weeks, everyone was in a festive mood.

I brought out the presents wrapped in butcher paper and twine with their names scrawled on each and presented these to the children, saying, "In honor of the Christ child's birth, I have gotten these birthday presents for you."

They were overwhelmed and more appreciative than an American child who might acquire a dozen popular gifts. Patricia gave me a hug, then they all hugged me, including the ordinarily self-possessed Harry. Little Joannie ran up to the girls' room, came back, and gave me her most prized possession—her pig rattle, saying, "This is for yeuw uncle Rand," then kissed me on the cheek." Colleen cried.

That night, we had a grand feast of goose, yams, rolls and green beans, followed by the delicious mincemeat pie. After numerous tries, Harry and I lit the yule log, which filled the room with luxurious heat and a delightful amber glow. While the children played with their toys, Colleen came over and said, "Thank ye-uw. They have not been this happy since John died. They needed this. I needed this. Thank ye-uw!"

I said, "I miss my family and friends, and Michael and Gwendolyn, but being here with you and the children has made me feel warm too. Thank you for welcoming me into your home."

Over the next few days, we played catch and kicked the ball; then, I taught them four square, kickball and hopscotch. I also taught them to high five, something they took to immediately as all kids do. Colleen said it had been a long time since she had seen them have so much fun.*

The day before I was to leave, Monsignor Albert appeared at our shop. He had heard I was sailing to Spain. Knowing how valuable the Spanish books would be to the Abbey's library, he wanted to ensure they had copies. He had a list of precious books and authors he thought might be there. We walked through the list, where I noticed that a few entries had stars, asking, "What do the stars mean?"

He anxiously replied, "Those are works the royal family would want. For these, I need a copy for both the Abbey and the royal family's libraries, especially for Queen Mother Margaret. If you can acquire these, I will not only pay a handsome fee but will do all in my power to give Colleen whatever she requires and waive half of the royalties."

"So, monsignor, I guess these books would greatly enhance your reputation."

Smiling nervously, he replied merely, "Yess!"

"Then I trust you will treat Colleen with dignity and respect until I return?'

"Oh, most definitely I will, Rand. You can count on me. She is indeed a remarkable woman."

As I packed my bag, I felt some trepidation. I had no idea how long I would be gone, how long it would take to sail to Spain and travel overland to Salamanca, or what travails I might encounter along the way. Travel is so glacial nowadays, and the world is so different and less homogenized than my time, which centuries of trade, common technology, and instant communication had provided to the world. When you stayed at, say a Hilton in the U.S. or Spain or Russia or China or Kenya you could expect the same type of room, food and services, but not now.

I had hoped to head to Bunkillarny, where I would see Michael, Gwendolyn, and all the guys at the Pub, and hopefully Marie if she was still there. I wondered how they were getting along if anything had changed. Still, I imagined all was just as I had left it—the cheerful, friendly people, the beautiful bay, rolling hills and farmland, the newly completed cathedral, and King Edwards's well-managed kingdom.*

Early the next typically foggy, dimly-lit London morn, Colleen, the kids, and I crowded into Stephen's cart and headed to the wharf. Once there, Stephen shook my hand vigorously and wished me well.

Each of the kids hugged me except for Harry, who shook my hand firmly. Colleen said, "Thank yeuw for everything yeuw have don fer me and my bairn. Without you, I don' know how we would ha survived. Don' worry about the books. We will work very hard. We look forward to your return. God speed! God bless and protect you, Rand!"

Then she kissed me on the cheek and hugged me for a long moment—not a passionate hug but rather one between two compatriots who care for each other on several levels—something I found reassuring. When it dawned on me that this would be a long journey, much longer than the voyage to London, the feeling of trepidation rose from my stomach. I would travel over the sea on an ancient ship and then an even longer excursion overland in an unfamiliar country where few would speak English, in a time before world travel became common. Not knowing anyone, I would be a stranger in a strange land, in an even stranger time. Still, I was looking forward to seeing a country I had never seen before, even if it was 500 years before my time. Unlike London, though, I would have nothing to compare it to.

Stephen had loaded the crate containing books that John had promised to Spain and samples of our work to show them. Then I climbed on board, where Captain Black welcomed me on the familiar polished teak and brass-laden caravel, Christine, with ice sickles clinging to her lines and spars and a frosty white coating over her decks.

We soon cast off, sailed down the pastoral Thames, and entered open water. My cabin, about the size of a small stateroom on a modern cruise ship, was relatively luxurious compared to Christine's other accommodations. With an inset washbowl and pitcher, it had a larger built-in berth that almost fit my too-long legs, ample storage space in drawers under the bed, and a small built-in desk and chair—a cozy little domicile. It even had a porthole, which I gazed out at as we sailed out of the Thames into open waters, where two to three-foot waves and a steady breeze behind us powered the sturdy ship. I could hear the tinkling sound of ice sickles falling onto the deck above as the morning sun broke them free and the fog clinging to the river vanished.

The young cabin boy brought my bags and introduced himself as Jack, and asked, "Is thar any thin I can do fir ye sir?"

"No thank you, Jack."

The next day, I heard Captain Black constantly berating and swearing at his crew, "Pull up the f___g gangplank! Hoist the mainsail you b____ds. Swab the ____deck you lazy _______."

From my previous trip, I knew sailors swore, well, like a sailor and that the captain had to maintain discipline, but this seemed excessively abusive. I never liked foul language anyway. My father never allowed it, and I knew if he ever heard me, I would face the consequences, which I never dared test.

While on deck one morning and wishing dearly I had a cup of coffee, I spoke with Jerome, one of the veteran sailors, "Do you mind that the captain berates you all the time? How do you stand it?"

He replied, "Oh, he's just that way, he is. All of us ha long sailed with 'im, don't pay no 'tension to it. We realizes he don mean much by it anyways."

"But it didn't seem this bad on my previous voyage."

"I'll tell ye that's cause we ha new swabs on this here crew. He wants to get them in line right away fore they picks up any bad 'abits. If they ain't going to make it, he wants to weed 'em out as soon as posble. We knows what's going on and want to see them get on or out too. Don ya worry Sir, he will settle down soon 'nuff."

That night, I ate dinner with the captain, first mate, second mate and a Spanish passenger named Francisco. It was as if the captain was Doctor Jekyll and Mr. Hyde, for there he was a perfect host and a gentleman, discussing a broad range of topics without any crudity and little swearing—less than many PG 13 movies that is.

Testifying to his more civilized nature, on a long shelf stood several books covering a broad range of topics.

Over the course of our voyage, he told several highly entertaining stories. On one such occasion, after dinner, I asked, "How did you meet Michael?"

Sitting back in his chair, sipping his sherry, he said, "Well, laddy, that be a long story. Then he settled into his chair with a reflective, self-satisfied grin.

Me mum died givin birth ta me and me dad worked as a tanner twelve hours a day, six days a week, so me brother Josh mostly raised me. When I was eleven, he went off ta sea. Six months later me dad got me a spot as a cabin boy like young Jack. After four years, I became a common sailor. Then I worked me way up to second mate.

That's when I meets Michael. When we were in Dublin, he had signed up fer our ship, and I taught him 'ow ta sail. No one I ever sailed wit' ere learned faster than himself. After two years sailing to ports round the Atlantic, the Baltic, and into the Mediterranean, I made it to first mate, and fast as the wind, he became our second mate."

His, goblet empty, he poured another round of the deep velvet liquid into our glasses, then, with an intense look to build suspense, leaned forward, raised one thick black eyebrow, looked at each of us in the eye, stroked his long, untamed black beard, and continued, "One day after picking up a cargo of silks from Venice, we were headin' back past the rock, the rock of Gibraltar that tis when out of no-wheres a black menacing ship headed directly fer us. It was pirates who wanted our prized cargo.

"Michael, who was at the wheel, tried to evade them, but they had the wind behind 'em and us facing into the wind, there was lil he could do. We sounded the alarm and quickly armed ourselves just before they came alongside, throwing hooks on our rail to close in on us. Don't mind tellin ya me blood was a pumping and my stomach was a complainin, but I girded me loins and was ready fer the fight. With long black beards and dark, filthy skin, theys looked fearsome as theys boarding us. When about a score of them reached the rail ready to jump in unison, Michael, who had faced us directly into the wind, spun the wheel to port, the sail filled, the yardarm swung fast round, and before they cud draw a breath, it sweeps them dirty pirates off into the dark sea."

"Now the odds war bettar and we lit into 'em wi or pistols and after firing, our swords. Just aftar I kilt one, another came from me back and wi his hand raised just as he was bout to cut off me head, Michael throws his sword into him, instantly sendin him ta hell. He saved me life, and I be beholden to im till I me last days."

"What happened next"?

"So I digs his sword out of the scoundrel and throws Michael's bloody sword back to him, and in a minute Michael kilt two of them as do I. He was one of the best swordsman I er sees, moving like a cat, stinging like a wasp. By now, thays had enough, they be scared as hell and thays jumpin back to their ship, many falling into the water, and since thay can na swim, drowning the bast____."*

Following a tasty beef and rutabaga dinner the next night, I asked, "What happened after you defeated the pirates." Captain Black, a great storyteller who, by varying his cadence, could captivate his audience, keeping them on the edge of their seats, told us:

"We had pretty much fair sailing after that one, but we kept an eye out for pirates. The cap'n and the owner of the line outfitted our ship with broadside cannons that could blast any pirates trying to board us.

"Bout a year later off the coast of Africa, some pirates tried us again. When they comes ta board us this time, we blasts them to 'ell," after which he laughed heartily, "har, har, har, we did."

"Michael and me became best o' friends, he learnin' me how ta read and all. When we stopped at a port, besides drinking and entertaining ourselves with the ladies, he would search for books, especially when in Italy. Spent most of his wages on' em. After he read em, he gave em ta me and we would discuss what we reads. I guess I caught his passion for it, something I ner thought would 'appen—me a tanner's boy with no lernin to speak of."

Pointing to his shelves he proudly said, "That's where I got all these. Cause of me education, I became a cap'n. "

"How did that happen?"

"While we's sailin back from Spain, captain Mark died of a heart attack. He were a good man, a family man with nine chillren, he were and it hit me harder than a hammer on a nail. Me being the first mate as should be done, I takes o're the ship. Since they always wants more refined types and gentlemen for being a captain, I knows I would no get the job."

"Michael worked me over well though, pounding manners into me and roundin off me abundant rough edges that were a plenty. When I brought the ship back to the port, using words like he puts into me, I went to the owner's offices near the dock and askt for the job, real politely and all, using the fancy words a tellin' 'em all I hads done. After talkin to em for a couple of hours, careful of me language and me manners, if you can believe it, I didn't swear once, they gives me the ship. Of course, they had a big load a finished woolens they wanted ta transport to France right off and did not have a cap'n fir it. So I ow's Michael for my position too."

"So, how long have you been the captain of the Christine?"

"Four years, I has"

Somewhat confused, I had thought that he had been sailing on the same ship all along, then adding up the years, realized that could not be the case and said, "Michael has not sailed for a long time, so you must have been the captain of another ship."

"Yes, this is me third ship. Me second one were for Portuguese, and I even sailed down the coast of Africa. That be another world, nothing like England or France or Italy or even Spain. You couldn't imagine what the natives be like and the animals, like no others I er heard o—huge gray elephants, fearsome leopards and lions with teeth the size o' daggers, chargin' rinos and snakes that cud swallow a man whole."

"But this here ship be mine, though," he said proudly.

"I made a lot of money from my share sailing for the Portuguese, and rather than spending it on gin and women at port following Michael's advice, I saved it. After several years, I still did not have enough till Michael came up with a third o' whats I needs. He's a third owner and gets a third of the profits. The best ships in the world arrr made in Portugal and tha's where I got this un – Christine, the dear girl, will last long afer I be gone."*

I spent my days strolling around the ship and reading the captain's books on deck. Wishing there was a deck chair, I found a spot in a cozy corner of the forecastle's deck where I would be out of the way. One day, I explored the lower deck. The captain had several cannons installed on the main deck to rake pirates when they tried to board, but under the forecastle in a room I had not yet ventured into, I saw a much larger cannon, where I met Gerald, a grizzled, rutty-faced, old veteran who was polishing the big gun. I asked him, "Why is this gun so much larger than the others."

He replied, "Well sur Rand this is a very special gun she is. The others arr fur killing the pirates when they's close up. This uns fur long range to get 'em fore they gets close ta our Christine. Fur the others, we'll be loadin 'em with grape shot and such that will rip them pirates ta shreds. She gets a 25-pound ball like this un 'ere. (He had me lift the heavy cannon ball)

There's only a handful of these guns in the 'ole world and the captain had to do some special dealin' to get it from the Portuguese gunsmiths. Thays the best in the world by leaps and bounds, they is. Don' think thars another one in England, or France or anywars other than Portugal."

The cannon that sat on four wheels was very long and, judging by its size, extremely heavy.

"We had to build up the structure below it to 'old 'er. We calls 'er Mary Rose and she's got herself quite a temper. We loads Mary back here in er breach with her 25-pound baby and powder. She's made o' the finest cast bronze. Not like all those iron uns made of iron bars in England that soon falls apart. This is something else new—she don't stay on deck. No this lady pokes her 'ead out the side when she's a ready to thunder."

A square window with two shutters opened to let the muzzle of Mary Rose out. I could see that he loved his cannon and asked him why she was so special, which he seemed offended by and, raising his voice, exclaimed, "Why those other guns on other ships can't hits a ship from a quarter o' a mile. Mary can hit one over a mile away, she can."

To calm him down, I replied. "That's amazing. She's a very special lady indeed," he smiled, nodded, and said, "Yes she is, she surely is! She's got's grooves in her that spins the ball that makes it go much farther and straighter too. With other cannons ye don know where thays a goin ta go after they leaves the muzzle. Ye could be aimin straight at a ship's midship only a hundred yards away and miss it entirely, whereas Mary will hits the target 3,000 yards away seven out a ten times. That is if she has one who knows how to treat her."*

The next day, while reading in my cabin, I heard a bell clanging and the clamor and footfalls of men running on the deck above, yelling, "Pirates!" I started running down the corridor until I remembered the matchlock pistols John the blacksmith had given me, so I ran back and grabbed them, the powder horn and balls, along with my BIC from my time. I had only fired the pistols once, but I hoped they would offer me some protection against the pirates I envisioned already boarding Christine. I quickly vaulted up the ladder to the main deck, where I saw Captain Black telling his men to man their weapons. In the distance, I saw a nasty-looking black pirate ship sailing quickly out of the fog, bearing down on us. After hearing Gerald the previous day, thinking I might somehow help, I flew down to the lower foredeck to see Mary Rose in action.

Meanwhile, the captain had turned the ship so the port's broad-side faced the pirates. They were still far away on the fluffy white-clouded, blue-skied horizon when Gerald ordered his gun crew to load the powder and ball into the breach then lock it in place. Standing behind her, he ordered the crew to position her so she was aimed ahead of the nefarious foe. With a screw, he raised the muzzle up a few notches and locked it in place, then stepped aside. Noticing that the crew covered their ears with their hands, I did, too. Then he lit the powder hole, and she exploded with a mighty roar that shook the entire ship and threw the mighty cannon backwards and me to my ars, which elicited a round of laughter from the gun crew.

I looked out a portal and, after a few seconds, saw a high splash, indicating the ball had landed a bit short of the pirates. By that time, the obviously well-trained gun crew had loaded the breach and were in the process of positioning Mary Rose for another volley. I saw Gerald raise her nose up just a little and then just as the ship reached the peak of a wave, fire again. This time the ball landed in front of the fast, oncoming pirate ship's bow.

Gerald urged his crew onwards, "Come on, lads load Mary quick-ly, thar ship will be in range o' us soon, and with all 'er guns she'll destroy our deck and sails fore we can get off another round."

They redoubled their efforts, and after he made a couple of minor adjustments, just as the pirates started to turn to fire on us, he fired. I looked out again and, similar to a large softball, could see the projectile headed for the greedy pirates cruising on the blue waters, like a baseball flying towards a running outfielder's mitt. This large cannonball connected with the center of the pirate's main deck, ripping through at least one of the lower decks, too.

With the pirates closing in, the next shot hit on their portside just above the water line, so the waves of the churning sea would enter and flood the lower decks. No doubt, surprised by Mary Rose's accuracy, reach, and destruction, wanting no more of her temper, the pirates began to turn as a third ball caught the bottom of their rear mast and ripped it to shreds to loud cheers from the crew, which the pirates could surely hear.

Captain Black ordered a keg of ale to be distributed to his men, and that night, we all celebrated. At dinner, the captain, in his glorious, story-telling mode, emphasized his words with vivid hand motions and animated facial expressions, re-lived every moment of the pirate's shel-lacking.

I told him, "I was standing next to the gun crew as they were firing and was impressed by how coordinated and quick they were," *like a NASCAR pit crew*, I thought to myself.

He whispered in my ear in a low, gravelly voice, "Thars no gunner in all of Christendom better than Gerald be. That's why I pays 'im a double share and wud pays 'im more. Don't tell him that though. Somehow, he is able ta figure the wind, the distance, the speed of the threatening ship, the pitching of Christine, and land a cannon ball a mile away. He's worth 'is weight in gold, 'e is. So is Mary Rose. We all loves that lady."

With that, we toasted Gerald and the Mary Rose with some whiskey out of a keg from Scotland, Captain Black saved for such an occasion. After several more toasts, navigating to my cabin on a rolling sea was challenging, but I slept like a babe, glad that Mary Rose would protect me.

Salamanca Library

Founded in 1254, the oldest university library in Europe. "Quod natura non dat, Salmantica non praestat," (What nature does not give, Salamanca does not lend.)

SEVEN

Spain

While on the voyage, I came to know Señor Francisco Marie Jose Ferdinand Alvarez of Castile, a very proud, lean, well-dressed man who stood tall and projected an air of sophistication and breeding. His looks, voice and mannerisms reminded me of Antonio Banderas. He had dark hair with a Van Dyke beard and had been to Holland and England establishing relationships for the sale of his "rare" sherry, something we frequently enjoyed during dinners with the captain on the long voyage.

Since other than myself, the captain and perhaps the first mate, Jack, there were few others he felt comfortable talking to. Throughout the journey, with little else to do, we came to know each other well. As it turns out, he was a second cousin of Queen Isabella, the scion of a noble family who could trace his lineage back numerous generations to the 9th century. He, as did all the family, attended her royal wedding to Ferdinand, which was evidently quite the affair. The marriage bound the two largest kingdoms of Spain, Castile, and Aragon, to each other. To him, Isabella was the fairest, most intelligent, most noble, best-dressed, finest woman in the world, and he could not resist talking endlessly about her, such that I felt I knew her too. He did not know her husband King Ferdinand, well, but thought they had formed a merger that would change the world. Indeed, they had already nearly transformed the Moorish nation of Andalusia into the Christian nation of España or Spain.

As I learned from Francisco, since the eighth century, the Moors, who invaded Spain from Africa, ruled most of the Iberian Peninsula, that included both Spain and Portugal. They also conquered northern Africa and parts of Italy. They were not terrible overlords and allowed the natives to practice their staunch Catholic or Jewish faiths, but they were still overlords who Isabella and Ferdinand had expelled from nearly all of Spain except the Southern portion near Granada, and Francisco thought they would soon conquer that too.

I said, "It sounds like they are a power couple."

To which he replied, "I have never heard that term before, but yes, they are. That is actually a good description for them—hmm, a, a power couple. I like that Señor Rand."

Francisco spoke excellent English, indeed better than most of the English sailors on the ship, but after a couple of days, I asked to have our discussions in Spanish. I would be on my own in Spain and imagined that few people would be able to speak English, which he confirmed. I had a year of Spanish in high school and another year in college, but I was exceedingly rusty. Other than a periodic vacation to Mexico, where I spoke tourist Spanish—enough to order food, tequila, cerveza, shop and greet people, I had not applied it. Still, similar to 15th-century English, I found it difficult to understand the current Spanish vernacular. Over the course of the voyage, my Spanish improved somewhat, and I hoped I would be able to get by without sounding too stupid. It would be forced immersion. I did not realize it then, but I would acquire Francisco's higher-class Castilian pronunciation, which would serve me well.

I told Francisco about my mission to obtain books from the University of Salamanca. Adding that before his tragic death, John, our agent, thought there were unique treasures he had planned to acquire, translate into English, and have us print, thereby ensuring their preservation for posterity so that we too might benefit from the knowledge they possessed. Enthusiastically, he said, "I graduated from there. Who will you be seeing?"

"According to Colleen, I should meet with a Monsignor Dominic, who I understand is in charge of the library."

"Oh yes, Dominic is a good man. He graduated a year behind me and decided to go into the seminary. He is from a good family near my town, a very intelligent man and a fine man too, as I recall."

Then, speaking Latin, he added. "Quod natura non dat, Salmantica non praestat (what nature does not give, Salamanca does not lend.) It is, after all the oldest library in all of Europe, even older than your fine libraries in Cambridge and Oxford."

"Well, that sounds like the place I would want to go to find rare books dating back to antiquity."

"Oh yes, me amigo. Of course, I was not so much into the books when I was in school. I was more into the wine, the women, and the song, but now I have more appreciation, and perhaps I should have spent more time in the magnificent library than the barras. If anyplace has such books, the Salamanca library surely would."

He continued, "I think you will find something I learned while at Salamanca interesting. That is why I think Salamanca's library appeared so early. As I recall from my classes, the first paper in all of Europe was produced around the end of the 11th century in Toledo, not far from Salamanca. Before then, you wrote on parchment made from goat, sheep or cow skin and, as a limited resource, was extremely expensive. You could make a leather coat or a few pages of a book, something only a king or the church could afford."

"We obtained the technology from the Moors, who, as I learned, had obtained it from the Chinese. Interesting how the art of paper-making traveled from the Far East to us. We were the only Europeans to have this prized paper for a century until the French acquired it from us. It took another century before the Italians had paper. So, when the Salamanca library opened, no other Europeans had the magnificent, transformative paper. This brilliant new technology facilitated our being better educated and, therefore, more intellectually advanced than the rest of Europe."

I added, "That is very interesting. The first paper mill in England just opened last year, over 400 years later than the mill in Toledo, and before that, we had to import our paper from Holland."

Francisco continued, "There are some very rare and ancient books in Salamanca, but I doubt Dominic will let you take these out of España."

"I think John had made arrangements to purchase the English rights to these books, have us print these and give them a share of the royalties. He also promised to return them to the library."

"I think not, me amigo, but you can see for yourself. The University is a wonderful place with spectacular views of the broad Tormes River, with the hills and the fields in the distance. I wish I was there. I spent many happy days there. You know the University was founded in 1134 and we are approaching the 250th anniversary of the library founded in 1254—the oldest in all of Europe."

"That sounds amazing. I look forward to seeing it."*

Francisco was a skilled swordsman who, since he felt they were beneath him, did not want to mix it up with the crew. Since I had no idea how to wield a sword, he decided to teach me. For, if I encountered pirates, I wanted to be able to defend myself.

Nearly being killed by Reginald, who held the tip of his sword to my throat in front of Marie, added to my motivation. Then I had mixed emotions of fear and embarrassment, but was able to save Marie from being raped by that psychopath. The serial killer even had a name for his sword, Megan, who evidently "liked to kiss opponents' necks or take their hearts." If it wasn't for Queen Catherine entering the room and yelling at him, I wouldn't be here today.

I was reasonably athletic, but dueling was not like any of the sports I had played, well maybe a little akin to racquetball or tennis. I had thought those iconic tennis matches at Roland Garros, Wimbledon, or New York were like duels with two superb athletes moving and swinging with all their might, trying to lure their opponent into a position where they could score. Still practicing an hour or two in the morning and another hour or two in the afternoon, I became, perhaps at best an intermediate swordsman—probably not that good. Compared to lounging around on the deck, I enjoyed the exercise and the adrenaline rush.

When we first crossed swords, the crew just laughed at my feeble attempts to thrust and parry, but later, from their eyes and nodding heads, I could tell I was acquiring a degree of mastery. At first, I just stood there and waved my arms and upper torso until he told me, "Half of being a good swordsman is in your feet and how you move," which seemed a little like playing defense on basketball, except that your opponent held a sword rather than a ball, an object that could kill you in an instant.

Besides there was not much else to do, and if we happened upon some pirates, I would be able to defend myself, that is after I discharged my two pistols. Captain Black was impressed by my progress, saying, "Before ye know it lad you will be one o' Christine's best defenders."

Francisco said that he had heard that vicious banditos plied the long road from Bilbao to Salamanca and that my training might come in handy, which further increased my motivation. From the London sales, I was carrying a substantial sum of money to buy books in Salamanca and did not want it to fall into criminal hands. So, I redoubled my dueling efforts. It was great exercise, and just sitting on the ship reading and eating dulled my body and my reflexes, which were steadily coming back to life. I enjoyed learning another sport that had previously seemed so foreign. In the back of my mind, I thought that if Reginald threatened Marie or me again, I would be better equipped to defend her and myself against the dreaded, deadly Megan.*

Halfway through our journey, the winds ceased blowing, and we became becalmed, which seemed similar to being in San Francisco traffic barely moving, but rather than hours, it might take days to make a little progress. Everyone on board was frustrated, but we could do nothing about it other than wait for the winds to pick up.

After ten days, we arrived in Bilbao. I shook hands with those in the crew I knew, such as Jerome, and enthusiastically thanked Captain Black, saying, "Captain, I greatly enjoyed your stories, especially about Michael. I will tell him how well you treated me."

He said, "Take care o yourself laddy, keep those pistols 'andy. Ye never knows where them land pirates may be." Then he handed me the sword I had been practicing with saying, "'Hope you do not need this, but if you do, I think you can 'andle yerself." Then, uncharacteristically for the stern captain, he embraced me. Interesting, how while being locked on a small ship for days, you become close to your travel mates. It becomes your world and they become your family. The experience was similar to a river cruise or a trip to Club Med, except that, absent the clamor of the ever-present Internet, there is no interference, and the bonds become deeper.

Jack, the cabin boy, had taken my bags down to the dock, and we said goodbye. Standing below, I tried to regain my land legs—odd how you become used to the rhythms of the swaying boat and standing on solid ground in the absence of that constant motion seems weird.

Standing there in a foreign land that did not speak English, I thought to myself—Now what? I had to somehow find a cart or wagon to take me and my trunk to Salamanca, which, as I understood, was a long trip. As he climbed up the gangplank, I called back to Jack and asked him to watch over my bags while I searched for some kind of conveyance in this unfamiliar land. Now, I was on my own in a strange land in an ancient time without all the convenience of a modern port. There was no information desk, no American Express, no currency exchange, no car rental agencies, no taxi stand, no Uber to call, no gift shop with maps. What now?

I saw Francisco coming towards me and prepared to say goodbye to my fellow traveler and new friend when he said, "Rand, I have not seen Salamanca in years. I will go with you, then onto my casa. It is not much out of the way, and we can share the expense of a fine carriage."

"Gracias. I would greatly appreciate that, and I would enjoy your company, my friend." Plus, I thought to myself, in case we encountered some robbers, it would be good to have an expert swordsman along.

Thankfully, he made the arrangements for a carriage that, unlike vehicles in London, actually had a roof to protect us against the rain and sun—a real carriage that did not yet seem to exist in London. Interesting that in this time it took decades or even centuries for innovations such as paper, printing or carriages to travel between nations and continents. I settled into the comfortable seat, glad to be on my way on this new segment of my journey. Its upholstered seats were definitely more comfortable than Stephen's cart, but I still felt every bump on the dusty, rutted, rough dirt road.

As we set out, he asked me, "Rand, how long do you think it will take to arrive at Salamanca?"

I replied, "I have not thought much about it, but I understand it is 200 to 250 miles. Maybe three or four days?"

"If the weather is good and the road straight, a couple of good horses drawing a carriage can do about 25 miles a day, so we can expect to be there in nine or ten days." All I could think of was that in my own time, there would be freeways spanning the distance between the two cities, and it would take no more than four hours—geeze! This will take as long as sailing here from London, which is four times as far. No wonder they sail everywhere they can.

Our driver, Pedro Martinez, a short, plump, cute-looking, dark-complexioned hombre, was reluctant to undertake such a long journey until Francisco offered to pay him what he would typically make in three weeks. Of course, counting his time driving this round trip would take nearly three weeks, but he thought he could secure passengers or cargo for the journey back. Plus, he knew of the Alvarez family, knew of their sterling reputation, and did not want to offend a senior member of the clan.

As we later learned, Pedro had seven mouths to feed, and after purchasing the expensive carriage was struggling to make the promised payments to his annoying brother-in-law, therefore he did not feel he could refuse such a generous fare. Evidently an astute judge of horseflesh, Francisco had looked over Pedro's two brown geldings and appraised them as being in excellent condition, complementing Pedro on them and buying 100 pounds of oats to keep them strong and to supplement their feed consisting of hay and grass they would graze on along the trip.

We stopped at Pedro's small casa on the way out of town. He went inside to explain his absence to his wife and packed a bag, then came out holding her by the waist, followed by five cute, little, dark-haired, bowl-cut children from two to perhaps ten. He introduced us as Señor Don Francisco Alvarez and Señor Don Rand, then introduced us to each of the children. As they were introduced, the boys, Pedro, Roberto and Juan, each respectively, bowed and shook our hands. After hiding behind their mother's skirt, the girls, Juanita and Maria curtsied. Señora Martinez bowed her head to us, gave us a large bag of delicious Spanish food, and had tears in her eyes. As we set off, Pedro turned and waved a sorrowful goodbye to his handsome family.

The first couple of days, we traveled through passes surrounded by mountainous terrain, where the going was slow and I appreciated Francisco's judgment regarding the horses. At times, we traveled through conifer forests more reminiscent of dramatic Swiss peaks than what I thought Spain would resemble. Going up and down through the passes, we were making no more than fifteen miles a day, and I began to think the trip would take even longer than anticipated; then we descended into a flat high plateau with gradual hills where the climate, although warmer than the mountains, was dryer and cooler than the coast. Here, we saw numerous farms, grape vines and olive orchards as we periodically passed through the small hamlets along the way. Since it was still early in the year, the fields were still barren, waiting for spring to come alive.

On our stops to feed and water the horses, I came to know Pedro better. He did not talk in Francisco's perfect Castilian accent but rather in a local peasant vernacular such that I could only understand about half of what he said, especially since he talked so fast, even after I asked him to slow down. He had a pleasant manner and quick wit. Trying to maintain his noble bearing, Francisco resisted laughing at his jokes but invariably had to break down and smile, which only encouraged Pedro that much more. Even though I did not always understand the jokes, I found Pedro's delivery and laughing infectious, so I had to laugh too, my laughter reinforcing his, which, in turn, resonated with mine.

I was so glad Francisco joined me on the journey because he knew the route and where to stay. The first three nights, we bedded down in Inns, where after introducing himself as an Alvarez, they treated us well. As a foreigner with a terrible accent, I am not sure they would have provided me with as nice accommodations or food. Still, the rooms were small with but one or two small beds for both of us. I would have found sleeping with a guy difficult except that I was used to being in a small tent with a friend while backpacking and riding all day was tiring. Pedro bedded down in his carriage, which might have been more comfortable and certainly was more private that the small rooms where you could hear every movement or snore.*

On the fourth night, when we were about halfway there, we stayed at a cousin of his, Diego Alvarez, who had a large family and owned an expansive olive orchard. Their large hacienda stood atop a hill with a spectacular view of their orchards and the rolling hills with a beautiful river valley encasing the silvery, meandering river in the distance. As we wound our way up to the hacienda through the carriage's window, I caught glimpses of the sumptuous broad estate. Embarrassed to be imposing upon them unannounced, I wondered what type of reception we might receive. Francisco saying that he had not seen his cousins in a long time did little to allay my concern. As we approached the portico, I felt a knot of embarrassment in my stomach. But Fransisco was immediately recognized, and the entire family came to door and embraced him, as they did me after he introduced me.

Overwhelmed by their hospitality, I found them kind and generous of spirit. Diego looked similar to Francisco, only older—tall, lean, proud, and noble with distinguishing touches of white and a very full turned up, waxed mustache. While sitting on an expansive veranda, the two immensely enjoyed each other's company and catching up on the family's activities and gossip, sipping Diego's delicious, slightly sweet, home-grown white wine with a gentle, warm breeze blowing and a view over the gradual, blue-green slopes leading to the glistening, meandering river. After a long, dusty trip, the atmosphere seemed heavenly.

Diego had also gone to Salamanca U, where they overlapped by a year and evidently, as I interpreted it, "fiested together." He remembered it fondly, saying, "It is the family University where many of us attend, as do many of the prominent families in España. Francisco generally talked slowly to me so I could understand him, but with his cousin and family, the cadence speeded up, and I had trouble understanding what they said. Of course, they talked about their mutual cousin Isabella, what a remarkable Queen she had become, and how much life under her and Ferdinand had improved. Since both had been officers in the army, they also talked about the Moorish wars of conquest—the Reconquista.

Before dinner, Diego and his oldest son, Carlos, along with his younger son, Jose, gave us a tour of the broad estate in our carriage, with Jose sitting above and telling Pedro where to turn while Diego and Carlos pointed out various points of interest on the magnificent estate, discussing the crops they were growing.

Along the way, they drove us down to the river, where Diego showed us a fascinating device he was very proud of—a windmill, the first I had seen anywhere on my travels. Powered by the wind, it lifted water forty feet into the air, where it deposited buckets full of water into a trough that fed a broad, shallow pond. At the end of the pond stood another windmill that lifted the water further up the hill to another pond. Through three cascading windmills and ponds, they pumped the water ever higher to a large holding pond. Controlled by gates, this final pond fed shallow canals with branching trenches that irrigated the fields.

Francisco said, "Diego, this is ingenious. I compliment you on what you have accomplished. I saw similar windmills on my recent trip to Holland but had not considered applying them here. Perhaps this is something I should do, too. We lost over half of our crop two years ago to a severe drought."

Diego explained, "Yes, Holland is, after all, one of España's possessions. Isabella sent Carlos there, where he acquired the idea. The credit goes all to him. Periodically, during dry spells, our crops would dry up, too, and we would struggle to make a profit and keep all of our hands and their families fed. We have doubled our profits and protected ourselves against such tragic droughts."

I complimented Carlos, and he replied, "When I was in Holland, I saw these windmills everywhere. Since they are below sea level, they use the windmills to pump water out of their fields. I studied the mills closely and thought we could use such mills to pump water to the fields. They pump water up and out of their fields, and I thought we could pump it up to our fields. To water all the fields on our high hill, I knew we would have to raise the water higher, hence the cascading windmills and ponds. Once at the top, I knew we could channel the water 360 degrees around our large hills. I brought a craftsman back from Holland with me, who helped us build the first mill, then, with the help of our men, we built the other two."

"Remarkable, Carlos," I said. The handsome young man smiled broadly.

Dinner became a feast as course after course appeared, with the exception of the dinner at Bunkillarny castle, by far the best meal I had had since being transported back in time, or for that matter, after working on that darned app, the best I had had in years. Diego's impeccably dressed wife, Salina, who, with a long, elegant, equine nose and long, jet-black hair, looked as regal as he had his impeccable manners. Lifting a bottle of red wine, Diego said, "This wine is our best. We have several hectares of grape vines along the western border of our property, where the grapes capture the heat of the afternoon sun. Even though it is still early, these vines are gathering energy from the warm afternoon sun, which is starting to green and will soon explode with buds, flowers, and fruit."

"It is truly delightful. Thank you so much for this incredible feast," I replied. "So you grow olives and grapes. Do you grow any other crops that we did not see?"

"Why yes, Señor Rand, up north, we grow wheat, and we also have a herd of sheep."

"How large is your property?"

"About 1000 hectares (2,500 acres)," he proudly replied.

"It is truly magnificent."

That night, I conversed with the male members of the family, who, knowing I could not speak Spanish well, occasionally slowed down their speech pattern for me. They asked me many questions about what I did, printing, books, and Ireland. When they asked me where I originally came from, I told Michael's story of how I had been robbed, had amnesia, and had been rescued by Michael and the fair maiden, Gwendolyn. The story was a hit, so I had to tell it more than once since several of the younger men, seemingly infatuated with my description of Gwendolyn, repeatedly asked me for more details and stories about her. Telling them about her reddish/blond hair, her height, impeccable posture, the way she carried herself, her caring manner, her diligent involvement in our business, her intelligence, her education, her grandfather being a lord, and even her Irish temper only made them more enamored with her.

As they continued to talk, still full from the incredible feast, my brain tiring from rapid interpretations and a long day, I strolled to the front portico of the broad hacienda. There, under a beautiful star-lit night, I sat on the broad white steps leading down from the large porch, the sound of happy people laughing, enjoying each other's company and the lamplight behind me casting a gradually fading glow on the expansive land. Below me, I could see the rolling hills heading towards the river, the windmills turning in a mild breeze, the sound of them slowly creaking, water sloshing down the slews. It was one of those wonderful, peaceful, unusually warm nights. What a marvelous relief from the dusty, bumpy road and crowded, smelly inns. I drank in this delicious, enchanting night.

Jose came out and sat beside me. His father had made arrangements with Francisco for him to join us on our journey to Salamanca, where he would enroll in the "family's" college. They had not planned to send him for another couple of weeks, but it made sense since we were heading that way anyway and had space. It would also give him additional time to settle into the city before his studies commenced. Considering their sterling hospitality, Francisco and I thought it was the least we could do.

Speaking in English, he asked, "Is it cold in England now?"

"Yes, it is generally much colder in the days but not much cooler at night than here. You speak English?"

"Yes. We have a tutor. All of my siblings and cousins learned French and Italian, but I wanted to learn something different, so I studied English. When cousin Francisco was last here, he told me stories of England. I know it is not as developed as France or Italy or Holland and is thought to be a most backward nation, but he thought it would be more prominent in the future. You said you are a printer. Are there many printers in England and Ireland?"

I enjoyed speaking English with this handsome young man, who looked like he could be part of a Hispanic boy band. "No, until recently, there was only one in England. Now, there are two. We are the only printer in Ireland."

"Good; I was hoping to read more English books in the future but have not found many up until now."

"What do you plan to do with your English?"

"I would like to be a trader like cousin Francisco so that we will have customers for our products up there like what he is doing with his sherry. Maybe I could sell our wine there. But I want to be a sailor first. In Valencia, I was fascinated by the port, the activity, and all the people from different lands. Here we are in the middle of nowhere. I want to see the world before I settle down."

My father wants me to go to Salamanca University, but I want to go to sea."

"How old are you?"

"Sixteen, but I will be seventeen next month."

"Could you not go to Salamanca first and then become a sailor? You would be older, wiser and perhaps obtain more from your travels."

"But why wait? Sailors don't need a college education, and neither do traders."

"Well, that's true, but the life of a common sailor is not an easy one. On the Christine, they lived a tough life and slept in hammocks stacked three on top of each other, all in a tiny room. If you went to college, you could be an officer or perhaps someday even a captain, and as a captain, your opportunities would be much greater, and I can tell you that in the future, the opportunities will be unlimited. Besides, what would your father and brother think, if you did not go to university?

Looking downwards and shaking his head woefully, "Oh, they would be greatly disappointed in me. My father wants me to be like him and Carlos, to fight for Isabella, or to work in her administration or help manage the estate. But I want to see the world."

I could tell he was very troubled, no doubt enhanced by his sudden departure, "Why not go to university? Try it for a year. See if you like it. Even just one year will expand your knowledge of the world and provide you with valuable knowledge. You are young with a world of opportunities out there. Going to college will help you in becoming a sailor. Since traders depend upon ships to transport their goods, having some college education and the experience of a sailor will enhance your trading. But as we progress in our chosen career, the road is seldom without obstacles, and as one path ends, new unforeseen paths will appear. However, we cannot see these new vistas until we follow the previous path to its conclusion."

I could see that he was a bright, considerate, well-mannered young man who would be a welcome addition to our little party.

Refreshed and rejuvenated, we left the following day. Looking a little worn, Pedro had stayed with the family's servants and said they treated him as well as we had been treated, "Señors, I did not wish to drink all of the wine, but they insisted. They had picked the grapes with their own hands and crushed them with their own feet. I could not refuse. It would have been an insult. So, you see, my current condition is not my fault."

We continued to follow the route of the Rio Pisuerga. To the left, the land laden with trees by the river looked green and lush. The land to the right, however, appeared arid with few trees. It reminded me of sunbaked Mexico. By now, we had become a jolly band of travelers, which was difficult to believe given our diverse backgrounds: a noble from a Spanish village, a peasant from Bilboa, a young student, and a misplaced time traveler from 21st-century America—allegedly from Ireland by way of England.

Diego had told us that there were few settlements and no inns for a long distance, but fortunately, Señora Alvarez supplied us with dried meat, cheese, bread, rice, and beans, along with some extra blankets. That day it was warm and very pleasant, perhaps in the mid-70s but as the sun set, due to the arid climate, it was cooling off quickly. We made camp on a picturesque, grassy knoll next to the river. Jose and I gathered up driftwood made a fire, then Pedro cooked the rice, beans, cheese, and meat in a kind of stew that tasted remarkably good, one that I complimented him on. He smiled and seemed very proud of himself. I would have liked to ladle it into tortillas to make enchiladas, but when I asked about tortillas, Pedro and Francisco looked at me strangely. Then I remembered that these, along with corn, probably originated in Mexico.

Afterward, we huddled around the fire and enjoyed the camaraderie. Passing the bottle around, we also savored some of Francisco's fine sherry, periodically poking at the roaring fire with a stick, sending embers flying up towards the star, the fragrant cherry smoke periodically blowing in our eyes. For me, after the long day's ride and excellent dinner, I became transfixed in the red, blue, and yellow flames—a mandala.

Then, we began to tell stories. Pedro told us, "When I was a child, believe it or not, I was not that big, me amigos, not as big and mighty a hombre as you see here before you today," flexing his muscles and growling through his fearsome expression.

Juan said, "You must be talking about your big belly, Pedro, because other than that, you are not so big." (We all laughed, Pedro being the loudest.)

Leaning in and speaking dramatically and slowly, so even I could understand him, "Well, there was this gigantic boy in our village, Sanchez, as big as an ox, that always enjoyed picking on me. Even though he was my age, he was a giant, nearly as tall as Señor Rand, but no so nice as you, Señor. So, one day, I had had enough, and I made up my mind that after that day, he would never beat me up again. When Sanchez came around the corner and saw me, he began calling me ugly names and a sissy-boy, and I snarled at him, which surprised him because he was used to me cowering or running away, so he circled me, and I circled him growling and growling and growling. Then he hit me in the arm, and I hit him in the chest—the first time I had ever done so. This made him very angry at me, amigos, and he looked like he would kill me. He hit me in the chin, and I punched him on his ear. So, then he hits me in the stomach, and I throw up on him like this." He put a mouth full of stew in his mouth, then spit it out.

"Oh, Pedro, that's disgusting."

"And, just as I had planned, Sanchez never bothered me again. In fact, he was now the one who would walk away, and that's how I became the hero of my neighborhood. Nobody would bother me after that."

Juan queried, "But he was obviously bigger and stronger than you. You couldn't have known you would beat him in a fight."

Oh no señor, I could never beat him. You see, I had a bag filled with frijoles and meat and rice and cheese like this stew, and when I first saw him, I put it in my mouth. Then, when he hit me in the stomach, as he always did, I spit it out on him. That's why all I could do was growl because I could not talk." Then Pedro began laughing uncontrollably, and we all joined in.

Francisco told us about when he was a major in the Castilian Army and the brutal battles they fought against the Moors to regain control of their lands and win back España. One key skirmish lasted an entire day, and neither side could dominate the other.

He recalled, "At one point, the Moors rushed our line high on a hill with an overwhelming force. As I surveyed the charge on my trusted battle-tested steed, Montoya, I knew if they broke through, they would capture the high ground and soon be able to encircle the rest of us Castilians and either force us to surrender or slaughter us, one by one, as they had done before, so I knew this would be a battle to the death. I had my cannons loaded with shot, which bit into their charging front lines, but after we fired the cannons and our matchlocks, and while we were reloading, the Moors overwhelmed us, yelling their awful, blood-curdling cries. It became a pitched battle, me fighting with the enemy after fearsome enemy until they shot my faithful, beloved Montoya. I then rose from the ground, angrily fighting face to gruesome, determined face. We were hopelessly outnumbered and surrounded, man after man going down, cherished comrade after cherished comrade falling. Exhausted, my arms tiring from the relentless clanging of swords, my lungs burning from the constant struggle, the smell of gunpowder sweat, and fear filling the air. Rivulets of blood stained the ground, wreathing and lifeless bodies everywhere, men yelling as they struck out, men crying out in pain.”

"Finally, the reserves arrived and beat back the Moors, who in the see/saw battle had risked all to break the deadlock and force an opening in our defenses—where we were. I had lost nearly half of my battalion, but we won the day."

"Me amigos, to my fallen comrades, I salute you who have perished so nobly for such a valiant cause."

We all raised our glasses and said, "Salud."

Although these sounded like glorious battles, despite his bravado, I could tell all the men he lost, as well as all those he killed, haunted him, for that night, he cried out in his sleep, reliving it all during a nightmare.

That night, it was in the low 40s or maybe upper 30s. It was, indeed, very cold. Pedro had extracted the seat cushions from the carriage for us to lie on. We built up the fire, wrapping ourselves in the blankets. As I looked up at the stars on the clear, cold night, my breath visible, remembering the last time I had camped at Hermit's Rest at the bottom of the Grand Canyon, I wished I had my down sleeping blanket. I missed my friends and thought it seemed like such a long time ago. Actually, it was a long time in the future—something I still could not fathom. Then I tucked my head under the covers and fell fast asleep.

In the morning, I felt as if I were a frozen popsicle. Dew clung to green shoots of grass while a hazy light fog emanated from the river, obscuring the details of the trees surrounding the knoll. Pedro and Francisco had already rebuilt the fire as I awkwardly climbed out of my blankets, and Pedro began cooking some ham and eggs. The delightfully fragrant ham frying over an open fire drew me out of my nest. Young Jose still slept. My thighs were frozen, and I walked stiff-legged like a toy soldier, pounding on them with my fists, then standing in front of the fire with a half-asleep expression, looking clueless. It took some time for my thighs to thaw and to walk normally. After a delicious hot breakfast under a bright blue sky, it rapidly warmed up, and we proceeded onward.*

Towards the end of an uneventful day, having run out of things to talk about, we zoned out. While looking forward to stopping for the night, we entered a rare enchanting forest—a verdant change of scenery possessing that delightful fresh fragrance of pine. Around a curve, a tree had fallen onto the road, and Pedro suddenly pulled the reins to stop the carriage short of the broad trunk, jerking us forward and shaking us out of our stupor. Two men on horses rode out of the woods. I looked out the window and saw they had pistols drawn and wicks lit, pointing these at Pedro and telling him to set the break and drop the reins. Three others on foot followed and surrounded the carriage. One of the un-groomed, vile-looking brutes on horseback rode over to the window, dismounted, and poked his matchlock pistol through the window. In a tough tone, he told us, "Get out of the carriage quickly amigos—vamos! I will only take all you have, and if you cooperate, we'll not have to take your lives, which would be such a shame for you fine, señores, vamos, vamos!

With my hands held high, as I began to exit, Francisco forcefully pushed the door open. The bandito pulled the trigger, causing the taper to light the primer, which produced an explosion, sending the ball flying rapidly out of its chamber. All of this took a second, within which the pushed door had forced the gun upwards, the ball ripping through the carriage's ceiling. By then, Francisco had exited the carriage, spun around, knocked the bandit to the ground, unsheathed his sword, and as the bandit began to rise, hit him in the mouth with its hilt, knocking the dastardly fellow out.

The other horseman aimed his gun at Pedro and shot him, with Pedro falling off his seat and flopping onto the ground. In shock, the horses shot forward until one of the banditos grabbed the reins and with all the force he could muster, held them in check.

The other two bandits descended upon Francisco, who began dueling with them. In the meantime, still somewhat in shock, I fumbled for my lighter somewhere in one of my pockets. When I found it, I grabbed one of the two matchlocks I had stowed beneath the seat and lit the wick with my BIC. The other horseman had drawn his sword and headed for Francisco. I aimed at the center of his torso and fired, but the shot missed. I could not believe how inaccurate these stupid things were, but at least it caused his horse to rear up. Just as he was about to strike Francisco from behind and possibly sever his head, I grabbed my other pistol, lit it, got out, and fired at point-blank range. This time, it caught him in the shoulder and knocked him off his horse.

A third bandit had come around the side to attack me, so I opened the door to shield myself, grabbed my sword from underneath the seat, took it out of the scabbard, and fended him off just as he was about to strike.

Francisco fought two desperados while I fended off the third, who struck me with a continuous barrage of blows—blow after blow after blow. All I could do was block his thrusts as he tried to wear me down until he could strike the fatal blow. Fortunately, I was quite a bit taller and had longer arms—my only advantage against this relentless foe, who was now, in addition to the downward blows, attempting to stab me from below, me barely fending these off. It seemed as if this one-sided stalemate went on forever, with me continuously backing up, until he sliced my arm, me tripping over a rock and falling to the ground, then raising my sword to fend off a fatal blow.

I popped up to my feet, then with adrenaline flowing, got mad and began taking the offensive, pushing him back with my strong blows, keeping him off balance with my thrusts. He began to tire and grabbed my hand with his as he swung his sword with the other. I dipped to the ground and threw him over me. His sword landed between us. Before he could grab it, I bounced up and hovered above his sword, daring him to go for it. If he reached for it, I would have run him through. Instead, he ran away, leaving me surprised that I had gotten to my feet so quickly.

By then, the bandit who had come to the window had recovered and was rising to his feet with a dagger. Jose called, "Behind you." Like a football, I kicked him squarely in the chin with my boot. Seeing the long sword attached to an unusually long arm aimed between his eyes, he, too ran off.

Francisco had no trouble holding off the two others, but he could do no more than hold them at bay and was finally tiring. Once, they saw this unusually tall hombre coming towards them, and Jose about to throw a rock. Not liking the odds any longer, they ran off along with their injured comrade.

Smiling, we hugged each other, Francisco saying, "Rand, you did amazingly well. I am so happy you learned how to fight with the sword."

Before celebrating our victory, we remembered Pedro, who was still sprawled out under the carriage. We were severely distressed with his death. Extremely dejected, we went over to check on him. When we turned him over, to our surprise, he said, "I guess I fooled them, hey, me amigos." Then he grimaced in pain and fainted. He had been shot in the left arm and was oozing blood.

I tore off the sleeve from my shirt, grabbed a stick, wrapped the sleeve above his shoulder, and twisted it with the stick until the bleeding stopped. We carried Pedro to the seat, and then Francisco corralled the bandits' two horses and tied them to the back.

Jose said, "There is a large village ahead where we can seek a doctor for Pedro. Someone there might recognize these horses and enable justice for these disreputable villains." Francisco drove the carriage slowly, trying to avoid rocks and potholes as much as possible to not cause Pedro pain, while I tended to Pedro supplying him with water.*

After about a very long, fraught hour, we arrived at the village, which fortunately had a doctor who tended to Pedro's wound by stitching it up. Aware of the problems with infections, I went to the carriage and procured the whiskey Captain Black had given me for the journey. I poured some over the wound as a disinfectant, gave Pedro a gulp, which he immensely enjoyed, and took a swig myself. Then I doused the wound on my arm before the doctor stitched me up, a procedure that, without a local anesthetic, was painful. Another gulp of whiskey helped, though.

We went to speak to the mayor and town constable the next day. Francisco introduced himself and asked, "Does anyone in this town know who owns these horses?"

The constable said, "I took the horses around town earlier this morning, and nobody recognized them. I suspect the banditos were from somewhere else. They have been preying on us, too, something nobody in town would dare do. We all know each other and are actually related to each other. You are not the first travelers to be robbed on the road. Thank you for vanquishing them, though. Hopefully, they will return to where they came from and not bother us anymore."

That night, since Pedro was recovering, Francisco, Jose, and I celebrated. When we sat at a table in the barra of the inn, the innkeeper came over and said, "Mayor Rodriguez told me that the town will pay for anything you order, including your room. We are honored to have you, mi amigos, the mighty heroes of our town, stay with us as our welcome guests. Mi casa su casa."

Throughout the night, various residents approached us, introduced themselves, thanked us for ridding the town of those awful desperados, and bought us drinks. Francisco toasted me, "Rand, you surprised me. You had improved much with your sword, but I did not think you were ready to take on someone as fierce as those desperados. You shot the one and saved my life; for this, I will be eternally grateful. Eventually, you overcame another. Unable to help you, I worried he might kill you. Occasionally, I looked over to you, and he seemed to be getting the best of you, and then suddenly, you transformed into a real swordsman. I toast to you, my amigo. Salud!"

"That took a long time, and if he had longer arms, I would not be here tonight." I tried, but I could not hide a broad smile. The fact that my teacher was proud of me meant a lot. Suddenly, it came to me. Perhaps all that racquetball and tennis helped. These did reward moving quickly on your feet and help to develop good hand-eye coordination.

I said, "Here's to you, Señor, my illustrious teacher. I was so afraid when you knocked the gun out of the first robber's hand, but I guess you knew it would take time for it to fire. Then, without hesitation, you knocked him out and lit into the others, dueling with two at a time. Salud!"

"I am not sure I would have done that if I had known, there were five of them. I thought there were just the three. Thinking you could have dispatched one with your pistolas, I thought I would only have to face one other."

Francisco said, "Pedro will not be able to travel for over a week. I think we should get another driver for the remainder of the trip. There are no such carriages in town, so we could have him drive Pedro's carriage the rest of the way to Salamanca. Then, drive it back here for Pedro to take back. The mayor said he would make arrangements for such a man, and they would compensate him. They will also arrange for a driver to take Pedro back to Bilboa, and we will pay Pedro for the entire trip as initially planned. Agreed?"

"Si, certainly, sounds fair to me."

"We will also take possession of the banditos' two horses, which we can hitch to the carriage. This will make the trip that much faster. They are great horses. I propose that you keep one. With it, you will be able to visit me in me casa. I will keep the other to ride there."

That night, I slept like a baby. In the morning light, while lying in bed, I thought about all that had transpired. The thought that I could have killed one of those bandits bothered me immensely, not that they did not deserve it. The other thing that bothered me was that those darned matchlocks took so long to load. Then, you had to light the wick before it could be fired. What would I have done if I did not have my trusty BIC? I could not imagine lighting it with a flint. That would take forever. And when you fired it, you had no idea where the bullet might go. I had to find a better weapon.

The mayor came to us late in the morning saying, "It will take the rest of the day to convert your harnesses from one that controls two horses to one that will work for four. We would like to have a fiesta in your honor tonight, and then you can leave in the morning." We agreed, and that night, the town held its fiesta. Perhaps it was in our honor, but it seemed more like they wanted to have a party, and our victory provided a good excuse. On the village square dramatically lit by candles, they roasted an ox, and the wine flowed freely. A band played local music, and nearly everyone from young children to senior citizens danced with each other. I enjoyed watching a couple of cute toddlers, a boy of maybe two and a girl of perhaps three, dancing with each other.

The mayor introduced me to his daughter, a dark-haired, sultry beauty with a voluptuous figure, Jacquelina, who soon asked me to dance. I said I did not know the local dances, but she ably coached me, moving her hips and toned torso rhythmically. She captivated me. When we sat down, after having me retell the story of our victory, she asked me questions about what I did, where I lived, and what I was doing in Spain, all of which she listened to intently, smiling sensually, coming ever closer. I sensed that my being a foreigner seemed somehow exotic to her, and of course, I was now evidently a hero for fending off the banditos, who plagued the town. Then, while stroking my arm and leg in a seductive, low, guttural voice, she inquired, "Being a printer of books seems like such an interesting profession, something that surely has a future. It is difficult to imagine that a strong, tall, handsome man, such as you, is also a smart hombre. Do printers make much money? Are you a wealthy man, Rand?"

The band still playing loudly, Francisco whispered in my ear, "Be careful me amigo. Her father is a large landowner in the area, a wealthy,

The merger of our two great families governed the only two areas of Espanola not controlled by the Moors that will eventually lead to their defeat and the Reconquista of Española."

On the last day, we figured we could make it to Salamanca if we drove forty miles without stopping. Taking no time for breakfast, we left well before sunrise, eating and napping in the carriage. After our driver tired, we took turns handling the team—a task that, unlike for the others, required my constant attention. In the distance, after the sunset, we could see the soft yellow glow of Salamanca's lights. By the time we checked into the hotel, I was so tired from the long, dusty journey, I was ready to drop. Gorges, our driver, took the hoses to a nearby livery, and Jose went to stay at a hostel for students. We ate a quick dinner, and I immediately passed out.*

Light streaming through the window woke me the next morning. Judging by the angle of the sun coming through, its bright yellow line slowly advancing along the wooden floor, it was around 11:00 am. I must have been exhausted, for I had slept for over twelve hours. With nowhere to go, after luxuriously lying in bed, I went to the window. There, I beheld the beautiful sight of a winding river flowing below with rolling fields in the distance under billowing cumulus clouds—the clouds shading some of the verdant fields while advancing streaks of sunlight spotlighted other fields. Resembling a captivating Dutch Masters landscape, the 180-degree view extended onward, seemingly forever.

Francisco entered the room joking about me being a Moorish Sultan with nothing better to do with my life than lay around all day. I said, "This is a wonderful room with a spectacular view. How did you acquire it?"

"The owner, Manuel, is a cousin. He gave us their best room. I have already eaten and taken a walk. Are you hungry?"

Having eaten only one small meal yesterday, I replied, "I am famished."

"They are holding breakfast for you, but you should go down immediately."

Unlike the small inns along the way with tiny restaurants/bars, I ate a leisurely, delicious breakfast in a bright, sun-lit, white-walled room overlooking a picturesque, deep green-grassy park. It was lovely, but I would have liked to linger there while sipping multiple cups of coffee. Even though I had long since passed through my painful caffeine withdrawal, I still missed the ritual of my morning brew, especially on such a halcyon day as this.

Jose appeared in the park and I hailed to him to join me, where Francisco soon joined us too. Jose said he would not be assigned a residence for another week and had never seen the university before, so the alumnus, Francisco, offered to guide the grand tour of the university and the historical city that surrounded it. Francisco pointed out that the centuries-old university had separate, independent colleges, similar to Cambridge.

As we toured the grounds, he relived his college days with pride and cherished memories. When we passed by some of its oldest buildings, Francisco proudly exclaimed, "The origins of the university date back to the 11th century when King Alfonso IX granted its charter in 1218. This is when Salamanca commenced to flourish. Salamanca is the oldest university in España and one of the three oldest in Europe. Along with the University of Bologna, the Sorbonne in Paris, and Oxford and Cambridge in England, it is considered one of the five most prestigious universities in the civilized world."

Along the way, Francisco, usually a proud, proper, stately man, seemed transformed. He stood even taller, seemed even prouder, had a relaxed, glowing, younger look to his face, and a happy, lilting tone in his voice. As if he were once again that happy young student attending university, his perfect Spanish diction began to sing.

When we entered a courtyard, he pointed to the law school, "There are two branches of the law school, or really two schools, one for the Church's canon law and the other for civil law. I hear they are pioneering new concepts that were unthinkable during the Middle Ages, such as the right to life, the right to own property, freedom of thought, and human dignity."

"You English with your Magna Carta seem to take your rights for granted, me amigos, but these are not absolutes in most of the world. In the feudal system that still dominates most of Europe, the king has dominion over your property and your life. If you offend him in any way, he can have your head. And the church controls what you think. The peasants, who make up perhaps 90% of the European population, are not thought to possess any human dignity and do not have such rights. They are, in effect, little more than slaves."

I wondered to myself if this is where the philosophy behind America's Bill of Rights originated. I knew our forefathers, such as Jefferson, Franklin, and Madison, were learned men who read such theories from France and England, but could they have also heard about such thoughts that originated in Spain? Could such thinking that originated in Salamanca have influenced the philosophers and statesmen in America and the rebellion in France? Of course, without the printing press, the spread of knowledge would have been glacial, and our forefathers may have never formulated our Bill of Rights, Declaration of Independence, or our constitution. Ben Franklin was a printer like me, and Thomas Paine published Common Sense, which was thought to be a major catalyst to the revolution, for which he was called the Father of the American Revolution. Even though there were only two million Americans at the time, most of whom could not read, I had seen that 500,000 copies of the forty-seven-page pamphlet were printed.

Walking further down the steep hill that most of the university occupied and upriver a bit, Francisco pointed out the medical school and the Hospital del Estudio, built in 1413. We passed many students along the way, indicating that this was indeed a large university. Francisco says, "You may think that only the wealthy, such as myself and you, Jose, attend Salamanca, but this is not the case. Many of the estudiantes you see passing by are poor. The schools are sponsored by families such as ours who pay for these poorer, bright estudiantes to attend. They may be poor, but why should that limit what they might accomplish? Isabella will need all the bright young minds like yours, Jose, we can provide her to run our expanded nation and our other possessions."

We sauntered down the hill to the river, where we stopped at a bridge spanning the Tormes River. "This is the Puente Mayor del Tormes Bridge. The Romans built it shortly after the birth of our lord and savior around 20 A.D. It is not amazing that here it still stands 1500 years later."

"Did you know that Julius Caesar conquered Espanola and that Salamanca was an important Roman trading center along the Via de La Plata, which crossed this bridge here where we stand."

Thinking about all the Romans from so long ago, we crossed the bridge halfway and looked over the edge at the river. To think that Caesar crossed over this same bridge boggled my mind, and I could envision legions of Roman soldiers dressed in armor, shiny helmets, and red skirts with their short, gladius swords accompanied by officers on horseback following their leader to conquer yet another land. To the left, we saw small, frothy falls, and to the right, a tree-laden island. We looked up at the rocky hills towards the city and the university above, with bright, tan structures under puffy white clouds slowly meandering across a brilliant, deep-blue, cerulean sky.

On the way back, Francisco insisted that we stop at the Catedral Vieja de Santa María, "To thank God for our successful journey and deliverance from those desperate banditos."

On my European vacations, it seems crass, but I was never much into cathedrals (I thought if you have seen one, you've seen 'em all). This one was built in the 12th century and, with a height of perhaps 12 stories, was by far the tallest building in the city. I must admit that the columns' height and ornate decorations inside were impressive. Plus, being back in the 15th century, before massive, motorized construction equipment, I was acquiring an appreciation of how challenging it would be to construct such monumental structures—why they took decades and sometimes centuries to complete, how expensive these were, and how proud the parishioners would be of such accomplishments—their vehicle to God and heaven.*

On the way back, we could hear Jose's stomach growling. After all, he was a teenager, so we decided to stop at a café for a late lunch. The tour stunned me, for it felt similar to touring the ancient ruins of Athens or Rome, except that many of these structures would be ruins in the future and were currently alive with activity.

Without looking at the menu, Francisco ordered for us. I was surprised to see the plates of food the waiter brought, exclaiming, "Are these tapas?"

"Yes, Rand, these are tapas," Francisco replied. "Have you had them before?"

"Yes," but thought to myself that that was 500 years from now.

Francisco launched into a story, "I know of two explanations for the tapas. Many believe it began with King Alfonso X of our Castile during the 11th century. While recovering from an illness, he could not eat full meals. He instead ordered small dishes with his wine. According to legend, to reduce drunkenness, he subsequently ordered that the taverns not be allowed to serve wine to customers unless accompanied by a small snack or 'tapa'."

"Another popular explanation goes that King Alfonso XIII stopped by a famous tavern in Cádiz near a beach on the coast where he ordered wine. Cádiz is a windy place, so to protect the king's wine from the blowing sand, the waiter covered the glass with a slice of cured ham before offering it to him. After drinking the wine and eating the tapa, the King ordered another wine with another tapa."

"As you know, tapa means cover," and as Francisco took a small piece of ham to cover his sherry, he said, "I use this to protect my sherry from the fruit flies, who drink a tiny sip of my wine, get drunk then die and end up in my teeth. Maybe this is really why tapas came into being."

Many of the establishments in the 21st century that do not have full restaurants offer bar food or appetizers. I wonder if this is where that tradition came from 500 years ago—now.

He continued to tell us more about the city, "The cool, dry air provides Salamanca with fantastic cheeses and delicious cured meats. Although not as good as ours, this sherry is also delicious. Salud, mi amigos!" We clicked glasses, and Jose and I replied in unison, "Salud!"

Over a delightful late tapa lunch of cheeses, olives, ham, boiled eggs, sautéed mushrooms, and mussels in a garlic, wine, and butter sauce, I asked Francisco, "So did the Romans establish Salamanca then?"

"Oh no. As I understand it, its origins go back to when the Celts settled here."

"Celts? Are these the same Celts that settled Ireland and Scotland?"

"They are the same except probably a different tribe. You know the Scotch and Irish Celts are still very tribal or clannish as you call it."

"Yes, they certainly are."

"Around 220 BC, Hannibal and the Carthaginians conquered the city with their elephants. Next, prior to the birth of our Lord, Caesar conquered her, which is when the bridge was built. Then, as Rome declined, the Visigoths came out of the north and invaded her. Around 700 AD, they were, in turn, conquered by the Moors along with the rest of the peninsula.

"For decades, this area became the main battleground between the Christian kingdoms and Muslim Andalusian rulers. The constant fighting between the Moors and the Kingdom of León first, and then the Kingdom of Castile and León against the Caliphate, depopulated Salamanca and reduced it to little more than a minor settlement. Who would want to live in an area constantly being fought over, so the people left? After the battle of Simancas around 940, when the Moors were finally driven out, the Christians resettled the area, and it began to thrive again."

My head spinning, trying to digest all of this, I stated, "My goodness, that is quite a bit of history—Celts, Carthaginians, Romans, Visigoths and Moors all ruling Salamanca. What a melting pot of European, Asian and African bloodlines. I guess that explains the interesting mix of architecture. And the handsome people all look so intriguing because they have a rich mix of ethnicities."

With a bright smile, Jose said, "Cousin Francisco, muchas gracias for this tour and the history lesson. I think I now have a feel for Salamanca and its university. It has inspired me. I will write to my father and tell him how enlightening and heroic my time with you two has been. I toast you mi amigos, Salud!" "Salud!"

Francisco said in a fatherly voice, "Study hard, Jose. I hope you know that Isabella and Ferdinand are counting upon the graduates of Salamanca, such as you and your brother, Carlos, to help them rule and expand our kingdom. Most of our ministers have come from here and will continue to come from here. That is why they have supported the university. Why we, the Alvarezes, support her, too. The future will not only be waged on the field of battle but by how we govern that which we conquer, which requires men of intelligence and learning. After the battles have subsided, that I sincerely hope is nigh, these men will be as importante as our soldiers, perhaps even more so, because if they do their jobs well, act fairly and with justice, maybe we will not have so many wars. This is an excellent time to be in school and start one's career. The opportunities will be unlimited, me cousin."

It was late afternoon when we returned to our hotel, whereupon the three of us settled into a delicious siesta in our spacious, airy, light, high-ceilinged, bright room—what a contrast to the days spent in the crowded, bumpy, little carriage and cramped inns.

Later that night, we went from barra to barra, visiting Francisco's haunts, sampling tapas, hearing stories of his college days, talking to locals about philosophy, local politics, and, of course, Isabella and drinking too much vino. Jose and I mostly sat back and enjoyed seeing Francisco enjoy himself. Jose was enthralled with his stimulating night in Salamanca.

When we finally bedded down, Francisco, while grabbing Jose's face in his hands in a slurred voice, told him, "Now remember, my dear cousin, every night will not be like this one. Some estudiantes get caught up in the drinking of too much vino, but you should emphasize your studies first, then have a little fun, mi handsome cousin. Unfortunately, it took me two years to learn this lesson, but without the constant guilt and worry of always being behind, I enjoyed my friends and the vino and the señoritas that much more!"*

The next day, we sauntered to the library under a cloudless, brilliant azure-blue sky that highlighted the tan and white buildings, casting contrasting dark shadows over the newly green campus. Sitting a half-mile above sea level on the high central Spanish plain with little humidity, the visibility and colors of the river and hills in the distance were enchanting.

When we entered the famous institution, we saw a long, high hall flanked by dark wooden bookshelves on either side along the walls with long tables in the middle. Francisco reiterated, "We are now in Europe's oldest library."

I always felt reverence when stepping into a library. Being so old and historic induced a double dose of that reverence.

Francisco spied Monsignor Dominic in a corner, perusing a book. At first, Dominic did not recognize him. When he did, he smiled, embraced, and kissed him on both cheeks, saying, "Oh Francisco, it is so wonderful to see you again, mi amigo. I remember when we were boys playing together. I heard from mi madre that you have done very well for yourself."

"Gracias, Monsignor Dominic, I would like to introduce you to my good friend Señor Rand Roberts, who has come all the way from London to meet with you."

As we shook hands, he said, "It is a pleasure to meet you, señor."

I instantly took a liking to the jolly balding friar with a quick smile and engaging wit, who seemed highly excited, saying, "Antonio de Nebrija just gave me a copy of his new book, Grammar of the Castilian Language. It is the first such book in España, something we dearly need. It will help our estudiantes so much, as well as our professors, who have been discouraged by the quality of their estudiantes' writing. It will give them all grammatical standards to follow for the first time. Oh, I am so pleased. See, here there is an appendix we can use to teach Spanish in the new provinces we have conquered to the south."

I explained my purpose in being there, "John Jones came here last year in search of rare books to translate and print in English."

"Oh yes, I remember him. He was a brilliant man who appreciates our fondest works."

"I am sorry to tell you John passed away."

"Oh no, he was a man of great passion for books and persistence, someone who will surely be missed."

"Yes, he will. I am here to further John's last mission in life. I understand that he had made arrangements to purchase the rights to some of your books, and I have come to complete the transaction and take these back to Ireland."

"Oh no, señor, we cannot let these precious items leave the library. Even our best estudiantes and professors have limited access to such works, and they cannot take these out of the library. I am sorry, but there must have been a misunderstanding. Perhaps there was a mistranslation. Mr. Jones did not speak Spanish as well as you do señor."

"I know I do not speak well, but I promise to take care of the books and protect them with my life. I will return them within a year, and we will pay handsomely for your loaning them to us. Plus, we will print copies for you to distribute in your library to interested students and faculty. And we will give you a percentage of the profits from selling the books, too, which you can use to fund additional acquisitions."

"My, that sounds like a wonderful idea, but I am forbidden from letting these go."

Then, to change the contentious subject, Francisco interjected, "Rand is a dear friend of mine. We have traveled all the way from London together. He has come such a long way and has risked his life to do so. If you please, Dominic, perhaps we can see these books."

"Why yes, certainly I can do that. I am so sorry, señor."

We walked to the back of the library, where Dominic selected a key from his large circular, clinking ring and opened a massive door. Behind the door stood another room with a long table, where a professor was transfixed on an ancient vellum scroll. The two greeted each other, and then Dominic proceeded to the back of that room, where there was an impressive steel-laden door, which took two keys to open.

The inner room, smelling of cedar and oddly of salt, had many shelves with manuscripts mostly lying down. Dominic said, "We lined the room in cedar to protect it from insects. Our climate is generally dry but we have a vat of salt and a vat of sand over there to keep the moisture level low."

I remembered that the Dead Sea Scrolls were discovered in a cave in the Judean Desert, and even though they were over 2,000 years old, they were relatively well preserved. This room provided similar arid, saline conditions.

Dominic proceeded to give an introduction to Spanish literature, which I greatly appreciated.

"Our literature dates back before the time when (crossing himself) Christ, our Lord and Savior was born, when Caesar and the Romans conquered the Iberian Peninsula. We have a few scrolls dating back to that time. During the Roman period and through the time when we were conquered by the Germanic Tribes in the fifth century, there were several renowned writers who wrote in Latin.

"Then, in the 8th century, the Muslims conquered our lands. Their civilization included Judea, Egypt, parts of Italy, Turkey, the Arab lands, Northern Africa, parts of Italy, and our Iberian Peninsula—all interconnected and trading with each other as the Romans had previously done. As you probably know over that period, during the Middle Ages, Europe struggled through devastating, desperate, debilitating plagues that wiped out half of our population. As if the plagues were not enough, there were constant wars. Therefore, in a near-constant struggle to survive, there was little time or inspiration to produce great works such as these.

"But throughout Europe's trials, the Arab civilization flourished with advances in mathematics, science and philosophy. They also preserved the reasoning of the great Greek and Roman great thinkers. The Muslims were religiously tolerant, encouraging the advancement of Muslim, Christian and Jewish thought.

"After the expulsion of the Moors in Northern Spain, Spanish prose and poetry emerged in the 12th and 13th centuries. One of the best-known works is El Cid, written around 1140."

From his remarkable description, I realized that Spain (Andalusia, as the Moors called it) on the Iberian Peninsula had much more going on with respect to literature than the rest of Europe combined. And substantially more than remote, backwater Britain. Indeed, some of the great works published in France and then England had been translated from Islamic to Spanish first and then to French, and finally to English. I hoped to acquire more of these works—why I had traveled so far—something, given the difficulty, I periodically regretted but now felt inspired to pursue.

I reviewed the stacks of old manuscripts and scrolls, and although they were very interesting, I did not think many would have a large audience. Most were written within the last couple of centuries and not on my list. I expressed my concern to Dominic saying, "I thought John had discovered some rarer and more foundational works, which do not appear to be here. Is it possible that these are on loan?"

"No, none of these works are allowed outside the library, outside of these rooms."

Francisco, sensing my disappointment, said, "Dominic, are there not other manuscripts somewhere? Rand has come such a long way—all the way from London, which took us nearly three weeks to accomplish."

"Can you vouch for him, Francisco?"

"With my life mi amigo. On the way from Bilbo, we were attacked by five treacherous banditos. When one pointed a gun at my head, I closed the door on him and knocked him out with my sword's butt. As another charged me on his horse, about to decapitate me, Rand shot him and then proceeded to fight another with his sword. He dispatched two of them and saved my life. He is one of the most principled, chivalrous, and courageous men I know."

Dominic asked the absent-minded professor to leave the room and brought in Padre Michael.

"Do you swear not to disclose what I will show you to anyone!"

Francisco – "Yes, I swear!"

Me – "Yes, I swear!"

He led us to one of the shelves that he astonishingly pulled on and rotated out of the way. Behind the shelf was a low, dark, arched alcove.

Dominic reached behind the door frame, flicking some kind of hidden lever that produced a clicking sound followed by a sliding noise. He lit the way with a candle that emitted no smoke, which I imagine was made with pure beeswax so as to not sully the precious documents we were about to behold. Entering the alcove, I looked up, where I saw a massive guillotine-like blade ready to crash down on an unwarranted visitor that the father had evidently disabled. He next told us to step over a large plank on the floor, which, after beholding the fearsome, shiny blade, we both gingerly crossed.

At the end of the alcove, there appeared to be a large, black, iron-safe door with two locks. Both priests inserted their keys. Screeching, the door swung open to reveal a small room about the size of a large walk-in closet. When they opened the door, I subconsciously stepped back onto the forbidden plank that immediately gave way, me falling into a void of darkness. After falling about seven feet, I grasped the floor with both hands, barely arresting my perilous descent. My aching fingers rapidly failing, Francisco quickly came to my rescue grabbing my forearm and pulling me up.

Before resetting the plank, Dominic shone the candle into the void, revealing rusted iron spikes that I barely missed, which he said were coated in deadly poison. At that point, I felt like Indian Jones in the Temple of Doom and hoped not to encounter any more deadly traps, for I wasn't that courageous or lucky.

Padre Michael departed. Peering into the room with Dominic's candle, we could see about a dozen steel boxes on shelves that contained scores of handwritten manuscripts. The first one he pulled out was the original El Cid. Handling the manuscripts very carefully, Dominic placed several papyrus, parchment, vellum, and paper manuscripts on a table. Dominic's face lit up, barely able to contain his excitement; he proudly explained the origins and significance of each one. I could tell he relished showing these—something that because of their value and fragility, he rarely had the opportunity to enjoy. He said, "Your John was the last one to see these. I normally would not have shown them to him, but his interest in literature, honesty, Christianity, and force of personality captivated me."

In the center of the small room, Dominic carefully placed papyrus scrolls written in hieroglyphics from the time of Cleopatra and Arabic parchment manuscripts by famous mathematicians, astronomers and scientists. To our amazement, after opening another metal box, he showed us manuscripts by renowned Roman playwrights and civic leaders, followed by Latin manuscripts by famous philosophers. Another box revealed carefully packed scrolls by renowned Jewish philosophers.

I noticed a corner of a smaller gray metal box on top of the shelves that being shorter, Francisco could not see. Reaching up, grabbing the smaller lead container, and bringing it down, I asked, "Father, what is this?"

"Oh, my son, this is something unholy." He hesitated, then lifted the top to reveal an elaborately embellished vellum book with a strap and lock. Above the strap was a skull and some red-edged, golden symbols that did not look like anything I had ever seen before.

Looking grave and concerned, the usually effervescent friar's tone deepened, and he spoke in a barely audible whisper, "This book allegedly comes from the infamous Cave of Salamanca, where it is said that the Devil masquerading as a holy man instructed seven students in the dark arts for seven years. It is written in a language that none of our scholars, whether Moors, Jews or Christians, could decipher. The symbols, the characters do not resemble any language on the face of the earth, not even the ancient hieroglyphs dating back to Egypt or the cuneiform of Mesopotamia. It is said that its incantations have irresistible evil powers beyond human comprehension."

"The church would not want its existence to be known, which is why it is hidden here."

I reached for the book when Dominic shouted, "Do not touch it! The foul book is cursed."

"What do you mean cursed," Francisco exclaimed.

"One of our professors, Manuel Ortega, an expert on ancient languages, spent weeks trying to decipher its symbols. Unable to do so, he became extremely agitated, could not sleep, became totally obsessed with the book, stopped teaching his classes, abused his children, went mad, stabbed his wife, and then cut out his eyes. She survived, but he bled to death."

Aghast, not wanting any part of the vile book, I stuck my hands behind my back, "But father, if it is evil and of the Devil, why not just burn it?"

"As the chief librarian, I preserve books, not destroy them, and this book appears to date back thousands of years. We do not know its true origins, but if it is of the Devil, there may be a time in the future when we will need to access its knowledge to defeat the Devil's hoard. Perhaps when Christ comes again and we engage in the final battle between good versus evil. Until then, we would not want it to fall into the wrong hands, for who knows what vile deeds they might perpetrate with it."

Francisco slammed the cover back on the box and handed it me to place back above the shelves, saying, "Push it to the back, Rand, so it is not visible. No harm can come from a book that no one ever sees, and even if someone opened it, they would not understand it."

"I guess the old saying of the University, What nature does not give, Salamanca does not lend, is truer than what I knew because this is certainly not natural. Perhaps the saying should be— What nature does not give and what is unnatural, Salamanca does not lend."

We all laughed—a nervous laugh that broke the tension enveloping the room.

Changing the subject, Francisco asked what was in one of the last remaining boxes.

Dominic opened the box, saying, "I can't believe I did not show you this." Taking a few manuscripts out of the box and placing these on the table, he said, "These are original Spanish manuscripts of some of Europe's first poets and romantic prose writers. Something we are most proud of."

As we left the small room, he closed the safe door, ensured we stepped over the trap, reset the latch for the guillotine, and restored the shelves guarding the hidden passageway.

As a nerdy STEMS major, I typically had to read non-fiction, and although I enjoyed it, I only read a handful of books a year, usually on a beach vacation, that is, if I was not totally absorbed in a project as I had been for the previous three years when I had no time to read anything other than technical manuals online. My literature appreciation extended as far as the required high school and college courses, which I would not have taken otherwise and now valued that much more.

Since arriving in Ireland and working for Michael, my appreciation has skyrocketed. When I met William Caxton and Wynkyn in London, I could not believe that I held the first books ever written in the English language. But what I beheld in front of me was a treasure trove of Western, African, and Middle Eastern literature over the last two thousand years, during a time when most of such thinking had been extinguished by wars, famines, plagues, carelessness, the ravages of time and the finality of fire. No doubt, these were the only remaining copies of many of these priceless works, whose monumental concepts may have otherwise been lost forever.

I suddenly felt that it was my mission to have these treasures printed in English, to make them available to others, to advance reasoning and civilization, and to save them for posterity. I fully understood the need to protect these fragile documents. If they had not been preserved, many would have been lost to mankind for all time. But just sitting in this safe did no good. They needed to be exposed to the light of inquiry to enhance the enlightenment of the human mind.

In a hushed tone, I said, "Father Dominic, these are truly magnificent. I am awestruck!"

After we exited the safe room and the less safe rooms, entering the main portion of the library, Francisco whispered, "Dominic, you honor us by showing us these precious works. We promise never to reveal what we have seen here today to another living soul! Right, Rand?"

"Yes, most certainly!"

After such a rare treat, still subdued by my awe, I resisted saying anything but had to; I had to force myself to speak before I lost the opportunity to do so, "Father Dominic, thank you so much for showing us those marvelous documents. I am still lost in wonder. Because I think it would be a service to mankind to print these so that any learned person may profit from their wisdom and to preserve their words for posterity, I must ask if there is any way we might have access to them."

"Señor Rand, I am sorry, but I am not allowed to do that. It is against the rules of the university."

Francisco interceded, "Can the President grant us such access?"

"Yes, he can, but I cannot imagine he would do so. But you are welcome to try; after all, your august family sponsors one of the colleges."

Before we left, Francisco invited Father Dominic to dinner at the finest restaurant in town. A coinsurer of fine wine and food, Dominic gladly accepted the invitation.

When we entered President Monsignor Don Emilio Cortez's office, we were met by his secretary, who immediately told us he was busy. After hearing that Francisco was an esteemed alumnus and his family was a major donor whose gifts "might not be as generous in the future," she reluctantly replied that he would see us on the following Tuesday—four days from now.

That evening, inspired by the rarified cerebral atmosphere, we had a grand time talking about a broad range of topics with the learned, entertaining, jolly friar. In the morning, Francisco said he needed to see his wife and family and would leave immediately. He invited me to visit him, saying that their land was south of the city, it was only a little over a three-day ride on my new horse, and he gave me a list of inns to stay at en route, "Remember to say I referred you to them and they will surely welcome you, mi amigo." We embraced; he expertly mounted the horse we had acquired from the banditos and trotted off with a remarkably straight back, carriage, and wave of his hat. I would miss the man I had fought with and had spent so much time with. I would have liked to visit him and the lovely family he had told me so much about, but it was difficult to imagine traveling for three days for what in my time would be no more than a two-hour drive.

Since Jose's rooms were not ready yet, he stayed with me in the large hotel room, and I spent the intervening days touring the city and the university and dining with him. Since I had acquired a horse, I also rode out into the beautiful surrounding countryside. As a kid, I had taken some horseback riding lessons at camp, but since all we did was ride around in a circle, I never really enjoyed it much. This chestnut gelding was surprisingly easy to ride and instantly responded to my feeble commands, such that I thought he was much better at this than I—me endeavoring to live up to his expectations, him sometimes looking back at me seemingly saying, "Get it together dude." Evidently, the bandit had trained him well, which I guess would be necessary for his chosen profession. Not knowing his name, I called him Chester because of his color.

After only a couple of hours riding in the country, my butt was sore, and my thighs ached, no doubt due to my lack of proficiency. But unlike all the bouncing around, when I galloped on Chester, it seemed so much easier and more enjoyable for both of us. When we came to an unanticipated fallen tree around the bend of the road, I thought I would be thrown to the ground until he cleared the 3-foot-high obstacle with ease. Evidently, the bandit had trained him how to do this, too. Anticipating the jump, I leaned far forward, which seemed like the right thing to do. Later, I realized that if I had leaned back, something I could have easily done when he rose up to jump, I would have fallen off and maybe never ridden again.

When I returned to the President's offices four days later, expecting to see him, the secretary officiously told me, "Monsignor Don Emilio Cortez has been called to Rome and will be gone for three weeks."

Severely disappointed, I asked, "I would like to schedule an appointment with him immediately upon his return. Senorita, it is a matter that will garner much funding and renown for the university. The Alvarez family, as you know, are major donors. I am sure he would not want to disappoint them." I was surprised I added the bit about Francisco's family, but she seemed so resistant.

"When he returns, he will be very busy, but I can fit you in for a short period of time in about four weeks. Come back then."

"But senorita, I had an appointment today that was summarily canceled; surely I should have an appointment immediately upon his return."

"Adios, señor"

Four weeks, I said to myself, this is insanity. After I turned and headed to the door, I glared over my shoulder at her, which was met with an even more vicious scowl. I would have liked to bawl her out, but I knew that would not help my cause.

NINE

Reconquista of Spain

Four Weeks! This development severely disappointed me. I thought about heading back to Ireland, but I had come so far and spent so much time and quite a bit of Michael's money to get here. I would hate to tell him I had failed, for I didn't even have his permission before I came. And then there was King Edward, his partner. Would he cut off my head? I didn't think he would, but...

Plus, my prospects of becoming a junior partner would be extinguished, as would my chances with the lovely Marie. My only alternative was to wait and hope my efforts would lead to success—it had to; Marie was too much of a prize to let go.

Having seen much of Salamanca already and having no immediate business there, I didn't want to run up a larger hotel bill. With Jose about to start his studies, I decided to take Francisco up on his invitation to visit him. Gorges had already left with Pedro's carriage and, to his delight, with a paying passenger and his new bride. I thought about hiring a driver or renting a smaller surrey, then reluctantly thought I might ride Chester all the way, which, given my novice horseback riding abilities, might be a mistake.

Worried about carrying that much money and being robbed again, I deposited the majority of the funds in the bank Manuel recommended, one run by his brother. Concerned about facing more banditos on my lone journey, I devised a plan to better arm myself. My large Swiss Army knife with a myriad of tools had a piece of flint I could slide out of its butt end. I visited a blacksmith who readily fashioned a new hammer for my matchlock that would hold the flint and ignite the power in the bowl that led to the charge in the barrel. When I tested it, after adjusting the angle of the flint, it successfully fired. I was proud that I had invented a flintlock; something, given how ineffective matchlocks were, would soon happen anyway.

The first morning, I was fine riding in the saddle, but after a couple of hours in the afternoon, my butt seriously hurt, so I stopped at the first inn I saw. The second day, it was a little better, but I was determined. On the third day, despite the soreness, I was able to settle into a better rhythm with Chester. I bedded down at the inn Francisco recommended for day two, using his name as a reference, which garnered relatively good accommodations, a nourishing meal, and friendly companions. I was pleased I did not have to sleep with a stranger in the same bed.

After a good night's rest, I woke to a pleasant day and felt more accustomed to the saddle. We climbed a steep rise, where on the road in front of me, I spied two men who I sensed might be banditos. I turned Chester halfway around ready to gallop back down when I saw another behind, who must have hidden in the brushes. I thought to myself, "Are all the roads in España plied by brigands, or is this just my bad luck—geez!"

With my adrenalin and heart pumping, hyperalert, as the three approached, I could see that they had no pistolas. Thankfully, most of our money was safely stored in the Salamanca bank, so I thought about surrendering my remaining funds to them, but these guys looked even more cutthroat and desperate than those others. If I was lucky and they did not kill me, they would take all I had, steal Chester, and leave me in the middle of nowhere, so I quickly drew the pistol from my saddlebag.

Seeing that it was not lit and had no fire to light it, they converged on me with swords drawn, the first one grabbing Chester's reins so I could not escape. I aimed and shot him in the leg, immediately sending him reeling to the ground. With me struggling to hold on, Chester reared up and lunged at the other bandits. They froze, for they had never seen a pistol fire without being lit first.

I drew the second pistol, quickly lit the wick with my BIC, and aimed it at a second robber. Surprised at how quickly the wick was lit, as if by magic, not wanting to die, he fled, as did the third when I pointed it at him. I was so angry I raised the pistol up, lined the barrel to my eye, aimed it at his back, and was about to pull the trigger when I thought better of it. Did I really want to kill someone, even if they deserved it? They were so thread-worn, bedraggled and emaciated; perhaps they were just hungry.

We galloped down the road for nearly a mile before stopping, where I extinguished my matchlock and reloaded my flintlock with powder, a new ball and paper, glad that it had performed so valiantly. Recognizing the amount of time it took to reload and how inaccurate these guns were, there had to be a better weapon than this.*

When I arrived at Francisco's the next day, I spied him in his newly green vineyard, speaking to a field hand. Attempting to surprise my friend, I slowly rode up behind him until he turned to see who was approaching, ran towards me, tore me off Chester, and bear-hugged me. "I am so happy you have come to see me, mi amigo, come I want you to meet my familia—your familia."

As we walked up to the large hacienda, Chester in hand, the family greeted me like a hero returning from the war. Señora Sophia Alvarez, a slender, voluptuous, young beauty with long, straight, black hair and elegant features that oddly reminded me of Sophia Vergara, hugged me, "Thank you for saving mi husband's life. You are always welcome here. You will forever be a member of our familia."

I told her, "Francisco is the real hero, for he disarmed the bandito with the pistola and then fought two desperate villains with his sword. I would not have been able to hold a sword properly if it was not for his excellent lessons."

Then, I met his three cute young daughters, aging from perhaps four to ten, the two older ones being very precocious and well-mannered. The younger one seemed very shy and hid behind her mother's skirts, periodically poking her head out, then retreated to the skirt's safety. Their two-year-old son, Francisco the IVth, was very rambunctious. With such a beautiful family, it was no wonder Francisco could not wait to return to them. They exceeded the lovely picture he painted of them during our travels. It was difficult to believe that someone as slender as Sophia had four young ones. Francisco had previously told me that she came from a noble family in Madrid that was also somehow related to Isabella, the exact relationship I could not follow, but they were no more than distant cousins.

An older lady came out to greet me, and I soon learned that it was his mother, Maria, a gentile woman who also praised my saving his life. Her husband had died as an esteemed hero in the wars against the Moors.

A highly animated Francisco asked me how long I could stay with them. I explained what had happened in Salamanca and that the president would not be available for over three weeks, which I thought might be too long to impose upon them. "Excellente, most excellente, you are our esteemed guest."

Over dinner that night, I told them of my escapade with the banditos along the way, the girls enraptured by my description. Later, in their immense, white living room young Francisco acted out the entire drama with a wooden sword on his stick horse, who he renamed Chester to the cheers of his family. They also had to hear the story of our encounter with the banditos on the way to Salamanca from me—a story they had heard before but could not hear enough of. I added as much detail and suspense as I could—acting it out. They gave me a spacious room overlooking the vineyards and orchards rolling off into the distance mountains under a peaceful, cool, starlit night.

On horseback the next day, Francisco provided a tour of his vineyards, pointing out the variety of grapes and commenting on his plans for the year. So impressed by what Carlos had done with the windmills, Francisco had arranged for him to come to his estate to help build windmills to bring water from the nearby stream to the fields during the hot, dry summer. We also toured his high-ceilinged, stone wine-making facilities with that distinctive earthy, yeasty smell of aging wine that stored numerous kegs from various years.

Showing me the implements used for each step, he ran through how they made their wines and sherry—the crush, the fermentation, the aging, the kegging and the bottling. I had obeen on several wine tours, but other than with Paul, my winemaker friend, I had never had a private tour.

He explained, "Sherry is a fortified wine, which means we add more alcohol. Here is the still we use to make the alcohol, where we boil the wine, which travels through these coils. The alcohol condenses then gathers in this jug here. The added alcohol helps to preserve the sherry. Would you like to taste it?"

I tasted it, and it tasted like pure grain alcohol or moonshine with just a hint of grape flavor.

That evening after dinner, while the elder Senora Alvarez watched the children., Francisco, Sophia and I sampled some of his prized wines and sherries in an oaken booth in his wine cellar bathed in candlelight, surrounded by hundreds of aging bottles on shelves. We had a great time, got a little tipsy, and told Sophia about some of the funnier moments on our trip, most of which revolved around the comical Pedro. Whereas Francisco was usually more reserved, she was genuinely fun-loving and had a funny snorting laugh that she tried to cover up, which made us all laugh that much more.

Now that I was a proven intermediate swordsman, Francisco could not wait to practice with me. So, we spent a couple of hours every day practicing. He continually corrected my form and showed me some of the more advanced moves, complimenting me on my "much improved" footwork. Like other sports, I now acquired a passion for swordplay, and eventually, the movements from my ball sports (basketball, racquetball, tennis) transferred to it.

One of the problems Francisco identified with my form was oddly due to the sports I had played, which required crouching down. For fencing, I needed to be erect and in balance with my core, which Francisco took much patience to overcome in me. As Francisco explained, what helped me understand the principle was riding Chester, where I also had to be erect and in balance. I did not know it then, but Francisco was one of the most expert swordsmen in all of España, by far, the best in the region. Therefore, I learned from a master.

One time, during a particularly long flurry of jabs and slashes, my arm aching, ready to drop from exhaustion, Francisco transferred his sword to his left hand, signaling with a nod of his head for me to do the same. This move gave me renewed energy, for I felt I could strike a winning blow. But after spending my last bit of reserves, I once again collapsed in defeat, for he was nearly as proficient with his left as his right hand.

He said, "If a skilled enemy used his right, it would not be likely I could soon defeat him with my left hand, but I could defend myself forever, allowing my right arm to rest then when the opponent became winded from his fervent attacks, I could strike the fatal blow. I have become nearly as proficient with my left, such that if I detect my opponent is unable to defend against the left, I switch and quickly dispatch him. In competitions, this is how I have won against many advanced swordsmen."

The next day, he taught me how to use my left hand better, which was not as difficult as I imagined. I had played baseball nearly every year since I was five, and since I was a switch hitter and caught the ball in my left hand, I had developed good hand-eye coordination with my left arm, too. When trying to attack with the left, though, I looked like a feeble clown. I could defend myself well but could not really attack yet.

Now that my skills had reached a higher level, Francisco taught me strategy, telling me, "Every adversary you meet will have his unique strengths and weaknesses. On the battlefield, I had to assess these, for my life depended upon it instantly. If I faced an unskilled opponent, I immediately vanquished him. If, however, I faced someone with obvious skills, such as a knight, I would have to be more careful, taking time to ascertain his skill level and finding his weakness before the fatal blow. Everyone has a different style, and everyone has at least one weakness. With a superior swordsman, while I was in a defensive mode, they often underestimated my skill, which was their undoing."

He mimicked several styles—aggressive, playful, defensive, overly frenetic, strong yet slow, fast yet weak, showing me how to assess and overcome each one. "To overcome your foe requires a degree of patience and intelligence, mi amigo. Be in control; use your emotions to your advantage. If you are in the proper mind and in the center of yourself, the battle will unfold as if it were in slow motion. You have exceptionally long arms and are, for a tall man, very fast on your feet—your strengths, but you present a large target and are a little wild—your weaknesses. You leave the back side of your shoulder exposed for attack and sometimes lack balance, but we will work on that." I was a little disappointed, for after so much practicing, in my mind I thought I was becoming an advanced swordsman. Now, I realized I still had much to learn.

I asked if he had killed many men. He said, "Unfortunately, si mi amigo. And I have lost many men, my comrades, both of which haunt my dreams. Unlike a pistol or a musket, when you kill someone with the sword, you are close, and you see their face their eyes as they perish, and often it takes multiple blows to kill them. If they are wounded and surrender, though, I have never killed such a man. The faces, the shocked eyes, when they endure the fatal stabbing is what I see in my dreams. The only thing that washes that away is to wake up to my beautiful wife and see the faces of my loving children. I am not sure I would be on this earth any longer if it were not for them."

Then he asked, "Is there someone you care for Rand? Perhaps the lovely Gwendolyn. I highly recommend marriage to you, mi amigo. You are a good man, and I can tell by the way you treat my children, you would be a good husband and father, much better than many I have known. You are too old not to have a wife and children."

"There is someone. Her name is Marie. She has beautiful soft brown hair, highlighted with streaks of sun-kissed blond, the most luscious red lips, expressive, sensual eyes, and a cute little upturned nose with a curvaceous figure that would drive any man mad. She is strong and athletic and loves riding her horses every day. She is a very intelligent French royal who speaks five languages and reads everything she can get a hold of. It's more than the way she looks, though, it's the way she carries herself. It's, it's something I can't describe. Every man in the kingdom, young or old, is infatuated with her, but she chose me. After I take those precious manuscripts back and I become a partner, I will ask her to marry me."

"She sounds extraordinary. I would love to meet her. And have my Sophia meet her too. We four would have much fun together, sí, yes?"

"Sí we would! Your lovely Sophia would become like a sister to my beautiful Marie."*

Even though Francisco had assured me that such robberies on the road to Salamanca were rare, I worried about my trip back and the additional banditos I might encounter. A major goal I hoped to accomplish while staying with Francisco was to improve upon my flintlock, which would not appear for another fifty years. When something like a flintlock seemed like such a simple extension of a matchlock, it always amazed me how long it took for some technologies to evolve. But I could not criticize this time period. The Internet was invented in 1969, but it took twenty-five years, until the 1990s before it caught on, the same amount of time for the TV invented in the mid-1920s.

I had shot a pistol at a rifle range once, but as a suburban kid, I did not know much about guns, so I fired up my iPhone and researched the history of guns. The battery was at less than 50% now, but I felt this was important enough to draw it down.

I found it interesting that matchlocks would soon replace flint-locks—not a radical change since they would just augment the s-shaped hammer to hold a flint and scrape against a metal protrusion, producing a spark. The spark would light the little bit of powder in the pan that had a weep hole leading inside the barrel, which, in turn, would explode the powder at the base of the barrel, thereby propelling the bullet forward. All of which is what I had basically accomplished relatively simply.

I wanted to be able to fire multiple shots from one pistol and found that there had been multi-barreled cannons since the 4th century and that a multi-barreled pistol would soon be invented in the coming century in Germany—called a pepperbox because they looked like big pepper shakers. What I wanted was a revolver that I saw would not be invented until the 19th century by Colt, among others, but I thought this would be too ambitious.

I asked Francisco if I could use the tools in his workshop. He replied, "All I have is at your disposal, mi amigo." I thought my large Swiss army knife, with tools not invented yet, might also come in handy.

I took the long barrels off my two pistols and sawed these in half, a task that was taking forever. I wish I would have had a hacksaw, but I found if I sharpened the saw teeth with a file and heated the metal, the job went much faster.

Francisco had a small forge used to produce horseshoes and some of their farm implements, operated by Diego the blacksmith/foreman. Using a clay mold, I had Diego pour molten metal to fuse the four barrels together.

The mold had a hole in the middle I used to pass a spindle through the barrels that would rotate around it. Afterward, I retrofitted the back half of my matchlock, carved out two additional pans in the new barrels, and drilled extra weep holes. I next screwed a clip onto the side that would snap each barrel into the exact position when I manually turned the barrels. With no power tools, all of this took a long time. Since it was early spring, Diego spent most of his time during the day tending to the vineyards and supervising the plantings. *

Between working on the gun, sword lessons, and riding, Chester, Francisco, and I went to town one day, where I picked up some parts for the gun from a local clockmaker. Since their vineyard was a half-day ride from town, the family had a smaller hacienda there, too, where we planned to spend the night.

That night, we went to Francisco's favorite barra for dinner and had quite a bit of wine. When the colonel he served under, Don Enrico Suarez, entered the bar, Francisco enthusiastically introduced me to him, and he joined us as we feasted on tapas and drank some more wine.

Earlier during the Moors wars, Francisco had been Enrico Suarez's second in command. After his father died, Francisco resigned to manage the family vineyards, and Enrico had been promoted to a general. He told us thrilling stories of the wars to the south. In early January, they had captured the last Moorish holdout in Grenada, thereby reuniting all of España, "Ferdinand and Isabella promised religious freedom to both the Moors and Jews, a concession that facilitated the surrender by King Boabdil. After many generations, the Reconquista of Spain had finally been accomplished."

We toasted to the Reconquista and to General Enrico and to his valiant troops and to Isabella and Ferdinand and to España. As they proposed each toast the rest of the denizens of the barra joined in—ever more fervently—it was infectious, joyous—the end of a war that had lasted over 775 years. By now, I had become a little tipsy, but it would have been an insult not to toast such a historic event.

Enrico had just returned from Córdoba, where the king and queen directed the Reconquista of Grenada. On his way home, he stopped here, hoping to find Francisco, his old friend and comrade in arms to share the glorious news.

Introducing a new topic, he asked, "Have you heard about this Italian Columbo?"

Francisco replied, "Well, over dinner with my friend, Father Dominic, he had said that he was asked to join a commission at the university to consider Columbo's proposal, but they did not think his plans were sound and advised the monarchs against the expedition. They thought it was too expensive and risky."

"Yes, he has been trying to promote his fictitious plan for six or seven years now. He says he can discover a new route to the Indies by going west and that he can do this because the world is round, if you can believe that. Of course, everyone knows that the world is flat. The church and logic says so. He even took his ridiculous plan to King John of Portugal. He's not even from here, he's from Genoa at the base of the Italian peninsula."

"What happened in Portugal?"

"They considered the plan, but since they had already discovered a route around Cape Horn of Africa, they were not interested in such an expensive, doomed venture.

Columbo had left Córdoba on his way to France to have them finance his expedition when King Ferdinand called him back. Even though the Queen thinks there is little chance of success, they do not want to risk another nation having such strategic advantages therefore, I believe she may fund his ridiculous expedition. As you well know, the Portuguese control most of the rich, spice-laden isles in the Indies and are becoming enormously rich. Columbo tried to sell the royals on the idea that there are more islands east of the Portuguese possessions yet to be discovered that would enrich Espanol without a war. I must admit this Genoan is persistent, but what a fantastical idea. I do not think they would go for the expedition if it were not for our victory. There is a sense of hubris and invincibility throughout Grenada and all the south. They want to conquer the world."

By now, I was the drunkest I had been since college and felt I had to defend Columbus. "I agree with you, my esteemed general. Columbo will not discover a new route to the Indies. Instead, I think he will probably discover an entire new world as large as all of Europe, maybe even larger. He will first discover large Islands southwest of España, similar to the Canary Islands. Then he and other Spanish explorers, encouraged by his success, will discover innumerable exotic new lands filled with gold, silver, natives, and exotic new foods. These riches will cause España to become the wealthiest nation in all the world."

"If what you say is true, that he will not come upon new Spice Islands, then the world is flat."

"Well no, eventually, other Spanish explorers will discover a much longer route to the East Indies. Have you ever seen the sea from the top of a coastal mountain?"

"Yes, after we conquered Granada, I was on top of the Rock of Gibraltar not far from Africa."

"Did you notice how the sea curves just a little?"

"Yes"

"That is the curvature of the earth."

"Have you ever seen a ship approaching you from a long distance?"

"Certainly, when I was at the base of Gibraltar, I saw ships bringing goods across the sea from Morocco."

"Did you notice that you could not see the bottom of the ship, then it gradually appeared."

"Yes, so."

"If the earth were flat, you would have been able to see the entire ship, from top to bottom, but the earth's curvature obscures the bottom portion."

He looked stunned, as if you see something often but don't appreciate its implications. I realized I had said too much, something I would not have done without so much red wine. "General Enrico, please accept my apologies for being under the influence of the vino; I have said too much."

Francisco said, "When Rand was in Ireland, he was set upon by banditos who stole all he had and left him for dead. Indeed, for a month, it seemed as if he would surely die. There is much he does not remember, but as if he were a profit, he has predicted some amazing things to come. He may be drunk, or he may have a vision of the future. If our dear Isabella does finance this Columbo, we shall soon see if his vision is true or just the vino talking."

Enrico stayed at the Hacienda for a few days, and our differences soon vanished under the influence of the beautiful and hospitable Sophia. While Francisco spent more time in the fields, Enrico and I enjoyed dueling. Whereas Francisco's style was more fluid and finessed, Enrico's style was aggressive and fierce. He, too said, "Each opponent I have met on the field has had unique capabilities, which I must immediately size up, assess his weaknesses, and conquer before moving on to the next foe."—a lesson that reinforced what Francisco had told me.

Before I left Francisco and his wonderful family, I assembled my pepperbox pistol. To test it, I loaded each barrel with powder and a ball. I would still have to prime each pan sitting on top of each barrel, something I could not do in advance because the powder would just fall off. Shooting would be faster than going through the time-consuming reloading process, but filling the new pan with powder from the horn would still take time. So, I drilled little holes into each barrel and screwed a dime-sized disk that would secure the powder in the pan. When I wanted to fire a chamber, all I had to do was to flick the disk and fire.

After filling the four pans, I clicked the first chamber into place, pulled the trigger, and the flint hit the metal, creating a spark that lit the pan, igniting the charge in the barrel propelling the bullet forward. It worked. I cheered jumping up and down several times.

Then, I spun the second barrel into position and repeated the process with similar amazing results. When I pulled the trigger on the third chamber, it blew up in my hand, burning my trigger finger and thumb, me immediately dropping it to the ground and cursing.

Upon examination, I realized the last barrel was misaligned. I hastily went into town and bought two more barrels, which I sawed in half and adjusted the mold for Diego to fill with molten iron. Since I would not have time to assemble the new pistol, at the gunsmith's, I also bought two more pistols to defend myself on the way back to Salamanca. With Diego's help, using the parts from my previous flintlock, I made one into a flintlock.

There was one problem I wanted to correct, though. Even if I had the flintlock loaded and ready to fire, I still had to use my powder horn to fill the pan before firing. If confronted by a bandit, I would not have time to do this. So, similar to my pepperbox, I drilled a hole next to the pan and screwed a cover over the pan. When I wanted to fire, all I had to do was flick the cover around and then pull the trigger, which would cause a spark to light the power in the pan and fire the pistol. Now, I would always be ready to fire.

Before I left, Carlos arrived to start work on the windmills, and I helped them as a common laborer, amazed at the cleverness of the growing, large machine. On my last night, the Alvarezes threw a grand fiesta filled with neighbors, friends, and relatives. After saying a sad goodbye to Carlos, Francisco, and his lovely family and thanking the beautiful Sophia for her wonderful hospitality, unsure I would ever see my gracious friends again, the next morning, I solemnly rode Chester back to Salamanca to gain permission to access the library's precious books.

Being confronted by robbers on my two previous excursions in Spain, I expected to be accosted by villains around every bend, up every rise, behind every bush. I kept my two pistols and my BIC handy, holding my flintlock in hand as I passed a particularly suspicious spot, ready to have Chester gallop forward at the least provocation, which I did on two such occasions where no one appeared. Despite my caution and tension, absolutely nothing happened.

TEN

Cordoba

Safely back in Salamanca, I acquired the same glorious room from Francisco's hospitable cousin, Manuel. The next day I went to the University to see the Presidente.

"Buenos Dias Sonorita, I am here for my appointment with El Presidente Cortez."

With an 'I can't be bothered' look on her face and a nasty tone, she responded, "Oh señor, that is impossible. He is far too busy to see (lowly) you." The secretary looked, acted, and sounded like an officious, too-busy, self-important bureaucrat to be bothered.

"But I have been trying to see him for over a month. You said I would be able to see him now. Surely, he can spare a few moments."

Seeming disturbed by my presence, she replied in a whiny, Lilly Tomlin, Ernestine voice, "Señor, you will have to wait! Maybe he can see you next week!"

"But, sonorita, I do not think you understand. I have a proposition that will increase the coffers of the University and will greatly enhance its reputation. The first time I came, I was with Francisco Alvarez, a distinguished alumnus whose family has generously funded one of your colleges for decades."

As if she were shoeing away a fly, "Señor, please leave."

Feeling that I was facing an immovable civil servant, the likes of which have existed for thousands of years with a plethora of such computer-aided characters still existing in the 21st century, I said, "I will not leave until I see the presidente. If necessary, I will stay here day and night until he appears." Then I sat at a bench with her periodically glaring at me, me glaring back. I felt ridiculous, but I had not come so far and waited so long at a considerable expense just to go back to Ireland empty-handed.

At the end of the day, the president left his office, saying, buenas noches Wauneta, to his petulant secretary."

I rose up, stood in his path, smiled, held out my hand, and said, "Monsignor Cortez, my name is Rand Roberts, a close friend of Alvarezes. I have come all the way from London to see you. Can you spare a few minutes of your precious time?"

"Why, certainly, come into my office, won't you? Wauneta, it is late in the day. Bring us a decanter of wine and two glasses." I could feel her daggers in my back as we entered his large wooden office. When she delivered the red wine with a scowl, and the monsignor poured it, I was glad she had not delivered filled glasses because she would have likely spit in mine.

"Why have you come all this way to Salamanca señor?"

I explained my long journey, including John's previous trip and the treacherous banditos, careful to prominently mention Francisco of the well-known Alvarez family and their endowment, from whose hacienda on their expansive estate I had just arrived.

"Oh yes, the Alvarezes are wonderful supporters of our institution and have graduated so many of their esteemed sons—very generous indeed."

I launched into the pitch I had rehearsed while waiting so many hours, "Father Dominic showed us Salamanca's treasures of literature that Francisco and I beheld." (The president looked astonished that we had seen these closeted, precious documents.)

"It is wonderful that Salamanca has been able to preserve such magnificent works of civilization from the great thinkers throughout time. I want to print copies of these wonders to spread the knowledge they contain and preserve them for all time. I am prepared to pay the university handsomely, return them in the same condition, plus give the university the first ten printed copies of each. In addition, we will provide you a royalty for every book sold, and given the importance of these works, I believe there will be many sales."

Then, having not thought of it before but desperately wanting to win him over, I added, "On the first page, we will print the name of Salamanca University and your coat of arms, which will appear in the libraries of top universities throughout Europe, such as Cambridge, Oxford, the Sorbonne and Barcelona." His interest perked up at the thought of having Salamanca books being referenced, studied, and discussed at such prestigious institutions. I showed him a couple of the books we had previously printed, noting our work's quality and the block-printed graphics. Then I showed him some of our pages with etchings, which no one else had done yet, and explained that process, which he found interesting.

Still smiling broadly but looking as if he had doubts, the president queried, "But these books they will be printed in English, which few of our estudiantes or professors read."

Then I showed him a couple of rare books we had printed in Latin for the church, something that sparked his interest, "We have preserved several of the books the Irish monks faithfully hand-copied throughout the centuries that otherwise would have been lost forever. This is what we want to do for your books, too. Our mission is to preserve and disseminate the great works of the ages to advance learning, thinking, and education throughout the world. I will make you a gift of these for the university, if we can reach an accord."

Wanting to allay his concern, I added something I had not previously considered, "We will print them in both English and Latin. Since Latin is the universal language throughout Europe and the language of scholars, the books will rapidly spread throughout Christendom, as will the name of Salamanca."

"Señor, you have offered generous and tempting terms, and I would like to help you, but I am concerned about having these delicate documents make such a long voyage to Ireland, as you say, and back. After all, many of these ancient papyrus and vellum scrolls are in delicate condition. If a fierce storm swamped your ship, they would be lost forever. I must, therefore, regrettably reject your offer. Buenas noches señor."

I took a large gulp of wine and, crestfallen, left the room dejected. I had traveled so far, so long, had almost been killed twice, and in the end, had failed. Perhaps John would have fared better. I felt I had betrayed his memory, had let Colleen and Michael and noble King Edward down.*

With nothing left to do, I had a dinner of tapas with Jose as he shared my misery over my failed mission. He was getting along well, had made friends, and had enjoyed seeing his brother Carlos on his way to Francisco's. He said to be sure that I stay at his family's hacienda on the way back, tell them how well he had adjusted to college life, and how much he enjoyed Francisco's introduction to the university.

The next dismal day, I bought a surrey and horse. I thought about hiring a driver and carriage but knew it would be too expensive. I wanted to get to Bilbao as fast as possible, which is why I bought the other horse. I had to have the surry to cart my trunk. I planned to sell the new horse and surrey in Bilbao but take Chester back to Ireland. Even though I never thought I would be a horse lover, I had become quite fond of the big, kindly fellow.

After a restless night, I woke up feeling depressed and awful. Matching my blue mood, there was a rare rain that seemed as if it would last all day—not the best day to travel, but I no longer cared, I just wanted to leave. In the dark, before the sun rose, I packed up my things and, while carrying my bag in one hand, clunked the trunk down the stairs.

In a playful tone at the small front desk, Manuel, woken by the racket, said, "Why so glum, Señor Rand? I am sorry things did not work out for you."

"Manuel, you have been very kind, and I appreciate your hospitality. I would like to pay you what I owe you and be on my way."

"Where are you headed, señor?"

"Back to Bilbao, then on a ship to London or, if I can find one, hopefully to Ireland."

With a curious smile, he said, "Maybe not," then he handed me a letter from Francisco that I opened with curiosity.

Dear Señor Rand Roberts,

I suspect that your meeting with President Cortez did not meet your expectations. If it did, I congratulate you and wish you Godspeed on your journey back to the British Isles, where I hope to see you on my next trip.

If Presidente Cortez did not grant you the books you desire, I have heard from General Suarez that Isabella will be traveling through our town and plans to stay with her cousin Francisco and our family. Perhaps you can meet her and she can grant you access to these documents. If you think this might succeed, come back immediately.

Your Amigo,

Major Federico Alvarez Esquire

Manuel asked, "Is this good news mi amigo?"

"Yes, it is! Wonderful news, Manuel."

"Will you be staying with us?"

"No, I will be traveling to your cousin Francisco's again—to meet the Queen."

"Oh, señor, what an honor that would be; she is magnifico."

Since I had already bought the new horse and surrey, I went to the stable where they had hooked up the horses, placed my bag and trunk inside, and set off for Francisco's hacienda. I stopped at the bank and withdrew all our funds. Fortunately, the surrey had a partial cover that somewhat protected me from the rain. Soon after, I left Salamanca. Early that afternoon, the rain cleared, the sun appeared, the moisture began rapidly evaporating, a cobalt blue sky materialized, and it became a beautiful day. Instead of the five days it originally took to arrive at the hacienda, thanks to two-horse power, more experience, and increased motivation, it only took me three days this time.

After Francisco enthusiastically embraced me, as did his enchanting wife Sophia, the children, and Carlos, he told me he had bad news. A messenger had just arrived earlier that day with a letter from Queen Isabella saying that she could not leave as planned due to extended negotiations with the Moors.

Francisco said he felt terrible that I had traveled so far. Then he thought—"If Isabella will not come to us, we shall go to Isabella." He recommended that we leave the next day for Córdoba, where, with his help, we could plead my case to the Queen and King Ferdinand.

Having never been to Córdoba, but hearing what a fabulous city it was, Carlos said he would join us. Francisco had a carriage and a driver. I insisted that we add Chester to the team so I could take him back with me. If we failed, since Córdoba was close to the coast, rather than traveling back to Bilbao, I would sail from there.

Under four-horse power, we made it to Córdoba in a little over four days. Two of the nights, we camped out, which I immensely enjoyed. Along the way, we talked about strategy. Carlos came because he had grown up near Isabella and had served her in Holland. His father, a first cousin of Isabella's, knew her well. He and Francisco wanted to help me by providing an introduction and giving me an indoctrination on how to approach her along with the appropriate court etiquette.

As the carriage proceeded along the dirt road, bouncing on the bumps stirring up dust over the noise, I asked, "Where is the capital of Espanola now? Where do Ferdinand and Isabella reside?"

Francisco replied, "They are constantly on the move. Before Córdoba, they were in Madrigal, Segovia, Averalo, and lastly in Seville. After the Reconquista, they will likely move their court to Granada."

"But why do they move so often?"

"For two reasons, mi amigo. First, because they have presided over the battles against the Moors, which, as we have pushed them out, has led the esteemed monarchs ever southward. Also, because we are a new nation, being in so many new cities helps unite the country. When the people live near Isabella and Ferdinand, the people love them."

"Tell me what she has done—a little of her history as a queen."

"This is a bit of a story—one that I think you will find interesting. She has been remarkable in unifying our nation, expelling the Moors, establishing a government, and reducing the crime. Our family members, the Alvarezes have supported her since the time when she first fought against her niece Johanna and Johanna's husband, the King of Portugal, for the throne of Castile."

"After her father died, her older half-brother Henry assumed the throne. He tried to marry her off to a prince of France and then to the prince of Portugal, but she refused. She instead eloped with Ferdinand. Now Ferdinand was her second cousin, and such a marriage required special dispensation from the Pope, which they could obtain."

"Portugal contested her assumption of the throne of Castile so we had a second war with them, which I fought in. She sued for peace by giving them most of the lands along the Atlantic Coast in Africa and to the west. Some thought she gave them too much, but she wanted to end the war."

"Her feckless brother, Henry, had caused Castile to be deep in debt, filled with corruption and rampant with crime. More than a pretty face and more than would be expected of a woman, she soon shored up the nation's finances and nationalized the mints, thereby stabilizing our monetary system."

"Henry had done little to enforce the laws of España, so the crime had become rampant. I know you faced banditos, but it was much worse then, with criminals preying on every city. She established a national police force that drastically decreased the crimes. One northwestern province was so bad she assigned a commission to clean it up. That was highly successful."

"Henry's government was also mismanaged. There were two branches of the government: one composed of nobles who did little other than to extract funds from the treasury and another administrative branch that did all the work. She practically eliminated the nobles' positions and ended the corruption, installing professionals, many from Salamanca, to administer the country."

"It sounds like she has done much to establish an effective government. What is she like personally?"

"She is very religious, honest, and virtuous—just, but not so merciful. She is an intelligent, tough lady, but not cruel. In addition to establishing a supreme court, she created departments of finance, state and public affairs. She also cut back on unnecessary regulations and had our laws codified."

"In addition to her propitious rule, she has had five children. Not frail of spirit or body, she is a strong woman."

Without thinking, I added, "Her daughters will likely become queens of important nations themselves." Then I regretted saying something about the future.

On the way to Córdoba one night, when we stayed at an inn, and I occupied my own room, I popped my battery into my iPhone and did some research on Queen Isabella. The battery was under 40% now, but I wanted to be prepared for our anticipated meeting. I remembered that one of her daughters, Catherine of Aragon, would become Henry the VIIIth's first wife. After something like twenty-five years of marriage, because she had not given him a son, he pleaded to the pope to grant an annulment. The pope would not allow the divorce and therefore, Henry would find the Church of England. She would be the first of Henry's six wives, one he would still love and one he would not behead.

After Henry's death, Catherine's daughter, Mary (Isabella's grand-daughter), would become the Queen of England and attempt to restore Catholicism to the nation. Two of Isabella's other daughters would become the Queen of Portugal and the Queen of Spain—thereby ruling in three of the most prominent and wealthiest nations of the world, three nations that would explore, claim, and control most of the land and wealth of the new world—what a legacy.

Until the Revolutionary War, Spain interacted with more tribes, found more cities, and held more territory in the United States than the English ever had, including California, Texas, Florida, the South-west and the Northwest. Whereas the English slowly spread out from Jamestown and Plymouth, starting over a century earlier, endur-ing similar survival hardships, the Spanish conquistadors established dozens of outposts in the new world, such as San Diego, Los Angelos, San Francisco, Sante Fe, St. Augustine, San Antonio, Phoenix and Las Vegas *

As we descended from the mountains, we saw a bright city on the broad plain below us—church spires and minarets reaching for the puffy clouds. It did not resemble the other Spanish cities I had seen but seemed more akin to an Arab metropolis, such as Damascus or Baghdad, that I had explored during my college backpacking trip.

After traveling so far, I was impatient to return to my home and friends in Ireland and, through the portal in Bunkillarny, find my way back to my own time and my friends and family there–Paul, Betty, Wes, Jenny, Mike, etc. I had enjoyed Spain, but whether successful or not, I just wanted to complete my mission here and return. I did not want to tour Córdoba or spend any more time than absolutely necessary.

As we rode through town, Francisco, realizing that neither Carlos nor I had been to Córdoba, provided an introduction, "Córdoba had been the capital of the Caliphate, which included nearly all of the Iberian Peninsula, what has been called Andalusia and, thanks to Isabella and Ferdinand will finally become España again. Then, it was the largest city in all of Europe. When Paris, Rome and London contained less than 40,000 inhabitants each, Córdoba had 400,000 - five times more than the three combined. In addition, up until 1,000 A.D., it was the most cultured city in Europe—the center of European culture and science."

With palm trees lining the broad promenade, it was decidedly warmer, more reminiscent of Florida than the cold mountains we had just crossed over or the Andalusian plain, where I had been for two months. It seemed at least twenty degrees warmer. It felt like taking a trip to Mexico or the Caribbean in the middle of winter that, when you arrived, felt so invigorating.

Francisco exclaimed, "You do not want to be here in the summer, though, when it is hotter than Hades, the hottest in all of Española. During my first year here, by August, I had to go up into the mountains to escape the heat."

We rode past a huge building that Francisco identified, "This is the Mosque de Córdoba, which was the largest mosque in all the world. Now it is the Church of the Assumption of Mary, maybe other than St. Peter's, the largest church in the world." The stunning architecture was an intriguing mixture of Arab and Spanish influences.

As he related, "Córdoba was the capital of Andalusia, and since the Caliphate was reasonably tolerant, it possessed large populations and rich influences of the Jews, the Christians, and the Muslims—why I enjoy Córdoba so much. I sell my fine sherry here but always stay longer than needed and have even brought Sophia and the children."

When we came to a picturesque, multi-arched sandstone bridge, Francisco announced, "This is the Roman Bridge built before the birth of our Lord and Savior." I marveled at the quality and resilience of the construction and artistic symmetry of a bridge built 1500 years ago—even before the one in Salamanca. I wondered if those Roman engineers and those who constructed it could have imagined how long it would last—what a contrast to America, where our infrastructure is rapidly deteriorating.

By the time we arrived at our hotel, despite my earlier resistance, Córdoba had cast her spell over me—I was enchanted. Being late in the afternoon on a hot day, being tired from our long journey, we all took a delightful siesta. That evening, we had dinner at a nearby restaurant that our tour guide, Francisco, recommended. We had not eaten well along the trip, and Francisco, a bon vi bon, wanted to make up for it.

I was not sure what to expect. Would it be Spanish, Moroccan, or Mediterranean cuisine? The first dish we had was one that Francisco greatly looked forward to, what he called Ajo Blanco—a soup composed of Sorento ham, bread, garlic, vinegar and olive oil. It was delicious.

Next, we had pinchinto morundo andaluz – saffron chicken, with cumin and coriander on skewers that resembled satay, along with bo querones en vinegar, which, when it arrived, I realized were anchovies.

Throughout the evening, as the leisurely dinner, accompanied by fine wines, unfolded, Francisco enlightened us regarding the history of Córdoba, a subject that, since he first came here as a freshman, had fascinated him.

"I learned about Córdoba in an Iberian history class, which Father Dominic also attended. He found it fascinating too, probably even more than me, since he is now in charge of the library. Having scores of institutions of learning and libraries, Córdoba was, no doubt, the most sophisticated city in all of Europe—the Paris of the first millennium. Indeed, it had the largest and the finest library in all of Europe. Specializing in medicine, mathematics, science, astronomy and botany, Córdoba far exceeded any country on the continent. The library reflected this intense intellectualism—its repository of culture."

Then we ate something I had before (well, 500 years into the future, that is) paella, which included rice, shrimp and ham mixed with various herbs and vegetables. I had become immersed in Spain in 1492, but periodically, familiar sights or, in this case, dishes reminded me of my place and time. I had to figure out a way to get back to America.

"The Sultan, then Al-Hakam II, himself an accomplished scholar, had an extensive library he wanted to expand. He, therefore, sent agents throughout the Muslim Empire to purchase books to populate his library. Many of the ancient texts were translated from Latin and Greek into Arabic, for which he formed a committee composed of Muslims and Christians to acquire and translate these."

"Then the library clerks, many of them women, carefully hand-copied the books. This was 500 years before your printing technology began to change the world, so each book had to be meticulously transcribed. Calligraphers and bookbinders created beautiful text and cover designs in leather. Al-Hakam's library was said to have contained more than 400,000 books, whose titles filled a 44-volume catalog. Under Al-Haim II, the library employed over 500 persons to accomplish all of this work."

"Elsewhere in Moslem Espanol, there were at least seventy libraries in the 10th century, with several in Toledo alone. Probably more than the rest of Europe combined. In addition to the royal library, there were libraries in the universities in Córdoba, Seville, Malaga, and Granada, among others. The people of Córdoba also collected books for their homes. Those who owned large, personal libraries were considered important figures in Córdoba society. Private libraries flourished, and it was said that Córdoba was by far the greatest book market in the world."

"With its specialization in medicine, mathematics, science, astronomy, and botany, intellectually, Córdoba far exceeded anything on the continent. This tradition peaked under the Moors but extended back to Roman times with men such as Seneca, a famous stoic, philosopher, statesman, dramatist and satirist. Much of his work is the foundation of modern philosophical and moral thought. Even though he was not a Christian, he was born around the time of Christ in Córdoba and was sympathetic to Christianity, which incorporated much of his philosophy. Some Christians even consider him a saint."

Francisco described the last dish as "Wild boar marinated in brandy and various herbs and spices." I hesitated to eat it until he and Carlos chided me into doing so. It tasted like gamey ham but was not that bad, as the spices and brandy greatly enhanced it.

For dessert, we had a mouthwatering Mallorcan Almond Cake - Gató de Almendras Mallorquin, after which we had a delectable brandy. Leaning back and tilting his chair, Francisco added, "All of the dishes we had tonight came to us from the Moors and are not readily available in northern Castile."

Swirling, sniffing, and taking another sip of my aromatic brandy, thoroughly immersed in Francisco's portrayal of Córdoba, I interjected, "Dominic showed us some of Seneca's works at his Salamanca library. These probably came from here, then."

"Most definitely, as did many of the other works Dominic showed us. Maimonides is yet another great philosopher born in Córdoba. His copious work comprises the cornerstone of Jewish scholarship. His fourteen-volume Mishneh Torah still carries significant authority as a codification of Talmudic law. The Torah comprises the Old Testament of the Bible, which includes the Garden of Eden, Moses's life, and other stories with which we are so familiar. It also includes the Ten Commandments and 603 other commandments, the most important of which is to love thy neighbor as yourself."

"Maimonides also figures very prominently in the history of Islamic and Arab sciences, becoming a prominent philosopher and in both the Jewish and Islamic worlds. We saw many of his works preserved in Salamanca too, including the Mishneh Torah."

"If you can acquire permission from the Queen, you should definitely print these. Many scholars throughout the world will drool over them. Well, hopefully, they will not drool on them; that would not be so good, but they would be very excited to read them."

"Since it was the major library during the Middle Ages, I should go there while I am here and try to acquire some of their works too. The Córdoba library sounds even more fantastic than Salamanca's. When can we see it?"

"Well, Rand, that would have been possible if you were here before 1,000 A.D. Then things changed. The Vizier at the time was Al Mazur. The Moorish Clergy feared that the intellectual influences of the Christians and Jews were devaluing Islamic traditions. So, they convinced Al Mazur to eliminate all the books. Inciting nationalistic fever, Al Mazur had most of the books in the city burned or sold.

"That's a tragedy—what a loss for humanity." Then I thought about how ISIS Muslims had destroyed the museums of Iraq. These museums housed the first relics of civilization from Babylonia dating back to 10,000 BC. I thought that the Muslims had built this incomparable library, seeming to be equal to or exceeding the Great Library of Alexandria. Then other Muslims burned it down—what a shame.

Of course, during the Middle Ages, through wars or neglect, Christians had destroyed so much more from the former Roman Empire. Throughout history, there seems to be a pull between the intellectuals and the uneducated people, between those open to other cultures and those who espouse nationalism. In the 21st century, over just the last hundred years, there have been persecutions and killings of tens of millions of intellectuals in Germany, in Russia, in China, in Northern Korea, in Afghanistan, in Cambodia, etc.

It seems that one of the first steps in the dictators' handbook is to extinguish the books and persecute the intellectuals who might oppose them. Looking beyond the unforgivable horrific persecutions, it almost seems that when we absorb the wisdom of preceding civilizations and stretch to advance civilization, rather than reaching successfully higher planes, those left behind rebel and, like a rubber band, react, sending us backward. The dictators such as Putin, Al Mazur, Hitler, Stalin, Mao, Franco, Kim, ISIS or the Taliban are the catalysts, but many of their people are their accomplices.

I wondered what had powered such an intellectual center, so I asked Francisco, "Why was Córdoba so successful?"

"They were noted for their silver, leather, metalwork, tiles and textiles. They also have a rich variety of fruits, vegetables, herbs, and spices here. As you can tell, their food is delicious. But being the capital of such a large, wealthy, long-lasting empire is the most important factor leading to its success."

"Yes, it was!"

Then he told us the tantalizing story of how, after Al Mazur had destroyed or sold the books and died, in a mere fifteen years, there were nine subsequent rulers of Córdoba, during which time there were also two slave rebellions—wow. From that time on, Córdoba began to deteriorate rapidly. It seemed like some kind of Karmic justice, I thought.

"Around 1250, King Ferdinand III of our beloved Castile conquered the city, and as you can see, the population is a fraction of what it was then."

"So, you might say that the burning of the books, signifying the extinction of learning and culture in Córdoba, led to its decline."

"Yes, but fortunately, over the intervening centuries, the library in Salamanca had rescued some of those great works. Others are no doubt, forever lost. Who knows how much knowledge, wisdom, literature and science those hundreds of thousands of books might have contained?"

Following our stimulating three-hour dinner, after Francisco and Carlos had bedded down for the night, to prepare for the meeting with Isabella, despite being exhausted, I went into the dark, unoccupied hallway, turned on my iPhone, and researched Queen Isabella, King Ferdinand and Columbus then quickly powered down the phone whose battery was now less than 30%. I always prepared meticulously for my presentations; this would perhaps be the most important one in my life. I had presented to associations, executives, VCs and college students but never to a powerful King and Queen. Although I thought my apps were so important, preserving these foundational documents was much more important.*

Following a full night's sleep, I arose to a cool morning and joined Carlos and Francisco for breakfast in the hotel's restaurant. After ordering a fried egg dish that also originated with the Moors, who Francisco said introduced frying to Spain, I smelled something familiar—coffee, ooh, coffeeee! When I anxiously asked the waiter for some coffee, he had no idea what I spoke of. I followed my nose to a table at the opposite end of the room where a dark-skinned man with a broad black mustache, white sashed robes and a red fez was sipping something out of a tiny cup. Standing there transfixed at his table, taking in a deep breath of the magnificent aroma, which must have seemed strange to this stranger, I introduced myself and asked him where he had acquired the coffee.

Looking at me as if I was insane, in an Arab accent, he replied, "I am not familiar with what you say is this coffee."

Trying to hide my growing anxiety at being so close to the elixir I had so long craved, I said, "But what are you drinking?"

"Oh, this, this is my Mecca."

Somewhat confused that my desired drink had acquired the name of the most prominent city in the Arab world, thinking with my deficient Spanish and his thick Moorish accented Spanish that I misinterpreted what he said, I hesitantly asked, "Where might I acquire some of this, um, um Mecca?"

"Oh, it comes from Constantinople."

"But the hotel must have some, no."

"No señor, they do not."

Feeling like a desperate drug addict talking to his dealer, frantically needing a fix, I said, "But, please, how did you get the Mecca señor?"

"Oh, I brought it from Constantinople with me. You see, they do not have Mecca in Andalusia. As far as I know, they do not have it anywhere this west of Turkey, but they may have it in Egypt. However, I am not sure of this."

Seeming more accepting, he continued, "Seeing your confusion, let me explain. I am a trader from Constantinople who has come here to trade for Córdoba's fine leather and silver works, currently in great demand in Constantinople. Since throughout the Ottoman Empire, we are not allowed drinks that have alcohol in them, I feel I must have my Mecca. So, I brought the beans with me."

The man, who did not say much, suddenly launched into a soliloquy, no doubt, fueled by the heavenly Mecca, with me mightily resisting grabbing his cup until finally, he said, "Would you like some?" He had the waiter bring a cup of the Mecca that he had requested be brewed in the pot he brought with him.

The first sip was heavenly, and I smiled with deep, dream-like satisfaction. It was extremely strong and thick—like a double shot of espresso but even more concentrated and even stronger.

"Judging from your satisfaction, you must have been to Arabia, no señor."

I had been to Turkey on a backpacking trip through Eastern Europe before starting on the app four years ago, so I honestly responded, "Yes, I have been to Constantinople, where I acquired the habit of drinking Mecca and have sorely missed it. Would it be offensive to you if I had some cream with my Mecca?"

"I have not heard of such a thing, but no, it would not offend me."

I had the waiter bring a larger cup and some cream, which I mixed with the Mecca. Farouck Al Azez, as I learned was his name, tasted it and liked it but preferred it dark.

We spent much of the rest of the morning on a delightful coffee high, talking about the expanding Ottoman Empire, which would eventually encompass nearly all of Arabia, Northern Africa, Israel, Greece, Hungary and the Balkans.

Later, when I checked my iPhone, with its capital in Constantinople rivaling the Roman Empire, it revealed that the Ottoman Empire would last for over 600 years—until World War I when the Turks were defeated. The lands they had previously controlled, such as Iraq, Syria, Israel, Bosnia and Afghanistan would spark constant wars in the 20th and 21st centuries, costing America trillions of dollars and thousands of lives. But we did not talk about all that but rather the culture, art and trade of this burgeoning empire.

Before he left, I asked if I might purchase some of his Mecca beans. He said since he had completed his business in Córdoba ahead of schedule, he could let some go "for the right price." He was a trader used to seeking the best deal, so we bartered a bit, but I still paid much more than I would in San Francisco, even at Starbucks, but far less than I was willing to pay for a small bag of the beans I would cherish, conserve and ration. Thankfully, nobody I would meet knew of or cared for my Mecca.

ELEVEN

Queen Isabella

Early in the afternoon, the three of us ventured across the Roman bridge to meet with the King and Queen in their current palace. Before entering the Alcazar, we passed through the most delightful, exquisite garden filled with flowers, fountains, pools, lemon trees, orange trees, and meticulously shaped topiaries. It being spring, the gardens had a delicious smell of citrus blossoms and herbs. The Moorish viziers who ruled here for centuries certainly lived in the lap of luxury. Judging by the garden, which rivaled those at Versailles or the chateaus of the Loire Valley in France, this was a spectacular place.

In anticipation of pleading my case to the monarchs, my stomach was tied in knots, but the stroll helped to relax me, and thanks to the Mecca, I was more awake than I had been in months. Francisco and Carlos had a jovial attitude that also helped me relax. We were the three musketeers off to see the queen.

The old fortress dating back to the Roman times in the 3rd century had been remodeled by each of the numerous victors. In contrast to the beautiful gardens, the outside looked austere and foreboding, but once inside, with its high vaulted ceilings, Moorish columns, and decorations, it became airy and truly inviting.

It was Friday, according to Francisco, the day the royals hear the pleas from the people—a marvelous custom they had introduced, which cast off the typical out-of-touch behaviors of the previous monarchs.

We passed through an open patio within the palace, stopping at a guard post. After Francisco related our purpose to the guards, emphasizing that he and Carlos were cousins of the Queen, who would undoubtedly want to see them, we were ushered into the packed reception hall. There the Queen and King sat on their high thrones surrounded by ministers and courtiers, hearing the various pleas.*

After standing for about an hour, we were ushered to the front. Isabella immediately recognized Carlos, enthusiastically greeting him, upon which he bowed and kissed her ring. It took a few seconds, but then she recognized Francisco, whom she had not seen in some time. Then they introduced me, and I, too bowed and kissed her ring.

Both royals wore intricate regal robes and crowns. Petite in stature, with a fair complexion, a long regal nose, rosy heart-shaped lips, and auburnish-strawberry-blond hair she possessed the classic beauty of the time. Her piercing eyes, brow and countenance projected the power of someone who had made crucial decisions that affected the lives of millions of subjects over the years and had accomplished so much. Besides nodding in recognition of them, Ferdinand did not seem very interested in her cousins and instead continued to speak to two of his ministers.

Weak in the knees, it was difficult to believe I was meeting such famous personalities who had taken back Spain and would soon become two of the most consequential monarchs in world history—wow! Feeling a little faint, I tried to stay focused and breathed deeply.

When asked why they had come to see her, using my full name, Francisco explained our purpose, "Your majesties, Don Rand, Daniel, Emmett, Roberts has come all the way from the British Isles to acquire the rights to certain manuscripts of historical significance from Salamanca University. He intends to print multiple copies of the documents. These will appear in renowned universities throughout the world, enlighten scholars, and spread the fame of Espóana as a leader of classical scholarship."

Noticing that neither monarch seemed too interested in what he was saying and feeling that my long journey might end in failure, Francisco changed gears, "This renowned scholar from London is also an excellent swordsman who terrorized bandits and has disclosed a vision to us of a venture you are about to embark on."

Perking up, Isabella said, "Is he a profit then Don Francisco?"

"Yes, your majesty, I believe he is. In the British Isles, he was set upon by banditos who stole all he had and left him for dead, where a beautiful noble maiden rescued him. Since then, during our travels from those northern shores, he has disclosed to me events in the future that no man could know, such as that your daughters will be the queens of prominent nations.

"Well, Señor Rand, tell us what you see for us."

I felt blindsided, for I did not think Francisco would do this to me, especially bringing up something I wished I had never said when I was drunk. Plus, I had ethical concerns regarding disclosing what I knew of the future because, ala all those Sci-Fi novels, I did not want to alter the course of history. Although I was in shock, I had to go forward.

Somewhat choked up, I proceeded, "Your gracious majesty, I had a vision of three ships sailing west from the Canary Islands to find a new trade route."

Isabella, in a commanding voice, said, "Speak up so we can hear you."

I realized anyone in court might know of the venture, so I had to be more specific. I took a few deep breaths and continued, "On the sterns, I saw the names of three ships—the Ninña, the Pinto, or it might have been the Pinta, and the Santa Maria. The image was blurry, so I could not quite tell. After a long journey sailing into the unknown, it seems they will discover large islands, but these will not be where they think they are. Instead, they will discover lands never seen by European eyes. These lands will surpass anyone's imagination in terms of their wealth. There, these explorers will also discover new peoples who inhabit fantastic cities larger than the biggest metropolises in Europe and new foods that will revolutionize the European diet. As a result of their discovery and the other Spanish explorers who follow, España will become the wealthiest and most influential nation in the world."

The story captured Ferdinand's attention, too. Isabella looked non-committal as her court, and I anxiously awaited her reaction. Then she smiled and said, "This is very interesting and encouraging. If your vision comes true, our new nation will be pleased."

"Thank you for disclosing your vision, what's this about manu-scripts?" she asked.

"Your majesties, the Salamanca library, which, as you know, is the oldest in all Europe, has preserved some of the most important documents of civilization from some of the most revered thinkers of all time—important documents regarding philosophy, mathematics, science, and literature, many of which originally came from the magnificent library here in Córdoba. I want to take these with me to the British Isles to print hundreds of copies in both English and Latin to preserve these so the whole world can benefit from the knowledge they contain. I promise to return them to the library, along with printed copies, and pay handsome royalties from the books we distribute. In addition, the first page will bear the name of Salamanca University and España for the rest of the world and particularly prominent universities to admire for your significant contributions to education and civilization."

"And why did the presidente of Salamanca not allow you to do this?"

Feeling I had no other alternative than to be honest with such a powerful, perceptive person, I continued, "He was afraid they might be unintentionally damaged en route."

"That is a valid concern, and I would not want España to suffer the loss of such important documents." She paused to consider the matter.

"This is what you may do. Under the guidance of the presidente and that funny fellow, Father Dominic, I think his name is; you may copy the text you desire and take these back to your northern islands. The rest of the stipulations you outlined in terms of payments, royalties, and copies shall, under my authority, apply."

"Gracious majesty, that is a marvelous solution, mochas gracias." Thrilled, Francisco and Carlos also thanked her. The three of us bowed to Isabella, then to Ferdinand, and proceeded to back out when she said:

"Francisco, Carlos, my dear cousins, and you, Señor Roberts, will join us for dinner tonight and be our guests in the Alcazar for as long as you like." She turned to one of the ministers and said, "Draw up a letter to Salamanca's presidente commanding him to release these documents to Señor Roberts, including the terms he mentioned."*

We practically flew back to the hotel, where we had to toast our success with a special brandy in the delightfully cool bara of the hotel, then packed our bags and drove our carriage back to the palace.

Isabella had her cousins sit next to her so she could hear the latest news of the family and the region she so dearly loved but had not been back to while fighting the war, something she planned to rectify soon once their business in Granada had been completed.

A man I had not met came, sat next to me, and introduced himself in a strange non-Castilian authoritarian accent, "Buenos noches señor, I very much appreciate your support of the discovery of the new route to the East Indies. I think the Queen is ready to support it, but has not yet reached a final decision. I was on my way to France recently to gain their support when Ferdinand called me back."

Struggling to interpret what he said, I was a bit confused until he introduced himself. "I am Capitan Cristóvão Colombo."

I was in a state of shock. Could I actually be talking to Columbus in the same year he would discover America, perhaps the most monumental discovery in human history? I could not let this opportunity pass me by, and I wanted to engage him and understand his motivation, "How long have you been planning this venture?"

"I first spoke to the king and queen seven years ago in 1485. Since then, I have also attempted to interest the King of Portugal in my quest. My brother also spoke to King Henry the VIIth of your England. The King of Portugal was very interested, but four years ago, they discovered a route around the Cape of Horn to the Orient, so they no longer consider my proposal. As you can see, it has been a long time, and I am so anxious to go and prove myself on my búsqueda."

"As I understand your plan, since the world is round, by traveling west, you will find a more direct route to the Indies."

"Yes, that is correct mi amigo. The Portuguese explorers discovered a route around Africa to India and the East. It has already become a rich trade route for them, bringing back goods and silks and precious spices from Cathay and the East. Indeed, much better than my countryman Marco Polo's overland route along the Silk Road, which took two years to complete for just one way. Under the Mongolians, this was a peaceful route. Still, since the Ottoman Turks' conquest of Constantinople, under their empire, it had become very dangerous, so the trade with the East has vastly declined, and the prices for the silks and spices have rapidly escalated."

"The Portuguese, who are marvelous navigators and sailors, made it around the Cape of Good Hope of Africa and back in sixteen months. This was a significant improvement over Marco's four-plus years. They may be able to sail to India and back in less than two years and avoid the dangers of the Silk Road, but they still have to face the treacherous maelstrom off the Cape of Good Hope—aptly named because you are at God's mercy when you enter this gauntlet."

"Following the trade winds, I will sail south to the Canary Islands, then west to the Orient. After loading my ships with gold, silks, spices and other treasures, I will follow the northern trade winds, discovered by the Portuguese, back to Spain. My calculations show that such a trip from the islands will take about two weeks, saving months of time. I could be there and back six times before the Portuguese have completed one round trip. And, with such high prices, all who support the venture will become wealthy."

From my research on my iPhone, I knew that Columbus's calculations were wrong and that it would take five weeks, which, considering the six weeks it took me to reach Salamanca from London, was not that long.

"You must have much sailing experience señor, to attempt such an epic voyage?"

"Si, I started sailing at ten in Genoa and have been sailing for over thirty years now. I understand you are from London. I have even sailed up to your Bristol."

"I came from London, but I started my journey in Ireland."

"I have sailed to Galway in Ireland, too, and as far south as Guinea with the Portuguese."

"If you are successful, what will this mean to you?"

"I am requesting the King and Queen to provide me with 10% of the revenues from the trip, which I think is very fair considering all the risks I take. I also expect to become the admiral of the Seas and for them to install me as a noble. I will become the governor of all the lands I discover, which I will pass on to my children. The Queen and I also want to bring the message of Christ to the pagans and convert them, so this is also a vital part of my mission. She plans to make them equal citizens of España, which I am not so sure of."

By then, we were on our second course, and after having a couple glasses of wine, we were both more relaxed. I asked Columbus, "Why do you think she will authorize this venture? I imagine she and Ferdinand think that it is very expensive, hazardous, and the odds of success are very long."

"There are perhaps a couple of reasons, Señor Rand. First, another nation, such as France might sponsor my quest, in which case they would have the rich lands I will discover. Once they tire of the long route and the treacherous cape, Portugal may also come back to sponsor my búsqueda."

"The deal their majesties struck with Portugal gave all the lands west of Africa other than the Canary Islands to Portugal, so if Espanola does not back me, they will have no additional territories, and I am sure there are many lands north and west of Africa. While the battles against the Moors consumed all their majesties' resources, I do not think they would have supported my mission. Now, as you can see, everyone is in a celebratory mood and wants to conquer the world. Once I find the gold, spices, and other treasures, they will be the richest monarchs in all the world. Of course, I will be very rich too."

"Why do you think these lands you will discover will be so abundant?"

"I believe there are many islands east of Japan that have yet to be discovered, Islands with the spices that are so valuable and precious minerals too. When I conquer these islands, we will possess these treasures. Plus, having a short route to Cathay and India will vastly improve our trade with these areas so that we can dominate these rich markets."

"Señor Roberts, what else did your vision show to you about my voyage, and how did you know the names of my ships?"

I had to be careful here, for I did not want to disclose too much. My 'vision' was not completely fabricated, for I viewed it on my iPhone on Wikipedia—still, I guess, a type of vision on the screen. I replied, "After I was beaten by the banditos and found unconscious, I have been able to see events in the future that others cannot. This is how I saw the names of your ships; for me, it is similar to looking into a cloudy mirror." But I do not see myself, but rather a blurry image of what will be.

"And your vision showed you that my trip will be successful?"

"Yes, but like any such mission, it will be fraught with difficulties and dangers. It will take longer than you expect. You will, however, be successful, and you will prove that the world is round. I believe your discovery will rank up there with Marco Polo's as one of the most important discoveries in 500 years. Perhaps even more so."

Anticlimactically, I added, "Be sure to take limes on your voyage. It is a natural remedy to help prevent scurvy—just in case your trip takes longer than expected."

"Thank you, Señor. I have faced so much scrutiny and doubt. It is refreshing to have someone support my quest. Good luck on your quest, too. Preserving such wondrous documents is a marvelous pursuit for mankind."

Francisco, who sat beside me on the other side, spent most of his time conversing with the Queen. Turning towards me, the Queen addressed me, "Señor Roberts, I see you have been discussing Columbo's venture with him. Do you still think he will succeed—that it is not just some fantasy?"

"Oh yes, your majesty, even more so. He is a man of great persistence and fortitude." Columbus smiled at her and at me.

"What are these new foods you speak of from your vision?"

By now, I was getting into my role as a visionary or a profit, something the superstitious society of the late 15th century fervently believed in. However, I still wanted to be careful of what I said.

"Well, Your Majesty, I saw a red fruit the size of an orange that will add much flavor to the typical Córdoban and Moorish dishes such as Ajo Blanco, making them that much more delicious. It will become a staple of Spanish and Italian cuisine used in your sauces too (tomatoes)."

"Another large yellow grain will grow on stalks and be used to make bread, porridge or just eaten as is (corn). I also saw a brown tuber found in the ground that, similar to rice, will become a staple: delicious baked, mashed or cut up into slices and fried (potatoes)."

"You also said that there will be many natives there. Did you see how many?"

"Your majesty, although I could not all, there may be as many as in all of Europe.

"What are your plans for the natives, your majesty?"

"First of all, they will be free men, for I will not allow slavery. As are those peoples in Holland and Sicily, they will become citizens of España with all the rights, privileges, and rule of law that implies. But most importantly, I want to bring the word of Christ to them and help them be good Christians, to save their souls, so they too may obtain ever-lasting life and dwell in the Kingdom of God in heaven."

"You said that my daughters will become Queens of Nations. What nations did you see?"

"Your majesty, In the blurry vision, I could not tell which nations or which daughters, but they will surely rule major nations such as England, France, Austria, Portugal or Espanola."*

I was anxious to return to Salamanca to start the process of dupli-cating the famous manuscripts. Francisco and Carlos, on the other hand, naturally wanted to stay at the Alcazar, catch up on the monu-mental developments there, and enjoy the halcyon atmosphere per-meating Córdoba following the Reconquista. Since they had made my mission possible, I certainly could not object. So, we stayed in Córdoba, dining and mixing with the nobles for another week. One of the disturbing things I heard from the courtiers was the possibility of an Inquisition that would attempt to either convert Jews and Muslims to Christianity or expel them. It was difficult to believe that after the Moor's progressive policies, people who had been in Andalusia for centuries would be persecuted or forced to leave.

Francisco said, "I hope they do not go forward with this atrocious plan. What has made España so rich is the diversity of its people. The Moors encouraged this diversity, granting us all freedom of religion. The Moorish and the Judean people have many valuable skills that we need—look at the richness and culture of Córdoba and its food; it's incredible food. I know the queen is against it, but I suspect Ferdinand is pushing the plan. Many of my friends are Moors; many are Jews. Indeed, many of those who work in my vineyards or help with my business are, not to mention the skilled artisans in town I rely on. Even though he has a Spanish name, Diego, my foreman is a Moor—he is my right-hand man, and I do not know what I would do without him. He is an important part of my business and a dear member of our family, who, as you have seen, dines with us every night. When I am away selling our magnificent sherry, he manages the estate and keeps things humming."

"I understand that this is a result of the protracted war, but it is a ter-rible mistake. Since the Queen talks about making the Indians citizens, it makes no sense to disenfranchise the Moors and Jews. I will speak to her about this and convince her not to persecute my friends."

During the day, I had the opportunity to tour the famous Great Mosque of Córdoba. Out of all the places of worship, with the exception of St. Peter's Cathedral in Rome, this was the most magnificent I had ever seen. In the main hall, which must be the size of three football fields, a feat of architecture I did not think existed now, row after row of high, red marble columns flowed up into ornately decorated arches that supported a colossal roof. This was as big or bigger than the enclosed stadiums of the 21st century. Because one arch would not support the roof, they constructed two arches between each of the 850 columns. The lower arch was in the shape of a horseshoe that, together with a higher arch, would support that much more weight and consequently the extreme height.

The fragrant wood panels were fastened with golden nails, and I enjoyed viewing the plethora of geometric designs set in a variety of rich, evocative materials such as ivory, onyx, jasper, gold, silver, granite, brass and copper. Exhibiting superior craftsmanship, this was more beautiful than any structure I had seen before. In the center of the massive area was a large cathedral with a high-domed ceiling flanked by a spacious garden.

Evidently, over the three centuries that Granada served as Andalusia's capital, rulers expanded the Great Mosque. After the Catalonians captured it, they, too enhanced it. By now, it had grown to its immense proportions for over 500 years. But it was not just its size but the attention to detail and its overall symmetrical, thematic sense of beauty that overwhelmed me.*

To counter our sumptuous meals with the King and Queen, for exercise throughout the week, Carlos, Francisco, and I practiced our dueling in a rather large marbled hall that resembled a gym, the sounds of clashing swords and screeching boots echoing off the walls. Carlos proved himself to be a master swordsman, too, which I guess is expected of all Alvarez men. Now that I had finally reached an intermediate status, Francisco endeavored to teach me more advanced moves. I told him how, back in Ireland, Reginald had disarmed me with a flick of his wrist and, in an instant, had the tip of his sword at my neck. With Carlos as his opponent, Francisco not only demonstrated the maneuver but how to counter the move and gain an advantage. They also taught me the principles of chivalry and not using swords to exploit the disadvantaged.

After several days of courtier living and large meals, I needed more exercise than just dueling. Carlos and Francisco met with some landowners to discuss windmills and viticulture. They asked me if I wanted to join them. I declined. I missed my runners high, so I put on my light hiking boots and hiked away from the river. I wished I had Chester with me so I could ride further out, but it did not take long before I was in the country, where I ran for a couple of miles through the newly green fields.

Along the way, a farmer who had been bent down tending to a furrow popped up and asked if someone was chasing me. Searching for an answer, I replied, "No, Señor, gracias for your concern, but I am trying to work out a kink in my knee," although his face showed that my excuse made no sense, he just went back to work—why would anybody run for no reason?

Walking back allowed me to think about what I had accomplished and those I had recently met—Isabella, Ferdinand, Columbus, and the court's intellectuals. Until then, I had been immersed in my goal and had become surprisingly used to this time and to Spain, but as I reentered town from the farm fields that were still familiar in the 21st century, I was astonished. I felt as if I was walking through a recreation of a medieval town, like a Society for Creative Anachronism gathering, where people dressed up in regal period costumes—except that few of these folks were nobles, but rather peasants. The streets I walked were similar to those preserved in some of the old towns of Europe, such as those in Germany, but many of these future antiquities were newly built.*

I returned to the room by midday and had just laid down for a siesta when a page appeared and said that Queen Isabella will see me, leading the way to her in the courtyard. Highlighted by the difference in our height, I was initially embarrassed to be alone with someone so famous, but she soon made me feel at ease as we walked through the fragrant garden. The queen asked me to discuss the books I had discovered, and I summarized the significant works the good father had preserved, something she seemed extremely interested in, asking numerous probing questions.

Wondering if it was proper to ask a question of a monarch, I reluctantly ventured, "Your majesty, I understand that you support Salamanca University. Why do you do so?"

Seeming to enjoy the uncourtly interplay from an unacquainted foreigner, as we turned a corner, she responded, "We are a brand-new nation, and we will need educated men to help administer our large country. You mentioned some books by Romans, such as Seneca. I have read several books about the great Roman Empire that extended into our lands. It was not just about the might of their army; it was also about how they ruled, how they administered that huge Empire, how they built roads and bridges such as ours in Córdoba, their coliseums, their marketplaces, aqueducts, and how many of those they conquered were assimilated as Roman citizens."

"It was also about how they administered these vastly different lands. The cities they conquered saw that their lives were much better because of the Romans and how they could acquire goods and sell their goods throughout the empire. To do these things for España will require engineers, scribes, bookkeepers, ministers, lawyers, officers, tradesmen, teachers, and even printers such as yourself to disseminate the proclamations and laws—all of which requires education."

"As Francisco may have told you, the Alvarez's support one of Salamanca's colleges and the admission of poor students. During my brother's administration, we had two branches of government, one controlled by the nobles, who did little other than sponge off Castile, and the other one administered by the people who did the work of Castile. I want more of these people to play a role in our government. To do that effectively requires education."

"My brother ruled in a selfish, imprudent way. He went into debt and had no vision of the future. I want our family and our nation to prosper for decades and centuries into the future."

Then the queen asked, "So, Señor Rand, evidently you are a seer. What else do you foresee for our new kingdom? Will we succeed in keeping our kingdom together?" I realized that this was the reason she had summoned me here. While submerged in the court, I heard that the royals and many nobles consulted with fortune tellers and soothsayers regularly. Compared to the modern world, there was so much that now occupied the unknown realm. It would be easy for me to criticize this. Still, many of their superstitions, such as cities of gold or silver, horrendous sea monsters such as whales, giant squids and killer whales, miraculous drugs, flying or venturing to the moon would come true.

I responded, "Yes, your majesty, España will remain whole. It will become one of the most prominent, powerful and wealthiest nations in all of Europe, perhaps even the richest. At some time in the future, one of its rulers will become the highest-ranking of Europe's kings, ordained by the pope (The Holy Roman Emperor). Perhaps it will be one of your descendants."

"And you foresee that Columbo's mission will succeed?"

"Yes, your majesty, beyond anyone's wildest dreams. It is a discovery like Marco Polo's of Cathay or the Portuguese exploration along the African coast and India, but even grander. But as any such discovery, it will be fraught with obstacles and difficulties." I did not want to disclose too much and risk causing some kind of time warp if such a thing existed, but I found her difficult to resist—she was compelling. As we strolled through the beautiful, fragrant, blooming spring garden, I was under her spell, something that no doubt many of the men she ruled had succumbed to. In this male-dominated, macho world, few women would possess the power and respect she commanded.

"And will he find much gold in the Indies?"

"I do not see how much gold Columbus will find, but surely Spanish explorers will find much gold, perhaps more than all the gold is in Europe."

We walked through the gardens, and I thought that this petite woman was the most remarkable woman I had ever met.

"And can you tell me which nations my daughters will be queens of?"

"No, Your Majesty, all I see is that they are wearing regal robes that some powerful nation must have provided."

We sat at a small gilded table in the garden, where a carafe of the best wine appeared, and continued our enjoyable discussion. At one point, she asked if I was married. When I said I had been too busy to seek a wife, she said she could find a lovely, highly suitable, attractive woman in her court for me.

"Thank you, Your Majesty, that is most generous, and I am sure any young lady you suggest would be magnificent, but I should return to the British Isles with the treasured books."

*

That night at dinner, she pointed out three exceedingly pretty women, Sophia, Selena and Angelina, saying that any one of these noble young ladies would be a suitable match for me, implying that I should choose one and marry her soon.

"But, Your Majesty, I am not a noble myself and would not make a suitable match for them."

"I could easily make you a noble, plus you would have a handsome endowment from their fathers, and we will install you with a large estate from one of those we have conquered."

"Your majesty, I am overwhelmed by your generosity, but my heart belongs to another, Marie, in Ireland, or she may be in England by now. She is originally from a well-known family in Normandy, and I hope to marry her if she will have me."

"Bless you."

TWELVE

Eurika!

Armed with the letter from Queen Isabella, we left Cordoba and returned to Francisco's hacienda. After resting for two days, I said goodbye to Carlos, Francisco, Sophia, and their marvelous family. Giving me a bear hug, Francisco said that after the harvest, crush, and bottling, he expected to travel to England in late fall or early winter to sell his prized sherry, for which he had found a growing market.

With the water Carlos's windmills provided, judging by how much the vines were already greening and budding, especially since they would have irrigation during the parched dry season, Francisco thought it would be a record growing season. I gave him Colleen's location in London and said I would either be there or, more probably, back in Bunkillarny by then.

"That is so close I might just go there to sell my abundant sherry."

"I greatly look forward to seeing you, mi amigo!"

I set off for Salamanca with Chester and Marie powering my surrey. With my pistols handy and my sword anchored to my waist, still on the lookout for brigands, my trip back was uneventful. Perhaps the Queen had indeed cut down on crime.

Once back in Salamanca, I walked up to the impertinent secretary. Upon seeing me, she, evidently remembering how I accosted the president, flushed red with anger. Sweetly, I said, "Senorita, is el presidente in?"

"Not to you, señor. Leave immediately. If you try to wait until he appears again, I will have you removed."

Smiling broadly, "But Senorita Juanita, I am sure he would not want to offend Queen Isabella, who I spoke with in Cordoba just last week. Tell him I want to see him immediately or risk her anger!"

Unsure of what to do, she begrudgingly and apprehensively ventured into the President's office. A minute later, two professorial-looking men left his room. With a scowl, she reluctantly ushered me into his office.

The previously gregarious president looked angry, saying, "Señor, as I told you before, under no circumstances can we let our precious documents depart the university."

"I agree with you, monsignor. I think you will want to read this, though." I presented him the Queen's order along with a bottle of Francisco's finest sherry, which he slammed down on his desk, indicating his disinterest. I brought out the sherry because, as Francisco explained, it is a way to lubricate business relationships. He noticed that I tended to get down to business immediately, which is how we worked in America, something that did not go over well here.

By the time he read her signature, his displeased countenance had morphed into the familiar, pleasant presidential smile. "Of course, Señor Roberts, we will do everything possible to facilitate your mission." Then he walked to the door, "Juanita, fetch us my sherry glasses and then bring Father Dominic here. She looked reluctant to follow his orders until, in a booming voice, he added, "Immediately, Juanita, vámonos!" Still scowling, she set off to her tasks.

We sat in an open area overlooking the dazzling, fast-flowing river, swelled by Spring rains, where he asked me a series of questions regarding the queen and king's health and victories. In his eyes, my status had greatly improved. When Father Dominic came in, somewhat confused by my presence, I shook his hand in both of mine and warmly greeted him.

Over the fine sherry, which they immensely enjoyed, I explained, "Dominic, thanks to Queen Isabella's cousins Francisco and Carlos Alverez, I was able to gain an audience with her noble majesty. After I explained the importance of the documents you have meticulously preserved, she recommended a wise solution to disseminate these to the world and thereby spread the wisdom they contain. She has granted me permission to translate these, copy them, and take the copies back to the British Isles to print.

"Oh, that is a marvelous solution, Señor Rand."

"According to the agreement, I will pay for the rights to these glorious documents minus the cost of translating and copying. Then I will provide you with ten of the first books we produce and give you 10% of the profits from the books we sell. Plus, the book's first page shall have the imprimatur and coat of arms of the university and that of Espanola. The books themselves will never leave the university or your library."

Both the monsignor and Father Dominic smiled broadly, Dominic responding, "Excellent, I felt horrible that I could not accommodate you, something I have regretted since you and Francisco left."

"By the way, Father, Isabella remembered you."

The President looked confused and evidently did not know of this chapter in Dominic's life. Splitting his gaze between us, smiling proudly, Dominic said, "After I completed my holy orders, I was assigned to her parish in Segovia and tutored her in Latin. She was a remarkable student, brilliant and inquisitive. Someone I thought would be an extraordinary Queen. That is where I met the Alverezes, Francisco's cousins, who fought for her from those first battles with the Portuguese."

Knowing I had the queen's support, the plan we hatched included the president recruiting the best university students and professors to translate and copy the texts. They would receive credit and a stipend. We would split the payment. Of course, it would be an honor for them to work on the "Queen's" project, which might help them later acquire a position and prestige in her expanding government.

The precious documents would be stored in the hidden vault until copied, then secretly transported to a secure room in the library where the transcribers would work. After they started, the process seemed to move slowly because they were conscientiously scribing beautifully handwritten letters. I stressed to them that the emphasis should be on accurately capturing the text rather than creating impressive-looking documents that would not be utilized other than to print from. They doubled their speed.

Translations to Latin would be provided for the Arabic and Jewish texts. Father Dominic, who spoke all four languages well, would personally edit each of the documents, and either he or a trusted guard would always be in the room to ensure none of the priceless tomes were pilfered.

I selected fifty scrolls, parchments, vellum and paper manuscripts such as El Cid to copy, including works by Seneca, Maimonides, and the early Spanish, Moorish, Roman, Greek and Jewish authors. There was even an ancient, pre-Ptolemy papyrus Egyptian scroll that one of the professors thought he could translate from the hieroglyphs. I would have liked to have purchased rights to more, but after all my expenses, that was all I could afford. I would be left with just enough money for the trip to Bilbao, where I would sell Marie and the surrey to fund my voyage back to the British Isles.

It took about five weeks for the monumental works to be translated and copied (something that would have taken one person a day on a high-speed copier). During that time, I checked on their progress daily, reading the Latin and Spanish versions, amazed at the wisdom they contained, proud that they would enlighten curious minds throughout the world over the following centuries. Glad that Dominic performed the primary edits, even though I was not much of an editor, occasionally, I even found errors that I noted on the transcribed page. Borrowing from my previous life as a systems developer in Silicon Valley, it felt similar to our last Herculean push to birth an app, when we all crowded into a conference room testing and debugging our work.

In the evenings, I frequently dined with Dominic when we discussed the essence of what had just been translated or dined with José, who now fared well at the university. He was delighted with the story of his brother, cousin Francisco, and my successful meeting with Queen Isabella. Being an Alverez, we also practiced our dueling, he saying that I had immensely improved. He had not found anyone at the university to challenge him until I appeared. Seeing his dueling skills, I wondered why he had not assisted us with the banditos, something I wanted to ask him about but did not want to embarrass the handsome young man.

After one of our sessions, in which he readily defeated me, he volunteered, "I wish I had my prized sword to fight off those banditos, but it wouldn't have been shipped in a trunk with my other possessions until a week later when I had a room in the dorm. This is something that has bothered me ever since, and I am sorry. I know I should have done something like grab the sword of the fallen bandito or maybe grab a club from the woods. I just froze. I am so ashamed of myself. I have shamed my family and am not living up to the ideals of the Alverezes." With tears starting to form in his reddening, downcast eyes, he added, "I am so sorry, Señor Rand!"

Laying my sword down and placing my hand on his shoulder, I said, "José, there is nothing you could have done. You were sleeping and didn't awaken until the pistol discharged. Anyway, we were able to defeat them, and at the end, you rushed the one bandito, threatening him with that rock, which caused him to scurry away. We all have situations when we do not respond the way we would like to and judge ourselves too severely. Please don't feel bad. You will have many opportunities to show your courage in the future, and I have no doubt you will perform well, mi amigo."

I rode Chester regularly into the warm, fragrant, welcoming countryside now filled with newly green trees, crops, yellow, red, purple, and blue flowers, which elicited their wondrous fragrances. José sometimes rode Marie with me. I was able to help him with his mathematics studies, something he struggled with.

We stopped at a scenic overlook with a beautiful view of the verdant valley and blue-green river below, tied up the horses, and sat with our legs overhanging the cliff on a sturdy granite rock. There, I said, "While I was in Córdoba with your brother and Francisco, I met a man named Cristopher Colombo, who I think the queen will support. He wants to find a new route to the Orient by sailing to the west rather than around Africa, which he thinks will take a fraction of the time. There, he thinks he will find unimaginable riches, gold, and rare spices."

"Oh, Señor Rand, that sounds so amazing. That's why I want to sail to such exotic lands and make my fortune. Do you think he will succeed?"

"I believe that Columbo and other Spanish explorers will succeed because of your steel and guns. I believe they will travel farther and discover more than any other nation in the world ever has, establishing many of the largest and richest cities in the world. It won't be easy, for these conquistadors will face unimaginable challenges to their survival, and many will perish. There are immense fortunes to be made there. However, true riches are not just measured in gold and silver but in how you develop your character and treat your fellow man in the face of adversity. It won't only be about the conquistadors, but also about how you govern the conquered lands, how you administer them, how you treat the natives, which is why the students here in Salamanca are so important."

He was already taking subjects related to navigation and shipbuilding—why he needed the math. No doubt, he would play an essential role in the discovery of the Americas.

Thinking of José as a beloved nephew and wanting to pass on some lessons to him, which he seemed to readily absorb, I continued, "As with any adventure, things are not always what they initially seem—opportunities evolve. The wise man works hard, works smart, and readily adjusts to unforeseen circumstances, keeping a vision of what the future may bring, willing to adjust that vision according to the realities presented. Queen Isabella means not to enslave the natives of this new world but rather treat them as citizens of España, convert them to Christ, and to save their souls."

From my reading, I knew the Spanish explorers would interact with perhaps one hundred Native American tribes over a vast expanse of North and South America, covering a much broader area than the French and English combined, from Florida to the Carolinas to the Mississippi and everything West of that long river. In many cases, they would treat the Indians well, trade with them, convert them, educate them and help them.

In other cases, they would exploit them, enslave them, kill them, and treat them terribly. Unlike the English and, later, the Americans, they would not continuously force them from their traditional lands but eventually merge with them. They would occupy such a large tract that it would be too difficult to govern effectively, whereas after the American Revolution, which Spain would support, the Americans, whose numbers were more concentrated, through the concept of "Manifest Destiny" would eventually control all the area north of Mexico up to British occupied Canada. However, unlike the reservations in the U.S., in Mexico, Central America, and in South America, the Spanish and Indians would eventually integrate, with many of the native nobles playing prominent roles. After all, the level of civilization attained by native Americans in many societies, such as the Incas, Mayans and Aztecs, far exceeded that of most of those in Europe.*

To celebrate the completion of our project, on the last day, I brought a variety of tasty tapas and wine for the group of intellectuals at the library. I looked over the books but did not find El Cid, thereby addressing Dominic, "Father, I do not see the copy of El Cid."

Then, he presented me with a bound book, saying, "We have two original copies of El Cid, one of which we will keep here. This one is for you, Señor."

"But Father, this is priceless. I cannot accept it."

"My son, would you want to go back to Britain without Cantar de Mio Cid d?"

"No, mochas gracias!"

He said he had another surprise for me, "Due to its age and delicate condition, one of the scrolls you requested had never been translated."

This is one that, because of how old it looked, I thought it must have some value, so I selected it. Dominic continued, "It is in an ancient form or Aramaic, which over the years, none of the chief librarians or myself could translate, but one of our newest Arab professors, who dealt with such ancient languages, with difficulty, was finally able to accomplish the translation. He was thrilled by what he discovered, what he considered the most significant accomplishment of his life, which he worked on day and night, finishing just yesterday."

By this time, I was so excited I could no longer wait. "Please, Father, tell me what it is.

"It is an account of Christ's life."

"Wow, one of the Gospels?"

"Well, maybe, but it is not one of the known Gospels by Mathiew, Luke, Mark or John. According to our remarkable professor, Abdur Rahim, it may have predated the known gospels and have been written by one of the earliest Christians, who may have witnessed Christ himself and knew the apostles. It is not as long as the gospels but has some remarkable stories that thus far are unknown, including a couple of illuminating sermons and inciteful parables.

All I could utter was again, "Wow!"

"Because he does not identify himself, we do not know who wrote it, but he does make references to specific apostles who he seems to know personally. For instance, at one point, he wrote: 'John (the apostle) told me the story of when Jesus held the sermon on the mount.' Unlike this scroll, the gospels were copied by hand by one person to the next until the third century so that something may have been lost or added during this time. This seems to be the original, and its accounts are slightly different, but the four gospels do not completely agree with each other either."

Then, when I caught my breath, I asked, "Where did the scroll come from?"

"It is uncertain, but Abdur thinks the precious document originated in Judea. Then he believes the Greeks transported it to Alexandria because there is a note on the outside in Latin that says it was taken from Alexandria to Sicily by a Roman general who served under Claudius Caesar. Since Claudius ruled until 54 A.D., it is believed to be one of the earliest accounts of Christ's life.

The professor believes that in the tenth century, when the Vizier had Jewish, Christian and Moors scouring the world for monumental manuscripts to acquire for the Cordoban Library, they came across this scroll and purchased it.

When the mullahs persuaded Vizier Mazur that the books were evil, a conscientious librarian in Cordoba rescued the document from the conflagration and hid it. We know this because there was a parchment note inside the middle of the scroll attesting to that fact written by Mohamed Atribi, dated June 17, 1003.

Later, it ended up in our library here in Salamanca, but we are not sure how it got here. We do know it was an early acquisition, though.

"That is a fascinating provenance, but wouldn't someone along the way have noticed how important and valuable a document it was and brought it to the church in Rome?"

"Well, if you think about it, none of those who we know possessed it were Christians: not the Greeks and certainly not a Roman general in the first century when they were persecuting Christians. Our research shows that he was awarded a large estate in Sicily, where he kept his considerable spoils from various wars, including numerous works of art. The Moors who acquired it or the librarian who saved it had little interest in Christianity. Perhaps we should have realized its importance, but we could not read it. At least we saved it, and unfortunately, like many important works, it remained obscured on a shelf, unread and unappreciated."

"Now, we will have to study it closely. It will create quite a sensation here at the University. The only other person who knows about it is the Presidente, and before he releases it, he wants Abdur and me to discuss its implications with him, for he is afraid it might contain heresies that the church would not want revealed.

"Father, this is truly remarkable. May I have a copy of it?

"We have a second copy, but the President does not want to release it to you."

"Why?"

"Because of what it might contain. You might print and distribute it throughout Christendom, which the church may not allow. They are extremely concerned about heresies and heretics at this time. I have even heard rumors of some kind of inquisition, which I hope does not come to fruition."

"Oh, I am so disappointed. But if it contains the words of Christ, how could it not be enlightening to the world?"

"That is not for us to judge. I feel that we never would have discovered this amazing scroll if it was not for you. Given its fragile condition, without your impetus, even given our care and precautions, it might have decayed beyond recognition. There are still segments that will require Abdur to do tedious reconstruction. I do want to give you the translation we have thus far, though, which is perhaps 80% of it. Do not let anyone else know of this, especially el presidente."

"That's wonderful. Thank you!"

Holding the prized pages containing the words of Christ before passing it to me, he added, "There is a condition you must solemnly agree to before I can give it to you, my son."

Puzzled, I responded, "Yes!"

"You must swear that you will not show or disclose the presence of this manuscript to any other living soul without my permission."

"I solemnly swear that I will not disclose the contents or presence of this document until you grant permission."

"Once we have determined its authenticity, I will write to you saying whether you can print it. If, according to the Church, it is not authenticated, you must swear to burn it."

"I do so swear."

As he gave me the treasured document and I started to read the first page, realizing it was not in Latin as I expected, he said, "One other thing, this translation is in Arabic—the professor's interim translation. I am giving you this so that if the document happens to fall into the wrong hands, they will not know of its importance. If I give you the permission, you will have to find someone to translate it, which will not be easy in Ireland."

"Excellent. I will protect it with my life."

In case someone like Gwendolyn accidentally saw it, I actually felt better that it would not be readable. It also had to be read backward. I was so curious about what it contained, what guidance, what wisdom it might impart that I was glad I could not read, for if I could, it would be too difficult to keep such revelations to myself.

Then I presented him with samples of the books I brought from London and a keg of sherry Francisco had given me, saying, "The wine is from your hometown, and these are for your esteemed library. I have learned much from you and have greatly enjoyed your company." Later, I realized that the books I helped lay out and print would occupy shelves in Europe's oldest library. Perhaps I would visit the library in the 21st century to see if they survived.

I packed the treasured documents into the wooden trunk that previously held the samples and drove my surrey back to the hotel. Early the next morning, I said goodbye to Manuel, thanking him for the marvelous room and his gracious hospitality. He saying, "I am so glad you succeeded on your mission to Salamanca, mi amigo. Is it not a glorious success?"

"Yes, it truly is. I have learned so much here." I had come a long way from my computer background, becoming something I could never have imagined—an enthusiastic bibliophile.

José helped me heft the precious cargo onto the surrey, which I carefully covered with sheepskins and tied down. He gave me a letter to give to his parents. We embraced, and I headed out somewhat verklempt.*

Wanting to purchase all the rare documents I could, I had little money left and could ill afford to stay or eat at the inns. Then, I thought that the gospel alone should have cost all I had. If it proved to be legitimate, every church, every clergyman, and most of Europe's reading citizens would want a copy. I had not been highly religious, but to read new words from

Christ would be amazing. Dominic had been very generous to let me have this.

I loaded up on bread, cheese, and sausages to eat along the way and camped out. Since it was warmer now, I enjoyed being outdoors more than being in a too-small bed in a cramped inn room, possibly in the same bed with strange, smelly, snoring men. I bought a feather quilt in Salamanca that would serve as my blanket on the cooler nights.

Along the way, I could have stayed in the village that welcomed us as heroes but worried about Jacquilina and her father. I worried about the mayor's reaction to my presence and possibly being pressured to marry her. Still, the road went through the village, so I pulled my wide-brimmed hat down, pulled my coat's collar up, and skulked through the village, trying not to attract attention, not looking at anyone who happened to glance my way. I camped on the other side of town, keeping one eye open for those banditos who accosted us the last time we were there, keeping my pistols and sword by my side.

The next day, a man rode by and stopped, dressed in the clothes befitting an artisan, and declared, "Are you not Señor Roberts who vanquished the banditos that plagued our village?"

"Yes, I am."

"Did you stay in our village?"

"No"

"Oh, señor, but we would have welcomed you with open arms as our hero and provided for all your needs. Our town has done so well since then, thanks to you and your valiant amigos. The fear is gone. We will tell the story of your heroic victory over those dastardly villains to our children's children."

"How is the mayor and Jacquilina?"

"We just had a grand wedding for her and Edwardo Sanchez. You should have been there."

"That's wonderful. Please wish them my best. Buenos Dias señor."

"Buenos Dias, Vaya Con Dios señor!"

Two days later, I spent the night at Diego Alverez's magnificent hacienda on the hill overlooking acres of fields, the vineyards, the river, and the twirling, humming, creaking, pumping windmills. They were nearly as excited to see me as Francisco had been. I gave them a long letter from their son José and, over dinner, recounted the story of their son Carlos,

Francisco, and I at the court of their cousin Isabella. Then, I recounted the stories I had heard of the conquest of Granada and of Columbus's planned journey. They were spellbound.

They were also thrilled to hear that I succeeded in my mission and had acquired copies of the precious manuscripts, praising Isabella for her support and wisdom. I showed them some of the documents explaining the importance and history behind each, for it was not just about what they contained but whence they came.

Diego and I spent a pleasant night on his patio, overlooking the panoramic view under a moonlit sky, sipping brandy, talking about the vineyards, fields, windmills, politics, literature and Salamanca U. It felt as if I was talking to an old friend.*

Feeling the urge to return to the British Isles as soon as possible, wishing I could have stayed longer, I reluctantly left early the next morning. Diego's wife, Salina, loaded me up with fruit, cheese, dried meats, cakes, bottles of their finest wine, and a casserole. Chester and Marie appreciated the feast of oats they had been afforded. Prior to my visit, the long road had caused them to be sluggish. Now, they had some pep to their step.

Warmed by their hospitality, driving that day and the next felt effortless. That night, I built a fire and reheated the delicious chicken casserole over an open hickory flame. It was one of those perfect, warm nights with barely a breeze, the peepers and crickets serenading, and a frog croaking. I felt good about the progress I had made; most of my journey to Bilbao behind me now. Not having seen a bandito in my last four trips, I settled in for a restful sleep under the brilliant stars that filled the sky with their innumerable pinpoints of light, able to see four large planets shining down upon me—brilliant Venus. red Mars. Jupiter and Saturn with perhaps a hint of its rings.

Out of a deep, restful sleep, I was woken by a hand at my throat, and my own matchlock pistol pointed at my nose. The filthy, nasty, dark, black-bearded face with missing teeth, half-lit by the pistol's wick, asked my name. In shock, I could not remember, and then I recognized the face as belonging to one of the bandits we had overcome—the one I had shot.

"So señor where are your amigos? I see you traveling alone. Don't you know desperados are plying this road? You should have been more careful than to ride alone, har, har, har. Thanks to you, we had to relocate down along this part of the road where the pickings are not so good." Then he slugged me with the butt of the matchlock, after which I spit out blood.

He kicked me in the side, then rolling back his sleeve, he showed me his wound, saying, "That is for what you did to my shoulder, señor. It hurts when it rains" Damn you!

"I see you are a bandito too, stealing my horse Gorges there. At least you have taken good care of him. Oh, and you have brought me another fine horse to make up for your crime."

He had the other two dragged me out of my warm blanket and held me while he pummeled me repeatedly in the stomach and kicked me in the groin. It was so, so, so painful. Before, there were five, and I guess that two had left his gang, or maybe they had been shot or arrested.

I fell to the ground, and as I rolled up into a ball with my hands over my head, the three began relentlessly kicking me. I looked for an advantage and tried to fight back but could not. If I were one of those action heroes, I would have jumped up and easily defeated them, but I was no Superman, and this was excruciatingly painful. Despite my fear and pain, events passing in slow motion, I was still aware of them and my surroundings but could see no possible escape.

As I lay, waves of pain washing over my entire body, their leader said with a smirky smile, "Please excuse my manners. My name is Rodriguez, Señor. What is your name? Now, don't be shy."

"Rand"

Pleased to meet you, Señor Rand. I see you have brought me a treasure chest, mochas gracias." While he pointed the matchlock at my head, his henchmen dragged the trunk out of the surrey. Please give me the key, Señor Rand. See, haven't I asked you nicely? If you do not, you will force me to chop this magnificent chest into pieces, and that would be such a waste of a good chest, no?"

I could not take any more beatings, so I reached into my pocket and, after surreptitiously turning on my iPhone, gave him the key.

They opened up the chest, and he said, "What is this just a bunch of f______ papers. I was expecting a little gold or at least some coins you b______." He grabbed a handful of the precious documents and was about to throw them into the fire—the texts I had worked so hard to acquire that held precious the wisdom of the ages.

I said, "Señor, those are much more valuable than mere coins. Some would pay mochas reales for them; burning them would be like throwing away thousands of reales." Searching for possible leverage, I continued, "I have acquired these valuable documents because of an order from Queen Isabella. You wouldn't want to offend your Queen by stealing them, would you?"

We have no love for Isabella. It is because of her and her policia that our livelihood has become so difficult. But we thank you for telling us the value of these old papers, which we will find a good home for, and mochas gracias for my horses and the surrey too, hombre."

"Now I think we are done with you." He came close and was about to pull the trigger when the jingle of my iPhone rang out.

"What is that? Bring it out...slowly, señor, slowly!"

After I brought it out, I told them, "This is a magic glass I acquired from a powerful wizard in Cordoba that possesses many magical powers, more valuable than even the papers, more valuable than gold. With this glass, I can see into the future." I quickly tapped the music icon, and it began playing Fire by Katy Perry.

"Listen, it is also a music box that can play many songs. There is a tiny orchestra in there that can play songs never heard before."

"That is not possible," Rodriquez replied.

Then, I upped the volume and changed to Happy by Pharrell. Amazed and captivated by the sound and video, they came a little closer, and even though they did not understand the words started subconsciously moving to the rhythm of the music, relaxing a bit.

"See, it also shows pictures, too." On the gallery icon, I selected a random picture of a previous girlfriend in a bikini when we were at the beach, then showed it to Rodriguez—something pornographic for the time. Amazed at what he saw, the other two crowded around to see each picture pushing and shoving each other as I swashed from picture to picture. Fascinated, they came even closer, pushing and shoving each other, and as Rodriguez reached to grab it from me, I tapped the flashlight app and pointed it directly at his eyes, blinding him and then his comrades.

I immediately did a backward roll, reached under my blanket, and grabbed my flintlock. His vision still blurry, Rodriguez fired at me as I rolled again. The bullet barely missed my head, puncturing my quilt sending feathers flying. Then, the three of them drew their swords and came at me. I flicked off the cover over the powder-filled pan and fired at the first short bandito, hitting him squarely in the chest and stopping him cold. Then I rolled back to my blanket and reached for my sword, barely fending off a forceful swipe while still on the ground. I sprang to my feet as Rodriquez growled, "As I recall, you are not much of a swordsman. It is good for us that you are not with that other one who was one of the best swordsmen I ever saw on the road. Chico, we will not have much of a problem with this one. Perhaps I will let you have him."

My left side throbbed with pain from the kicking, but with adrenalin flowing because of my long arms and practice, it took only five maneuvers to stab Chico in his side with one of Francisco's patented moves—he instantly folding up. Rodriguez faced me and began relentlessly thrusting and slashing at me. Being weakened by the relentless beatings, I struggled to fend off each blow. Francisco taught me how to defend such advances well and how to wait until they had spent their energy and I could assess their weaknesses before attacking. The dastardly and more skillful Rodriquez kept advancing with me continuously warding off his attack, backing up and circling, him thinking I was an easy mark until I had caught my breath, then I launched a merciless attack that caught him off guard, wounding him in his good shoulder.

He somehow recovered and lunged repeatedly at me, me continuously backing up. Then I tripped on a root and fell. He was about to stab me in the chest when I beat him to it and stabbed him in the side, causing him to drop his sword. With surprise and terror on his face, after hesitating, he ran and jumped on Chester. As he started to ride off, I whistled to Chester, and he reared up and threw the brigand off, who ran into the darkness of the woods after Chico.

Enraged, adrenalin flowing, my heart rapidly pounding, I wanted to reload, ride Chester to hunt them down, and finish the job, but thought better of it. For all I knew, the other two could be somewhere out there in the darkness, perhaps at their camp. Then, the pain of the beating hit me. My left arm was numb with excruciating pain, and I feared it had been broken, but fortunately, my right sword arm had saved the day. The third bandit lay on the ground dead. I had never killed a man before, but he and his dastardly gang were about to kill me, so I knew I should not feel bad about it. I prayed over him, asking God for mercy on his soul.*

Even though I hurt badly and needed desperately to rest, I did not want to risk their return. I prioritized my actions and first reloaded both of my pistols, relighting the matchlock from the fire, then packed up camp. My side screaming in pain, I struggled mightily to leverage the trunk into the back of the surrey with my one good arm. I could not lift it, so I took out half of the documents, placed a rock on these to prevent them from being blown away by the periodic strong gusts of wind, laid one side of the trunk on the back of the surrey, then, accompanied by a loud scream, I hefted the other side into place, and restored the rest of the documents. With one arm, I hitched up Chester and Maria and quickly drove off.

Struggling to keep my eyes open, aching more after each mile, I made it to a village by mid-morning. There, I talked to the local police, giving the approximate location of where I had thwarted the attack and the dead men, saying that both of the others were wounded on foot and would not likely go far. I also said they were three of the five men that had plagued that town down south that we had defeated. Then I checked into the inn, which would likely cost all of my remaining reales or more.

In my room, a doctor, who coincidentally had graduated from Salamanca U, came to check on me. He bandaged my bleeding mouth, checked my side, and mercifully found that my ribs were not broken, just fractured, something that would heal over time. He wrapped the ribs so they would not move. He noticed that most of my back was black and blue, as was my left side and arm, which had absorbed most of the blows, and it would also take time to heal. Fortunately, the bones in my painful left arm had not been broken. He recommended that I stay at the Inn for several days, then gave me pills made from willow bark—aspirin.

I said, "Señor, I cannot pay for your wonderful services, but I can pay with some of the food and wine Senora Alverez provided me. The wine is very good."

He responded, "Considering the service you provided to the police, I did not plan to charge you. But I will take a bottle of the wine."

"Gracias!"

I collapsed into the bed, struggled to eat something from my bag, and then slept throughout the night until afternoon. Following a late breakfast of sausage, hard bread and cheese, I felt I had to be on the move. I knew I would be in pain but desperately wanted to make it to Bilbao. After the stable boy hitched up Chester and Marie, when I went to settle with the innkeeper, I saw the policia riding into town with a cart that held Rodriquez and Cisco. When they stopped by me, the two bandits looked desperate, their wounds and the skirmish with the policia evidently taking much out of them.

The Capitan said, "Señor, you have done us a great service in stopping these desperados. We have been hunting for them for weeks, and during that time, they have committed numerous crimes and murder not only here but also down south. We will try them in a week when the judge comes and will require you to testify against them.

After being in Spain for so long, I was anxious to get home. Besides, I could not afford to stay here for a week. "Capitan, I must get to Bilbao. I cannot afford to stay."

"Señor, we do not wish to delay you, but unfortunately, we need your testimony and must insist that you remain. Pablo (the innkeeper), we will pay for all his charges. Is there anything we can do for you, señor? You do not look so good. You should stay in our village and heal."

Searching for something that would release me to continue my journey, "El Capitan, I am on an urgent mission authorized by Queen Isabella and must continue." Then I reached into my bag and handed him the document signed by the Queen."

Coming to attention, in an instant, his attitude changed from that of an authoritarian bureaucrat to that of a conciliatory subject. "Señor, we would not want to delay you. Did you really meet the Queen?"

"Si."

Treating me as if I were a celebrity, "What an honor! What was she like, señor?"

"She is a very intelligent, strong, caring, gracious, and wise leader. I cannot imagine a better person to lead Espana at this critical stage in your long history."

"Perhaps I can make a statement that can be used in court. I assure you that these are the two that accosted and beat me. As I had told you earlier, they bear the wounds I inflicted upon them."

After completing the statement, the captain offered to send me off with a guard, to which I replied, "No el capitan, mochas gracias!"

I felt a little like the Lone Ranger riding off into the distance after performing a good deed, but each bump on the road hurt too much.*

Besides being in constant pain, the next days on the road were uneventful. Hurting extremely badly by the end of each day, not wanting to be a lame victim on the road, still somewhat traumatized, the first night I stayed in something that more resembled a rundown B&B rather than an inn, which was very cheap, so I could afford it.

The following nights, I camped on the road. The mornings when I was stiff were very painful as I stretched, but found that by midday, the pain would subside a little. Heading down the mountains to Bilbao went much faster than coming up, although there were a few treacherous spots where I had to apply the brakes or plunge off the side of the mountain, which caused my ribs to scream out in pain.

My funds exhausted, I checked into a hotel near the wharf and readily found a buyer for Marie and the surrey. I went down to the docks each day to see if a boat was sailing to London. On the third day, I found an English ship that had just arrived and would have a cargo heading for Calais, France, and then back to London. It would leave the next day.

I stopped in to see how Pedro was doing and found him and his family in excellent spirits. He proudly showed me his wound, which he wore as a badge of honor. From what I heard from his son, he was the hero of Salinas, something I had no intent of disputing. Pedro said those in Salinas treated him extremely well, and after a week, when he was healed, one of them drove him back to Bilbao in his carriage. "Emillio's sense of humor was nearly as good as mine, and we laughed most of the way back." The locals in Bilbao also treated him as a hero, and his notoriety added to his business. With our payment and the rides he had taken since then, he had paid back his brother-in-law and planned to add another carriage and a second driver. I was heartened to see he was doing well.

Pedro thanked me, saying, "Señor Francisco said he would fund my eldest son, Pedro's, education, something that was beyond mi and mi wife's wildest dreams. I cannot believe my son will go to Salamanca University. Pedro said he will study very hard and make us proud."

THIRTEEN

Back in London

Not certain whose ship I would have sailed back on, it is re-freshing to board one from a British line. On the fourth day, sailing on the open sea, seemingly out of nowhere, dark, churn-ing clouds well up, looking more threatening and blacker by the minute. The wind picks up, then blows harder, whipping the sails and blowing untethered items off the deck. While the temperature drops precipitously, it becomes dark as night, and the waves crest at eight, then ten, then fifteen feet. Putting out the sea anchor to steady the ship, the captain commands his crew to bring down most of the sails and lash down all else. With serious, worried faces, the skilled, efficient crew, fighting against the rising and falling, twisting deck, attacks their tasks in hyper-mode, ordering me to my small cabin below so I would not be washed overboard—not something I resist.

Lying on my bed, trying to calm my frazzled nerves as the cabin radi-cally pitches up and down, left then right, I look out my small porthole and see copious rain-driven sidewise and mountainous, dark waves crest-ing at perhaps twenty-five feet. The wind howls fiercely and sounds like freight cars rumbling by. When a monster wave hits us from the other side, after tumbling into the wall of my nearly vertical bed, I look out the window into the sea, the surface above the portal, where I glimpse a great white shark thrashing against the turbulent forces. As if the vulnerable ship was a roller coaster, I become progressively more seasick, wondering if the ship will ever make it out of this fearsome storm intact and if I will survive. I can hear a mighty roar as a large rogue wave runs over the length of the ship and hear the sloshing of water pouring into the lower decks.

Concerned about my trunk being inundated with water and all my efforts lost, despite my trepidation, I had to check on it, something that is not easy as I bang against the walls and frequently fall onto the soaking wet floor desperately trying to reach the hold. There, I find the trunk on the floor, already seeping in several inches of water. I see several crates nearby that seem securely lashed down. So, I push the trunk to them and, with all my might, lift it upwards, just as an immense wave smashes into the ship, causing it to list at a 45-degree angle, and the trunk flies off, narrowly missing my head.

Now, six inches of water are in the hold, and I must get the crate up immediately. Timing the waves, I wait until the ship lowers, then, with as much force I can muster, lift the precious cargo up onto the crates again. When the vessel climbs up the other side of a gigantic wave, bracing my legs, I struggle mightily to hold it in place. Waiting for the wave's descent, I quickly slosh through the water to the other side of the hold and grab a rope just in time to prevent the trunk from sliding off. Working feverously, as the ship descends, I tie it down, thereby protecting it from the eight inches of water in the hold that crests up to two feet as the ship climbs the successive sea-mountains—splashing just a few inches below my treasured trunk. Feeling as if I were sloshing around in a washing machine, I know that it would not be long before my trunk would be infiltrated by the salty sea water and my precious documents ruined.

I know there has to be a sump pump somewhere and see a circular iron tube leading upwards to what I assume is where the pump is located. With difficulty climbing the steep ladder out of the hold around a corner, I see a young, thin apprentice sailor named Paul manning the pump. The captain needs every experienced hand to manage the sails and keep the boat afloat as he guides the ship through the angry, storm-tossed sea and can only spare one man for the pump, who, although he tries mightily, is tiring. I man the other handle of the teeter-totter-like pump that sucks water out of the hold and spits it out into the sea.

Seeing how drained he looks, I tell him, "Rest for a bit, Paul."

I pump by myself until, in perhaps a long ten minutes, he rejoins me. Pacing ourselves, bracing ourselves against the constant rise and fall of the deck, together we significantly increase the flow of water streaming out of the hold, hoping our efforts will be enough to save its contents and not weigh the ship down. After another hour, Fred comes to relieve the exhausted pumper, who eats, rests and returns to duty on deck.

Realizing the overwhelming extent of the storm, similar to a coach, the experienced captain rotates his crew to keep them as fresh as possible, though he stays at the helm for the duration of the fierce storm that seems to never end. Periodically, someone comes to relieve me. After I lie down, eat, drink some water, and meditate a bit, I return to the pump, for there is little else I am qualified to do.

One benefit of helping is that because I am actively involved, I am no longer seasick. After nearly a day, the storm eventually abates, and the captain hands the wheel to his first mate. He is not able to open the hands that had grasped the wheel for the duration. Without the wheel's support, he drops to the floor and is assisted below deck, where he has his first meal in a day.

The current ten-foot waves, by comparison, seem like molehills. As if nothing had happened, the sea eventually calms, and the sun shines, bringing that fresh after-rain smell. Fearing the worst, I venture down to the hold. There, I see a four-foot water line that missed my precious cargo by an inch. If I had not raised it or manned the pump, all of my prized manuscripts would have been soggy, matted, paper mâché clumps.

The outside of the trunk is wet from the constant water sloshing around the hull, but the inside is perfectly dry. I wipe off the outside with a towel.*

Later, after everyone has had a chance to rest and recover, at a joint dinner with the officers and crew, everyone has that sallow, gaunt, spent look that accompanies such horrors but is relieved and proud of what they had accomplished. Captain Horn orders up a triple ration of spirits and, waving his glass, says, "I toast my magnificent crew and her officers, who, without your extraordinary efforts, our noble ship, Grantham, may be lying at the bottom of the deep with us on 'er. I have the highest admiration and gratitude for each of you."

He then goes from man to man, looks them straight in the eye, shakes each one's hand, pats them on the shoulder, and individually thanks them for the specific tasks they performed. When he comes to me, he says, "I understand you provided a Herculean effort at the pump. As a man of letters, I did not realize your strength. If you ever want to sail the seas and see the world, I would love to 'av ye on me crew."

Being blown so long by the storm, the captain had no idea where we were until that night when the sky was clear, and he could tell our location by the stars. It turns out the storm blew us near the coast. I sleep deeply and awake to a beautiful sun-drenched, yellow morn, grateful to be alive. When I look out my porthole, I can see the bluish coast of France and, on deck, see Britain in the distance. We dock in Calais by mid-afternoon.

Having survived the fearful storm, it is wondrous to be alive. After discharging some of his cargo in France, Captain Horn will head to nearby London. I had been thinking about Marie nearly every day, and now that my long journey was winding down, I desperately longed to see her, hoping I would find her at the court in London, or if not there, back in Bunkillarny. I hoped that after securing these valuable literary treasures, thereby becoming a partner and improving my financial prospects, she would consider marrying me. Still, realizing how desirable she is, I worry that some handsome, young royal may have swept her up and captured her heart in the meantime.*

Somewhat depleted by the fierce storm, by the time I arrived back in London, it was late summer. When I knocked on Colleen's door, all five children mobbed me, calling me Uncle Rand, warming my travel-worn heart.

Colleen said, "I hope you don't mind that I let them call yeuw uncle. They so much looked forward to yer return. I thought 'bout it while ye be gone, and since you live with me, dear cousins, Michael and Gwendolyn, ye be like a member of our family.

Where have you been all this time? We expected you months ago."

"It's a long story. I will tell you later."

"I have much to tell you too. Albert, fetch a roast of beef from the butcher and a blackberry pie from the baker. We shall have a feast tonight," after which the children jumped up and down, cheering boisterously!

When I walked into the shop, it was so much larger than before. There had only been a couple of shelves containing a few books. Now, there were several bookcases, and as I perused them, I saw that they contained more than just our titles. I looked to Colleen with a puzzled look.

Realizing my confusion with a big grin she exclaimed, "Twas a dream of John's to expand our lil shop, which we were close to doing when he died. As I will show you when you see the books, our business has prospered. And I am not only selling just our books but those of the Caxton's shop too, and they sells ours. Wynkyn has been marvelous."

I am sorry to tell you that Mr. William Caxton died shortly after you left. What a monumental man he were for printing the first books in the English language. It were he that John learned so much from and had so much respect for."

"I am so sorry to hear that. What an honor to have met him. Michael will be crushed."

After saying a prayer for his soul, beaming and talking quickly in a high-toned voice, Colleen continued, "With our share of the profits, I was able to buy the widow's townhouse next door that suddenly was for sale, her son wantin' to sell right off, so I got a good price, I did. So now the shop occupies all of this house's first floor, and we live in the other house. When Captain Black came back from Bunkillarny, I asked him to bring back many more books from Michael for us to sell, because the demand has increased that much more. Since we are in Westminster, and tis near where all the bureaucrats and nobles live, they frequent the shop now and purchase books and they tell others about our shop too. Some says the heard 'bout ar books when they met ye at the pub."

"Colleen, what you have done here is amazing—a couple of minor suggestions. I see you have the books grouped alphabetically according to who printed them, either us or the Caxton shop. You could group them by subject with a sign for each, such as history, religion, poetry, novels, etc. I see that you have quite a bit of space over here. Something else you could do is lay a few of the most interesting or newest titles on a table for customers to peruse."

"I will surely do that, and since we gained two new bedrooms, we have a guest room for you. And Harry has his own room too. He has been such a 'elp."

She gave me a tour of the new configuration, connected by knocking down a wall in the former kitchen on the first floor and the hallway on the second floor. I had bought gifts for the children in Salamanca that

I distributed, something that made them giggle with delight. One had a ball attached to a string and a thin cup that you tried to catch the ball in, something I played with as a kid 500 years from now.

Colleen said, "You spoil them. Few of their friends have such toys. I asked Harry and Albert if they would like to go to school, and Harry said he would rather work for the business. Albert said he would go. Albert will still spend much of his time helpin' out, but with his education, he will be an asset to us. Since I spend so much of me time away from home, Patricia is teaching the younger children and doing a marvelous job."

During dinner, because I was with Colleen and her family, I could not be any happier. It felt like a long, yearned-for visit home. After dinner, Colleen told me that she had shipped manuscripts back to Michael to be printed and had sold many books throughout London and the rest of England, too. She asked about my long journey and if I was able to acquire the books that John wanted.

I told her about my adventurous expedition, "The library at Salamanca would not release the books because they feared they might be lost at sea. Fortunately, I met a wonderful gentleman named Francisco Alverez on my way to Spain, who helped me. We ended up traveling to Córdoba in the south of Spain, where, thanks to Francisco and his cousin Carlos, we had an audience with Queen Isabella. (Colleen's expression showed how surprised she was by my meeting an actual queen.) She granted us an edict that stated the library would give us copies of the wondrous documents. Back in Salamanca, translating and copying the treasures took six weeks, after which I traveled back to London. I have these in my trunk, and I want you to see them. They are absolutely marvelous, truly a testament to John's legacy.

"Oh, along the way, I was apprehended by bandits three times, beaten badly and survived a fierce storm."

"I see that your eyes are still a little blue and yellow. Must have been quite a fight."

"It was, but fortunately, I survived."

The children cried out for me to tell them the stories about the bandits and about the storm. I told the stories with as much detail and embellishment as possible, about how, on the first encounter, Francisco, and I fought off five menacing banditos and about the time I had to fight three, highlighting my growing skills with a pistol and a sword, which the children loved, their fresh faces looking at me as if I was a hero. Since I was so beaten up, I did not feel like a hero, though, more just lucky to be alive.

Colleen showed me the ledgers the next day, and I could not believe how well she had fared. She said, "Much of the credit goes to Harry, who has been working tirelessly. He's even turning into a literary man like his father, something he showed no inclination to do before. He's a good salesman too, traveling around England, interesting other merchants to stock our books. At Cambridge and Oxford, he sold a lot of books.

"Thank you for sending Captain Black here. He was very helpful in transporting the books from Bunkillarny, saying that you wanted him to visit here whenever he sailed to London. He's a fine gentleman; he is."

I had asked the captain to look in on the family to see if they needed any help, and although somewhat surprised, I was glad to hear he was on his best behavior.

I asked her how her relationship with Monsignor Albert had gone.

"He was invaluable over the first few months but not at all helpful over the last months. He has visited us several times asking about when he will be able to see the books you acquired, which is why I think he has been so resistive."

"Well, he should be ecstatic with what I was able to bring back. I will show him what we have acquired and smooth things over."

I opened my trunk and showed Colleen my treasure trove of Spanish, Moorish, Roman, Greek and Jewish literature. When I showed some of the manuscripts, explaining their origins, subject matter, and purpose, she spied a wooden box at the bottom, which she picked up and asked, "What be this one?"

This was the box that contained the missing gospel that I had promised not to disclose to anyone. Since it potentially so valuable and secret, I had purchased a wooden box in Salamanca to store it in. Given my oath to Father Dominic, I could not disclose its meaning. "Oh that, its not in Latin. Not exactly sure what it is. I plan to get it translated sometime."

"Maybe I can make sense of it?"

"Do you know Aramaic?"

"No, but I can probly find someone who does here in London, perhaps at one of the universities."

"That's all right. I won't worry about it until I arrive in Ireland."

She said, "I cannot wait until these are printed. I want to read them all. I'll sell hundreds of them, if not thousands. I especially want to read El Cid to the children. The monsignor will be very pleased."*

The next day, Colleen and I went to nearby Westminster Abbey. There, I showed Monsignor Albert a few copies of the manuscripts I had brought and his list, of which I had about half of what the royals wanted. Then I showed him another list containing all the other works I had found, transcribed into Latin and copied. He was ecstatic, saying, "The Queen Mother will love this. I will arrange a meeting with her, and you will show her what you have acquired. She will be particularly interested in the writings of Seneca. Please be sure to bring these."

After the meeting, while eating lunch at the Hamstead, I asked Colleen, "Who is the Queen Mother? Wynkyn and Albert talked about her, but I don't know much about her."

She informed me that, "Albert was referring to the king's mother, Margaret Beaufort. She had sponsored Bill Caxton and currently sponsors Wynkyn. Without her patronage, Caxton's press would never have survived. She is intensely interested in literature and has sponsored the translation of the great works into English. She has even translated some of these herself, and from what I hear, she did an excellent job. One was entitled the Imitation of Christ, the other was The Mirror of Gold for the Sinful Soul, which was originally written in Flemish then into French. When she was but a wee girl, she translated it from French to English."

Back at the shop, Colleen walked through the door, causing the tiny bell on a spring to tinkle, to one of the Caxton shelves and pulled off copies of both books, which we apparently sold, and handed them to me. As she waited patiently, I skimmed a bit of each book and thought they seemed interesting. It felt as if I was in an actual bookstore like the ones I used to enjoy while wandering around the tables and shelves, looking at various displayed titles and thumbing through the pages of actual physical books, with no place to go or deadline to meet. There, I would lose myself in the experience—something while being encased in the digital world I had not had the opportunity to enjoy for a long time. If only Colleen had an espresso machine, I would be in heaven.

Then, she told me about the Queen Mother's other translation, the Imitation of Christ, by Thomas A. Kempis, a Dutch monk. "This book is full of God's wisdom, love and power. The author appears to have an intimate relationship with his creator and savior, Jesus Christ. He seems to have found the secret which is to believe, and obey Christ's commands, but says our carnality is a hard thing to overcome. The devil comes into your life to kill, steal and destroy you, but Jesus comes into your soul, mind and spirit to give your life more abundance. In reading it, I could tell the Queen Mother was a very spiritual and intelligent woman. I want my children to read this when they are ready for it."

I asked, "What is the Queen Mother's role within the monarchy?"

Colleen responded, "King Henry the Seventh would not be on the throne if it were not for her, for his claim was very weak. I would not understand much of the story except that John ha' done research on the Tudors for a possible book that Michael would print and would likely be a best seller here in London. I have his research and maybe someday, I will work on the book meself and maybe after Albert's education, when he is more involved, I will finish it.

"It all started with the War of the Roses, which lasted for over thirty years until 1487. Back then, there were periodic battles for the throne. Even here in London, the war impacted us, but the peace over the last five years has been most welcome.

"The Plantagenets had ruled England for a long time, but after the death of the king, there was no clear heir. Two branches of the family claimed the throne. One branch was from Lancaster, who were represented by the red rose. The white rose from York represented the other branch. It's a long story with many battles and outcomes, which you will, no doubt, find confusing, so let me try to summarize it all."

"Sounds like a soap opera or a Shakespearean play," I said, to which she responded with a confused look.

"Soap opera, shake a spear and play?"

"Sorry, it must be my amnesia coming back. Please continue."

"It began with King Edward IV of the House of York, who was married to Elizabeth of Woodville. They had ten children, but two are particularly interesting—their first child, Elizabeth of York, and Edward, their first son."

When Edward IV died, his son Edward was to become king. Edward IV's brother, Richard, became the regent and declared that the marriage between Elizabeth and his brother was invalid because they were cousins. Richard assumed the throne. Then he imprisoned the young Edward and his younger brother, who might at some time claim the throne too. Under questionable circumstances, both soon died in prison. As you would expect, their mother, Elizabeth of Woodville, was furious."

"Here is where Margaret Beaufort, the Queen Mother, enters the picture. She married Edmund Tudor and was pregnant when she was only thirteen years old. At one of the numerous battles of the roses, her much older husband died before Henry was born. They were from the house of Lancaster. At court, she conspired with Elizabeth of Woodville. Elizabeth had her eldest daughter, also named Elizabeth, marry Henry."

"With the help of France, Henry's Lancaster forces defeated Richard's at the battle of Bosworth Field in 1485, where Richard was killed. Afterwards, Henry became King Henry VII. By marrying Elizabeth, he united the two houses—the Yorks and the Lancasters—the white roses and the red roses. The new house of Tudor's symbol became a white rose within a red rose."

"Since Margaret is only thirteen years older than her son, the king, she has played a key role in ruling England and smoothing things over. She is his main advisor."

My head spinning from all the details, half-jokingly, I said, "Thanks for not making that overly complicated. So, we will meet with a powerful woman who unified the country and sponsored the first printing press in England. What an amazing woman!"

Wanting to be prepared for our meeting the next day, I took my dying smartphone from its case, where I looked up Margaret Beaufort. I learned that she founded religious chairs at both Oxford and Cambridge. In addition, she founded Christ's College and Saint John's College at Cambridge. She also founded a grade school and was one of the first fervent and highly effective supporters of expanding education in England. Margaret also sponsored the press that would distribute more affordable books to vastly more people, thereby increasing Britain's level of education, intelligence, and, soon, its standing in the world.

FOURTEEN

British Royalty

I presumed our meeting would be just a few blocks away at nearby Westminster Castle, but Colleen informed me that it would be at Richmond Palace, Henry's primary residence now. Since Margaret wanted us there for a meeting in the morning and it would take over half a day to get there, we decided to leave a day early and stay at a nearby inn overnight. Stephen drove us in his cart, and of course, it rained.

Since I had traveled so much for work up in the 21st century, I was used to the typical three-star hotels, which seemed remarkably similar, all with the standard accouterments including a large-screen TV, dryer, iron and mini fridge with breakfast included. Accommodations these days, however, were very Spartan and quirky. This inn looked like it had additions that stretched back a couple of centuries, with incongruent sections in stone, brick and wood, doorways that I had to duck through, with low ceilings and steep steps that seemed more like ladders. Upon checking in, I learned that there was no such thing as a queen or full-sized bed, and although we were able to obtain a separate closet-sized room for Colleen, Stephen and I were forced to occupy the same cramped room, with two small beds that I hung over. The beds were no more than a foot apart and located under a steep, slanted roof on top of a slanted floor that creaked with every movement. The room had a tiny parallelogram-shaped window. Even though they had extra rooms, they refused to give us separate rooms—"Why would two gents traveling together need two rooms—preposterous?" The bathroom was an outhouse in the back of the hotel, but we did have a washbasin on the tiny set of drawers that barely allowed the door to open halfway.

The next day was beautiful as we completed the delightful passage through the spacious, tree-lined grounds to the palace overlooking the surprisingly clear blue Thames River. The palace resembled an enormous, classic, five-story, 19th-century resort hotel with numerous spires, such as the Del Coronado in San Diego or the Greenbrier in West Virginia. To me, it more resembled Downton Abbey than Westminster Abbey, except that it was much more ornate and fanciful.

Colleen and I were led through spacious halls into an extensive library where we met Margaret, whom I bowed to and addressed as "Your Royal Highness, Lady Margaret." Along with Monsignor Albert, the four of us sat at a long table where Albert gave us a surprisingly sterling introduction. I brought out the list of books I had acquired from the Salamanca library, which Colleen had made a hand copy of and gave to Lady Margaret. As Albert had surmised, she looked extremely pleased with the list, noting that many of the authors she had hoped I would find were on the list but that there were also many others she was interested in. She had the delighted countenance of a child at Christmas opening her presents.

Her long, strong face with a long, sharp nose and blue eyes seemed joyous as I described some of the titles to her. I showed her the works by Seneca that Albert had asked me to bring. Then Albert said something that concerned me, "Your majesty, we can have the Caxton's print shop start printing these books immediately."

I had gone to all that trouble so we would be able to print these in Ireland. Still, knowing that she was a woman of formidable power and influence that had ended a 30-year war, brought together the two sides, and made her son the King of England, I did not know how to proceed. She might be able to command that the documents be confiscated and printed in London by the Caxton shop she sponsored. Therefore, I proceeded cautiously.

"Your Majesty, I am so glad you are pleased with what I acquired from Spain. I procured these for our print shop—the McCarren Press in Ireland."

"I was not aware that there was a printer in Ireland. Still, I think we should have these printed at Caxton's."

"Your majesty, I had the honor of meeting Mr. Caxton and also Wynkyn de Worde, who I assume will be his successor. There is no other than Wynkyn who I would trust with such an important job other than ourselves. But it took me several months, at great expense and danger, to acquire these works for our shop to print. Indeed, I was nearly robbed and killed on three occasions, including once by three bandits I faced alone, who wanted to burn and destroy the manuscripts."

"I understand, and I am sure we can reach an arrangement that will adequately compensate you for your efforts."

It did not look like I could succeed in my quest until a thought occurred to me, and I blindly followed it, hoping it would not land me in jail.

"Your majesty, I could only acquire these manuscripts through the intercession of Queen Isabella of Spain. It was only through her decree authorizing the acquisition of these invaluable documents that allowed me to obtain them. According to the decree, I entered into a contract with the president of Salamanca University, in which, in addition to paying for the manuscripts, I agreed to give the university the first ten copies of each and a portion of our royalties."

Even though I had not thought this out thoroughly and had no legal background, I hoped my agreement with Spain would work in our favor.

Her expression and pleasant mood suddenly changed, which I found unsettling. Perhaps she would send me to the dungeon. Instead, she said, "How is Isabella? Tell me more about her."

"She is a splendid, intelligent, caring, highly religious, strong, yet fair monarch who, as you do, supports education, particularly at Salamanca University. I met her in Cordoba just after they had conquered Granada and unified all of Spain. As you might imagine, they were ecstatic. While there, I met a captain named Christopher Columbus, who is on his way to discover an eastern route to the Indies. I believe he will succeed in discovering many new lands that will vastly increase the wealth of Spain."

"Well, young man, if you have a contract with Isabella, we would not want to interfere with such an arrangement."

"Thank you, your majesty. I will ensure that you receive some of the first copies of each of the manuscripts you are interested in. Colleen here is our representative in London and throughout England, where we have distributed many of our titles, some of which came to us from the monasteries in Ireland and do not exist anywhere else. If you like, Colleen could bring you some of these."

"Yes, I would like that, and it is good to see that you have a woman involved in your business. I will have my minister pay for these."

It struck me that Henry, likely advised by Margarette, would eventually arrange for the marriage of his oldest son, the heir to the throne, Arthur, to Catherine of Aragon, Isabella's daughter. Thereby uniting the two emerging kingdoms. After Arthur died, Catherine would marry Arthur's younger brother, Henry VIIIth.

As I learned on Wikipedia, Margaret was perhaps the only woman allowed to hold property in England, which testified to the state of women in England and, indeed, the rest of the world at this time. She understood how difficult it was for a widow like Colleen to survive in the male-dominated society.

Margaret continued, "There is one other matter I would like you to tend to... I am having our monthly meeting with my royal literary soiree this evening, and I would like you to speak about what you found in Spain. We will arrange for you and Colleen to spend the night."

As we walked out, me extremely anxious about the last-minute commitment I was not the least bit prepared for, Monsignor Albert, who would attend the soirée, informed us about the meeting, "The group consists of writers, intellectuals, professors and royals who have an interest in literature and intellectual pursuits." His description only heightened my dread, for it sounded like I would have to perform a last-minute presentation with no preparation to many of the country's most influential and intelligent people.

"But, monsignor, I am not prepared for such a meeting with such an esteemed group. I am just a lowly printer's assistant. I would not know what to say or what their particular interests might be. Perhaps we can do this another time."

"I am sorry, Rand. This was a surprise to me, too, but she is, after all, the Queen Mother, and we would not want to disappoint her. I am sure you will do well. Just talk a little about the books you brought, like you did for her, and you will be fine."

A servant, who introduced himself as Jeeves, met us and said he would lead us to our rooms. My spacious room on the third floor overlooked the Thames River with a spectacular view of the farmland and hills in the distance—quite a contrast to the previous evening's digs. He asked if we had any servants with us, and I said, "We have our driver, Stephen.

"I will find accommodations for him too. Do you have a personal manservant, Sir?"

"No, I do not. "

"Then I will serve you. Do you have a suit of clothes suitable for the soirée, Sir?"

In a high-pitched, nervous voice, "No, I did not know about the soirée, and these are the only clothes I brought. We thought we would be leaving for home by now."

"Then allow me to find you a suit in your size."

"Thank you, Jeeves."

"Is there anything else you desire?"

"Well, since we have not eaten today, we could use something to eat." Then I thought about the presentation that had just been thrust upon me. I had performed scores of PowerPoint presentations over the years, sometimes with little notice. Back in Silicon Valley, Steve, the CEO, had sometimes wanted me to give a presentation to a venture capitalist, or a tech billionaire investor, or an executive of a software company the next day. I would customize a previous presentation overnight, but this was different, for there would be no PowerPoint for hundreds of years, and this wasn't a tech presentation, but it was about literature—certainly not my area of expertise.

Those presentations regarded subjects I worked on daily, was highly familiar with, and had materials I could draw upon. I did not have any canned graphics from which to work for this presentation. I had no idea what they would expect, and I was not used to speaking extemporaneously. Instead, as a graphically oriented nerd, I depended on the slides—something I knew was a weakness I worked around. I was no good at just reading stuff.

Trying to build a presentation these days, I asked, "Jeeves, see if you can find me an artist's pedestal and twenty sheets of the largest paper you can acquire. Also, something large to write with, perhaps a half-inch wide paint brush, black and red ink or a long piece of charcoal."

I had faced tight deadlines before, but I had no idea what would appeal to such a distinguished 15th-century audience. I had performed presentations to vice presidents and CIOs of major companies but never to royalty, who might, for all I knew, cut off my head if it did not appeal to them. I realized that these types of thoughts would only increase my anxiety level and undermine my effectiveness. I needed to focus all my energies on the presentation that would occur in just a few hours. Therefore, I needed to concentrate and start working on an outline. I took a deep breath and focused.

Jeeves was able to find everything I requested, but I realized I needed something to attach the sheets of paper to the artist's easel, so I asked him to find some small nails and a hammer, which Colleen would use to attach the paper to the easel, where the picture would usually be painted.

When Jeeves appeared again, he had brought a very splendid 15th-century black outfit to wear, insisting that he would assist me in putting it on, which I resisted but went along with. I was glad he helped me because I may have put on the vestments backwards, and I still was not used to those dang tights. I looked at a presentation similar to an athletic event—something you prepare for, get up for, react as well as you can during it, and do your best. Putting on a suit is similar to putting on a uniform, and the tights were similar to tight-fitting football or baseball pants—so I told myself, after all, under their shorts, Lebron and many NBA stars wear something that looks like tights, and even though I never paid attention to them it, I was told that I had a great pair of legs.

Then, Jeeves said we needed to leave immediately because the soirée would be at the opposite end of the palace. Jeeves guided us through the maze of halls, through which, without his help, we would've been thoroughly lost and never made it in time. Once there, I set up my easel and did not have any time to rehearse my presentation before people began entering the room. The large maple wooden hall had a tall ceiling with many decorations adorning the walls. One wall was filled with windows that let in quite a bit of light, which would have been a concern for my PowerPoint projector because it would've been blanched out, and there was no way to darken the room.

As they entered the large hall, Monsignor Albert introduced me to them. There were three professors from Oxford and two from further away, Cambridge, who happened to be in London. I wish I could have asked them how they taught their classes, and I wish I had spent some of my time at Salamanca University going to a lecture where I could see how they did it now.

He also introduced me to several lords and ladies who apparently evidently had an intense interest in ancient literature. As the room filled, there was a pause in the introductions, and my nerves started to fray until I saw the familiar face of Wynkyn de Worde, who, although surprised to see me, enthusiastically greeted me. Seeing him helped me to relax, at least temporarily. Then two other friendly faces appeared—Abbott Philip and Brother Martin, who had helped Colleen so much in her efforts to acquire texts from and distribute our books to religious institutions.

After everyone had settled into their seats, Lady Margaret appeared with two other regally dressed women. Everyone stood then bowed to the three royals as Albert whispered in my ear that they were Elizabeth of Woodville, the previous queen, and her daughter, Queen Elizabeth, King Henry's wife. These were the women who unified the two Houses of Roses and England under the Tudors, no doubt saving thousands of lives from the continuous battles.

Lady Margaret spoke, "Rather than our usual free-flowing discussions, which we all find enlightening, I have invited someone I just met earlier today to speak to us, which is why the chairs have been arranged as if you were at an Oxford lecture. He has just returned from Spain, where he discovered some amazing manuscripts that date back to the time of Seneca, the Romans, and the Greeks over two thousand years ago. I think that you will also find it interesting that he operates another printing press within my son, Henry's realm—in Ireland of all places (which drew a reaction of surprise and 'ah hahs' from the audience). Monsignor Albert will introduce the young man.

As he introduced me, my nerves ratcheted up. I often felt nervous before a major presentation, which I thought was a good sign, for it helped me to focus. This time, as I stood at the center of the intimidating large hall with a large audience, I felt as if I would faint. With my mixture of American, Irish, and Spanish accents, would they even understand me? Would using an improvised flip chart and drawing on it with charcoal and ink be offensive to them? Would I be able to speak loud enough to fill the huge room without a mic and speaker system? All of these thoughts danced around my brain, debilitating my body.

When I began my speech, I was choked up and had to take several deep breaths to calm my nerves. Sporting dour faces, the professors, noble lords, and ladies looked like this would be a waste of their time, some even yawning and looking at each other with disappointment. This was nothing like my previous speeches, for these people were not dressed in suits, dresses, or business casual. The ladies wore long, stylish, low-cut gowns, while the gentlemen wore tights and what looked like miniskirts—talk about gender confusion. I looked at my friends in the front row, who gave me encouraging nods. Lady Margaret also looked my way, smiling encouragingly, waving the back of her hand at a 45-degree angle, and nodding, encouraging me to have courage.

I began by telling them a little bit about my adventure in Spain—the long trip to Salamanca, in which Francisco, a cousin of Isabella's and an excellent swordsman, one of Spain's best, fended off five brigands, the understandable refusal of the president of Salamanca to release the treasured books, the trip to Cordoba where Queen Isabella devised a suitable compromise, the translation to Latin from Hebrew, Arabic, Egyptian and Greek and the trip back to the coast, when I faced the same fearsome bandits, who would have burned the precious manuscripts, whereupon they would have been forever lost.

I also told them about the ferocious storm that nearly sank our ship and ruined the priceless documents. As I told the story, I could sense that my audience, especially Lady Margaret, was paying attention to me. As I listened to myself, the portrayal seemed as if I was Indiana Jones hunting for artifacts in Egypt—not that I thought of it that way, but I went with it.

I next spoke about Salamanca University, along with Cambridge and Oxford, one of the top five universities in Europe, and its prestigious library—the oldest in Europe—a treasure trove of ancient wisdom and knowledge. Then I spoke of Córdoba 500 years ago when it was conquered by the Moors, when England was still a poor, warring, divided nation, Córdoba had been the center of culture in Europe, when merchants, nobles and guildsmen measured their status not by the size of their bank account, or the size of their house, but by the size of their personal libraries. This is where many of these treasured books that date back to Greco-Roman times sprang from. From the surprised looks on their faces, I could see that they had not heard much about Córdoba.

I spoke about the evolution of Spanish literature from the time of Seneca and the Romans through the time of the Moors in Andalusia, who ruled the world of art, literature, astronomy, and science, to the famous Jewish authors such as Maimedees, to our "modern" times when Spanish literature produced some of the first romantic titles such as El Sid.

I also spoke about the tragic extinction of books in Córdoba in the early 11th century, of a library that employed 500 people and had 400,000 titles, which I could tell by the expressions on their faces they were enthralled by. As I spoke, I used the flip chart to draw graphics and outline much of what I portrayed, which seemed to amaze them. At the end of the speech, I fielded several questions, many asking for more details about my encounters with the brigands. A splendidly dressed lord asked how he might acquire these books.

I turned to the back page of the flipchart where Colleen had scribed the titles of the books I had acquired. I pointed to some of these, explaining their subject matter and importance to modern European literature, philosophy and culture. Then I said, "Colleen, please stand. Colleen will take orders for any of the books you care to acquire. This list will help determine which books we should print next. Once printed, Colleen will deliver these to you."

The audience seemed to enjoy what I had said, but there was an uncomfortable pause at the end until Lady Margaret applauded, followed by thunderous applause by all. As she stood, she said, "Well done, I hope you all enjoyed that stimulating discussion."

A nurse entered and handed Queen Elizabeth an adorable little toddler who seemed to be a little over a year old. The three women (mother and two grandmothers) who now stood, as the rest of the audience stood at attention, smiled at the handsome little fellow with a round face and rosy cheeks. I smiled at him before I realized I was smiling at the future powerful, consequential king—Henry the Eighth—something I could hardly believe, seeing someone who would dramatically change England, its role in the world, and lead the Protestant Reformation as a cute little baby.

Her highness, Lady Margaret, congratulated me again and, gathering Wynkyn to her side, asked me, "I would like to have one of Seneca's works so I could read it soon. Do you think it would be all right with Isabella if you leave a coup this with us for Wynkyn here to print? We promise to deliver whatever portion of the profits you feel are appropriate for you and for you to reimburse Isabella."

"I will certainly do that, Your Majesty."

After the three royal ladies left the room, I talked to the professors and others, who complimented me on the speech and had more probing questions about specific manuscripts. When we exited the room, Colleen showed me the list of orders with over 150 entries. She said that she had met some of those at the soirée who had previously stopped by the bookshop, and she made sure to inform the others of its existence. She said, "I will have Wynkyn print up sheets with the shop's location, and I will slip them into their books when Harry or Albert delivers these. Some of them were delighted to hear that our little bookshop even existed, was so close to them in Westminster, and promised to stop by."

I told her, "We could make a woodcut of a map that shows where the shop is relative to some of the better-known landmarks, such as Windsor Castle, within the flyer."

"Excellent!" she replied.*

While walking down the long corridor, I felt a tug on my elbow and turned to see an overwhelming sight. It was Marie, my Marie! Despite palace protocol I hugged her tightly—I could not resist. After longing for her over so many months, sometimes thinking about her nearly every moment of every day, embracing her felt wondrous.

In an excited tone, she said, "Oh, Rand, I have so longed to see you again. After riding, I was walking down the corridor when I heard your voice and sneaked in through the servant's entrance at the back of the hall."

"But, I did not see you?"

"I was behind Lord Buxton, a very corpulent man. What you said was absolutely magnificent. I had no idea you were traveling to Spain on such a dangerous mission. Oh, mon chéri, such a heroic venture, one that should not surprise me after your wonderful performance at the Bunkillarny games when you ran, when you threw the spear. I had hoped to see you here in London and you are finally here. The books that you acquired in Spain, it's simply magnifique. Are you staying the night?"

"We are staying here at the palace." I introduced Colleen, who seemed confused by Lady Marie's presence and my reaction to her."

"Where are you staying? Where is your room?"

"In the west wing on the third floor, the fourth room to the left. "

"I have to go now, mon chéri, but somehow I will see vou tonight. We have much to discuss."*

Lady Margaret had invited us to a dinner with the bibliophiles.

When I returned to my room, Jeeves said that my current attire was, in no uncertain terms, unfit for evening wear. He had laid out some more appropriate clothes, which he helped me don, including black tights, a turquoise tunic with a gold braided belt and a black and gold cape. The shoes resembling slippers were remarkably comfortable but not suited for wearing outdoors in the often-muddy pathways and roadways. I thought I would be more used to these outfits by now, but I still felt like a ballet dancer in tights and tutu about to perform.

When I knocked on Colleen's door to take her to dinner, my jaw dropped, for she looked stunning. Evidently, Lady Margaret, seeing how poorly we dressed, had ordered the servants, including a lady's maid for Colleen, to spare no effort in making us presentable. Her hair was professionally coiffed into an updo under a stylish triangular black hat. A regal purple gown fit tightly around her surprisingly thin waist and ample breasts, leading to white and purple trimmed sleeves. A gold belt tightly fit her waist that cascaded to a green triangle in the front, trimmed in ermine accented with complementary black, vertical triangles. She also wore two gold necklaces, one tightly around her neck and the other leading to her low-cut square, revealing bodice.

I told her, "Colleen, you look absolutely amazing. You will be the belle of the ball."

Her face displayed a mixture of embarrassment, pride and excitement, for she had never attended such an affair in her life. As a mother of five children from humble Ireland trying to make a go of it in a male-dominated business, dreams of attending such a ball had long since vanished.

When we reached the reception, I could see many of the lords and ladies' heads turn toward Colleen. She stood straight but still looked uneasy until someone she knew who had visited the shop, a Lord Baltimore, approached, complimenting her on her stunning appearance, then engaged her in a discussion regarding one of our books he had just read. This did much to relax her.

A steady stream of nobles approached me, asking a variety of questions regarding the Spanish literature I had acquired. At one point, I found myself locked in a discussion regarding Seneca, Maimonides and Greek philosophy—not subjects I felt I was an expert on. Still, at least I had perused their books, which no one else would have the opportunity to do until we printed them. Rather than them instructing me, it felt odd to be lecturing learned professors. We spoke about Greek philosophers, my favorite being Aristotle. Then Edwin Smith, a Cambridge philosophy professor, asked me about Seneca and Stoicism, something he was unfamiliar with. Fortunately, I had dived into the works of Seneca while waiting for the transcriptions in Salamanca and found these fascinating.

I told him the little I knew about the subject, hoping I would not embarrass myself, "According to Seneca's teachings, the Stoics believe one should live in the moment—that the path to happiness is found in accepting the moment as it presents itself. They also preach that we should not allow ourselves to be controlled by the desire for pleasure or the fear of pain. Happiness can be cultivated by using one's mind to understand the world, to do one's part in nature's plan, by working together, and treating others fairly and justly."

Professor Smith thought what I said was enlightening and asked me to "Please, continue." Since I had not yet embarrassed myself, I plowed onward.

"Professor, according to my understanding from reading Seneca, the Stoics are especially known for teaching that virtue is the only good for mankind and that external things, such as health, wealth, and pleasure, are neither good nor bad in themselves but have value as material for virtue to act upon. For instance, if you are wealthy and you are charitable and use your wealth to help others, this is virtuous. Or, if you are healthy and help, say, an elderly widow repair her leaking roof, this too is virtuous."

"What is unvirtuous then?" another professor inquired."

"The Stoics say that certain destructive emotions resulted from errors in judgment, and they believed people should aim to maintain a mindset that is in sync with nature. Because of this, they thought the best indication of an individual's philosophy was not what a person said but how a person behaved. In other words, what they did. Since they thought everything was rooted in nature, to live the good life, one had to understand the rules of nature."

I found these texts particularly interesting because they reinforced my love of being outdoors and hiking in the woods, for these restored my soul and provided balance to my digitally-dominated life.

"Seneca emphasized that because virtue is sufficient for happiness, a sage would be emotionally resilient to misfortune."

"Throughout our lives, we all face adversities, but, as I understand, if we were to live a stoic life, we would be in a better position to persevere. Think about those who you know who have endured terrible misfortune. Isn't it amazing how some can endure such trauma, complain little about their troubles, and still be relatively happy? Those who weather the pain and misfortune we all face well are stoic. This belief is similar to the meaning of the phrase "stoic calm"—a Stoic views that only a sage can be considered truly free, and that all moral corruptions are equally vicious."

The second professor said, "This all sounds very interesting. How would you summarize what he thought?"

I paused to jog my memory, collected my thoughts, then with emphasis, said, "As I recall, some of Seneca's key teachings are:

First: Live Every Day as If It Were Your last.
Second: We should Eat to Live rather than Live to Eat.
Third: Focus on the Small Things.
Fourth: Failure Is Natural, Regret Is Foolish.
Fifth: Throw Away All Vanity."

By then, I had acquired an enthusiastic audience, who nodded approvingly as I completed my impromptu dissertation.

It seemed interesting that 2000 years earlier, the Stoics pondered the same kind of questions we did in the 21st century, which appear in self-help books, or on talk shows, or on the Web or in podcasts. From the little I knew of Buddhism, which sprang up some 500 years before the Stoics, Stoicism seemed somewhat similar. I wondered if the Stoics got some of their ideas from Buddhism, perhaps after Alexander conquered India. Maybe.

During the discussion, I noticed a steady stream of nobles approaching Colleen, who had become more comfortable, having been introduced to them during the presentation and who had ordered books from her. Cleverly, she had Jeeves acquire a table, a chair and several quills and inkwells, then lined paper for the lords and ladies to list the books from our easel behind her, adding their name and address of where to deliver their orders.

After introducing himself, the Duke of Baltimore asked me, "Is Colleen your wife?"

"No, sir, she is an associate who runs our operation here in London."

"She is a ravishing beauty, but there is more to her. She seems so different from the typical courtier ladies consumed with gossip, politics and the latest fashion. Tell me more about her."

"Well, her husband passed away a little over a year ago, and she has five adorable children. She had helped her husband John, our agent here in London. When he died, I came to London to find a suitable replacement but could find no one nearly as qualified as she. Since then, she has blossomed and has proven to be a valuable asset to our thriving business. I have found her to be a strong, intelligent, kind and capable woman. Oh, and she is perhaps the best-read woman in all of London, for she consumes all of our books on various subjects and Caxton's too."

"Perhaps that is why I find her so enchanting. I know of no other woman who is so accomplished and is so stunningly pretty, and she has an enticing, soulful look that can only be acquired by such readings."

I did not realize it until dinner was announced, but I was the guest of honor, seated next to Lady Margaret, who sat next to King Henry. Sitting next to me on my left and feeling more at home, Colleen smiled her brilliant smile, grasped my hand, and said, "This is a dream that I never want to end. Across from us were Queen Elizabeth and her Mother Elizabeth, the former queen.

I noticed the large array of servants tending to the dinner—perhaps as many as one per every two guests. Without modern conveniences or appliances, I could not imagine how much effort it would have been to put on such a feast. I saw the servers bringing dish after dish, serving wine and ale, but there must've been a regiment of servants behind the scene in the kitchen preparing it all. The nobles paid little attention to them as if they were invisible, but I remembered from binging on Downton Abbey what such a feast required.

Regally attired, tall and slender, with thin lips, long nose, and face, the king bore a remarkable resemblance to his generous, intellectual mother. I remembered that she was only thirteen years older than him. From my iPhone research, I remembered that he was about 45, which would make her 58.

When King Henry first spoke to me, I was flustered. "Sir Rand, you seem like such a large man to be so involved in literature. Might you be a man of arms, too? "

This was a question that I had previously faced, the first time from King Edward, but this time I could better respond. "Your majesty, I cannot honestly say that I am an accomplished warrior, for I am a man of peace, but I am adequate with a spear, and I have recently learned how to wield a sword from one of the foremost swordsmen in Spain, which came in handy when I recently fought three bandits there." Then, at his request, I told him the story of how I saved the Spanish manuscripts, which he found entertaining.

"And how far can you throw a spear, he queried. "

"During the Bunkillarny games, I tossed it over 180 feet."

"And did you win the contest?"

"Yes, I did, Your Majesty."

"Oh, that is marvelous. I want to see you compete against one of our best javelin throwers. I heard about these splendid games from one of your countrymen, Sir Reginald, a magnificent warrior he was. Surely you know him?"

Hearing the name of my nemesis filled me with disgust, which I tried mightily not to reflect to King Henry. "Yes, Your Majesty, I do indeed; he conducted the games and gave me my awards."

"I hear that you have the gift of sight. What do you foresee for my kingdom?"

I was not sure how King Henry knew about this. Since this was the king, I could see no way of avoiding the question, but I wanted to be very careful about what I said. I certainly did not want to offend him, but I did not want to give too much away that might alter the course of history. While at the Spanish court, I visited a couple of popular fortune tellers, primarily because I was being asked such questions there and wanted to respond appropriately. Many of the nobles consulted them regularly, which seemed to be a popular service of the time. They were very vague, which helped me respond similarly.

"What I foresee is somewhat clouded, but it appears that the house of Tudor will last for over a hundred years."

"And what do you foresee for my dynasty?"

"One of your heirs will be a mighty king who will be part of a major European transformation (Henry VIII, his son.) This king will have many wives."

"What kind of transformation? Are you foreseeing a revolution?"

Not wanting to speak about the Protestant Reformation, which would be shocking to the fervent Catholic royals, "No, Your Majesty, certainly not. Rather, it is an offshoot of the new technology of printing. The spreading of knowledge across the continent over the last fifty years has already resulted in a renaissance that is gaining momentum in Italy and is spreading throughout Europe." I smiled at Lady Margaret and continued, "Your lordship's mother has done much to encourage this renaissance here in London."

"Yes, she has spoken to me about this, and what are your thoughts on this renaissance?"

"The Renaissance traces its roots back to Rome and Pax Romana 1000 years ago, before all the plagues and wars. It will result in a revitalization of the accomplishments of civilization with amazing advances in the arts, sciences, philosophy, and literature. It will be a time of discovery, exploration and expansion. The center of the Renaissance is on the Italian peninsula, where amazing artists and writers are currently working on their masterpieces. Our printing will play a major role, for we can print a hundred in the time it takes to copy a couple of books. Since millions of books are produced throughout Europe every year, the knowledge and wisdom they contain will spread like wildfire throughout Europe. By sponsoring Caxton and expanding education at Oxford and Cambridge, your noble mother is greatly expanding the intelligence of your realm that will serve you and your heirs well. You will be better able to conquer the challenges to come."

"There is also a revolution in art, the results of which are much more realistic paintings and sculptures by magnificent artists."

"As with Pax Romana at the height of Rome's power, will there be an end to the wars?"

"Unfortunately, no, my lord."

"And, what of my other heirs?"

From what I learned from Colleen of the War of the Roses and all the challengers to Henry becoming king, I could tell this was an important subject to him. "One whom you would not expect to rule will have the longest reign in England when the nation will become truly mighty (Queen Elizabeth I)." Recognizing how much power his mother and mother-in-law applied, despite his son Henry the Eighth's unsuccessful quest for a male heir from his six wives, it was not surprising that a woman would rule for so long. Still, I dared not tell the king that one of his successors would be a woman. Actually, including Mary, the granddaughter of Isabella, two of Henry the Eighth's daughters, Henry the Seventh's granddaughters would rule England.

"How do you know these things? Do these come to you in a dream or a vision?"

Since I saw these on my iPhone, there was some truth to what he said, "Yes, Your Majesty, it is like that. For me tis like reading a book or looking at a painting."

After a couple of ales, I became more relaxed talking to the king. I found him to be very amiable, friendly, intelligent, and dignified. He exhibited the kind of personal magnetism that drew people to him, and as the dinner proceeded and he too had more ale, he became highly spirited.

The table setting did not contain silverware, which is why Jeeves supplied me with a knife and spoon. There was no fork yet. I could have brought my Swiss Army knife with its fork, but this would have seemed out of place and drawn unwanted attention. The meal consisted of poached salmon and then several courses of meat – lamb, beef roast, capons and pork from a whole pig that actually had an apple in its mouth and was roasted in honey—all accompanied by constantly flowing ale. Other than a squash soup at the start of the meal, there were few vegetables. With no fork, I noticed that I should hold the meat on the platters we all shared and with my left thumb and fingers, cut it with the knife in my right hand. Surprisingly, I thought the fare at Bunkillarny castle to be more elaborate, but Lady Catherine had employed two French chefs.

Marie sat at the opposite end of the table, whom I occasionally stole glances towards—she enticing me with her enchanting eyes and as usual she was the object of affection of all the lords in her proximity. All I could think of was her. I wanted to crawl under the table to her but knew, according to protocol, I could not leave until the king did.

Since this was the Queen Mother's intellectual group, there were many enthusiastic discussions along the long table. Those who attended were extremely animated and there was a copious amount of cerebral energy filling the room fueled by ale and wine. I enjoyed the discussions, but all I could think about was Marie. My heart was full of Marie, and I could no longer wait to see her, but she had seemed so mysterious when we met in the hallway.

When the dinner finally ended, I was approached by my professor friends. I lost sight of her and when I went to where she had been and then anxiously searched the rest of the hall, I could not find her. I did not know where she went. I thought about wandering around the palace asking for her, but the palace was so immense and confusing, and I was not sure that my inquiries would be welcomed by her—that somehow, these might cause her harm. After dinner, before departing, while the discussions were still percolating and seeming like they might continue late into the night, I stopped to thank Lady Margaret, "My dear Lady Margaret, thank you so much for your reception of the Spanish manuscripts. I have greatly enjoyed sharing these with your soirée. This is a marvelous group and such a marvelous meal."

"Thank you for bringing these to us, Mr. Roberts. I wish you Godspeed on your sail back to Ireland and enthusiastically await your books' arrival back here in London. "

"Your majesty, there is a lady here who is related to our sponsor, my lord King Edward, whom I met in Bunkillarny, Lady Marie. I was wondering if you knew where she might be?"

With a broad smile, she said, "Oh yes, Lady Marie, she is such a delight and so enticing to our young lords. Since she is so interested in literature, I expected to see her at our soirée. You might find her in the western parlor."

"When I finally ferreted my way to the parlor, I found a large group of lords and ladies milling around, but no Marie. I wandered the maze of halls searching for her for what seemed like a desperately long time, what seemed like a nightmare, where you wondered aimlessly never able to find what you seek. Then, as I turned yet another corner, I saw her down the distant hall and ran towards her just as she disappeared around a perpendicular hall. I ran as fast as I could and called out to her, but she did not respond. When I caught up to her and grabbed her elbow, she turned, and I realized that the person with similar hair and gown was not her. Dejected, I headed back to my room. *

My head down, resigning myself to a restless, disappointing night, I eventually found my way back to my room, opened the door and there she was! There she was, more beautiful than ever with her cascading lemon-highlighted-brown locks, deep, beautifully shaped brown eyes, flawless white skin, firm chin, dainty upturned nose, high rosy cheeks accenting her perfect white, glistening smile—features that fit together so well, one complementing the other—the face that had brightened my dreams and inspired me over the last months. There she was in a royal blue gown trimmed in gold around her ample bodice, caressing her too-thin waist and shapely figure sculpted by years of riding. She was more beautiful than I remembered, more beautiful than I could imagine—she took my breath away.

She asked if I would like some port from an elegantly shaped crystal decanter she had brought with her, along with two crystal goblets. Then she poured the velvety, dark purple elixir and toasted my success that day, "Here is to vou Rand," mon cheri." I wanted to scoop her up into my arms and kiss her but was unsure if my forwardness would be met with acquiescence, for I detected an unwelcome awkwardness between us."

She stepped back and sat at the small, circular maple table with two matching chairs. In her enticing French accent, she said, "Randalle, I must tell you about what has happened in Bunkillarny. (She paused.) With Reginald ogling and threatening me, it was not long before I had to leave. First, I went to Scotland, where I heard that Lord Edward, your sponsor, had died in a hunting accident."

The news shocked me. He seemed indestructible. "I can't believe he's dead!"

"I immediately sailed for Bunkillarny and was there to comfort dear Aunt Catherine and her lovely children—my cousins, but because of Reginald, I could not bear to stay."

"As you know, it takes a long time for news to travel from Ireland to here. I heard his son, John, would soon be king, but there was some discord. The O'Donnells supported Edward's younger son, Patrick. They did not want John to be crowned because he was the son-in-law of King Albert of Nealland, and being king of Bunkillarny would upset the delicate balance between the two powerful northern clans. Then I heard rumors that John had been deposed, and I imagine that cousin Patrick had assumed the throne. I don't know if this is true, though. You know how these things can become so muddled like the houses of the White and Red Roses here in England have been."

"I certainly hope that John succeeded Edward, for I hear he followed in his father's footsteps. Patrick is a fine lad, but he is too young, bashful and small. Besides, John is older; isn't this how the successions should go?"

I could not help but notice that she seemed nervous and that her glass of port was empty, whilst mine was still half-full. As she filled both goblets, I asked, "What have you been up to lately?" a question no doubt inappropriate in the 15th-century vernacular.

"Well, I spent some time in Glasgow with a marvelous couple, where I met many Scottish royals and nobles. They are delightful, although staid, people who are even more reserved than the English and much more so than us French and the Irish." Then, I came here to London hoping to find you, but you were no longer here, and I heard you had gone to Spain. You were gone for so long."

Attempting to change the subject, she asked how I found the Spanish? "It is unwise to make generalizations about individuals, for each person is unique, but in my travels, I have found certain characteristics that apply to their populace.

"They are a warm, friendly people, probably more like the Irish than the English. Francisco Alverez and his family were very hospitable and immensely helpful. I would never have been able to acquire the treasured texts if it were not for them.

I would also have been robbed and likely killed if not for Francisco. He taught me how to duel. Without having learned to do so, I do not doubt that I would have lost my treasure and my life. I also must thank John the smithy who gave me two pistols. Those really came in handy. I even refitted one of the matchlocks, so I did not have to light it first." In the back of my mind, I hoped that given my pitiful performance against Reginald, my learning how to wield a sword and an improved pistol would impress her.

I wanted to ask her what her plans were. Sensing that she did not want to tell me much, she asked, "What do you plan to do with the treasured documents?"

"These will keep our print shop busy for over a year, and judging by the reception here today, they should be well received and highly profitable. Just today, Colleen took orders for 150 books. I am sure there are many titles you would like to read, such as El Cid and the works of Seneca. Once these are printed, I will give you copies. I think Michael will make me a partner in his business, which will be very successful and afford a fine life for a wife and a family. There will be immense opportunities over the next decades, especially after Columbus's discoveries. I plan to invest in such highly profitable ventures."

"Columbus's discoveries?"

"Oh, I met a fascinating captain in Córdoba from Genoa. He plans to sail east to the Orient, which will vastly reduce the required time. He will find a land laden with gold, silver, rare foods, exotic animals, billions of game—an immense fertile territory far greater than all of Europe, sights beyond belief, and unimaginable riches.

"Is this something you see with your sight? It sounds too unbelievable to be true."

"Yes, but there is no doubt what I say is true, for I have been there."

Despite the preposterousness of what I just told her, she seemed to believe me. I was considering popping the question to her at that point, and I wanted her to know more about me and who I really was so that she could make an informed decision about our life together. I had been worried that not being from a royal family and having a modest income would not be attractive to her, but I now thought that my prospects had greatly improved and that she might consider such a proposal when she again changed the subject.

"This Colleen I met, she seems very, oh, I cannot think of the words, very accomplished and very attractive. Are you in love with her?"

When she said this, she did not seem jealous but rather relieved, which worried me. I assured her, "No, Colleen is our agent here in London. We are not involved."

"Oh mon cheri, vou have such a funny way of expressing yourself." Seeing the dejected look on my face, she continued, "I find it delightful, for I have not met anyone on my travels that compares to vou. Someone so strong and virile yet so intelligent and interested in literature, too. Then she came over to me, caressed my face with her hands, looked into my eyes with a sultry look melting any resistance I might have had, then daintily, suggestively sat down on my lap, very slowly moving closer until our lips met in an explosion of passion.

As if I was being transported to another world, I lost all sense of time and was in a state of ecstasy kissing those desirous thick, perfectly shaped lips, then caressing her more fervently as she responded in the same ancient rhythms, becoming closer and closer becoming as one—lost into each other. Minutes seemed like hours; hours seemed like minutes as we entwined. Then I scooped her up and lifted her into the bed.*

After a long, passionate night and exhausted sleep, I awoke hoping it was all not just a dream until I saw her beautiful, sleepy face next to mine.

I caressed her, and after she awoke with a smile and a yawn, not wanting to wait any longer, I told her I loved her and asked her to marry me.

"Oh, me amore, I love you too, and there is no one I would rather spend the rest of my life with, but I am afraid this is impossible."

"But I can find a way to work it out. Whatever you need, I will find a way to make it happen. If it is a noble you want, I will find a way to become a noble. Queen Isabella said she would make me one. If it is a fine manor house you desire, I will acquire one or two or three in Paris, in London, and maybe a chateau on the Riviera. I know what is to come, which will grant us whatever you want."

"But it is not up to me. I am sorry, but my life is not my own. When I had not seen you for so long, my uncle, King Charles, betrothed me to a Hapsburg prince. Someone I knew as a child. I had refused two others, who, because I found them unacceptable, he forgave me. But even though he is not as magnifique as you, this prince is kind and acceptable, and I could not refuse. I thought you might be dead, and I had mourned your loss."

"But what about last night? I, I thought you cared for me deeply."

"I do care more than you know. I love you, too. Please forgive me, but I wanted you so much. I have never given my heart to anyone else but you. I did so at great risk. If anyone were to catch me in your room, I would be disgraced forever, and my family would be disgraced. Accept this as my gift to you, something I will forever cherish. I leave for Paris tomorrow."

"Is there nothing I can do to convince you we would be happier together? The world is changing, and there will be many opportunities in the future. We can create a life that will bring you much happiness. Trust me. I can make it happen."

"But me amore, unfortunately, I have been cast as a royal, a pretty creature of the court, who is unsuitable for anything else. I have been given much, but much is required of me too, especially from my family, whose wishes I must honor. My uncle, the king, feels that this alliance is important for the security and future of my beloved France. I am not suitable as a merchant's spouse, not even a very wealthy merchant's one. Even though I would be with you, I would eventually be unhappy, and neither would you. Instead of helping you as your partner in life to acquire your fortune, I would deplete you, and I could not stand to do that. You will find someone who is more suited than I. Someone who will be your partner and help you to obtain your destiny. Someone who will magnify your copious abilities, not drain you."

I racked my brain to find an argument that would convince her, but just could not think of anything. She made herself ready, we caressed one momentous last time. I peered out the door to ensure no one was in the corridor and she vanished.*

Feeling dejected and depressed, I hastily packed my bag, thanked Jeeves, gathered Colleen and Stephen, and quickly left the palace. Befitting my dour mood, it was a dim, foggy, cold, rainy ride back to London. I felt as if part of me had died, and a future that just the previous day seemed so bright, I now cared little about. The clipitty-clop of the rhythmic horses' hooves, the whirl of the wheels against the ground, the swishing of droplets spinning off the wheels, the bouncing on the dirt road, the muted, dreary scenery passing by seemed reassuring. Life would go on, and I might be OK, but I oscillated between a sense that nothing had really happened and total despair. I had hoped for so much, which seemed within my grasp but now had vanished.

I thought about traveling to Paris and making some grand gesture similar to those in those romantic comedies, but given Marie's steadfastness, I realized such an attempt would surely fail and would only serve to embarrass her and jeopardize her position. That may have worked in the 21st century, but not here in the 15th, not in this situation.

Expecting me to be thrilled with the previous day's successes, Colleen sensed that I had been rejected and sympathetically wrapped her arm around my back. She was still flying high from the night's activities, which she had said was the highlight of her life—thrilled to meet the king, the queen, and the Queen Mother, who surprisingly supported her career, not an experience someone in her class would ever expect to happen. I felt badly that I could not share her excitement, but I was just too depressed.

Back at her home, I went to bed early, feeling that my dour mood negatively affected the children. The next day, I stayed in bed until afternoon. When I came down, Patricia was busy teaching the younger children, and Colleen was at the books.

I went to the nearby stables, saddled up Chester, and rode in the country. Only a few blocks away from the center of Westminster, the long, dusty, aimless, winding ride over the hills and valleys on the dirt road, through the fields, woods, and hamlets fit my dour mood.

I knew I did not have much battery life left in my iPhone, but played my blues list. I did not care much, but after a few minutes, I shut it down. The last song, the iconic theme from the old Midnight Cowboy movie with Jon Voight after down-and-out Dustin Hoffman dies on the bus to Florida, kept playing over and over in my head.

Upon my return, Colleen showed me a handful of invitations from various countesses and duchesses to have dinner with them. She had received one from lord Baltimore to accompany him to one of those dinners. Evidently, our presentation the previous day was a stellar success within London society.

I knew attending these dinners would greatly improve our business prospects, but I just could not get up for these events. I needed to go home. So, I packed up my trunk and retrieved the treasured multimillion-dollar books from Colleen's hiding place. Colleen had also acquired some books from the monasteries around London to have printed at our shop. I split these into two trunks, putting half of the Spanish document in each in case one was lost at sea, damaged, or stolen. Harry found a ship leaving for Dublin the next day that I would be on. Colleen gave me a letter and a present for her brother Tommy, who still lives in Bunkillarny.

On one of our trips, she asked if I had met her brother, who I recognized was our younger apprentice, someone whom Gwendolyn had taught, showed promise, and had been hired by Michael. The package contained a new suit of clothes for him from a fine London haberdasher.

Bukillarny Castle

Bunkillarny Castle high upon the hill overlooking the town and its pic-turesque bay.

FIFTEEN

The Troubles

Early the next morning, I said goodbye to Colleen and the children. Stephen drove me to the dock with Chester tied behind, who would join me on the journey. With smooth sailing, the voyage to Dublin was relatively uneventful. I still felt depressed and rejected, but trying to focus on the future, I thought about how we would print the Spanish documents—which ones we should print first, what artwork we should add, etc., making notes on the pages with my quill pen. I also thought about Michael and Gwendolyn and all of those I had met in Bunkillarny. It had been nearly a year, and I was anxious to see them again.

I missed my own time and place even more and thought about how I might get back there. If I could only travel through that portal in the cave, I could sell my books for tens of millions, or who knows how much, and use the money to rehire everybody from our team for that next, even more, spectacular app, which would change the world.

After Marie rejected my marriage proposal, I desperately wanted to forget what had happened. Going forward in time 500 years, would be the ultimate way to move on.*

Upon my arrival in Dublin, I found a small room at an inn close to the wharf, where the sailors stayed and each morning sought a ship sailing to the northern part of Ireland that would agree to drop me off at Bunkillarny. After three days with no success, I thought I might ride

Chester up north but realized riding would take three times as long, and besides, in the cool, damp Dublin weather, I had contracted a cold that would only get worse on such a long, wet, cold ride. I thought about doing it anyway but was too miserable to ride that far.

I had my dinners at a nearby sailor's pub, decorated in ship paraphernalia such as wheels, blocks and tackle, yard arms, sails, nets, oars and flags from the seafarer's various countries, where I sat at the bar by myself, drowning my sorrow in my ale, something I found therapeutic. Typically, I would tour the ancient city I had never seen, but I did not have the inclination to do so. One of the stout-drinking denizens engaged me in unwanted conversation, telling me a bit of the town's history.

The overly cheerful, smiling Irishman said, "I ken you're not from these parts, laddie, but perhaps you'd like to know something 'bout it." I said I really didn't, but he continued anyway. "Don' ya know, way back in the 10th century, when Dublin were settled by the Vikings, it served as the center of an active slave trade. The men, the women, and the children they captured from England, Wales, Normandy, and beyond were brought here. Then in 1171, King Henry II conquered Dublin and declared himself king of all o' Ireland. Dublin is now part of the English crown, called the Pale, which includes the other coastal towns along the eastern shores of Ireland such as Belfast. Us Irish always been an independent lot, and since the new 'enry be far off in London town and has plenty 'o problems o' his own, after they fights over the throne fer thirty odd years and all, he don think much 'bout us, so we do pretty much as we pleases. But, the rest o' Ireland has always done all they pleases ta do anyway, ye ken?"

After five days, I finally found a ship that, after docking in Belfast, for a steep fee, would drop me off in Bunkillarny on its way to Glasgow. Compared to my other sailings this trip would be short—less than two days.

With placid seas of no more than two or three feet, it turned out to be a mild, pleasant voyage. Hanging over the rail, breathing the fresh sea air, I greatly enjoyed viewing the unfolding Irish landscapes, scenes of farm fields and seaside villages flowing to the ocean with gentle, rolling hills and mountains sloping upwards to the horizon. The land around Belfast appeared to be atypically flat and fertile. For the first time since being rejected by Maria that night, I slept like a babe, rocking to the gentle roll of the ship, inhaling fresh sea air. As we turned western into the northern sea, the coastline became very rocky, enhanced by steep limestone cliffs. The light and dark contrasting cliffs set in emerald-green Irish soil popped out under an intense sun shining through an indigo-blue sky between puffy white clouds reminded me of the exquisite scenery along Route 1 in California—truly spectacular.

I counted down the hours until I would be home, looking forward to seeing Michael and Gwendolyn and John and all my friends and just resting for a solid week, reading in the green backyard by the peaceful river, listening to the rushing falls, zoning out. We arrived late that night. After the crew deposited my trunks at the bottom of the gangplank and cast off, I checked them for water damage, but they were fine. Fortunately, I found a surly carter I didn't know, who, with my help, deposited the heavy trunks in the back of his wagon. Normally, everyone in town was friendly, but this guy was nasty—not the welcome I expected.

We wound up the familiar hill to the main street and took the accustomed left. It would only be a few more minutes until I was home, at long last home. As the horses' hooves pounded the dirt road in a rhythmic tone, we passed two women outside an old house. The one with dark hair had a revealing red dress, whilst the one with the red hair had a skimpy, low-cut, black dress. As we passed, the brunette, walking along the side of the cart, said, "Want a go of it yer lordship?" I noticed two new pubs across from each other, a fight spilling out of one just as we passed. It seemed strange that even though it was Saturday night, McNab's pub was already closed. Even though it had been less than a year, much seemed to have changed.

Getting ever closer, I could now hear the roaring falls in the distance, my long sought-after goal coming ever closer, time compressing. With baited anticipation, I knew it would only be a minute more. Lifting the heavy Brass knocker pounding on the door, I had a heightened sense of expectation. After such a long, demanding journey, I was finally home, home at last. Seamus opened the door and was surprised to see me. Smiling broadly, I told him to go and tell Michael and Gwendolyn I had arrived. He said, "Michael has been arrested, and Gwendolyn left this morning."

Shocked at the news, deeply disappointed that I would not see them before I could ask the obvious questions, a sleepy-eyed, large man came up behind Seamus and said, "What's all of this commotion 'bout?"

"Master Hugh, this is Rand Roberts. He used to work here."

"Oh yes, I remember you from the games. You did rather well at the throwing of the stone, as I recall. Sorry, but we have no need for your services any longer."

Puzzled, I asked, "Where is Michael, and what are you doing here?"

In a sleepy, matter-of-fact, flat voice, he replied, "He's bin arrested for sedition, and I be running the shop on behalf of the crown now."

Before I could say anything, the door slammed resoundingly in my face. I felt a large hand on my shoulder and turned around to see that it was John, the smithy. He shook my hand vigorously in both of his large, callused ones and said, "'Tis good to see you, lad, I'd imagine you have a lot of questions. Come with me."

He led me to their kitchen, poured three fingers of whiskey into each of our glasses then told me, "Michael's bin arrested by Reginald for publishing a sheet called the Truth. He wrote about what was really 'apnin in the shire. Since it reflected poorly on ole Reginald he arrested 'im and locked 'im up.

"But why would King John allow that?"

"I suppose you heard that King Edward allegedly died in a hunting accident?"

"Yes, I did. Why do you say allegedly?"

"Well, the only ones to witness his death were Reginald and Boston. To many o' us, it seemed questionable. But thas not the kind of thing Michael wrote about because there was no evidence otherwise. Sadly, Prince John is not the king. At the battle of Neilland, Reginald was supposed to 'elp John 'gainst the O'Donnells, but he turned on them and instead fought the O'Neals. We are not sure whether John was killed or escaped."

"Then, wouldn't Patrick become king with his mother as regent?"

"Yes, Patrick was crowned, but in addition to his mother, Reginald is co-regent."

"Well, why would Patrick allow Michael to be arrested? They were close, and Michael was even his tutor."

"Soon after Reginald conquered the O'Callaghan's, Patrick's health began to worsen and supposedly Queen Catherine took 'im to a warmer clime to recover. That left Reginald in charge of the kingdom. Since then, he and Boston have cloistered all the troops and doubled the taxes to support their wars o' conquest. I suspects it won't be long til he wars agin on some other unsuspecting shire."

"Is that why I saw so many troops in town and what looked like a brothel."

"Yes."

I took a steep slug of whiskey to help me digest all I had heard, then asked, "Who is the big fellow who showed up at the door of the print shop?"

"That be Hugh. He is Reginald's right-'and-man, who has been overseeing the press for some time now. Boston has been writing articles favoring the new regime for the Bunkillarny Reader."

My head was spinning, and not from the whiskey. "Where has Gwendolyn gone?"

"She went to her grandfather's castle. Don't let Seamus know, though. Gwendolyn suspects he may have had something to do with Michael's arrest and does not trust him. Besides, he and Hugh are very close."

"I will ride there immediately."

"But it's a long ride and it is late at night. You can stay here and leave early in the morn."

"Thank you, John, but I feel I have to go to her. There is something you can do for me, though. Can I store my trunks somewhere where Hugh and Seamus will never find them? They contain very valuable documents I hope we will be able to print soon."

"Of course, I know just the place where no one will find 'em."

We awkwardly carried the trunks down the steep stairs into the basement and deposited them behind a false wall.

After saddling up Chester and thanking him, I told John that the pistols he gave me saved my life more than once. Then I galloped away.

Fortunately, by now, I was better able to ride Chester. After being cooped up in the ship, he seemed to enjoy the exercise, and since I could barely hold him back, we galloped most of the way there. At the fast clip, we made it to the O'Flannery castle by the middle of the night. I knocked on the large door knocker opened by a yawning, sleepy-eyed servant. At first, he refused my entrance, but after my insistence, he went to fetch his lordship and Gwendolyn. As soon as she saw me, with her white nightgown rippling in her wake, she ran to me and embraced me. She would not let go for a long time, saying, "I am so happy you are here! So, so happy!" Then she kneeled on the stone floor, crossed herself, and thanked God that he had answered her prayers.

Even though she was sleepy, she looked incredible—more like a woman than the girl I had last seen on the dock—a vision of beauty. I guess facing adversity tends to mature you, which for some brings out their character.

Including the lord, the three of us went into the library, where they confirmed what I had heard from John, adding that if Gwendolyn did not marry Reginald, Michael would be executed.

They would be leaving later today for Bunkillarny to attend his trial, which would commence the following day. After saying that I would be joining them, which seemed to relieve Gwendolyn, Lord O'Flannery insisted that I get some sleep and had the servant lead me to a room. After a couple of hours, tying Chester to the back of the wagon, we left for Bunkillarny. Sitting beside her, she smiled and laid her head on my shoulder. I felt a magnetism between us, realizing how much I had missed my "little sister."

Once there, we met with Kevin Stanforth, Esquire at McNab's, a lawyer from Dublin who would defend Michael. Kevin had worked for King Edward, advising him on legal matters and assisting him at the king's court and council meetings. I had met him before but had never gotten to know him well. He had a formidable profile with a large upper body that resembled a cube, a large bald head, unusually thick eyebrows, and a deep, resounding voice—he looked imposing, just how you wanted a defense lawyer to look like. When Reginald took over the kingdom, he dismissed Kevin, who had returned to Dublin.

Commonly, cases would be heard in the throne room. But Boston and Reginald, realizing the magnitude of this case, decided to hold it in the main hall, which, by the time we arrived was filled with perhaps two hundred people. Reginald, having enjoyed the success of his rallies, along with Boston, decided that such a large trial would enhance their power by making Michael an example, thereby discouraging any other challengers to his absolute authority. We sat on the front bench next to

Michael, who was ecstatic to see me, the two of us hugging; he telling me how much it meant that I was there and how glad he was I had returned safely.

There was a loud buzz in the hall when the disreputable Boston appeared. After a flourish of trumpets, he introduced Reginald, who now wore luxurious, regal, purple robes flowing to the floor. He sat behind a tall table similar to a lectern on the stage that had been used for the band and awards ceremony during the games. With Boston seated on a tall stool below him, Boston read the charges consisting of sedition against the kingdom and King Patrick.

Reginald asked how Michael pleaded, guilty or not guilty, upon which Stanforth rose, stood on the stage, and authoritatively, in a booming voice that filled the massive hall, said, "Your lordship, I am Kevin Stanforth, and I will be representing Michael McCarron in this case. He pleads not guilty. As I am sure you are aware, under English law, Michael is entitled to a jury of his peers to decide this case, which I assume you intend to select before we conduct the trial."

Confused, duplicitous Boston and Reginald looked at each other, each seeking an answer from the other. They had intended to have a quick trial, convict Michael, and then have a wedding, or if Gwendolyn refused a public execution. They did not expect that Michael would have a lawyer or that they would face any obstacles.

Deceitful Boston took the stage and said, "We do not need a jury. As the regent, standing in for the king, Lord Reginald will decide this case."

Stanforth replied," According to the Magna Carta signed by the King of England in the early 13th century, he is entitled to a jury of his peers."

"But English law does not apply here in Ireland!"

"My dear sir, it certainly does, for, at approximately the same time, we had the institution of the Irish Magna Carta, which established the same justice system."

"But those laws only apply in the Pale—those Irish coastal towns under the direct control of King Henry."

"Your lordship, as you well know, I served under King Edward, and as a precedent, he followed the Hibernian Magna Carta."

Looking exceedingly extremely disturbed by this unwelcome intrusion, duplicitous Boston continued, "But that law only applies to Norman, male landholders. McCarron, the accused, is a pure Irishman;

therefore, such laws do not apply to him. According to an act passed earlier this century that forbade marriages between Normans and the Irish, even if he was half Norman, it would not apply to him."

"But that law has not been followed, and even in the Pale, few pure Normans are left. Besides Michael McCarron, has all the rights afforded to the Normans."

"That's not possible!"

"I have a document here registered in Dublin that grants him all the Norman rights. King Edward filed and paid for this a year ago for all of his council members and several of the prominent merchants in town, including Lord Reginald. I filed the papers myself on his behalf."

Looking highly confused, Boston conferred privately with Reginald. Reginald stating, "He shall have his jury, which shall consist of the council members who, since he was a council member, are therefore his peers. I see that many of them are in attendance here. My men will round up the others, and we will reconvene later this afternoon." He took his staff and pounded vigorously on the hollow stage floor creating a booming sound resonating throughout the hall.

"But your lordship, as I understand, some of the council members are soldiers who are not his peers."

"Overruled!"

With that, people began filing out of the hall. We decided to adjourn to the inn for lunch, where the four of us would be staying. Other than a speeding ticket, I had never been in a courtroom and had not watched many legal shows that populate TV. I needed to clear my mind, so I elected to ride Chester back to town. Besides knowing that the Magna Carta was a famous legal document, I knew nothing about it or even that there was an Irish Magna Carta, but was glad Stanforth did.

Somehow, I thought everyone had the same rights we did in the 21st century, something that greatly troubled me. So, the laws only applied to Norman male landowners. With half the population women, the vast majority Irish or a mix of Irish and Norman blood, and only a handful of wealthy landholders, doing the math in my head, these laws would only apply to something like 5% of the population.

As I rode on, I remembered that on PBS, I had seen that after the Normans conquered England around 1066, the Anglo-Saxons had been discriminated against, and the Normans had taken over much of the land in England—the Anglo-Saxons' land, making them in effect serfs on the land they had owned, little better than slaves, with virtually no rights. The Normans became the landed gentry and their oppressors.

I was glad that we all had such rights in the United States. Then I remembered that similar to England, the United States had been established as a republic and that initially, the only people who could vote were white, protestant, male property owners. Women, Indians, Blacks, Asians, Catholics, the poor, Irish, Germans, Eastern Europeans, Italians, etc., were frequently denied such rights. It was not until the 1920s that women could vote, and not until the late 1960s that Black Americans were guaranteed the right to vote!

So, initially only about 5% of Americans could vote too. Indeed, the first thirty-four U.S. presidents, up until John F. Kennedy, were wealthy, white, protestant males. Come to think of it, only one other was not a white, protestant male—Obama, until Biden. Ironically, this all helped me feel better about the state of justice in 15th-century Ireland and how much the United States had evolved over its relatively short history.

At the inn, I joined Stanforth, O'Flannery, Brogan, and Gwendolyn discussing the trial strategy. There were fourteen members of the council, two of whom Stanforth felt should immediately be disqualified, Reginald and Boston, because they were presiding over the trial.

He would also attempt to disqualify the three knights loyal to Reginald, which left nine. Lord Brogan said they had a solid two votes and probably another two who would not want to convict Michael. Two others held positions given to them by Reginald, so they would vote to convict. Of course, three more would have to be selected to replace the knights, and Stanforth was sure he could get at least one for Michael.

That left the tally at five in favor of Michael and three against, with four undecideds. He would try to require a unanimous vote but realized that Reginald would likely not go for that. Since a majority would be needed to convict, he would be innocent if just one of the two undecideds went with Michael.

Back at the trial, with hundreds now in attendance, dastardly Boston called the noisy hall to order. The ten council members sat at a table on top of the stage, who, along with himself and Reginald, would comprise the jury.

Stanforth–"Your honor, I object that you have included yourself and Lord Boston as jury members. The judge cannot be on the jury, and neither can the prosecutor." Surprisingly, Reginald allowed the motion without objection and selected two more jurors seemingly at random from those in attendance.

Stanforth–"Your honor, three of the jury members are knights who directly report to you as their general. These men should also be disqualified from serving on the jury. Besides, they are not peers of Michael McCarron's."

"They shall remain on the jury because they have been council members for some time now and occupy more than just a knight's role."

Stanforth, "Am I to understand that a conviction requires a unanimous vote by this jury?"

Enjoying his power in front of such a large audience, Reginald ruled, "No, all that shall be required is a majority. And I will hear no further objections." Disgusting Boston smirked at Reginald.

I did the math in my head, which made the score 6 to 6, provided that the four swing votes went for Michael, enough for a hung jury.

Boston, moving to the center of the stage and with a copy of the Truth in his hands, stated, "In this spurious document, Michael McCarron cast aspersions on the character of Lord Reginald, doubting the reason for King Patrick and Queen Catherine's departure."

Stanforth read the article out loud and argued that it merely questioned the reasons for Catharine's departure. It did not question Reginald's motives or impugn his character. "Therefore, Michael should be released post haste."

Reginald glaring at Stanforth, pounding his staff on the resonating stage floor, said, "Motion denied."

Then, the dishonorable Boston displayed three other copies of the Truth that Seamus had likely pilfered, saying that Michael had undermined the reign of Patrick and his regents for a long time.

Boston then proceeded to produce two of Catherine's maids, and two of her ladies-in-waiting testified that Patrick had indeed been sick and that Catherine had considered departing to the south of France for some time, where the abundant sunshine and warm springs would heal him.

Deplorable Boston questioned a third lady in waiting Lady Winifred, "Dear lady, how concerned was Queen Catherine for her son?"

"Oh, she be very worried for the dear boy. Day by day, he appeared to be wasting away. I had lost my oldest son, Andrew, to the plague, and Patrick was starting to look like that gaunt, pale, gray around the eyes, moving slowly, listless. You never know when someone with such a serious malady might seem fine one day, then be gone the next as me, dear Andrew were."

"And what was she like? What was her mood?"

"Catherine had not been herself since Edward died. She just moped around all day, dressing in black, not wanting to see any of us, her ladies-in-waiting. When I went to comfort her, she chased me out of the room as if she were a banshee, she did, like a crazy woman, but under the circumstances, I could no blame her. She was just starting to come out of her mourning when this strange sickness caught hold of Patrick. Then, she seemed to be worried and regressed. Not talking to any of us agin."

"Did she speak to you about her plans to depart to a warmer climate?"

"Not specifically. Like I said she wasn't talking to us much, but we knew she had a royal cousin near Monaco who had a palace on the Mediterranean and thought that would be the best place for her to go. There are also healing hot springs nearby. We all thought that would be the best thing to do for poor Patrick."

On cross-examination, Stanforth asked, "So, Lady Winifred, did you trulysee Catherine making preparations or see her and her children leave the castle."

"No."

"Did you think it was odd that neither you nor the other ladies saw her making such preparations or were aware of her leaving? I mean, as the queen mother, caring for a king, one would expect that there would be much luggage and an entourage involved, would you not?"

"Normally, that would be the case, but Queen Catherine was not acting normally. She had been behaving very strangely for months, talking to herself, roaming around the castle in the middle of the night in her nightgown, singing sad dirges, moaning, sleeping all day, snapping at us, her ladies, who were only trying to help her. So, we weren't surprised that she just got up and left. It was impulsive, but she had been so up and down day by day. One day, she seemed happy as a lark; the next she would be so despondent, disagreeable, and dour. Patrick probably took a turn for the worse, and as a mother, she would do all she could to save the dear boy. As a mother, I could understand that."

After Boston called him up, a night guard at the scene testified, "I seen her leave with four of the other palace guards with her bags, a maid, King Patrick, and her two lil' ones, who did indeed seem to be in distress. Comes ta think o it, they all seemed distressed, as if they needed to get Patrick to a better climate right off. It had been raining for days and was unusually cold, with mold and mildew growing green throughout the castle, which we all know can make any sickness worse. She, no doubt, thought she had to get away quickly. I know if I could, given how miserable the weather has been, I would have left too."

To those who supported Michael, it was obvious that as members of the court, the witnesses had been coerced or bribed by Boston and Reginald, who controlled their positions. Stanforth rose to object, but Reginald cut him down, saying, "That is enough from you. This trial is over. The jury will now decide Michael McCarron's fate."

Stanforth was furious at the miscarriage of justice and objected, saying, "This is a travesty. I want to call witnesses that will testify to Michael's character."

"That will not make any difference. We know some like him, while others do not. You could call witnesses, and then Lord Boston could call witnesses, which would only delay the inevitable. I have had enough of you, Mr. Stanforth. If you say another word, you will be expelled from the hall and imprisoned." Then he pounded his staff onto the stage three times, the thumping sound echoing throughout the hall.

"But at least my client is entitled to defend himself. There is no court in all the British Isles that would not allow that."

Reginald looked to Boston, who shrugged his shoulders and raised his hands halfway up, indicating that this was true. "I will allow the disreputable printer to speak," Reginald reluctantly conceded, "But that will be all."

Michael rose, walked up the stairs to the top of the stage, and turned towards the large audience sitting on the lines of benches in the massive, resonating hall. He had not prepared anything, and for some time, during a long, awkward silence, it seemed as if he had nothing to say. Then he coughed and began speaking, "My friends, most of you have known me for a long time; indeed, I or my dear Gwendolyn have taught many of you how to read. And, even if you could not read, you have heard from those who are able to read the Bunkillarny Reader, of the news of our shire. I sought to make the items in the Reader as unbiased and truthful as I could until one day when Reginald came to our shop and smashed our press and type, threatening to burn the place to the ground. He took over the press, and since then, the Reader has published articles that favor him and make him and his administration look perfect. You have all read these or heard of these articles and can tell the difference before and after they took over the press."

"Well, as you know, things have not been as rosy as the new Reader portrays. Many of your shops have been damaged or pilfered by the drunken hooligans roaming the streets at night, who have harassed your daughters and wives. Our town has changed. Think back to the earlier days and contrast that with today. Is it better, as the propaganda in Reader suggests, or worse? And you mothers and wives, whose husbands or sons have been conscripted into the army, robbing you of their labor on the farm or in your shops, you all the time worried that they might die in some unnecessary war to enhance Reginald's wealth. And for you farmers, think back to when Edward was king. Back then, only a small portion of your crops went to fund the government; now, many of you struggle to get by after paying the tax. That is why I felt I had to tell the truth, why I published the Truth."

"Two days before Queen Catherine's departure, I went to see her. She was in good spirits because King Patrick was making a remarkable recovery. She suspected that there was something in his ale that was hurting him, and after he stopped drinking it when he drank pure mountain spring water, he seemed to be recovering. I spoke with Patrick, and although he was a little weak, he seemed much better. His color was back to normal, he seemed positive, his stomach didn't ache, and he was eating all his favorite foods, building up his strength. He had already resumed his lessons and looked forward to starting to practice his swordsmanship with Reginald the following week."

"I..."

Before Michael could say more, Reginald pounded his staff loudly three times, "That's enough from you. The trial is over." Then, in a hateful tone, "The jury will now decide your fate, Michael McCarron."

The jury conferred at the table and, in less than a half-hour, was ready to disclose their verdict. Rather than reading it, Reginald had each in turn say whether Michael was guilty or innocent. With me keeping track of the tally on my fingers, the vote preceded as follows:

"Guilty,

Guilty,

Innocent,

Innocent,

Innocent,

Guilty,

Innocent,

Guilty,

Innocent,

Guilty,

Guilty,

Guilty.

Reginald ruled, "That makes it five for innocent and seven for guilty. Michael McCarron, you shall be returned to jail and hung by your neck in a fortnight."

Gwendolyn hugged Michael before two of the knights dragged him off. I stood in their way, stared them down, shook Michael's hand, and gave him a man hug.

The verdict hit the crowd like a thunderbolt. They were stunned and motionless. Some of the women, obviously upset, were crying. Most of those in attendance were from town, most friends of Michael's, who learned how to read from him, read his books and the Reader. They were incensed that he could be convicted so quickly and, after prolonged booing, rushed the stage. Anticipating possible trouble, Reginald had stationed soldiers behind the great hall who poured into the room and formed a line with swords drawn and spears facing outward in front of the stage as those on the stage, including Michael, were quickly whisked away.

The crowd pressed forward, shouting at the soldiers to stand down. Many of them had relatives in the crowd and, having doubts, started withdrawing their weapons, "Billy O'Brian, you won't stab yer ma would ye!"

Quickly assessing the situation, Reginald ordered his knights to stand behind the men and force them to respond, then slowly push closer to the mob. At the top of his voice, in a deep, commanding tone, Reginald ordered them to stand their ground. When one of the protesters got too close, arm raised with a clenched fist, Hugh, in one mighty motion, sliced off his hand. The sight of the blood spurting out of the unfortunate young man's stump caused the others to stop in their tracks. When Reginald ordered his men to advance again, the crowd dispersed.

We just sat there throughout it all in shock.

We left the great hall, descended the steps and gathered at the bottom. One of Gwendolyn's students, who was a page, came up and told us that during the lunch break, he heard Boston threatening the two lords who were on the fence leaning towards Michael with the loss of their titles and lands if they voted to acquit him. They reluctantly acquiesced since they had seen this already happen to Lord Buckingham.

Because he did not have the opportunity to call his own witnesses, Stanforth was seething.

I asked him, "It seems that you have cause for a mistrial. Will you appeal?"

"If we were in Dublin, I could appeal to the King of Ireland, or if we were in London, we could appeal to King Henry, but here out of the Pale, there is no one to appeal to. Reginald has the ultimate authority, so I can't appeal to him."

I was thinking in 21st-century terms. Apparently, there would be no formal appeal process for who knows how many centuries.*

Following the trial, Reginald went to Michael's cell and said, "I told you not to persist, and you disobeyed me. You asked for this." Then, exerting his power over Michael, finally having him under his control, taking out his pent-up rage on him, he proceeded to give him twenty-one excruciating lashes until Reginald's arm tired and Michael passed out, leaving Michael bleeding profusely, bent over in a fetal position, unable to stand. Feeling invigorated by the exercise and exertion of power over his rival, as Reginald left, he ordered Hugh to have a doctor tend to him—"So he would not miss his appointment with the executioner or the wedding of his daughter, which now depends upon that fetching

Gwendolyn. Whether she sees the light or not, I shall surely have my way with that voluptuous wench."*

Two days later, Reginald traveled to the O'Flannery castle with a dozen of his knights. Trying to assuage their frazzled nerves at the injustice done to Michael, Lord O'Flannery and I were out hunting at the time and Reginald demanded to see Gwendolyn, who was still very upset. Reginald, on the other hand, was on his best behavior, acting as if he was chivalrous. Gwendolyn was shivering while he attempted to gently calm her.

"My dear Gwendolyn, I am so sorry that this whole mess has turned out the way it has, but on behalf of King Patrick, I felt it was my duty to proceed. My affection for you, however, has not waned in the least, and if there is anything you would like me to do for you, all you have to do is ask."

"Please release my father."

"That is the one thing I cannot do. Unless you agree to marry me, then I will grant him a pardon. We would be so happy together. Imagine being the queen of Bunkillarny, being the most admired and powerful woman in the kingdom, with a dozen servants and ladies in waiting tending to your every desire, looking up to you with envy. Imagine all the gowns you could have, the silver, the gold jewelry, anything your heart desired. You would be the belle of every ball and such a beautiful queen you would make.

I know you like books, so you will be able to read all the books in the extensive castle library and any new book that is printed. And your son would be the next King in a long line that would remember you as the first queen of the new dynasty, not just here but throughout all the lands I shall conquer with you by my side. You will not only reign over the castle but in our summer palace overlooking the spectacular bay, and my castle to the east and at the hunting lodge deep in the woods on the lake. And we will be able to travel—to Paris, to the Bavarian Alps, to Rome, to Venice to the French Riviera. You'd like that wouldn't you?"

Gwendolyn started to imagine herself in the glorious life Reginald portrayed until she recalled what he was doing to her beloved father and felt the Devil was tempting her, as Jesus was before he was crucified.

"Will you at least let me see him?"

"Of course, just let lord Boston know when, and you can see him the following day."

"I would like to see him tomorrow."

Realizing that Michael was in desperate shape from the whipping he inflicted on him, Reginald said, "You may see him a couple of days after tomorrow." *

We had just arrived from our successful hunt, having slain several quail as Reginald exited. With his knights looking on, Reginald grabbed my collar and threw me against the door, saying, "Oh, Rand, I see you have returned from your long journey. Do not dare interfere with my plans, or you will end up like Michael. I know you remember the last time we fought, not that you had the least bit of skill. You were remarkably pitiful. Then I would have slain you if not for Queen Catherine's intercession."

I could feel my blood pressure rapidly rising and dearly wanted to slug him in the face before he could reach for his sword, but I realized his bodyguards would be on me in an instant, so I merely grabbed his hands, pressing against my chest and crushed them within mine until he withdrew in pain, trying to hide his grimace, not wanting me to know I hurt him in front of his knights.

We were both horrified when Gwendolyn told us of Reginald's proposal, saying that she had to marry him, both of us persuading her to wait until we could figure out an alternative plan. Lord O'Flannery said it would be better if I stayed in town so that Reginald would not be unduly angry. After comforting and hugging Gwendolyn, I rode to town and stayed with John.

Reginald had Michael cleaned up, tended to, and transferred to the best cell they had with a window, to which Boston added a bed, a candle, a chair, a desk and a chamber pot. Then they fed him nourishing meals of beef, chicken, porridge, cheese and bread. Michael, still dazed, appreciated the care but realized there had to be ulterior motives, such as keeping him alive until the execution.

Still, when Gwendolyn appeared, he looked horrible. She asked what they had done to him, but keeping his injured, bloody back hidden in the newly requisitioned shirt, he refused to let her know of the flogging.

"Father, I cannot stand to see you doing so poorly. Reginald has said he will release you if I promise to marry him."

"No, under no circumstances can you do that. I would rather be tortured and die. He is vile, and I cannot imagine you being with him even for a minute. As your father, I forbid it. I would never give my blessing."

"But, I can na let you die. You mean too much to me."

SIXTEEN

The Rescue

Following a delicious dinner of roast beef, buttered turnips and mushrooms that John's wife cooked, I asked John if we could talk in private. He led me to his blacksmith's shop, which, even though it was cool outside, was still hot, smelling of molten and hammered metal—since my summer jobs working in a factory, a smell as delightful as the roast, for it meant that something useful was being manufactured there—the smell of productivity.

I asked him how the shop was faring.

"We are busier than we have er been. Me youngest son, Sean, is helping now. I have promoted the two apprentices to journeymen and hired two more. Reginald insisted that 'alf of our effort be dedicated to making weapons for him. A quarter of our profits are supposed to go to Michael, and I am afraid that since Michael has been jailed, they will take these too. Plus, they have asked for a rebate, which I am sure they are keeping."

"Reginald has said that if Gwendolyn agrees to marry him, he won't hang Michael."

"That would be terrible. Can't imagine what I'd do if me only daughter wanted to marry that hooligan."

"Yes, we have to come up with a plan to rescue Michael so it does not happen. I have something in mind that you can help with."

"Of course, I would do anything fer Michael and fer Gwendolyn, too. I've known her since she were a wee babe. She be like a niece ta me."

I brought out the pepper box pistol and showed it to him. "Each barrel holds a ball and powder, same as a matchlock. Here is the bowl and weep hole for the primer, but so the powder will not fall out, I added this little disk that slides over it like this. After I open it up, rather than a lit wick, the flint will strike the steel and create a spark. So, if you were being attacked and did not have your wick lit, you would be ready to fire and fire up to four times before reloading."

"My lord, what an ingenious device. You know I've used flint to light a fire and even to light the wick, but this device saves all that. Should ha' thought of that years ago. Does it work?"

"Well, two of the four chambers fired successfully, but the third one blew up in my hand, which burned my fingers. I think it was because the weep hole was out of alignment or something like that. But I have a plan for a new type of pistol, one that might come in handy in an attempt to rescue Michael. Something beyond even this pepperbox."

"My son Ryan is the one who makes our pistols and is an excellent gunsmith. I will have him work with you starting tomorrow, and it will be his top priority."

"Great!"

Later that night, I took out my iPhone and fired it up, searching for the design of a revolver. I hastily sketched what I saw as my iPhone repeatedly told me that the battery was dying and I needed to plug it into its charger. I finished the sketch and realized I needed to manufacture cartridges that would fit into the revolver.

Shortly after I clicked on a link for 'cartridge' on the Wikipedia page, the phone died. I had seen the basic design but needed to know the chemical formula for the primer. When I pulled the trigger, the hammer would hit the back of the bullet, igniting the primer, which would, in turn, explode the gunpowder in the cartridge and propel the bullet out of the barrel. I imagined that this was the same kind of stuff that was in my six-shooter cap pistol when I was a kid—I wish I had a roll.

Without that formula, my revolver would be useless. And, there were no stores in the 15th century that could help me. I had to find a way to charge my phone. But while I tried to figure that out, I would work with Ryan to build the revolver because it was only a few days until Michael would be hanged. I redid my sketch several times from different angles to show it to him.

The next morning, just after I started working with Ryan over the noise of the pounding of metal at the forge, I heard a familiar voice at the open door. It was dastardly Boston asking for me. I hastily gathered up the diagrams and had Ryan take them away.

As Boston approached, he said, "I trust you had a good trip to London and Spain Randdd?"

"It was OK, I guess."

"What do you mean OK?"

Realizing that I had once again unconsciously used 20th-century slang, I recovered, "That is Spanish for all right."

"And were you successful in finding what you sought in Spain?"

I suspected that he had insider information about my trip. I thought that Seamus or Hugh may have rifled through Michael's desk, found the letters from me, and given these to Reginald. I had to be careful what I said.

"I did find some of the documents I was searching for in Spain, but they would not allow me to take them out of the library. Indeed, very few people had ever seen or handled these documents. I could understand their concern, but I was very disappointed." I was not sure he believed me.

Oh, too bad. "Did you bring back new books from London to print?"

Not wanting to be tripped up, I said, "Yes."

"But we have not yet received these in the print shop."

"Without Michael there, I was unsure whether the shop would be able to handle any new printings."

"I assure you we will be able to handle these. Hugh and Seamus are doing a splendid job running the shop."

Biting my tongue, I said, "I will bring them over later today."

Feeling he had cornered me to get what he wanted and to demonstrate his superiority, he said, "Very well. Bring them over after we are finished here."

"And, what of the funds you collected from Colleen Jones?"

I was unsure of how he knew about these, but as an accountant, he had obviously rifled through Gwendolyn's books and had seen previous entries from London. "Yes, I have these and planned to give them to Michael."

"I will take them."

"They are not yours; they are Michael's," I said in a deep, raised voice that caught him off guard for a second.

"Michael has been convicted of a serious crime. All his assets and revenues are the crowns now. As you may or may not know, King Edward was an equal partner in the business, which is now Patrick's. As our new King's financial minister, I look out for his interests and insist that you turn these funds over to me or face the consequences. How much money did the London operation take in?

I wanted to hit him and then take on that formidable Hugh, who looked like an NFL offensive tackle and stood behind with his arms crossed but thought better of it. Even if I succeeded and ran away with Michael's money, it would jeopardize our plans to rescue him, which had to be my highest priority.

Realizing he was an accountant at heart, I took out a sheet of paper and a quill pen and showed him how much revenue Colleen had taken in, minus my expenses and commission, which resulted in a substantial profit of 22 pounds.

"That is excellent, much better than before. But what are these added expenses and commission."

"Well, the expenses are for the trip back from London, without which the books and revenues would not be here."

"All right, I will pay these, but I will not pay you a commission."

"That is for the books I helped sell in London."

"As I understand, your salary was two schillings a month. You have been gone for 11 months, which amounts to 22 schillings or 1 pound 2 schillings, which is what I will pay you and no more."

"But when I was in Spain, I used the funds I had won during the games to fund that, which was much more than 1 pound and 2 schillings. And Michael had intimated that I would become a partner in the business."

"Be that as it may, all you're entitled to is what I have said. You should feel lucky you are getting anything at all. I expect you to have the funds when you appear with the books later today. And by the way, you no longer have a position with the shop. You're fired Randdd, fired!" he added with a sleazy self-satisfied, superior smirk.

In actuality, I had used the funds from the earlier sales to fund the purchase of the Spanish literature, and most of my travel was funded by my winnings, except for the Gutenberg Bible. Seemingly, Boston did not realize this, so I felt I had gotten some of what I wanted. I did not want to work for Hugh and Boston and Reginald anyway, but including my Silicon Valley job, this was the second time in a little over a year that I had been fired, and it stung. With John's help, we fetched the books out of the well-hidden hiding place behind the wall in the basement, placing all the London books in one trunk and the Spanish documents and my priceless Caxton first editions in the other trunk that we again hid.

Together, John and I carried the trunk to the print shop, where Hugh, with muscular arms folded, glared at us while Boston glared and smirked, dropping the heavy object at his feet with a resounding thud that startled the emaciated, scraggy figure. Then I handed him the funds from Colleen. Seeing all that money, not able to catch himself, he said, "Thank you, Randdd." His always adding an extra d to the end of my name infuriated me. I, again, wanted to punch him in his sleazy, thin mouth but held my right hand down with my left.

Then, to my surprise, since I thought we were done, he continued with a smirk, "Oh, one more thing before you go. I think you forgot something."

"No, I have brought you all I promised. You should surely be satisfied."

"Not quite! Our enterprising young printer here, Seamus, had a hunch that there was more. When you arrived, he saw that you had two trunks in your cart that you and John the smithy carried into his house. He suspected these were the valuable Spanish documents you referred to in your letter to Michael. So, when you left, the good lad followed you back, entered the house, heard rustling in the basement, and sneaked a peek down there, where he saw you were taking books from one trunk and putting them in another. Now, don't tell me that this was souvenirs from Spain or some other lame excuse. In any case, we want to see what was in the other trunk."

Hugh and Boston led us outside to where six soldiers were waiting, then led us to the back of John's house attached to the blacksmith's shop down to the basement, where the soldiers began searching among the infrequently used Smith's possessions. Not finding the crate. Boston said, "Now, where is that second crate?"

John and I said nothing. Then Boston said, "You three, go to the blacksmith's shop and bring back the one with the red hair."

When they arrived, Hugh stood behind Ryan and held his dirk's blade across Ryan's neck, causing drops of blood to seep out, snarling, "I would hate for my blade to slip on such a fine young man's neck, especially since Ryan is the finest gunsmith in all the land. Now, where's that crate?!"

I nodded to John, who was ready to take them all on. Concerned for his son's life, he reluctantly opened the hidden wall and slid the crate out.

Boston opened up the crate and, seeing its contents, said "Now that wasn't so hard, was it? But these are just poorly written pieces of paper. I don't know why these would be worth hiding, but still, hiding them from the crown, who owns the press and all its contents, is surely a crime. Hugh, arrest them!"

After four soldiers grabbed each of our arms and were about to lead us out, I turned and exclaimed, "John had nothing to do with the crates. He was merely storing these for me and knew nothing of their contents. Besides, I do not think Reginald would be pleased if his main arms supplier were in jail, unable to fulfill his orders, would he?"

Continuing to rummage through the Spanish copies, disappointedly, slimy Boston said, "These don't even look old. I was expecting parchments or velums or even scrolls, but evidently, they must be worth something, or you would not have gone to all that trouble."

"You have no idea how valuable those are. Oh, and unless you want to risk a war between Bunkillarny and England and Spain, I would treat them with the utmost care. The Queen Mother is expecting books to be printed from these, and as you may well know, King Henry owes his throne to her, and they are very close. Oh yes, and there is a contract with Isabella, the Queen of Spain to supply printed copies of each one, plus royalties. She would not be pleased if you do not live up to the contract between Spain and McCarron Press. They might send a squadron of ships and hundreds of men to collect the books and promised payments."

Boston looked taken aback and confused. Not sure of what to do, Hugh asked, "Do you want us to throw John and Rand into the keep?"

Boston just walked up the steep stairs out of the basement, shaking his head repeatedly and mumbling to himself. The soldiers were following behind, carrying the crate with them.

Glad to be free, John and I soon climbed up the steep stairs, and then I checked to make sure they were all gone and that Seamus was not skulking around somewhere, after which I said, "That danged Boston has the books I acquired from William Caxton's shop, the first books ever printed in English."

"Those must be very valuable. I remember putting those at the bottom of the crate, so they might not find them for a while."

"My friend, you have no idea how valuable they are." I had used most of my winnings to buy the Gutenberg Bible, which alone would be worth a great deal. I had to somehow get my books back before I traveled back to my time, but knew Boston would not just hand them over.

He took me aside and whispered, "Rand, they are out to get you. You should stay low! Do you remember O'Leary?"

"Yes, Tim O'Leary, the butcher. He was with us at the royal ball after the Bunkillarny games, and I would frequently talk to him at the pub. He certainly had the gift of gab."

"Well, Tim was at the pub complaining loudly about the high taxes and having all the soldiers in town always causing trouble. He also lost his only son in the war and holds Reginald responsible. He constantly complained about such things every time he be there. Well, Tim liked to go fishing early in the morn before he opened up the shop, he did. He would sell any fish he caught at the shop. One day Tim just up and disappeared with no sign of him or his rowboat. The first thing ye wud ha thought were that a rough sea wud ha swamped him and carried his body and his boat out ta sea, but the sea were clear as glass that day and Tim never went fer from shore. So, we thinks Reginald had him kilt for complainin'. He has spies like Seamus everywhere, so be careful."*

That afternoon, I again began working on the diagrams with tall, slim, red-haired, freckled Ryan, who resembled a 19th-century cowboy. He was still irritated for being taken by Hugh and having his dirk at his neck, especially since he had served under him during the Nealland War. He became inspired when I told Ryan that I had a weapon in mind that might help free Michael. Compared to the matchlocks he had worked on, the revolver might blow his mind, so first, I brought out the flintlock—a minor improvement over the matchlocks he had produced.

"Wow, I could easily make these," he said. "Just a flint, a curved hammer, a sliver of metal and a spring is all I'd need ta add."

I next showed him the pepperbox pistol, saying that variations of this had existed for some time, such as cannons or crude long guns. I emphasized how the four barrels spun around the spindle and showed him how I had fastened little ha-penny-sized disks over the wells to prevent the powder from falling out when these were upside down – "Wow! I ner heard o' these. That be ingenious!"

"Unfortunately, it blew up," I added.

"Yes, I can see that. Maybe with an adjustment or two, it might work, but that one barrel is ruined."

Before I showed him my revolver design, I was concerned because I did not want to start an arms race throughout Europe that might change the course of history. Therefore, I said, "Ryan, what I am about to show you next is a secret that must never be disclosed to anyone, for if it is, many thousands of people and perhaps millions will die. No one else can ever know what I will show you—not even your father or brothers or your future wife or children—no one. **Do you understand**?

Realizing the import of what I said very solemnly, he said, "Yes, I understand!"

"Will you swear to God, our Lord, Jesus Christ, and the Holy Ghost that you will never reveal what I am about to disclose to you or ever produce another without my consent?"

"I swear to God, Jesus Christ, and the Holy Ghost and to our Holy Mother too that I will never reveal what I am about to see or ever produce another without your consent! Upon my honor, you can trust me."

"If someone such as Reginald ever got a hold of this, he could destroy Bunkillarny and the rest of Ireland."

"Rand, I am not someone who tells secrets. Even if someone asks me to, I don' disclose their secrets. Whatever it is, I will take it to me grave."

Spinning the barrels of the pepperbox, I explained, "With the four barrels, this is very heavy, which is why the barrels are so short, thereby limiting the range and accuracy of the pistol. It could miss a target from as little as thirty feet away. So, I thought, what if I only had one long barrel and multiple chambers to hold the balls? It would be lighter and more accurate." Then, bringing out the diagram, I said, "This is what I came up with."

Ryan was flabbergasted by what he saw, "It does not look much different than my pistols, but there is so much more in there, and there are six balls in that small cylinder—my goodness! Do you truly think this will work? So, it will hold six balls and powder at a time, but where are the weep holes and the pans to hold the powder? How would you ever fire the thing?"

"There are none. Instead, there will be a cartridge that holds powder and ball. I have not quite figured that out yet, though. The ball, what I will call a bullet, will be made of the same molded lead, like what you manufacture today, but with a point and flat bottom, similar to a church steeple. We will make cylindrical containers for the powder out of copper or brass. This will be easier to produce than the printer type you and your father already fabricate."

We walked through each assembly for the revolver. The barrel would be easy to manufacture—he would use one of his pistol molds for that. The frame would be somewhat similar to those in Ryan's pistols, too.

Using a mold, he thought he would be able to create the cylinder, but making it as precise as it would need to be would take some experimentation. He did not think he would be able to handle the trigger and firing mechanism, though, "This seems like something a clockmaker would craft. You should have Kevin McCarthy down the street look into it."

I told him that we had to produce this in a little over a week—"In time to save Michael before they execute him." He said he would devote days and nights to the project and have his journeymen and apprentices work on the orders for Reginald so he would not get suspicious.

I worked up a separate design for the trigger mechanism on another piece of paper, which I reviewed with Kevin, who did not thoroughly understand what it was for—my intent. There would be small holes in the cylinder (one for each chamber) that would line up with the barrel that the trigger mechanism would rachet to. I did not show Kevin the cylinder design or the rest of the gun so he would not be vulnerable to inquisition or be able to produce the lethal weapon on his own. It would be similar to a clock ticking away the minutes—something Kevin understood well. Because it was to help save Michael, Kevin also promised to work on it immediately, night and day.*

With Ryan and Kevin working diligently on the revolver parts so I could figure out a way to produce a cartridge, my first task was to find a way to generate electricity to recharge my cell phone battery. I thought about building a generator that I would turn with my hand, but that would require a lot of wire and time to build. In my high school chemistry class, I remember making a potato battery that generated electricity, but potatoes came from the Americas and would not be around until after Columbus discovered America. I also recalled that any acidic fruit could generate a little electricity but thought that, say, an apple would not produce enough to charge my phone. Maybe a twelve-apple battery would—no, probably not.

Then I thought about the car battery, which used sulfuric acid. If I could find some sulfuric acid, I could construct a battery. I walked down to the apothecary/alchemist down the street, David Duffy, a thin, blond, middle-aged man whom I knew from the pub, and asked if he had any sulfuric acid.

He said, "I have ner heard o' that, Rand."

"Do you have any sort of acid?"

Then, with a puzzled look on his face, he replied, "I do ha' vitriol, which, come to think of it is made with sulfur. Do you think this will do?"

I asked him to drop a little on a piece of wood, which it immediately started eating through, emitting a little plume of smoke with an acrid odor that smelled like rotting eggs.

"Yes, that will be fine." I purchased the large beaker (all he had), he telling me to be very careful with it.

I remembered seeing the clockmaker/jeweler using wire to make jewelry when I recently visited him. On my way back, I stopped there and bought a few feet of copper wire.

I remembered that to make the potato battery, we used copper and zinc. All I would need to assemble my battery would be the sulfuric acid, copper and zinc. The copper would be the positive terminal, and zinc would be the negative terminal. In the print shop, we used copper to mold our printing type, so we had plenty of that, and as had been done for a couple of thousand years, John mixed zinc with copper to produce brass. I asked John to forge two bars—one of zinc, one of copper.

I drilled two holes in the lid of the largest glass container I could find in the kitchen, Daisy adamantly saying, "Rand what are ye doin to me vessel, and what do ye expect will 'old that barley ye took out o it? Give it back."

I replied, "Daisy, this will help to rescue Michael, but do not tell anyone. Do you understand?"

"Oh, ye can have anythin' you wants. I don' like cookin' fer these interlopers anyways. And be assured I will no tell a soul. I would do anythin' to get Michael back. He has treated me so well. Even teaching me ta read. Can you believe that—me a readin'?"

I slid the bars through the holes and tied the copper wires to each terminal. I poured a small amount of the acid through a third hole, which immediately started bubbling. I held one wire between my left index finger and thumb and holding the other wire in my right, touched the tip to the first joint of my index finger. Eureka! I felt the tingling of a current. I felt it when I touched the second joint but did not on the fourth. I was eliciting a current—electrons were flowing from the positive copper terminal to the negative zinc terminal.

I had no idea how much voltage I was generating, though. I looked at the cellphone's description on the back, which said it would require 5 volts—something I had no way of measuring.

Fortunately, I still had my USB cable from when I nearly drowned in the Grand Canyon, which I kept in the waterproof pouch along with the phone. Using the wire cutter on my Swiss army knife, I stripped back the wires about an inch and tied them to my copper wires. All I could think of doing was to add increasingly more sulfuric acid until my cellphone indicated it was charging. After adding a quarter of the beaker, I could see the solution bubbling away at a furious rate, but the iPhone still did not register a charge. I added progressively more acid but became concerned that the beaker, which was eliciting a lot of heat and that terrible smell, might explode, dousing me with acid and glass, permanently disfiguring me. Still, I persisted until only a third of the solution was left. Knowing I had all of the alchemist's sulfuric acid, I did not know what else to do.

Finally, the icon on my phone indicated I was getting a charge. I stayed there for hours, adding more acid when the red light went off. When I turned on my phone, after I heard the amazing, momentous jingle, it said it was 60% charged—eureka! what seemed miraculous to me. I quickly searched my offline copy of Wikipedia for the precious cartridge formula and immediately turned the phone off.

I went back to Dave and, as the formula indicated, asked him for mercury fulminate, something he had never heard of. So, I walked behind his shop, away from the street, where no one would see me, and fired up my precious cell phone again and searched for other primer compounds. Starting in the early 19th century, several compounds that were either too volatile or too corrosive had been developed. None of these existed in nature. I found one that I thought I might be able to acquire—potassium chlorate. I saw that it was the same compound used in my cap gun when I was a kid. Then, we would take a role of perhaps twenty-five caps and shoot at each other with our mock cowboy pistols.

I saw that potassium chlorate could be produced by mixing a common salt substitute, potassium chloride, with bleach, but chlorine bleach had not been invented yet. Then I saw that I could make it using electrolysis and found pictures on my phone that described how to do it.

As a result of my research, I went to Dave and asked him for potash—a common fertilizer with potassium made from burned trees. I put a solution of potash and water into a similar circular glass container and inserted my two terminals into the solution. I used my homemade battery to generate electricity and, after a few hours had a white precipitate at the bottom. I boiled the solution down further, producing more white powder.

Reminiscent of that high school chem class, feeling like the cook I never was, according to the formula, I mixed the powder with sulfur and charcoal, which hopefully would result in my desired primer. When I lit the mixture, it exploded—voila- just what I wanted. When I hit a little bit with a hammer, it exploded like my cap gun. My half-assed, MacGyver-like imitation of a chemist actually worked. Hearing the explosion, Ryan came over to where I was working at a table in the blacksmith's shop and wondered if I had succeeded. I hit a little more of the mixture, resulting in another cap-gun explosion, after which he smiled and patted me on the back.

Working 16 hours a day, I assisted Ryan as he completed the pistol. I made my lead bullets and the brass jacket for my cartridges, inserting my primer cap and powder to assemble the finished cartridges. I installed the trigger mechanism from the jeweler and, the day before Michael was to be beheaded, tested it all. I wanted to prevent the revolver from being duplicated and Ryan from potential harm. Since only I knew about the primer formula and the final assembly, even if Reginald or someone else captured Ryan, he could not figure out how it worked.

Ryan and I went deep into the woods, back into the hills, near a grassy clearing by a stream to test our revolver. We tested it, and of course, it did not work. After adjusting the place where the hammer hit the cartridge, it operated remarkably well—all six chambers fired without exploding, and I was able to hit a bottle from 50 feet away. This was much more accurate than a matchlock or a flintlock. *

In the meantime, Lords O'Flannery and Brogan had hatched a plan to rescue Michael. After our successful test, we rode to Lord O'Flannery's that evening to discuss the plan. Gwendolyn was a nervous wreck. She did not want to take the chance that her father would be killed, but she did not want any of us to be killed either. She said she was going to Reginald and would marry him. "What is my life worth versus that of any of yours?" With a desperate, resigned expression, she continued, "I am but a woman. Please, please do not do this! Let me go!"

Lord O'Flannery said, "It is not just about you, lass; it is about all of us. We do not want to live under Reginald's rule any longer. This will be a blow against all he represents: his tyranny. How he is ruining our beloved Bunkillarny."

One of Brogan's nieces, Bridget, a voluptuous redhead, worked at the castle in the kitchen and was responsible for bringing meals to the night watch. Understandably, the handsome captain of the watch had a crush on her.

According to the plan, dressed in a low, form-fitting gown, she flirted with him. While they were necking, she suddenly stopped, saying, "I can na kiss ye with them damn keys constantly a jingling. What do these open anyway?" He proudly explained the function of each key, she feigning fascination with his explanation. Then he placed them on the table, where her younger brother, who also worked in the kitchen, had hid under the table.

As they were passionately making out, something she didn't mind since he was an attractive young man, the brother grabbed the keys and made an impression of the one that opened the back gate in clay. When he lifted the keys back up onto the table, they made an unmistakable jingling sound. With his back to the table, the captain was about to turn his head until Bridget, sitting on his lap, turned his head back with her hands and kissed him even more fervently. The lad carefully restored the keys to the top of the table. John would use the impression to forge a duplicate metal key.

With masks on, John, Ryan, I, and two of the Brogan boys, Paddy and Daryl, would sneak in through the back gate and make our way to the jail. The Brogans wanted revenge against Reginald for killing their esteemed brother Thomas, and this was their chance to get even. Lords Brogan and O'Flannery wanted to be in on the raid but were too old, slow, and too recognizable. Instead, since they would be the first suspects, they would be at McNab's drinking. We would be armed to the hilt with pistols, swords, and dirks each. Of course, I would have my new revolver. Ryan would have my pepperbox, which he had fixed, tested, and trained with, back in the woods.

When Bridget appeared at the jail at midnight with his supper in her lowest-cut dress, anticipating making out again, the jailer could not wait to let her in. With his undivided attention on her, we entered through the back gate, came up behind him, grabbed him, gagged him, tied a bag over his head, and then tied his hands and legs. We tied her up and bagged her, too, so she would appear innocent. John grabbed his keys, and we made our way to Michael's cell, where we found him beaten and incoherent.

As we ferreted our way through the labyrinth of halls, somehow, the guard got loose and rang the alarm bell. We hurried down the maze until we arrived at the back gate, where a dozen guards were waiting for us. When they started firing, we returned their fire. Even though they outnumbered us, we had an advantage because they were in the open, whereas we hid behind the gate's walls. The nearly full moon on the cloudless, cool night clearly lit the field in front of us, showing our foes. Out of my six shots, I wounded three—my revolver so much more accurate than their primitive matchlocks, but unfortunately, Daryl was hit. We heard the sound of boots running down the hallway towards us and had to hold them off, which, given the time to reload a standard matchlock, would be a losing proposition. As soon as we fired another round, they would rush us. We had to do something, and we had to do it fast.

As the others barely kept up the fire at both ends, I took a rod from my pocket to eject my spent cartridges one-by-one and reloaded. I told the boys we would have to make a run for it. Ryan had just reloaded his pepperbox and said he would keep the soldiers down the hall at bay. I threw open the gate and, running towards the surprised guards, began firing, shooting at those who had reloaded and were about to shoot me. I kept an eye on their wicks; when they fired, it took a full second before the explosion. I dodged like a halfback, thereby avoiding the bullet. I did not bother with the one who just fired, for it would take time for him to reload, instead, I concentrated on one soldier who was about done loading and hit him, then another. When two were about to fire at the same time, I dove to the ground and shot the two next to them. The rest of our group followed behind me firing their single shots as they ran.

I hit four in all. As we converged upon them, ready to fight them with our swords, they, in various stages of loading, seeing me point my empty weapon at them, thinking I had an endless supply of bullets, were so shocked, one by one, they peeled off and ran away. By then, Ryan, after causing those in the hall to stay back by firing his pepper box, being the fastest of all of us had caught up. We made it to the woods, where Danny Brogan waited for us with our horses, and under a barrage of bullets, we rode away. *

Reginald had been in bed with Brehana when he heard the alarm bell. He hastily put on his robes and ran to the back of the castle, where he saw six men running into the woods. Along with his men, he chased us, grabbed one of their pistols, and shot at us as we rode away on our horses. One of the men stood considerably higher than the others, taller than anyone in the shire. He was convinced it was Rand and that the broad one was John.

Once out of range, John and Ryan doubled back to Bunkillarny and McNab's, where everyone would say they had been all night.

Gathering a couple dozen men, Reginald thundered into town, broke down John's door, and had them spread out and search for him and Rand throughout the shop and attached quarters, but they were nowhere to be found. He asked John's son Christopher where John was, who said he must still be at McNab's, whereupon they galloped to the pub. Reginald threw open the door and as his men shoved the inhabitants out of the way, headed directly for John, who had just arrived, snuck through the back door and chugged a pint of stout.

Grabbing the large, strong man, who could have knocked him out in a single blow, he challenged him, "Where have you been all night, John?"

Seeming a little wobbly, as if he had drunk numerous pints, John said, "O hello there lordy Reggie, why thank yeuw fer askin... Why,,, I've been here all night. McNab give us a pint for me handsome, Lord Reggie, me best customer will yeuw." Then he teetered a bit, smiled stupidly, breathed beer breath into Reginald's face, and patted him lovingly on his face.

Lord O'Flannery appeared and asked, "What has happened? "I assure you that John has been with us all night. Right, boys?" The entire bar, now focused on the scene before them, answered in various slurs, "Yes, John ha' bin here the whole time, since 9, no, 8, no 7". Lords O' Flannery and Brogan had bought several rounds and had frequently referred to him, so that no one knew how long John had been there.

Even though he saw both at the pub, Reginald split up the soldiers and had a dozen go to Lord O'Flannery's while the other dozen went to Brogan's to search for the perpetrators.*

With Daryl wounded and Michael dazed, we made our way to the Brogan manor. Once there, Lady Brogan hid us in their wine cellar, where she tended to her son's wound. With the oft-practiced skills of an army medic, she extracted the ball from his shoulder and sewed up the hole.

We had just nodded off when we heard a loud knocking at the door. It was Reginald commanding his troops to search every corner and cranny of the manor. Paddy led us through a hidden passageway behind a wine rack that led to the back of the manor above a ravine. Me guiding Michael and he helping Daryl, we slid down the bank, tiptoed over the rocks to cross the stream and climbed up the other side. Fortunately, expecting Reginald would search his abode, Lord Brogan had previously instructed the servants to hide our horses, tying them up on the opposite side of the ravine. Reginald would likely have the stables checked to see if any of the horses had been ridden hard and would be looking for Chester, who would be a sure giveaway that I was implicated in the attack.

As we rode through the moonlit woods, the tall old trees casting long bluish moon-shadows over the leafy, multicolored ground, we saw a lone rider approach. It was Christopher, John's oldest son, who told us that Reginald had raided their blacksmith's shop and suspected I was part of the raid.

Paddy and Daryl would wait until Reginald left, then return to the manor. With no other hiding place, I decided to take Michael to the cave, where I first materialized in Ireland.

As he rode away, I told Christopher, "Tell Gwendolyn we're headed for the cave. She will know where to find us."

Exhausted from the ordeal and the beating that Reginald felt entitled to deliver, narrowly escaping his execution, Michael looked as if he might faint at any time, therefore, I tied him to his horse and, grabbing the reins, led the way. The first morning light was beginning to illuminate the tips of the trees, and I wanted to be off the road before others started traveling on it. Hearing galloping in the distance, I quickly turned the horses off the road behind some fir trees just before one of Reginald's patrols stormed by. We arrived at the cave a little after sunrise, carefully guiding Michael through its small, hidden hole.

SEVENTEEN

The Cave

Once inside the dark, cool cave, Michael lay down on the damp dirt floor and, in a weakened voice, thanked me for rescuing him and saving Gwendolyn from a fate worse than death (having to marry Reginald). Then, midsentence, he fell asleep. I folded my jacket and carefully placed it under my friend's head. He slept soundly with an expression that seemed to convey that although he was thoroughly exhausted, he felt secure and at peace.

Careful not to be seen, Gwendolyn arrived after dusk. She began crying when she saw how weak, beaten up, and clinging to life her father appeared, so glad he was alive, yet very concerned about his condition—crying tears of joy and sorrow at the same time. She covered him with two warm blankets, after which, tired from the exertion, he immediately dozed off. Then she gave me a long, intimate hug, thanking me profusely for rescuing her father.

I said, "Thank you, dear Gwendolyn, but four others made this possible: Daryl, Paddy, John and Ryan." There is no need to thank me, after all, you and your father saved my life."

When Michael instinctively turned from his side to his back, the pain of his whipping caused him to scream out in pain. She went over to comfort him and placed another blanket under him to insulate him from the ground. When she saw the ugly, mangled tissue and red scars, Gwendolyn was outraged at what Reginald had done to her beloved father. As she tended to his wounds, she thanked God that she did not have to marry the Devil, although, she thought, if she had, she could have slit his throat on their wedding night with the dirk she had slid into her garter.

She brought several blankets, candles, enough food to last a week, and some whiskey and wine. I walked her out of the cave, thanking her and told her to be careful, "Gwendolyn, I know you want to come here every day, but that risks someone finding us. I will care for your dad. After he has some rest, he will be fine. Thanks to you, we have plenty of supplies; please do not return for five days. When you come, leave the road at least a half-mile from here and proceed through the woods. Do not tell anyone where we are; be sure no one follows you. If it is safe, ask Ryan to give you my bullet supplies—he will know what these are. She gave me another intense hug and a kiss on the lips, saying, "I am so glad you are here and are safe. I missed you so, so much!" I played it down, but being a hero, especially to such a beautiful, young maiden, felt pretty good.

With no light source, the cave was extremely dark, not that it mattered to Michael because he slept most of the time anyway, but it was nice to finally be able to see by candlelight. When I was first mysteriously transported to Ireland, adapting to how dark everything was took a while. I was used to 100-candle power or more, and most lighting at this time was one, two, or three-candle power. With just a couple of candles lit, our cave was as bright as the castles. I could acquire water in the stream below, but since it ran alongside the road, someone might see me, so I explored another passageway in the cave, where I heard a trickling sound and found an underground stream whose water was pure, cold and delicious.

After a couple of touch-and-go days, Michael had recovered, physically and emotionally—as much as could be expected. Being in a cramped jail cell for so long had caused his muscles to atrophy; therefore, I had him doing exercises, something he had never done before—not that anyone in this time exercised, since they worked so hard. I enlarged the hole a little and dragged some logs in to serve as benches so we would not have to sit on the damp ground. I also found a passage that led to the top of the rock face where I could observe those traveling on the road at the top of a distant exposed green hill and periodically saw their progress through clear spaces between the trees below.*

Over the next few days, Michael did little other than sleep. When Gwendolyn appeared again, in addition to more food and supplies, along with my cartridge-making equipment, she brought Michael's sword, and in our cozy cave, we began practicing. He was impressed with my nascent abilities but was extremely rusty himself. I was amazed at how fast he improved, though, living up to the reputation that Captain Black had painted of him as an excellent swordsman.

We had plenty of time to discuss my adventures in London and Spain. He was astonished at all the classic literature I could secure and wished he could read and start printing these treasured works. Unfortunately, with Hugh in charge of the print shop and in possession of the documents, that was not an option. Hugh and certainly Seamus would not be able to translate these from Latin or Spanish, so they would not be able to work on them until they acquired a translator. Because Reginald had killed his nephew, Thomas, our translator, Jimmy Brogan, left the shop when Hugh took over. Since the manuscripts were not the originals, they would not know their value or how to market them. At least they knew they were valuable and prized by two queens, so they would surely protect the treasures. Since the fifty or so documents would be confusing to them, they might not find my prized Caxton original books at the bottom of the trunk for some time. At least, that's what I hoped.

We were very bored, though. We found some cards at the bottom of the supplies, and I taught Michael Texas Hold Em. If we lost, we had to take a sip of whiskey and eventually became silly—a welcome release.

Meanwhile, Reginald was furious with what had happened and told Boston that he would see that everyone who aided in the escape would be tortured, drawn, and quartered. He wanted my head more than any other and, according to Gwendolyn, had posted broadsides with my name and description throughout the shire, offering a substantial reward for my capture. He knew that the O'Flanneries and Brogans were somehow behind it, too, and threatened to attack them, confiscate their lands and imprison them all.

Boston said, "Reginald, we must be careful with the two lords. If you arrest them, we will lose the support of the people and the other lords. We might even risk interference from the King of Ireland or King Henry. Be patient; we will catch the vermin. We should post guards outside their manors to see who goes in and out. I have already bribed servants at both domiciles, who will apprise us of their activities, for which they know they will be handsomely rewarded. Once we catch them conspiring, we can try and hang them and then confiscate their estates. These are the largest lands in the shire, which will make us even wealthier," he said with a glint in his eye and a smirk on his thin lips as he wrung his hands in anticipation of the ill-gained windfall."

Reginald reluctantly agreed but, as a man of action, had to do something. "Since Michael escaped, I will force Gwendolyn to marry me. That was the deal, and since they took Michael and we cannot hang him as he deserves, I will take her. It's only fair."*

After seeing her father at the cave, Gwendolyn sat in her grandfather's den reading when Paddy Brogan entered. The handsome young lad with sparkling blue eyes, copious black hair and dimpled cheeks had recently taken a rare bath, combed his hair, wore his best outfit, and shined his Sunday go-to-church boots, for he, like many of the young men in the shire, had a crush on the fair Gwendolyn.

When Gwendolyn saw him, she immediately went to give him a hug and a kiss on the cheek, something he misunderstood. "Thank you, Paddy, for helping to save me da. I be so grateful to you and your brother Daryl, too. Please thank him for me."

Even though he resembled his older, dead brother Thomas, whom Gwendolyn had loved, she was not interested in the younger Brogan.

Somewhat verklempt, red in the face, Paddy said, "I have a message for your grandfather from me da."

The lords knew that Reginald was surveilling them. They also knew from their loyal servants that Boston had tried to bribe some of them. Therefore, they did not meet in person; rather they communicated through trusted messengers such as Paddy.

"My grandfather is out in the forest to the West hunting," Gwendolyn exclaimed.

His white, freckled, Irish complexion still glowing from her presence, Paddy bowed to Gwendolyn and awkwardly backed out.

Soon afterward, Reginald suddenly appeared in the library. He had heard from one of the bribed servants that Rand had previously been at the castle and had brought a dozen of his knights with him, who were now noisily searching the castle.

"Where is Rand? I know you know where he is."

"He is no here. After he returned from London, he was fired from the print shop. He spent a couple of days here, but that be all. Perhaps he went to Dublin in search o' work. He may be trying to open a print shop there."

"Was he involved in the criminal act that helped your father escape? Is he with your father now? Where are they, Gwendolyn? Who else was involved? I ken you ken where they are."

Feeling assaulted by his inquisition, Gwendolyn nervously responded, "I ken nothing about all this. I am just a woman. No one would include me in such plans, but I am glad that, as you said, my father has escaped. I thought he might have been killed by your men by now. This is the last place they would be. If it be me, I would ha' been in Nealland or Dublin long ago."

In a time when sexual abuse was rampant, and there was little or no justice for the victims, when an abuser, similar to modern times, might despoil dozens of innocent victims, when the rich and powerful had no fear of retribution when a king could claim the right to sleep with a virgin bride on her wedding night, when the victors expected to rape the defeated army's young maidens, Reginald, the relentless, remorseless, serial rapist's face dramatically changed. Gwendolyn's feistiness brought out his lust and abusive nature.

"Since your criminal father has escaped, even though your family has been disgraced, I will take mercy on you and marry you to save your reputation. Come to me, kiss me, give me some of your honey."

"I would never marry you. How could I possibly marry someone who wants to kill my father? You disgust me!"

Her comment set Reginald off. He was used to having his way with women and thought that they all wanted him. Even if they resisted, he knew they wanted him—they just needed a little coaxing to inspire their passions and set their hormones on fire. He went to her, put his hand behind her neck and long red locks, then forced his lips upon hers.

She began hitting him relentlessly with her fists and pushed him away, to which he just laughed, "You excite me, you lovely wench. You will marry me whether you want to or not. If you resist, I will confiscate your grandfather's lands for harboring a criminal and hatching a seditious plot."

"You have no proof."

"I am the all-powerful king NOW! I need no proof. I know the plot is true. I want you. Gwendolyn, I need you to be my queen. You are an exotic, beautiful creature that has piqued my desire. I need you. I want you now. Come to me."

"No, go away!"

He came at her and, with the leather from his sword's belt, tied her hands behind her back. "I will bestow on you pleasures that you have never tasted before. When we are married, you will learn many ways to please me."

Then he pushed her up against the bookshelves, hiked up her skirt, grabbed her derriere and began grinding on her as books fell from the shelves above, one hitting him on the head, which caused him to pull his lips back from hers, so she could shriek in horror.

"Reginald, you surely would not want to marry a woman who had been spoiled, would you? That is not the way of a true Christian king or a chivalrous knight."

This caused him to stop and let her skirt fall. Instead, he ripped the top of her dress and began plunging into her breasts.

Unable to find her grandfather, Paddy returned to say goodbye to Gwendolyn. When he heard the books falling and the shriek, he immediately ran to the room, opened the door, and saw Reginald upon her, shouting, "Stop you maniac!"

Reginald turned, saw the young man, grabbed Megan from the floor, unsheathed her, and, without hesitation, stabbed Paddy in the stomach.

In horror, Gwendolyn screamed at the top of her lungs, a blood-curdling yell. The knights, the servants, and the rest of the household converged on the den, where they saw young Paddy on the floor, bleeding through his shirt. Reginald left the premises with his bewildered knights trailing behind. Gwendolyn caressed Paddy's head and ordered the servants to call for the doctor and take him up to a bedroom.

When Lord O'Flannery returned from the fields and saw his beloved granddaughter so disheveled at the hands of Reginald, he ordered the servants to assemble all the men from his lands and all his relatives, including Gwendolyn's sisters' husbands. He checked on Paddy, who, although he was in terrible pain, barely able to talk, gave him the message he carried from his father.

The lord donned his armor and grabbed his broadsword. As he walked out to join his forces, he was met by Gwendolyn, who said, "Grandfather, don't do this. I am not completely together after what happened to me, but no real damage was done. My virginity is still intact. If you attack Reginald with all his troops, he will slaughter you all. That's what he wants. Then he will confiscate your lands and have his way with me."

O'Flannery took a deep breath, realized she was right, and reluctantly dismissed the men, vowing to himself that he would find a way to get even with Reginald. He knew it would take hours for him to calm down and days to move on, but eventually, he would get even.

One of the servants hastily rode to the Brogans, where the lord and lady were in shock, and immediately traveled to the O'Flannery's. There, they beheld their dying son, who the doctor said could not be saved.

Gwendolyn stayed by his bedside, holding his hand throughout the night until he passed at dawn as the yellow sun lit the dew—a scene that was too familiar to her since she had been in the same position when the love of her life, Thomas, Paddy's brother, perished.

The Brogans were incensed, for this was the second son they lost to Reginald. They promised revenge, not an idle threat, because they were a formidable clan. Lord Brogan was the oldest of fifteen children, eleven of whom were male. Lady Brogan hailed from an adjacent clan with nearly as many brothers. Other than a priest, a nun and a son who had died in an accident, each of their siblings, in turn, had between four and twelve children. Nearly everyone in their neck of the kingdom was related to them, as were many throughout the rest of the shire. With a limited amount of land, the Brogan's had spread throughout the shire and Ireland, many in Dublin and some in England, but if the lord of the clan called upon them, they would come to avenge the dastardly act.

The funeral for their youngest son was a somber affair attended by nearly all the shire's lords, who felt the Brogans' pain and outrage at Reginald. Gwendolyn could not stop crying for Paddy, who had come to her rescue. If he had not done so, she would be permanently dishonored and might even be pregnant. But, if she had given in to him and not screamed, Paddy would still be alive. She was confused and conflicted.

Following the funeral, the Brogan's servants prepared a reception for the attending nobles. There was to be a council meeting next month, and they promised to press for justice for Paddy and Gwendolyn.

Lord O'Flannery had a servant call Gwendolyn into the den, "Gwendolyn, I am highly concerned about you, and I want you to get away before Reginald returns. One of my brothers, your uncle Finbar, lives in Dublin. He is a lawyer there, and since he personally knows the king, he will be able to protect you. I want you to leave before first light tomorrow morning."

"But Grandfather, If I go, who will tend to me da and Rand? I am the only one who knows where they are."

"Surely you can find someone you trust to care for them; how about Ryan the smithy?"

"But he is in town, and Reginald may surmise what he is doing and the forge is next to the print shop where Hugh is."

"Well, I am sure there is someone here."

"I do know someone who no one would suspect—Kieran. He is the stable boy I see every day when I go riding. He is loyal to a fault and full of character. Besides, he goes to town regularly to get horses shooed by John or to bring back oats. Reginald's guards are used to seeing him on the road with the wagon."

"Yes, I think Kieran is a good choice. I like the lad meself."

"Then you will go to Dublin. I will write a letter to Finbar for you to carry with you."

"Thank you, grandfather, but I will go to be with my da and Rand."

"You can't go there. Do you want to live on the run, afraid that any minute someone will find you?"

"They are perfectly safe, where no one will ever find us. I appreciate your concern for me. It means so much, but I will be fine."

Realizing, akin to his red-headed, departed wife, her grandmother, how headstrong she could be, Lord O'Flannery relented.

She hastily packed and told Kieran about her plan. They would leave before dusk. She would ride her horse through the woods and meet him on the road. After she was sure no one was following them, they would drive to the spot where he could turn the wagon off the road and hide it behind the pines. He would do this every five days and then proceed into town to obtain a load of oats.*

To break the monotony of being cloistered in the cave, I regularly climbed to the top of the ancient rock formation and look down over the cliff to the road about a third of a mile away. In a sense, I felt like an old, nosy grandmother who looked out the living room window onto the street, but I told myself I was doing reconnaissance to see when the busiest periods were, to see who traveled along the road and when Reginald's troops passed by on their regular patrols. Looking for patterns, I recorded these in quill on paper, for it was my analytical nature to do so. Out of the dimly lit cave, my perch on the flattened, massive, gray rock carpeted in green moss became my special place. Above the trees, which were just turning from green to reds, yellows, oranges, and a dozen other variations of color, I could look out over the broad valley, be by myself, and meditate. It also provided separation from Michael, not that I did not enjoy being with him, but being with anyone, 24x7 could be a little draining. I think he also appreciated the separation. Below, I saw a periodic stream of traffic: traders with wagons full of goods, farmers taking their produce to market, merchants from Bunkillarny journeying to the smaller hamlets with their products, and some young lovers out for a drive to see the nearby scenic lake with their chaperone in tow. I even saw Tommy riding out to deliver the Reader.

One dewy morn, looking between the trees coming over the hill, I saw a rider with a wagon in tow. They turned off the road at the bottom of the hill into the clearing behind the blue-green fir trees. Then, I caught a glimpse of Gwendolyn's blondish hair shining in a spot of sunlight. Since it was not our pre-appointed day, I was alarmed and scurried through the cave into the woods to see what had occurred to risk her trip. When I encountered Gwendolyn coming our way, I met her, holding her horse's reins while she said, "We have a new arrangement. Come with me to gather the supplies, and I will tell you about it when we return to the cave."

I shook hands with Kieran, who took boxes and bags out of the wagon and deposited the supplies on the ground. After Gwendolyn checked for traffic on the road, he headed for Bunkillarny. We disguised the wagon tracks. Winding through the forest and boulders, I carried as much as possible, as did Gwendolyn, but it took two trips, which seemed like a lot, considering it had only been three days since the last supply run.

Once back in the cave, she hugged her father, exclaiming how much he had improved.

"Rand has been keeping me busy doing all of these ridiculous exercises, but once again, I have become a formidable swordsman," he said as he lifted his sword, swished the air, and demonstrated some adroit moves.

Gwendolyn declared, "I am staying with you." We both looked stunned until, seeing our expressions, she explained, "Since you escaped, Reginald came to the castle and demanded I marry him, so Grandfather thought I should get away."

Realizing how vile Reginald could be, in unison, we said, "Did he hurt you?"

"No, not really. I'm all right."

But I could tell by her countenance that something terrible had happened. "Are you sure you are all right? You seem upset."

"I'm fine and so happy ta be wi' you two."

"Gwenn, tell us what happened," Michael demanded.

"...Well, Reginald started to attack me. When Paddy came to my rescue, Reginald stabbed him. He died the next day. I feel so awful, so dreadful awful!"

Michael responded, "I will kill that bastard. Rand, let's ride to the castle, and I will challenge him to a duel. You can be my second."

"Da, that be why I did no want to tell you. He would have both of you immediately thrown in the keep and hung. The reason he came to Grandfather's was to capture Rand. It would do no good to confront him. Grandfather will figure out something that we can help with. Oh, as you might expect, the Brogans are threatening to start an uprising."

I was worried about having her with us, namely, that our rough bachelor accommodations would be too Spartan for her, but she turned out to be a real trooper. She cleaned up the cave, made it into distinct rooms, had us make some rough furniture, and cooked real meals for us. Our lives definitely improved. She adapted to outdoor living as well as any of my backpacking friends, though cave living was much more civilized than living out in the woods, and it was nice to have a pretty face around. Having her there made me feel good, and I could see how it lifted Michael's spirits, too.*

When Reginald told Boston what happened, he asked, "What have you done? Can't you keep it in your pants? She's a noblewoman. You can't just have your way with anyone. You are jeopardizing everything we have built up!"

"But I have had many a noblewoman, and they all love having sex with me."

Searching for an answer, Boston just stood there looking up, not saying a word for a long time, which greatly concerned Reginald, for anytime he got into trouble, Boston always seemed to have an immediate solution.

At the council meeting, the lords pressed to have Reginald tried for the murder of Paddy.

Deceptive Boston replied, "There is no precedent for trying a king, and Reginald stands in for King Patrick."

Lord Harold—"But there is precedent—after all, that was what the Magna Carta was about. Then the lords challenged King John for his misdeeds in 1215 and later formed parliament."

"I move to have a vote."

"But, you are not in parliament. You are merely an advisory council to the king, to Reginald. You have no authority to try him. Besides, he has done nothing wrong. He was simply protecting the lady in question from a prowler. She had lured Reginald into the den, where she kissed him and pressed her body next to him. Reginald, as a renowned man of arms, as you know, has lightning-fast reflexes. Being surprised, thinking it be a prowler, he immediately reacted. Unfortunately, Paddy did not mean any harm, but by then, it was too late. Surely, somebody who is standing in for our king and therefore has absolute power cannot be tried."

Since Reginald chaired the council, there was no vote, which angered many. Not all the lords protested, for some owed their positions to Boston and Reginald and didn't want to upset those who provided them with more influence, power, and wealth. The others were disappointed that the council they had so fervently believed in devolved so quickly.

Lord McGlinchey pressed onward, "As previously agreed, the harvest is upon us, and it is time for our men to return home so they can bring in the crops."

Reginald—"We still face threats from our neighbors, the O'Neals, and there is a possibility of an insurrection by the Brogans. I need all of my troops here to defend the shire."

Harold –"If we do not harvest the crops, you will not be able to feed or pay those troops. You will still have those attached to the castle and the conscripts from the O'Callaghans. If needed, our men will return after the harvest in time for the games."

Devious Boston, disgusted with Reginald's recent behavior that had jeopardized their positions, sensing that he could not win this skirmish too, acquiesced, adding, "Any soldier who is not involved in the harvest shall stay here. The others may depart."

Reginald gritted his teeth but said no more.

EIGHTEEN

Prince John

After sailing from Scotland, when Lady Catherine and Patrick finally arrived in London, they acquired a suite at the Royal Hotel near Westminster Palace. Catherine was disappointed to learn that Marie had already left for Paris. Upon settling in, they went to the palace and requested a meeting with King Henry on Patrick's behalf, and the next day, they went before the king to plead their case.

"Your majesty, I am Lady Catherine of Bunkillarny, Ireland, the widow of Lord Edward. This is my son Patrick, who was installed as the Lord and Marquess of Bunkillarny. I serve as his regent. I came here to charge General Reginald Van Cleve the Third with undermining the authority of the marquess, attempted regicide, and attempted rape on my person."

"Those are serious charges, mi lady. I know the man of whom you speak, who has performed valiantly in the War of the Roses and whom I awarded a silver cross. What evidence have you?"

Catherine knew that because Reginald had fought for Henry and knowing that it was a man's world and that women's pleas against such glorified men of war were typically ignored, worried that Henry would not rule in her favor. She continued, "When Reginald returned from an unjust war waged against a smaller shire to the south, ruled for hundreds of years by the O'Callaghans, he began meeting with my son, and I believe that he was slowly poisoning him with the ale he was drinking. Day after day, my son became sicker and sicker until he ended up in bed and no longer saw Reginald regularly and did not drink any more of the poisoned ale. Then he began to improve. As you can see, Patrick is strong now."

"Do you have proof of this, Lady Catherine? Perhaps this was just one of the many ailments that regularly plague us all."

"No, your majesty, not yet. If it pleases you, may I continue?"

"Proceed"

"Reginald insisted I marry him, in which case he would have all the authority over Patrick, Bunkillarny, and rights to my lands in Normandy, for which I am a cousin of King Charles of France. (Henry's interest peaked upon hearing this.) When I refused, this enraged him, and he began to rape me. Patrick came to my rescue and drew his sword on Reginald, who soon had the sword's tip at Patrick's throat and was about to slay him until I beat him off. Fearing for our lives, we attempted to escape, whereupon we were pursued by Reginald and a dozen of his men. My palace guards defended us courageously until they were all killed by Reginald's superior forces. We barely made it out alive with them shooting at Patrick and trying to kill him as we sailed away. I am suspicious that in his quest for our kingdom, he might have also killed my beloved husband, Edward, who you knew, majesty."

"This is indeed very serious. What would you have me do?"

"I would like you to send your army to help us arrest Van Cleve, reclaim the throne for the legitimate heir, and obtain justice."

Henry whispered to one of his ministers, who left the throne room and asked Catherine and Patrick to stay while he heard other petitions. Catherine felt that this action indicated that she would be ignored and wondered what she would do. If the king refused her, they would have to remain in London as exiles, but how would she support her children?

About twenty minutes later, Henry interrupted the current petitioner and bade someone from the back of the massive hall to come forward. As the crowd of courtesans parted, Catherine and Patrick turned and saw Prince John. They were ecstatic and, forgetting court protocol, simultaneously hugged him from either side.

"I can see that you appear to be a happy family. Is this true?"

"Oh yes, Your Majesty, we love John; he is a remarkable man, a good man. Instead of coming to John's aid at the battle of Nealland, as he was sworn to do, Reginald betrayed John and attacked him."

"Well then, we seem to have a problem here because John has also petitioned me to help his cause as the legitimate heir to the throne."

"Your majesty, we support that claim. Patrick will abdicate the throne in favor of John, for he would be a splendid king with all the noble qualities of my dear departed husband, Edward. He is, after all, the oldest living son."

"Patrick, will you renounce your claim to the throne in favor of your brother John?"

Patrick stepped up before the king and, without the shy reluctance he previously displayed, put his arm on John's shoulder and, in a strong, sure deep voice, said, "Your noble majesty, I, Patrick, Daniel, Emmit, Edward, the Lord and Marquess of Bunkillarny, do formally renounce my throne in favor of my august brother John, who except for salacious, untrue slander and an unjust war should have been the Lord of Bunkillarny."

"Madame, I sanction your cause but, unfortunately, cannot afford to send an army to Ireland at this time. What I shall do, instead, is give you a document recognizing Prince John as the legitimate heir of Bunkillarny, which will be signed by myself and the archbishop of Canterbury and will be transmitted to Bunkillarny along with my emissary and an accompanying honor guard."

"Oh, thank you, your majesty, you are certainly a noble and just king." The three of them bowed low and backed out of the room.

Unbeknownst to them, three suspicious men dressed as nobles, which granted them entrance to the throne room, had followed Catherine and Patrick to the court and stood at the back of the hall, where they heard King Henry's pronouncement, then followed them at a distance back to the hotel.*

That night Catherine, Patrick and John went out to dinner to celebrate their success. John introduced Catherine to a wine that, even though she hailed from France, she had not had because it came from another region—Chardonnay. She loved the tasty, oaky, creamy white wine. There, they discussed their return and their strategy for restoring the throne to John. Something that Catherine said would not be easy, for Reginald and Boston would not give up their power without a fight, and Reginald controlled all the armed forces.

John said, "I know that the O'Donnells support Reginald because they fear I will align Bunkillarny with the O'Neals. I will go to King Rory and pledge that I will never make such an alliance and renounce all claims to any titles or lands in Neilland, which should hopefully assuage any concerns Rory has."

"But John, isn't that very dangerous?"

"It is, but I trust King Rory as a man of honor."

John continued, "With the support of King Henry's emissary and your support, I believe we have a chance."

"But I thought you loved your life and your estate in Nealland. You seem to have done so well there, nurturing it, growing it, and inspiring those who tend to it. You would give all of that up?"

"Dear Catherine, I never coveted the throne and would have been happy raising a family in Nealland with my lovely wife, but my duty is to Bunkillarny and my father and family's legacy—a condition of the benefits I received when I was born. I wish my brother Edward were still alive and had assumed the throne, then none of this would have happened, but fate never follows a straight line, and as my father taught me, we must be prepared to meet such challenges."

"How shall we defeat Reginald? Since the battle of Nealland when you escaped, he and Boston have moved to consolidate their power. Reginald controls the armed forces and has been giving speeches throughout the shire to enhance his reputation. Many are enamored with him and his lies. He and Boston have been handing out positions, no doubt demanding loyalty in return. They both have added to their wealth. My husband, the king, thought Boston was skimming money from the kingdom and was about to fire and exile him. With no one to check on them, they have doubled the taxes and are probably taking much more."

"I don't think we can waltz in and claim the throne. As you say, they have too much power. We must work with allies to sense the situation, assess who is still loyal to the crown, and hatch a plan."

After a couple of bottles of the delicious Chardonnay, the festive trio left the restaurant. It was late at night when three men, now dressed in lowly garb, greeted them with lit matchlocks and ordered them into a nearby darkened alley.

To avoid conflict, John offered up his purse and said to let the woman and child go on their way.

In a thick Gaelic brogue, the leader said, "We will be a taken your purse and madam's jewelry, but tha' is no what we came fer."

"What do you want?"

"We came fer your life, Prince John, and that of yer brother. Unfortunately, madam, you will have to forfeit your life too. Not something we had planned, but there can be no witnesses to this here 'robry'."

Realizing the desperate nature of their predicament, John rushed the leader, and after the trigger was pulled before the explosion, he knocked it out of his hand, then spinning around the portly brigand, shielded himself from the others so they could not fire at him. Without thinking, Patrick unsheathed his sword and knocked the pistol out of the second man's hand. Just as the third man raised his hand to shoot Patrick, John pushed the portly one into him, the bullet firing down into the dirt.

The three grabbed their swords and began fighting with the brothers, who stood back-to-back, fending them off, pairing and thrusting but mostly fending off their foes' blows for what seemed an eternity. John was an expert swordsman, but these were three of Reginald's best, battle-tested warriors who had the advantage of numbers.

Impressed by Patrick's unexpected skill, sensing that he was tiring, John needed to take action. Seeing an opening, executing a risky move, he lunged forward and struck one in his side, taking him out of the fight for a while, but the leader, seeing him exposed, stabbed him in the chest. John, staggering to defend himself, fell helplessly to the ground. Patrick, seeing his brother down having a surge of adrenalin, wounded the third man in the arm but now faced two who knew it would be soon over.

Suddenly, four soldiers appeared at the end of the alley and commanded the men to drop their swords immediately. Recalling they had passed a pub where several soldiers were, Catherine ran back and begged them to come to her aid, saying that bandits were accosting two nobles. The soldiers arrested them, one of whom had been mortally wounded.

John was still alive, but with the wound so close to his heart, it did not seem as though he would make it through the night. Catherine and Patrick were severely distressed and, realizing that Reginald had, no doubt, sent the assassins to kill them, wondered how many more they would have to face and if they would ever make it back to Bunkillarny.

Revolt!

Through trusted couriers, Lords Brogan and O'Flannery had been exchanging encoded notes for weeks. Brogan was becoming more and more impatient, insisting that they meet face-to-face or that he would have to act on his own. He had put out a call to his extensive clan to return to Bunkillarny, who had been arriving from throughout the British Isles and even Holland and France, along with several sailors who sailed the Atlantic, Baltic, and Mediterranean. Reginald, fearing reprisals following Paddy's death, had doubled the guard on the roads to the two lords' lands, watching both continuously—day and night. Some of the lords' peasants had even seen the soldiers skulking through the woods. The entire shire was tense. Subconsciously, they sensed there might be a civil war brewing but oddly went about their daily lives as if nothing would happen. The shire had been at peace for so long such a possibility was beyond imagination.

Not wanting to attract attention, Lord Brogan had the out-of-town clan members hidden in Mariah Canyon, on the outskirts of the shire near Neilland, in an inhospitable, uninhabited portion of the shire that, because of the deep gorge and depleted soil, had no commercial value. There, the clan practiced with sword, spear, pike and lance, honing their skills, rekindling their bond, preparing for a war of revenge for their two fallen kin. They dared not practice with guns, though, for fear that the explosions would attract attention from some passerby.

By way of a trusted messenger, Lord O'Flannery agreed to meet at Mc Nab's and sent a note to John, the smithy, asking him to join them. They would have liked to invite Michael and Rand but realized that was too risky. Whenever they were in town, they would stop at McNab's, so that would not attract suspicion; plus, as the night wore on, as the noise level escalated and the men continued to mix or relieve themselves of their ale, no one kept track of anyone. Without needing to say anything, as if they were going to the privy, each of the three left their tables separately, walked to the back, and looking around to make sure no one observed them, climbed the stairs.

They met in the Mc Nabs' small kitchen in their rooms above the bar, sitting at the kitchen table on rickety chairs, the noise of the boisterous crowd below masking their desperate plotting. Since the harvest was in process, nearly all of their men were home, but the harvest would be completed soon and Reginald would likely call them back for a war on another helpless inland shire. There was little time left to overthrow Reginald. They figured that Lords Harold and Mc Glinchey would definitely join them, but that still left nine lords that were either in Reginald's camp or undecided, some of whom, for fear of reprisals if they could avoid it, would surely not take sides.

O'Flannery opened the discussion on the subject of weapons, "When the men were allowed to go back to their homes, Reginald ordered that their weapons be stored in the arsenal at the castle until they returned, preventing any possible insurrections. Our knights and some of our merchants still have their own weapons, but very few of our peasants do."

Brogan said, "Maybe we can sneak into the castle and seize the arsenal, but since Reginald suspects we are up to something, it is, no doubt, well-guarded."

John said, "I may be able to help. I have been working on a large order for Reginald, and since the army is away in the fields and Boston did not want to pay for these yet, they are stored in my shop. I have produced many additional weapons, just in case—swords and spears, along with Ryan's new flintlocks. These ingenious pistols are adapted from the matchlocks that do not require a wick and will certainly come in handy they will."

Brogan enthusiastically replied, "That sounds marvelous, John. Just what we need."

O'Flannery had some doubts, "With Reginald surveilling us, it will be impossible for us to mass our troops without him finding out about it. That will give him time to gather men from the other lords, and we know that at least three owe their positions to him or Boston. Besides, with them controlling the Bunkillarny Reader and all the speeches Reginald has been making, I am not sure the people are with us."

"Well, most of the merchants certainly are," John said.

Brogan, feeling he was losing support, added, "We only have a week before our men return. We have to act now. We do not have any more time and cannot live under this corrupt ruler any longer. We have the element of surprise. We can take out Reginald's guards and be ready to mass our troops at night. With all my clan ready to go, I have the largest force, most of them hidden, armed and training in the canyon. I will go forward alone if I have to."

"No, you will not have to," O'Flannery exclaimed.

"We will be ready; I have been waiting for this day. Let's go!" John exclaimed, and clicking glasses, they toasted to success.*

We had grown used to our little family life in the cave. Thanks to Gwendolyn, I was eating better than when I lived in San Francisco—no TV dinners or fast food, and the accommodations were larger than most studios in the city, which cost $3,500/month. Living in the cavern was free, and when I climbed through the passageways up to the top of the cliff, I enjoyed my little perch above the tree-tops with a fantastic view of the valley below and the winding river in the distance—on sunny days, a nice respite from the cool, dark cave. While up there, I had noticed more patrols and wondered why—perhaps old Reggie was getting nervous. Drama permeated the atmosphere, and it felt like something, whatever it was, was about to happen.

Gwendolyn had brought with her some tools, including a saw, hammer and nails, urging Michael and I to fashion crude furniture so we would not have to sit on the ground or logs. Together, we sawed the end off of a large fallen tree deep in the woods for a tabletop and, using sawed-off branches, made a crude table. Using similar techniques, we also sawed and hammered three chairs together so that we could comfortably eat, read and play cards.

I was amazed to see how their cards looked remarkably similar to those I was familiar with, except there were four face cards instead of three, representing what she said were a king, queen, knight, and knave. The suits were similar except what I called diamonds, clubs and spades, which Gwendolyn called tiles, clovers and spikes. The hearts were the same in the deck of fifty-six cards with no numbers printed on them. I taught them Texas Hold 'em, which we played for river pebbles of various sizes representing various denominations. Somehow Gwendolyn seemed to win most of the hands, thereby accumulating most of the pebbles, which she lorded over us, telling us to go to the creek for more pebbles for her to win.

The first room of the cave was relatively small, but the second, roughly the shape of a geodesic dome, was twenty feet high and thirty feet in diameter. This cavern became our great room, Michael's, and my bedroom, where we slept on hay that Kieran had brought for the horses. When we put out the candles at night, the cave became totally dark, and the first one up would have to stumble around to light the first candle with a flint. If I happened to be the first up, I cheated and used my BIC. So, he would not see my lighter, I had my back to Michael. One day, Gwendolyn got up just before me and saw my BIC as I lit the candle.

"What be that Rand?"

"What be what?"

"That little device you used to light the candle"

I quickly hid the BIC in my pocket, "Oh it was just a flint and taper."

"No, it were not. Show it to me."

I showed the BIC to her and said, "This is the flint that strikes the wheel that lights the oil in this little cylinder."

"Ingenious. I ha' ner seen anythin' like that before."

I replied, "I guess it came from me old country," but could tell my standard excuse was running thin with her."

The third room contained a rough bed we constructed for Gwendolyn. An alcove off that room became our workshop where we made our furniture, and I assembled my cartridges—far enough from the cave's entrance so that our sawing and hammering could not be heard outside. Considering that most castles at the time were dimly lit, cool, and made of stone, seeking positivity, we told each other we lived like Kings.

Gwendolyn asked me, "What are all these strange symbols on our cavern's walls?"

I responded, "I am not sure, but they may have come from some ancient tribe who lived here."

"You mean the Druids?"

"Possibly"

"I have heard tales of the Druids—tales of little green men, banshees, and pagan ceremonies before Saint Patrick came here to save our souls. What do they mean?"

"I really don't know, but they certainly are elaborate, aren't they? Thousands of years ago, all of the British Isles were connected to France, and you could walk to Scotland, London and Paris."

"How could that be possible?"

"Back then there was, what was called, an ice age and the water in the North Sea froze as a huge sheet of ice."

"How do you know these things?"

Realizing I had said too much, I blamed it on my amnesia, but I could tell by her expression that she was no longer buying that either, so I immediately changed the subject. "I was sorry to hear that Thomas had passed away. He seemed to like you very much, and I think we could have become good friends. Was his passing difficult for you?"

"Oh yes, very difficult. I stayed by his bedside until he died. At one point, it seemed as if he would recover, and he asked me to marry him, to which I said yes. I was so happy and looked forward to our life together and having bern with him."

"Oh, I am so sorry, Gwendolyn!" and with that, I hugged her.

"And how is Lady Marie?"

Somewhat off balance, not thinking she knew about Marie, feigning ignorance, I replied, "Lady Marie?"

"I saw the way she looked at you when you won your awards and when you were dancing with her. Then you disappeared and did not get back home until the next morn. I believe that the day before you left for London, when you were gone so long, you had gone to see her. Did you see her in London?" she said with a penetrating look."

After what she had told me about Thomas, I felt I had to be honest with her. "Everything you say is true, and I did see her in London. We spent an incredible night together, and in the morning, I asked her to marry me. She said she loved me but that King Charles had promised her to a Bavarian prince. I pleaded with her to run away with me, but she said that since she lived in another world, the world of the court, and that she would not be a good wife for me."

"Are you still in love with her?"

"Yes. It was not that long ago—the wounds are still fresh."

Gwendolyn gave me a much-needed hug.

Throughout our time in the caves, we explored many of its passages, finding one that led to the back side of the mountain, where we could forage without risking being seen or heard by those traveling along the main road. This is where we found the fallen trees and branches for our furniture, which we could see without fear of being heard.

On one such occasion, Gwendolyn and I found berries we brought back to Michael, who encouraged us to wander by ourselves. He said he preferred to stay back and read the books that Gwendolyn had acquired from her grandfather's library.

I told Gwendolyn of my adventures in London and Spain—of the attempted robberies, Francisco and his family, the marvels of Salamanca and its famous university, the culture of Cordoba, the precious books I had found in Spain, dating back to Grecian times and the honor of meeting Queen Isabella. Gwendolyn could not wait to read the priceless manuscripts and was entranced by my description of the famous queen.

I told her about Colleen and her family, who, since they, in essence, worked for the same venture, she considered a sister and wanted to meet her again. She remembered that her father had taught Colleen how to read, but she was just a toddler then. I told Gwendolyn that the next time I went to London, she should join me. Then I told her about Margaret, the Queen Mother, her soiree, and the privilege of feasting with King Henry. Gwendolyn marveled at the concept of a soiree—being able to discuss so many interesting topics with knowledgeable professors and learned people. I suggested that when we went to London, perhaps Lady Margaret would invite us to one. "Oh, that would be marvelous," she expressed.

While walking back through the passages one day, carrying a rabbit I had snared, I felt a strange electric tingling. The only other time I had felt this was at the bottom of the Grand Canyon when I had been transported to the cave. The cave walls were luminous, just as they had been back there. This was the moment I had been waiting for—to return to my own place and time—something I had longed for so long. But I felt very close to my friends here and wondered if I could leave them at this critical time. I was torn. I started walking towards the back of the cave where I would be transported until I heard Gwendolyn's sweet voice calling for me, and without hesitation, I went to her. When the electric tingling began to increase, feeling faint and stretched, I ran until I saw her.

"Rand, what is happening? Look at those bright blue and green lights. Isn't it magnificent? What causes it?" She seemed mesmerized, and she was starting to tremble and looked stretched. I grabbed her by the arm, lifted her over my shoulder, and carried her away until we reached the main room, which, with the hieroglyphs glowing, was starting to fluoresce. Michael was sitting there reading by candlelight when I told him we had to leave immediately, and before he could get up, I swept him up, too."

Outside, Michael, in a stern voice, asked, "What's going on Rand?"

"Being in the cave now is dangerous."

Crossing his arms with a determined look, he queried, "Why Rand?"

Not wanting to tell them something I did not think they would believe, I said, "I can't tell you why, but I know the cave could kill us. Did you feel the tingling?" Gwendolyn had, but Michael had not.

Looking confused and somewhat disheveled by the bum's rush, Gwendolyn probed, "Does this have something to do with how you got here and why you were injured? After all, this is near where I found you, and it seemed like you were saying goodbye that time we first went into the cave."

"Yes, it does. But if I told you, I don't think you would believe me, and I don't truly understand what happened."

"Whatever it is, I would believe you. I trust you." The look she gave me from that beautiful, beaming, honest face melted my heart, and I so wanted to confess all to her.

"With so much going on now, this is not the right time. I will tell you later. Trust me."*

Overlooking the road from my perch, I noticed a wagon coming down the road and turning off. It was Kieran riding into the clearing, and since it was not our pre-appointed supply day, I wondered why. Unsure where we were, not wanting to call out, he started wandering around in the woods. When Gwendolyn and I intercepted him, he gave us a coded message that we were not able to decipher, but Michael was:

We take back Bunkillarny tomorrow.
Come to the manor immediately!
Be careful!

We had kept our horses in the back of the cave surrounded by rocks on three sides, where we retrieved them and saddled up. On this cool, crisp day under a sea-blue sky, the sun illuminated the multicolored trees around us, many leaves having already fallen to the ground beneath our feet. In the middle of the forest, the pungent odor of fall filled the air.

Despite our protests, Gwendolyn insisted that she join us, "I'm as good with a sword as any man and can ride better than most."

I said, "I cannot believe you could be that good."

Michael replied, "She is, indeed, outstanding. I taught her."

"I was supposed to be a boy, and I liked playing with bows, knives and swords better'n my sisters' dolls."

I still could not believe this, so we had a go of it. Moving adroitly, crunching the leaves under her well-placed feet, her arm raised, back arched, sword superbly balanced, she successively thwarted my advances and unexpectedly forced me to defend myself against her dramatic parries—she was indeed very good excellent. Except for all my practicing and the instruction I received, she could have easily beaten me. We agreed to let her come along on the condition that she stay at her grandfather's castle, to which she reluctantly agreed.

To avoid detection, we rode through the woods as far as possible, but because the cliff walls were too steep, we could not cross a stream. Therefore, we had to ride along the dugout road below. After we crossed the ford and with our horses' hooves slipping and struggling for purchase, we climbed up the other steep side. We heard horses galloping towards the stream and quickly turned off into a much-appreciated crevasse in the rock face above the ravine. One by one, over a couple of dozen of Reginald's men galloped by. We could see them, but fortunately, with their attention on the steep road ahead, they did not see us.*

Meanwhile, the four rebel lords were marshaling their forces. The Brogans were forming up and moving out of Mariah Canyon. Liam, the oldest Brogan son, and heir apparent, was gathering the peasants from the fields, while Breandon, the second oldest, gathered up the male servants in the castle and outbuildings. Five of their other brothers, along with their older sons, had gathered in the canyon. One servant was unaccounted for, though—Markus, who, crying out in anguish, had told another servant that he had a toothache and had to go to the doctor in town. The preparations were similar at the Harrold's, McGlinchey's, and O'Flannery's, where they were gathering up not only their men at arms but any man between fifteen and sixty, some to be armed with John's weapons, others to carry homemade bows, pitchforks spears, or repurposed scythes that the lords had been surreptitiously producing.

In town, John and his three sons were carefully loading their wagon with arms so that they would not attract attention from Seamus next door. Fortunately, Hugh was off somewhere doing Reginald's bidding. The constant noise of the printer and hammering at the forge kept their occasional clanking masked. They would rally on the other side of Bunk Hill, where they would hand out their pistols and swords to the assembled clans before they moved on to the castle that night. A portion of the weapons would be reserved for the town's merchants, who would pick these up after nightfall and stealthily make their way to the castle. John still had the key that would allow them access to the back gate. The Brogan niece had checked to see that the lock had not been changed—it hadn't.*

As we approached O'Flannery castle, we entered the woods to avoid being seen by Reginald's roaming guards. We tied our horses to trees, then stealthily sneaked through the woods some distance to the edge of the forest, where we could survey the main gate below. There, we saw several soldiers who had Gwendolyn's grandfather in chains, roughly throwing him into a wagon with Lord Brogan. When we snuck to the stables, Kieran told us that, evidently, someone had gotten word of the planned attack and warned Reginald of it.

Knowing that the attack was off and its two leaders were headed for prison, realizing that we did not want to be seen, we retreated back to the cave. The harvest would end in less than a week when the Bunkillarny Games would commence. The last chance to retake the shire had evaporated—score another win for Reginald. Somehow, he always seemed to win.

Reluctantly admitting defeat, Michael thought it was time to travel to Dublin, to his uncle-in-law's, where we would be safer.

Gwendolyn said, "But what about Grandfather and Lord Brogan? We canna just let them rot in jail or be hanged. We have to do something. We should rescue them, just like you were rescued, da."

"Dear Gwendolyn, I do not think the same plan could work again. Reginald likely has the castle on high alert and has posted guards at the back gate, too.*

Meanwhile, Reginald and the deplorable Boston plotted in the King's quarters behind the throne room. Boston had published several weekly articles in the Bunkillarny Reader regarding the McGowan clan, who had supposedly been stealing sheep along the border to gain support to take over their lands—the next move on Reginald's chessboard of conquest. Of course, the stories had no basis. Some of Reginald's soldiers had painted their faces black, disguised themselves in McGowan tartans, and stolen the sheep in the middle of the night. The invasion was scheduled to occur after the Bunkillarny games when the soldiers would return, and patriotic fever would be high.

But before they invaded, Reginald would lead his forces to take over the Brogan and O'Flannery estates. Boston told Reginald, "In the case of an insurrection, you, as king, or acting king, ha, could assume extraordinary powers and dispense justice at will, superseding those darn restrictive Hibernian laws. There will be no show trial this time. After you declare Marshal Law, the two imprisoned lords will be unceremoniously convicted of treason and immediately hanged. If their heirs resist, they would also be hanged on the spot, and you would take control of their vast lands, replacing them with vassals loyal to you after they pay substantial consideration, that is."

One of Reginald's senior knights entered the room. Reginald had relied upon his gang of twelve knights to implement his policies and had promoted them to what he called his "Loyal Senior Knights," who would command his army and undertake "special assignments" such as stealing the sheep. Donal had just returned from London and told them, "We slayed King Patrick and Prince John. Unfortunately, I lost my two men in the fighting, and regrettably, I had to kill Queen Catherine, for she was a witness. I made it look like a robbry, so there would be no incriminations against you, me lord."

Reginald replied, "This is excellent news! Now, no one will interfere with us, and I shall surely be king. Boston, please announce the tragedy at the games that Patrick and John and Catherine were ruthlessly killed by robbers in London. We will have a brief mourning period and then tell the bishop to arrange my coronation. Oh, what a great day this is!"

In advance of the games, Hugh would print a special edition of the Reader, which contained an article by Boston regarding the heinous plot orchestrated by Lords Brogan and O'Flannery. Supposedly, the two lords had previously plotted against King Patrick and had been arrested for it. They then conspired with Nealland to have Patrick killed, for which they would receive a vast amount of gold and land. Queen Catherine caught wind of their plan and fled with Patrick before they assonated them both. They sent men to London, where they killed Patrick, Prince John and Queen Catherine.

Surprised at how gullible the people were, Boston had become skilled at weaving lies—it did not matter how outrageous it was if it was in the paper, people believed it. The Reader would be handed out freely throughout the shire and at the games. Twiddling his fingers, Boston said, "This insurrection will actually work in our favor. Our main enemies will have been eliminated. The people will be behind us, and we can do what we please."

Later, Brehana stormed into the room. "Why have I been moved from my rooms to much smaller quarters in the castle? And, why has that peasant, that young, buxom, blond maid, moved in?"

"Don't worry, you will still have a place in my court."

Reginald had an unquenchable sexual appetite and, like a bull, thought any woman in the castle should be his to do with as he pleased. Visiting her less often, he had grown tired of Brehana and moved on to the voluptuous, enticing, ambitious, voluptuous maid, Sheila, who had become the main object of his affection. Boston wanted him to settle down, marry, and put an end to all the gossip. Of course, he could still have a couple of mistresses—more appropriate behavior for a king.

Brehana continued, "Reginald, I helped you to dispose of the king and have kept your secrets that I am sure you would not want anyone else to know."

"Yes, and you have been handsomely rewarded for that." Lifting Megan out of her scabbard and resting the tip on her shoulder, he said, "I would hate to see that pretty little neck of yours severed; besides, you are as guilty as me. After all, it is you who supplied the poison. If I go down, you go down!"

Brehana stormed out of the room. She thought about telling on Reginald but realized since he would be king, there was no one she could tell who could ultimately help her, and she faced deadly consequences if she did. She thought about opening a shop in town, but there was already an apothecary there, and her patients in the castle had much more money to spend on her potions. Still, she was a woman scorned who wanted vengeance.*

Over the next two days, the three of us cave-dwellers racked our brains trying to figure out a plan to rescue Lords O' Flannery and Brogan but could not do so. In preparation for our journey to Dublin, we began packing up when we heard the cry of a distant wolf—the signal that we had arranged with Kieran. The decoded message Kieran delivered said that we should go to the docks that night. We asked him why we should go, but he knew nothing more.

Wearing black, hooded capes to disguise ourselves, riding through the woods as much as possible, we rode to Bunkillarny. We stopped at the entrance to town, wondering how we would pass by the two raucous soldiers' pubs without being detected. There was no other route to the docks, so tensely we rode past, keeping our heads down and a hand on our swords, me ready to draw my revolver. We passed by two soldiers who had just relieved themselves on a nearby building, and when they looked into Gwendolyn's downturned face, they recognized that she was a woman. One grabbed hold of her reins, saying, "What is such a pretty lass doing out so late at nigh'? You should come wi us, so we's could buy ye a whiskey ta chase away the chill there deary."

Michael and I turned our horses and, seeing that Gwendolyn was about to draw her sword, not wanting to talk because they might recognize us, nuzzled our horses up against them causing one to fall, flailing like an upturned crab, whereupon Gwendolyn signaled her horse to trot away.

"Hay govnor, what ye do that fer?"

As I turned, in a muffled voice, I said, "Sorry." And we too, trotted away.

After we turned towards the port and made our way down the road, around a turn, I could see a ship with lights aglow. It was Captain Black's Christine, which Michael, unable to contain the excitement of seeing his long-lost friend, had galloped towards, with Gwendolyn and I galloping after him.

Evidently expecting us, the captain was waiting at the end of the gangplank, quickly ushering us on board. We all exchanged fervent handshakes and hugs, Gwendolyn bestowing a much-welcomed kiss on his cheek, Michael saying, "I can't believe you are here, you old scallywag. You are just the tonic I needed. I am so glad to see you, my friend!"

When we climbed up to the main deck, I was enthusiastically greeted by my shipmates—Gerald, the illustrious gunner of Mary Rose, young Jack, Jerome, the deckhand and Marcel, the first mate—all with big smiles and welcoming handshakes. The captain led us down to his stateroom where, after pouring sherry, toasting, and ensuring we had a stiff drink, he said, "I have a couple of surprises for you. Are you ready?..."

From behind the small closet door, two male figures appeared. It was Francisco and Carlos. I could not believe it and did something I had never done before—I started to tear up as I ran to greet them, lifting Francisco far into the air before he could do so to me— just the tonic I needed. I introduced them to Michael and Gwendolyn, who, having heard stories about them, were thrilled to meet them. In his gallant manner, Francisco kissed Gwendolyn's hand. Carlos said, "Mi amigo, she is even more beautiful than the picture you painted of her," which caused Gwendolyn to blush.

"Yes, she is," I declared.

After several minutes, Captain Black said he had another surprise for us and left. When he returned, he held the door open, and to our amazement, Patrick, Prince John, and Catherine walked in. Having been through so much since their departure and having heard the rumors that they had perished. Michael could not believe his eyes until he hugged each in turn, as we did.

Like a reunion of long-lost comrades, we spent the rest of the evening telling stories of what had happened to each of us over the last several months, featuring Reginald as our common antagonist. After successfully selling a record number of his wines and sherry in London, Francisco had planned to visit me in Bunkillarny. As directed, he stopped in at Colleen's to ascertain my whereabouts, whereupon he met Captain Black, who was planning a trip to Bunkillarny to visit Michael to bring back more manuscripts from Colleen and Michael's share of the profits. Carlos had joined Francisco to understand the London market better and to sell his father's fine wines, the results of which he was highly pleased.

Another soul joined our group for a delicious late dinner of fish fresh from the dockside market—Sir William Southwick, Henry's emissary from London. Before coming to Bunkillarny, they stopped to see King Rory at the O'Donnell castle, where John pled his case with Southwick's help. They won over the king by promising to renounce all claims, lands and titles in Neilland in return for Rory's pledge not to interfere in the Bunkillarny succession. The fact that Patrick testified on his brother's behalf sealed the deal. The document Sir Southwick witnessed, under Henry's authority and signet proclaimed their agreement.

The games would commence in two days, so we had little time to hatch a plan. Catherine wondered why the games would not be held the following year as usual, but we explained that Reginald planned to use the games to support his ascension to the throne.

Fearing that if they presented themselves at the castle and demanded investiture, Reginald would oppose them and possibly kill them, they decided on an alternate course of action. Most of the people from the clans throughout the shire would assemble on the large field behind Bunkillarny Castle for the games. With so many witnesses, this would be an ideal occasion to appear and demand restoration.

About that time, John the smithy joined us along with Lords Harold and McGlinchey, who informed us of the previous plans, which they thought could be reactivated. We all gathered around the captain's table to hatch a plan, the excitement and determination palpable, exponentially multiplied by the feelings we had for each other on this glorious reunion.

John said, "My son Ryan and the printer Seamus have been friends since they were wee ones. After some coaxing, Seamus told Ryan that Reginald had already sentenced Lord Brogan and Lord O'Flannery to be hanged at the conclusion of the games—as a grand finale and a gruesome lesson to all not to rebel. Seamus had just set the type for a flier that announced the charges against them and the hanging, something Seamus thought would be a great spectacle. Bragging, Seamus told Ryan that because Reginald was so fond of him, the shop would become his, he would become a wealthy man, and Gwendolyn would beg to marry him."

In an angry voice, Gwendolyn declared. "That will never happen, never, never, never!"

Michael asked, "So there is to be no trial of our friends?"

"No!"

"And they are ignoring the Hibernian Code, which demands a jury trial?"

"Yes, they are. Reginald claims that since Brogan and O'Flannery conspired to create an insurrection against him as the ruler of Bunkillarny, he could assume extraordinary powers and have them hung. Plus, he claims he will be able to do the same to anyone else who conspired with them or anyone who speaks up against him in the future."

"So, all of us here are, therefore, subject to hanging," I added.

"Yes, so we have to succeed. Or else!"

Lords Harold and McGlinchey, whose lands lay next to each other along the Irish sea in order to avoid detection, left the same way they came, sailing on the dark, moonless sea upon a black picard—a small single-masted ship.*

The next day before the games were to begin, before the sun rose, John had taken a wagonload of weapons to the other side of Bunk Mountain. There, he met representatives of the four clans, who gratefully unloaded the wagon that supplied them with a significant number of arms. Iron-ically, the pistols, halberds, and swords ordered by Reginald would be used to overthrow him.

The Brogans, determined to free their clan leader, had already been on the march. Since the entire shire would be on the move, heading to Bunkillarny castle, this large force of men did not cause much alarm. They hid their weapons within their supplies and the tents they brought to the games in their carts. Arriving early, they took their places up on the hill next to each other on that portion closest to the viewing stands. This was nothing unusual because members of the same clan had always camped together, the games serving as a kind of biannual family reunion.

I desperately wanted to compete in the games but knew, as a want-ed criminal, I could not do so. Instead, we cloistered ourselves in the ship. Since they would not be noticed, Francisco, Carlos, Captain Black, and his crew attended the first day's activities. The dueling was under-standably of particular interest to Francisco, the master swordsman. We planned our insurgency for the second day when Reginald and his forces, settling into the excitement of the games, would be less on guard.

The night before we were to overthrow Reginald was a sleepless one, laying in my hammock, constantly turning from side to side, worrying about how the critical day would unfold. I had spent similar nights worrying about a major corporate presentation, but this was different, this was a matter of life and death, something I had never had to endure before. As the night unfolded, I desperately wanted to sleep, for I knew I would need it but knew from previous experiences that just lying there offered a measure of rest. Random thoughts kept bouncing around in my mind. Would the normally shy Patrick be able to assert himself? How would the crowd perceive Prince John, who had been unjustly portrayed as their perverse enemy? Would they support us, or because of Reginald's propaganda campaign and lies, would the people support him? Could the four clans really assemble and be armed by John without any of Reginald's troops detecting it? Would the untrained merchants join the cause? Would they be slaughtered? Would all my friends be killed? Would I die here, never to see my beloved 21st-century friends and family again?

I had my revolver, which would give us an advantage, but would I have the courage to stand up and shoot someone? Would we all be victorious, or would Reginald again detect the plot, thwarting our efforts and hanging us all? No matter how evil his actions were, he always seemed to win.

Rather than face this challenge, I wish I had taken advantage of the opportunity in the cave to return to my place and time, away from all this turmoil. There had not been enough room in the ship's cabins. Indeed, the royals had priority, so I was sleeping in a hammock, similar to bunk beds three to a column with a restless sailor above and below me, hearing the various sounds the crew made and their never-ending snoring. As soon as one stopped snoring, another would start up just as I was about to nod off. Sometimes, two or three created a cacophonous snoring concert. Unable to sleep, I finally grabbed my blanket and went up to the top of the forecastle above all the decks, under the stars. There, in the fresh air, I soon fell asleep. When I arose to the sound of commotion on the decks, under the damp, dew-kissed blanket, I felt that our cause was just and that these were my friends, who I was going to fight for. Rising deep from within my core, I felt a welcome sense of courage emerge.

TWENTY

Rebellion

Reginald peered imperiously out his castle window down to the town below blanketed in a white fluffy cloud that glowed golden under the rising sun, thinking that this would be his day of triumph when he would finally become the official King of Bunkillarny and all those down there would worship him. After the games, he would regain his army and, with all the weapons he had won and made, capture more defenseless shires, vastly increasing his army, his wealth and his power. After he conquered those shires, he would take on Nealland and then the feckless O'Donnells, for even though they supposedly had an alliance, he had little respect for King Rory, who could have crushed Nealland and taken all they had. Good, he hadn't, though, because that left the weakened shire for him to capture and plunder. Those farmers and herders stood little chance against the fearsome, professional army he had been training for years. *

Fearing recognition, John, Patrick, Catherine, Michael, Gwendolyn, and I dressed in monk's robes with the hoods shielding our heads. We left early that cool October morn when the fog still obscured the town, the dew drenching the ship's decks, dripping off the ropes, its riggings and moorings, obscuring the docks, such that all we could see had a ghostly, blurry appearance. In the fog-shrouded town, diffuse star-shaped lights emanated from homes. The people had woken and were preparing for the coming coup, each girding their loins, each bracing themselves for whatever might transpire.

As we carefully stepped down the damp, slippery gangplank, we could see stripes of sunshine poking through the fog: a faint blue tinting the milky whiteness. To hide our identity, the crew surrounded us on the way up the hill to town. Lord Southwick's royal guards led the way, marching in time, dressed in green and white jackets with the Tudor red and white rose on their chests, black caps with white plumes, and black tights with green garters, some with halberds, all with swords. Even though only twenty of them represented the crown, they made me feel more secure in our just quest. When we walked through town, the merchants and their families gathered around us, providing an added layer of protection from recognition. Unlike last year's games, the mood had changed from that of a light, carefree group of friends and neighbors climbing the hill for a day of fun and celebration to that of a determined force of insurgents marching to take their town and their kingdom back, their determination painted on their faces.

The merchants stopped at the blacksmith shop to arm themselves, where John and his three sons were handing out the remainder of the weapons they had fashioned and reserved for the townsfolk. Hearing all the commotion next door, Seamus poked his head out the back door and asked what was going on, whereupon John, knowing he would run to warn Reginald, promptly tied and gagged him, telling him, "This is none of your concern." Colleen's one-armed brother, Tommy, wearing his new suit for the first time, seeing what had happened to Seamus, asked to join the rebellion.

After we climbed above the fog into the sunshine, wound around the castle, and down to the field below, we went to where the jousting competition would be held. Earlier, some of the Brogans had occupied the closest spots, forcefully making way for us monks to move close. We stood across from the nobles' viewing stand, the other side of the jousting lanes on that portion of the field with a slight downslope so the massive crowd could view the coming main attraction below.

Following a flurry of trumpets, the dishonorable Boston moved to the center of the stage and, speaking as loud as he could, shouted, "My dear friends and subjects of Bunkillarny, I welcome you to the second day of our games. We have just learned some tragic news..." Pausing as the crowd braced themselves for what was to come, "King Patrick, Prince John and Queen Catherine were killed in a heinous robbery in London. Two of the bandits were killed, while a third escaped." A hush emanated from the crowd, and all were silent.... "Given these heinous circumstances, we are fortunate to have such a fine leader during these tumultuous times to guide us along the way. Here is our esteemed, noble, chivalrous leader, Reginald Van Cleve."

Reginald, expecting possible trouble from the dissident clans, particularly the Brogans and O'Flanneries, had scores of armed men under the viewing stand and behind the back gate, so in the unlikely event some difficulty arose, troops would be there in a minute. Plus, he had his twelve loyal knights on the stands. Therefore, he spoke with confident assurance.

The thousands in attendance applauded but not as loudly close to the viewing stands where we were. "My dear subjects of Bunkillarny, I would like to start with a moment of silence for our dear King Patrick. What he lacked in age, he made up for with heart.... I spent many a day with him, teaching him how to use our weapons: the bow, the sword, the lance, the ways of warfare, and how to be a good king... Thank you. Please, let's have another moment of silence for our dear departed Queen Catherine, who was a bright light for our shire and served us well. After King Edward died, I comforted her and her adorable children, getting to know what a wonderful woman she truly was. We will all miss her....

Over the past year, our shire has suffered losses of those we hold most dear, but despite these tragedies, under my leadership we have managed to prosper. I have won critical battles against Nealland and the O'Callahans, both of whom envied our success and coveted your productive farms, herds and markets. I ensured they would not take these from you (applause stimulated by his shills). Thank you.

And now our Bishop will lead us in prayer for the souls of King Patrick, Queen Catherine and poor misguided Prince John, may they rest in peace." Everyone bowed their heads and said the Our Father.

"I am pleased to see so many of you here. I have never seen so many attend these games. The hills are filled. This surely must be an all-time record."

"Under my guidance, the kingdom has fared well over the last year. I understand that our harvests will be the most productive ever, and I have conquered another shire, which has added immensely to our wealth. Our army is stronger and better equipped than ever and has proven itself in formative battles under my leadership and that of my twelve loyal senior knights (who rose to the applause). We defeated the devious O'Neals and have been constantly vigilant against them, something we will unfortunately need to continue. Before they could attack us, we also thwarted the O'Callaghans, who were stealing our sheep.

Lord Boston here has done a marvelous job of improving the management of the shire. (He bows to applause). As you know, I have visited all the towns in the shire and have informed you of our remarkable progress. I enjoyed meeting you and your leaders personally and appreciated all the support and cheers you gave me. It truly warms my heart. No past king has visited all the towns and hamlets and spoken to them as I have or had such overwhelming support for the programs we have initiated." Applause!

"We will soon commence the highlight of the games, the jousting tournament (loud resounding cheers). Some have said that since my leadership is so important to the shire at this critical time, I should not compete. But I could not let you down, and I shall compete and perhaps win, as I have for the last three tournaments (more applause).

As you may know, I won the grueling sword competition for the fourth time yesterday. Others have said that because of my stellar leadership, I should assume the kingship (rousing applause), but I shall leave that to the council. If called upon, I shall serve. (The council was stacked with members already committed to his coronation). We will now commence the jousting."

The trumpeters were about to blow their horns when Lord McGlinchey, who purposely sat next to them, raised his arms and then lowered them, signaling that the trumpeters should put their horns down. Lord Harold walked to the stands, smiled, and placed his hand upon a confused Reginald's shoulder, then spoke as if his speech was a planned portion of the event, "My dear friends, I would like to introduce you to some notable personages who are here today. Sir Southwick is an emissary from London who represents King Henry and his royal guards." (He came to the stand to applause, and the guards moved closer.) Reginald, who was ready to sound the alarm, thinking he should have known about them and introduced them himself, relaxed.

"Our noble lady, Queen Catherine, who miraculously survived the attack in London, could also attend today." She threw off her monk's robe, exposing a regal purple gown, and came to the stage to thunderous cheers, resonating off the hills. Reginald looked to Boston, both thoroughly confused.

"Now, I would like to introduce our king, Patrick, who also survived that brutal attack." Patrick threw off his monk's robe, revealing his royal, kingly blue, gold-trimmed garments. As he vaulted up the stairs to the stage, the king, now a strong young man resembling King Edward, donned his crown. On the flat field and up to the top of the hill, as word spread, "Patrick lives. Patrick lives!" the crowd, like a wave, jumped to its feet and roared, a deafening roar. Reginald and Boston looked afraid of what might happen next, but he had the reserves nearby, and he placed his hand on Megan's neck, signaling his loyal knights to be ready.

The young man, who previously spoke meekly at his coronation, now spoke in a strong, deep, loud, commanding voice, "My dear subjects, it is with the sincerest gratitude that I am here with you today. We were able to survive an attack in London by three men-of-arms. They came from Bunkillarny to kill us. Reginald orchestrated this attack! (who Patrick pointed an accusatory finger at as a hush came over the multitude.) One of his knights who led that attack, Donal, will testify to this fact." Donal stepped away from the other knights and stood resolutely, raising his hand so all could see him on the stage. Glaring, Reginald looked back at him, ready to cut him down on the spot.

"Furthermore, we have testimony from his mistress, Brehana, who says that Reginald administered a poison that debilitated me and would have led to my death if we had not fled. After trying to rape my mother, Queen Catherine, in her rooms, Reginald followed us, killed our guards, and attempted to kill us too." (Rumbling and intense boos filled the arena.)

"As my first act upon my return to the throne, I remove Reginald from his office as regent and the general of my armies. Secondly, I hereby pardon Lords Brogan and O'Flannery (cheers from their clans on the hill), and I so order that they be released immediately." He turned to the first knight and said, "Do as I say. I want to see them here beside me in five minutes. Go! Go!" The knight, not knowing what to do, followed his command and ran to the jail to have them freed.

"I also officially pardon my good friends, Michael McCarron and Rand Roberts. Would you please come to the stage?" We proceeded to the stage along with Francisco, Carlos, Captain Black, John and Ryan. We surrounded Patrick, serving as his guards.

"Now I would like to introduce my brother John, who has been maligned by scandalous rumors regarding his character. Let me assure you that none of those rumors are true. I have known my brother all my life. He is the most honest of men, the most faithful husband, and the kindest, most charitable Christian I know. All who have served him will testify that he is as noble as our august father, Edward!" Reginald attempted to assassinate John twice—on the battlefield and in the failed coup attempt in London, where his men also tried to kill me and my mother, the queen."

John came to the stage and shook his brothers' hand, "You have heard salacious rumors about me that are totally untrue. I have a document here in my hands from King Rory of the O'Donnells testifying that I renounce all claims to any lands and titles in Neilland. It has been witnessed by Sir Southwick, King Henry's emissary." Everyone applauded and roared wildly.

The despicable Boston looked as if he was going to faint, and Reginald was purple with rage, his hand squeezing Megan's hilt tightly, impatient for action. This was something he had not anticipated. He thought that John and Patrick were dead, something one of his most loyal knights testified to—a knight who betrayed him, who he would soon slander as a liar and have summarily executed. Reginald felt as if their world and the kingdom he and Boston had worked so hard to build was crumbling before his eyes. But Reginald, anticipating a possible insurrection by the Brogan and O'Flannery clans, had a contingency plan.

Turning to Hugh, he raised his hand, and Hugh, taking a trumpet from one of the trumpeters, bleated out three long blasts. Suddenly, scores of armed men streamed out from beneath the stands and the backside of the castle. We looked at each other fearfully, braced for a fight, but were hopelessly outnumbered.

Patrick waved his hands like a bird about to fly, causing another trumpet to bleat in the hill above, triggering 200 arrows to climb high into the deep blue sky, towards the stands, eliciting a mighty rushing sound, then falling to the empty field behind the stands in a massive sustained thump—an intended warning to the soldiers not to advance, stopping them cold in their tracks at the side of the stands. Then, we could hear a massive explosion coming out of the bay, followed by a large cannonball slamming into the Bunk Ravine's cliff wall below the field, causing a landslide of shale to cascade down to the river, eliciting a sustained rippling sound—a warning message from Mary Rose on the Christine. The troops looked towards the crash and took a step back. Meanwhile, Henry's Royal Guardsmen advanced.

Reginald ordered his loyal knights to seize Patrick and John, but by then, Michael, John, Ryan, Francisco, Captain Black and I stood between them, swords unsheathed. Gwendolyn adroitly jumped onto the stage and unsheathed her concealed sword, too. Reginald laughed at the sight of this motley crew against his skilled, war-forged knights. As they advanced with their swords drawn, Ryan and I began shooting, he with his pepperbox, me with my revolver, wounding them in the chest or shoulder as they raised their arms to attack. Within seconds, six of them were stopped, and the others stood mystified by pistols that could spit out that much lead.

Reginald ordered the hundred or more men assembled at the base of the steps to attack. As the ten of us began to fend them off, some stayed back. Others were blocked by the King's Royal Guards, who they would not fight. To advance on them would bring down the wrath of King Henry, something they did not dare risk. I stood next to Gwendolyn to defend her from the wave of approaching soldiers, but I had to defend myself. After I knocked my adversary's sword out of his hand, I looked toward Gwendolyn, who faced a large, fearsome, fat foe intent on taking on the easiest target he could find. Moving at lightning speed, Gwendolyn had no trouble outmaneuvering him and stabbing him in the kidney—a look of shock on his face. She immediately moved on to her next victim. Those in the audience, many men disguised as women, took off their robes, revealing a myriad of weapons. The four armed clans in the hills began running for the stands, yelling a blood-curdling cry as they ran, and the Royal Guards moved towards the stage. Reginald realized that he was hopelessly outnumbered.

Prince John grabbed a trumpet, blew as loud as he could, and yelled at the top of his lungs to stop. Looking and sounding like his departed father, he said, "We are all brothers here, men who have known each other all of our lives. Men who have fought side by side. How can you attack your brother? How can you attack your neighbor, your friend? We are not enemies. We are all the men of Bunkillarny. Step back and lower your weapons." In a resounding tone, "Patrick added, "As your king, I command you to lower your weapons. **Now!**"

Reginald's men and officers looked confused. They had sworn an oath of allegiance to the king. They were hopelessly outnumbered, and they really did not want to kill their neighbors or friends and certainly not their king. Realizing the situation, they did not want to die for such an unworthy cause.

Reginald, sensing defeat, said, "I claim the right of challenge. Rather than have our men kill each other as the lawful regent of Bunkillarny, I challenge the criminal, John, to a duel."

"As you should know, he has been critically wounded by one of your agents and cannot fight you," Patrick declared.

"Then I acknowledge this as a defeat."

Realizing that Patrick was about to accept the challenge, something Reginald expected next and relished, with my adrenalin still surging, I reluctantly said, "I will represent John," after which I wondered what I had gotten myself into. Did I really want to duel with Reginald, who just won the sword competition for the fourth time yesterday? Oh well, might as well make the best of it.

Looking pleadingly at me, Francisco said, "Rand, I should be the one to challenge Reginald, and after seeing him in the sword competition, I know I could make mincemeat of him."

"Thank you, Francisco, but this is my fight, one you have prepared me well for."

Reginald smiled broadly—a smirking, knowing, egotistical smile. "Grand! Hugh shall be my second."

"Francisco shall be my second. I assume that I choose the weapons, and I choose spears."

"No, Rand. As your superior, according to our laws, I have the choice of weapons and swords."*

Francisco takes me aside and tells me, "Mi amigo, I watched him at the competition at the castle yesterday. He is very good, aggressive, and impatient. He will expect to defeat you in the first minute. Take the defensive posture I showed you and guard against underhanded slashes and stabs until his initial attacks subside. He will try to get you off balance with overhand strikes, then come underneath. He will think you are an easy opponent. This is his weakness and your strength. Bide your time and stay centered. Go dispatch him, mi amigo, Via con Dios!"

One by one, my friends – John, Ryan, Carlos, Captain Black, Prince John, King Patrick, and Michael come up and pat me on the back or shake my hand, urging me on to victory. Gwendolyn comes over with tears in her eyes, hugs me, and gives me a fraught smile, a deep hug, and a big kiss, saying, "Don't you dare die. You mean too much to me!"

They back up to make room for the duel, and I am left alone in the middle of the stage in front of thousands, who, given Reginald's perennially demonstrated skills, expect the duel it to be over quickly. I flashback to when, with Megan's tip puncturing my neck, when he promptly mastered me. I am nervous. I stretch and practice some thrusts to warm up, as Reginald looks at me as if I am a fool just delaying the inevitable.

We square off, and after bowing and clicking swords, Reginald furiously lights into a relentless assault that, by keeping my arm and wrist loose, I am barely able to fend off. He keeps backing me up, me evading his advances by stiffly moving to one side and then the other. Playing to the cheers of the audience who had now overwhelmed the jousting area, he toys with me until I strike out—he smirking as if I were a petulant child. I feel pitiful, but know, after all my practicing and instruction, I am better than this. After what seems like an interminable time, his blows lack their initial ferocity.

Francisco calls out to me. "It is time mi amigo! It's time."

This is the moment I have been waiting for, and I relentlessly strike out at him blow after loud clanking blow while he retreats.

"Printer Rand, I see that you have been practicing. Maybe this will be an interesting duel after all, and Megan will have a suitable suitor's neck to kiss. Or maybe she wants to steal your heart. We shall see. We shall see."

The duel enters a new phase as we trade jabs and slashes, each one met successfully by the other's sword. Then he launches into another attack, pushing me towards the end of the stage, where the only option I have is to step onto the steps, something I really do not want to do because

I might lose my balance. With him above me, he has the advantage as he forces me further down the stairs. At the bottom, as the audience scrambles to get out of the way, I stumble and barely hold off a fatal slash aimed at my eyes.

I switch my sword to my other hand and, with my right hand on the railing, vault myself up four feet, landing successfully on the stage. Now, he must fight his way back up the stairs. Once on level ground, he adroitly slashes my arm. Under the influence of adrenaline, I cannot feel it, but after such a long time and with the blood draining, my arm is tiring, so I switch my sword over to my left hand. Sensing that it will be over soon, as if he were a matador about to stab the bull with the fatal blow, Reginald turns, raises his sword into the air, and bows to the audience. Gwendolyn quickly tears off her sleeve and wraps it around my wound before Reginald comes back towards me, sporting a demonic look on his face.

He relentlessly charges me, continuously trying for the final blow, me defending myself and using my legs to avoid being backed up.

Francisco says, "That a boy." My friends cheer me on as does the audience.

Finally, after what seems like hours, Reginald's blows lose their force. Wanting to reclaim the advantage of my long arms, I switch my sword back to my right hand and unleash a series of slashes and parries, backing him up to the edge of the stage, where I pierce his shoulder. For the first time, he has a look of fear. But he recovers, and we fight onward.

Hugh sticks out a foot, and I trip and fall to the floor, Megan's point immediately at my neck. Before he plunges forward, Reginald raises his other hand and smiles, relishing his final victory.

With all my might, I grab Megan with both hands and break off her tip. Reginald is aghast; how can you dare do such a despicable thing? Before he can recover, I bounce back to my feet, knock the wounded weapon out of his hand, grab him around the collar and his crotch, lift him above my head, and throw him eight feet across the stand, where he lands with a resounding thud. Then I grab my sword and am on him in an instant. Hugh makes a motion to stab me from behind, but Francisco readily fends off his futile slashes as if he were a child.

I have the tip of my sword at his heart and, under the heat of the battle, am ready to send him to hell. After wrestling with my conscience, I ask if he will yield. His face wrinkled up, looking as if he will cry, he says, "I do, I, I, so yield."

I cannot believe it, but the exhausting fight is finally over. While sucking in air, my friends come over to congratulate me, and Gwendolyn passionately kisses me—what a kiss!

The crowd goes wild, and Sir Southwick orders his guards to arrest Reginald. He orders Reginald's knights to drop their weapons, then orders that Boston be arrested and jailed along with the loyal knights, many of whom will be treated for gunshot wounds. *

In a booming voice, King Patrick announces to all that the banquet will still be scheduled for that evening. Before then, we gathered in the Kings' reclaimed dining room for lunch and discussed what had just happened. Lords Brogan and O'Flannery, having just been released, join our celebratory group along with Lords Herald and McGlinchey. We were filled with relief, satisfaction, and joy.

Lord Harold said, "We were lucky that the other clans did not oppose us, especially those loyal to Reginald, but I think they were surprised, and since Reginald had kept all of the arms, most of them were unarmed. John, I think your weapons made all the difference."

Lord McGlinchey, "Did you see the expressions on Reginald and Boston's faces when Patrick came up to the stage? He was caught totally off guard. The bastard knew he had been caught like a rat in a trap. I was concerned when Reginald ordered his knights to attack, but then you, Rand, and Ryan stopped them in their tracks with those magical pistols. Could you make me one?"

"Sorry, lord." Winking at Ryan, I said, "Those are one of a kind from my country that I cannot reproduce."

Then, attempting to change the subject added, "After Reginald's signal for his men to come out of the castle, some seemed uncertain and did not want to attack their king."

It was an exhilarating lunch, during which time we talked about the strategy for that evening. Smiling multiple times, with glasses of ale, we toasted each of us.

Even the servants seemed ecstatic. They were not supposed to express their feelings, but one by one, they told Patrick how glad they were that he was back and how much they hated Reginald and his haughty, demeaning attitude.

Patrick wanted to relinquish his crown immediately in favor of John but was advised to wait until a new council was formed—"After the events of the day, it would be too much for the kingdom to absorb."

I sat next to Gwendolyn, who caressed my leg and said she was terrified but was so happy I had defeated Reginald and was still alive.

"I would never have been able to equip myself as well against Reginald if not for all the training I had received from Francisco, Carlos, Jose, General Suarez, and Michael. Even though Reginald was the better swordsman, I could hold my own thanks to Francisco's excellent strategic insights. I am very thankful and fortunate to be alive. A toast to Francisco for teaching me how to duel! Salud!" Clicking their glasses, they all responded, "To Francisco, Salud!"

Queen Catherine assigned me to the same spacious room I had occupied during the last games. While we were at lunch, Michael had dispatched Tommy back to the print shop to reprieve our costumes for the evening. As I changed into my peacock plumes, I had a chance to reflect on all that had transpired, which resembled one of those Hollywood fairytale endings. I always thought those were contrived and that real life never happened that way. But I remembered those epic last days before releasing an app, when with adrenaline flowing, working into the wee hours, we accomplished Herculean feats. Of course, this was much more dramatic than building yet another app to occupy the virtual world, for this was real, and many lives and the future of a people were at stake.

Still, my life had changed dramatically since my first nervous visit to this imposing castle, when I feared meeting the domineering king and could not wait to leave. Now, I felt at home in the castle, and the royals, whom I greatly respected, were friends who I felt respected me.

I thought about all the sports I played. The coordination I developed in those helped. Sports showed me how to find and occupy the zone where actions and time move in slow motion and reflexes are highly tuned. I imagined that if America ever faced a major war, all the sports we played in high school and afterward would provide strong, coordinated, team-oriented, disciplined, tech-savvy male and female troops.*

Thanks to the castle's servants and volunteers throughout the land, all the preparations for the evening went on as planned. Seated at long tables, the assembled nobles of the various clans and merchants rose and roared when King Patrick entered the room. You could see that the Brogans and the other three clans were especially excited to see Patrick, but so were the other clans, even those who aligned with Reginald. After the benediction, as everyone feasted, the buzz was palatable.

Patrick, who had grown five inches since the last games, rose to address the assembly and, in a deep, commanding voice that surprised many, exclaimed, "My dear friends, this is a day that will live forever in the lore of our great shire. It would not have been possible without the cunning, bravery, and courage of those you see before you—my brother, Prince John..., Lord Brogan..., Lord O'Flannery..., Lord McGlinchey... and Lord Harold... I would also like to recognize Rand Roberts..., Ryan Smith..., John Smith..., Michael McCarron, Gwendolyn McCarron .... and my dear mother, Queen Catherine..." Without their help, courage, and cunning, we wouldn't have succeeded in our noble quest. After each name, there was applause followed by a roar after the last, as everyone in the spacious hall stood and cheered wildly.

"I would also like to thank the King's envoy, Sir Southwick, and the Royal Guards for all their support during this trying time. They stood to the applause. And our esteemed guests from Spain, Major Francisco Alvarez and Captain Carlos Alvarez, both expert swordsmen and who actively fought for the recent Reconquista of Spain from the Moors. (applause) Reginald and Boston have been arrested along with his loyal or, should we say, disloyal knights. This was the fourth time he tried to kill me, first by poison, then at the docks and in London with his assassins and, as you witnessed here earlier today.

He also tried to assassinate my older brother three times; plus, he attempted to have his way with my mother. Although we cannot prove it yet, given his vile nature, we believe he committed regicide by killing my father, the honorable King Edward, who I feel is here in spirit with us all tonight. Reginald is the most despicable, evil person I have ever known. And, he will be tried for his crimes."

"We will also try his accomplice Lord Boston, who we suspect has looted the shire's treasury for his own enrichment, something his chief accountant has already intimated. Sir Southwick, who is unbiased and an excellent judge, will lead an investigation into the Shire's finances and his activities over the last year."

"I would like to announce that my new regents will be my mother, Queen Catherine, and my brother, Prince John. Since several of the council members are in the keep, it will be reorganized.

"Now, you all may realize that the printer Rand Roberts, who won all those contests at the last games and who has come back to us after traveling to Spain, where he acquired priceless treasures and the smithy John Smith, who supplied us with armaments that helped win the day are not nobles. Well, I would like to remedy that situation. Rand and John, come forward and kneel before me.

Totally surprised and overwhelmed, we both did as he commanded, kneeling in front of him as Patrick unsheathed Edward's bejeweled, royal sword and, placing it on each of our shoulders said, "By the powers vested in me as the King of Bunkillarny, by the grace of God, I pronounce you Sir Rand Roberts a knight of the realm of Bunkillarny, and you Sir John Smith a knight of the realm of Bunkillarny with all the duties, rights and privileges according your rank." Then he placed a signet ring on our index fingers proclaiming, "This ring declares proclaims your noble stature for anyone to see."

Sir Southwick rose and said, "Since you two participated magnificently in an action under the auspices of King Henry VII, in his name, under his authority he vested in me, I recognize you as knights of the realm of Britain with all the rights and privileges accordingly applied.

This shall thus be recorded in the books of the court at Westminster." These honors were beyond my wildest expectations, and I felt a mixture of humility, pride, and joy. In the back of my mind, I wished Marie was here, but I had finally, gratefully, moved on.

As was customary at the conclusion of the games, we all went back to the viewing stands where Patrick delivered a similar message to the throngs of people gathered there, which was received with thunderous applause that could be heard all the way in Bunkillarny, out to sea, and for miles in the fields and hills surrounding the castle. With pigs and oxen roasting on the spits, the air smelled delightful as each of us rose to the crowd's cheers in the unusually warm, enveloping fall night. It felt wonderful to receive such adulation, especially since it was shared with my friends and companions. I could only imagine that this must be what it feels like to be on the medal stand at the Olympics, or as Super Bowl champs, or high school state champs, something you would remember for the rest of your life.

Rather than immediately returning to the hall, I decided to peruse the torch and campfire-lit grounds to gain a sense of how the other clans were taking the overthrow. Throughout the grounds and in the hills above, the mood was even more celebratory than the previous year. I was not completely sure where the clan boundaries were, but had the opportunity to talk to several men as I walked around, asking which clan they were from and how they felt about what had just happened. The general consensus was that they loved King Edward, were unsure of Reginald's assumption of power, thought what he did was appalling, and welcomed Patrick as Edward's son and legitimate heir.

Other than a couple of disgruntled people that would occur in any such informal survey, I could not detect any animosity or bitterness regarding the overthrow. I think the huge celebration helped to allay people's fears. I was less certain of the lords who benefited from Reginald's and Boston's rule, but their loyalties could be ascertained, and they could be weeded out over time.*

When I returned to the hall, they were handing out the awards for the various contests, which took me back to last year when I had done so well. For a split second, I regretted not being able to participate, especially since I had won so much money and was now totally broke, but being honored as a knight was so much better, and I had used those funds to purchase the most valuable books of the English language. The award ceremony proceeded similarly to previous years, reinforcing the festive continuity everyone enjoyed and looked forward to.

The royal family still presided over the ceremony, with Prince John announcing the winners, King Patrick presenting the prizes, and, to my surprise, Gwendolyn being selected to don the sash over the participants' necks and kiss each one on their cheek as they passed by as Marie had done. Wearing a splendid golden gown she had obtained from Queen Catherine, Gwendolyn looked radiant with her long, streaming reddish-blond hair and perfect alabaster skin. As the prettiest noblewoman in all the shire, I could see why she was selected, but I felt an unaccustomed sensation as the various young men looked at her with loving eyes, relishing her kiss as if that was the ultimate prize. I looked around the hall and saw all the other young men seeming envious of those who had won, wishing they were on the stage with her.

When the band started playing, everyone began dancing—there were certainly no wallflowers waiting for someone to be the first up. Michael took me aside and said, "I can't wait to get my hands on those documents you brought back and start printing them. It shall be a glorious venture that will likely be highly profitable. What an honor to deliver such classics to the Queen Mother in London and Isabella of Spain. You have done very well for us."

"I have spoken to the king, and as a reward for your service, we will grant you a junior partnership in the print shop. The crown shall have a 40% share of the profits, I will have a 40% share, and you shall have the remaining 20%."

"Michael, that is very generous, thank you."

Occasionally, I looked at the dance floor and saw Gwendolyn enchanting a series of amorous suitors, her figure swaying rhythmically to the music, her beautiful locks flying, her eyes and smile enticing her prey. When I saw Carlos take her in his arms, I felt an unfamiliar tinge of jealousy, realizing how the tall, dark, classically handsome, perfectly mannered Spaniard could be. I tried to assuage my jealousy by thinking of how good a friend Carlos was and how he helped me acquire the prized Salamancan documents from Queen Isabella, but that didn't help.

Mercifully, Gwendolyn grabbed my arm and dragged me onto the dance floor, teaching me the various dances until we were ready to drop. I was amazed at her endurance. Instead of rejoining our group, I asked if she would like to get a breath of fresh air. I took her up to the opposite tower from where I had been with Marie. There, we saw the people below in a festive mood, the glow from campfires extending into the hills, reflecting happy faces. We heard the joyous sounds of laughter, cavorting, and half-lit people dancing around fires, to various sounds of discordant music mixing together. In the distance, we saw the sea's whitish waves lit by moonlight kissing the shore, our sturdy ship, Christine, docked at port, and the vacated, darkened, shadowy Bunkillarny below.

Captain Black had brought back a cargo from Italy along with some fireworks, which Marco Polo had discovered in China a couple hundred years ago. As I took Gwendolen's hand in mine, suddenly, the fireworks lit up the sky, the hills, and the castle. I stroked her long hair, looked into her willing eyes, and kissed her deeply; she responded in kind. We made out passionately and were lost in each other's embrace. When we finally paused, she said, "I have never experienced anything more glorious than that in my life. It was delicious. And we did it under the fireworks. I'm not sure how you arranged that, but wow! Rand, you mean so much to me. I missed you more than I can say!"

I wanted to ask her to marry me, then thought that was what she wanted me to do. She was like a sister to me. How could I do that? She was too young. A few years before, I had dated an attractive, refined, intelligent girl fresh out of college who seemed relatively immature. Not that there was the least bit wrong with her, it's just that we were at different stages in our lives. How could I marry someone so young?

The romantic moment passed, and I said, "We should return."

Looking dejected, her previously glimmering face now looked pale. With a hint of a tear in her eye, she said, "Yes, it's getting late. I guess I should go."

She walked through the turret's arched portico, down the sturdy, triangular, winding stone staircase that previously having been entwined in each other, I hadn't noticed, which now seemed so endless, going forever down, down, down. I felt terrible, for she was someone I greatly cared for, the woman who saved my life, and seeing her with her head down, despondently plodding down the staircase in front of me, not sure what I would say, I thought we needed to talk.

"Gwendolyn," I said, but she did not respond, so I said it louder, "Gwendolyn!" Still no response. With a seemingly broken heart, she ignored me, stepping ever downward now at a faster pace.

As she vanished around the curve, something unfamiliar from deep inside of me whispered, "You fool. Don't let her go!" Walking ever faster, she trying to escape me, as we finally approached the landing, I leaped down the stairs, grabbed her arm, stopped her, and stepped around her down to the landing, blocking her attempted escapes. I looked into her beautiful eyes that blinked away her tears. Then she turned her head so I could not see how upset she was. I was not sure of the protocol at this time, but knowing it must be much less involved than in the 21st century, I got down on one knee and asked her to marry me.

At first, stunned, she did not respond and looked angry as if she would reject me, and I felt I had lost her; then she struck me across my left cheek with her right hand, and the shiny brilliance returned to her face. Overjoyed, she replied, "Yes! Yes! An infinity of yeses!"

Hand in hand, higher than a bird, we flew back to the hall, and I asked Michael for his permission, which he enthusiastically granted, saying, "I have always wanted a son and could not imagine a better one. What took ye so long?"

She spread the news to our group of merchant friends, who were all overjoyed for us, the men vigorously shaking my hand, patting me on the shoulder and cracking Irish jokes about the pitfalls of marriage, the women congratulating me, telling me there is no better wife and either hugging or kissing me on the lips, which I guess was their custom.

Next, we went to the royal table and told them the news, and they, too, were elated. Queen Catherine took Gwendolyn into her arms, saying, "This will be a glorious wedding. After your marriage ceremony at the cathedral, you shall have the grand hall for your reception and anything else you desire. My dear, since your mother is in heaven, I hope you will allow me to help with the plans?"

"Yes, my queen, thank you so much!"

Carlos shook my hand vigorously, declaring, "If you had not proposed to her, I would have tried to win her hand; she is magnificent, mi amigo; congratulations, you are a mucho lucky hombre."

Francisco gave me a big bear hug and lifted me into the air, proclaiming, "I hope you are as happy as I am with my family. She is truly a beautiful woman, mi amigo. You have done very well for yourself."

Captain Black said, "You may not know this, but Gwendolyn be me goddaughter. Welcome to the family, my boy! I guess you be my godson-in-law, har, har, har!".

Lord O'Flannery grabbed my hand in one hand and with the other, patting me on the shoulder, said, "Yes, my son, welcome to the family. You are truly a welcome addition, and I will make this wedding grand."

Prince John, congratulating us, said, "I cannot imagine a better-suited pair. This will be a royal wedding, a celebration that shall help heal the shire."

King Patrick looked giddy with excitement, "What a fantastic day this has been. I cannot imagine a better ending."

I told Gwendolyn that we could honeymoon in London if she wanted. She said, "I do not know what a honey moon is, but I'd love to go to London and see cousin Colleen and meet Wynkyn, and I love you so, so much!"

"I love you! More than I could have imagined."

TWENTY-ONE

Victory

A page came to my room the next day, inviting me to attend the council meeting that afternoon, saying, "Queen Catherine decided that since all the lords had attended the games and witnessed the rebellion while they were still in the castle, she would hold the first meeting under the restored monarchy."

After wandering the dimly lit halls, I grabbed a passing page who showed me to the council room. It was yet another of the many rooms I had not yet seen at the far corner of the castle on the top floor with a pristine view of Bunkillarny, the blue bay, and the patchwork of farm-dotted hills rising up to the sky on the other side of the bay. Not much larger than the conference rooms I was accustomed to, except it was two stories high with coats of arms from the various clans and various armaments, including swords, spears, pikes, and halberds, each crossed with another, lining the walls.

King Patrick, Prince John and Queen Catherine were already there. I looked admiringly at the large, oval, walnut table in the middle when Patrick pointed out that the center consisted of a seven-foot-wide, oblong inlay cut from an ancient oak that was hundreds of years old. As I marveled at the polished grain and innumerable rings, Patrick said, "It was thought that the Druids worshiped this tree before St. Patrick's conversion back in the fifth century, and it wasn't until a fierce storm took it down that it had been cut. That was several hundred years ago. It is thought that deliberations over this table have power, and with the holy tree as our witness, we should conduct ourselves with dignity, understanding and fairness."

As each member arrived, they enthusiastically greeted each other. In his regal robes, Patrick introduced Catherine, who took control of the meeting, which was impressive in this male-dominated era. However, she was the remaining regent and King Edward's most trusted adviser, who knew the shire's political inner workings and customs. After all, she managed the large castle's staff, leaving Edward to deal with matters of state. I thought it might be difficult for the men to follow her lead, but they all had immense respect for her. I also wondered how a 15th-century meeting might transpire, but similar to any meeting, that depended on the leader and Catherine was up to the challenge.

The first order of business was to select the council members, which included the four rebel lords, the bishop representing the church, and Lord Buckingham's heir whose lands Reginald had confiscated, which would be restored to his family. As expected, Michael would return to his role on the council. To my surprise, I was to be a council member; Queen Catherine saying, "Edward had a great amount of respect for you and liked you. Given your valuable knowledge, Edward had considered adding you. After your role in regaining the crown, we wanted you to provide your wisdom, and you seem to have insight into the future." I was incredibly honored that someone who I had so much respect for cared for me.

Three other lords would be added, according to their loyalty and performance, to be determined at a later time. There was skepticism regarding some of the other lords due to their positions and closeness to Reginald—no doubt they would deny their involvement with Reginald, which would require purposeful deliberations to ferret out.

A trial of Reginald and Boston would be scheduled. Lord Southwick, who attended the meeting as an adviser, would be the judge, who said he required two weeks to gather evidence. The "loyal" knights, including Hugh, would also be tried.

Patrick interjected, "I will abdicate the throne in favor of my brother. The only reason I was installed was due to Reginald's scheming and betrayal of John, which was not legitimate." The lords and bishop advised him to wait until after the trial, giving the shire time to heal and organize a suitable coronation, which would further help restore confidence in the kingdom.

Other than those normally attached to the castle, the troops would be restored to their clans. The castle's troops would be assessed and asked to pledge loyalty to the crown. The new pubs and brothels would be closed, something that would greatly please the inhabitants of Bunkillarny. In addition, Michael's printshop would be immediately restored to him, as would the lands that Reginald had surreptitiously seized along with their valuables that he and his loyal knights seized.

I was so glad to see how fast all of these decisions were made, for in my time, it seemed to take months or even years for the wheels of justice to turn, something I could not understand when our economic sectors and computerized systems moved so rapidly. An item ordered from Amazon would arrive the next day, whereas it might take months to prosecute a murder or years to prosecute illegal business dealings.*

Queen Catherine and Michael prevailed upon us to hold off on our wedding until after the coronation. This gave us plenty of time to get to know each other as a couple. Michael said it would be scandalous for me to live any longer in the same house as Gwendolyn, so Catherine insisted I stay at the castle.

Riding Chester back and forth to the print shop every day resembled my usual commute in San Francisco, except it was much closer, and thankfully, there were no rush hour traffic jams to endure.

While there, Queen Catherine invited me to dine with her, Patrick, John, Lord Southam, and whatever nobles happened to be staying at the castle. I enjoyed the stimulating, intellectual conversations, especially during this heady, optimistic period in Bunkillarny's history. Although appreciative, I cautioned myself not to become too used to royal living, for I knew it would not last. One fortunate outcome of attending these dinners was that the educational program King Edward had commenced would be reinstated and many children throughout Bunkillarny would have the opportunity to read, write and learn math.

As we dined on roast duck in a plum sauce, I told them about my experiences in Spain and London, "While in Salamanca, I stayed near the university, including Cambridge and Oxford, one of the five most prominent colleges in the world, where King Edward and you, John, attended. Their library, where I acquired all those fabulous books, is the oldest in Europe. Prominent Spanish families, such as the Alvarezes, sponsor various colleges within the university, and Queen Isabella herself funds the entire university. She feels that after conquering all of Spain, they will need many learned men to build their new nation."

King Henry's mother, Margaret, sponsors a soirée with intellectuals. Similarly, she funds colleges within the famous universities and even a primary school."

Queen Catherine said, "I can see how education will help our shire, especially in this changing world. We should expand our college here and ensure it has the best professors and books. In fact, we should endeavor to entice professors from Oxford and Cambridge to teach here. If they will not come permanently, perhaps they will come for a year or two and enjoy our Irish hospitality. And with your print shop right here, we should be able to supply our students with the best books that will accelerate their learning."

"Edward loved reading books, funding books for the university, and would want to sponsor such programs. During this time of Renaissance, my homeland in France is embracing many new ideas and printing millions of books. There, reading is spreading like the plague, and I have heard the same is true on the Italian Peninsula and the Germanic provinces. Plus, I can see how expanding our education will give us a strategic advantage over the other Irish shires, beefing up our intellectual capacity thereby making us more able to deal with adversities. As it is now, the university attracts students from throughout Ireland, as well as Scotland and England. As they have before, some of these students will stay, enhancing opportunities for our shire. Similar to Margaret and Isabella, I shall sponsor education here in Bunkillarny, and we shall start by funding our university. We shall build King Edward Hall in remembrance of my dear departed husband. It will be immense and will be established to educate teachers, promote literature, and advance the study of science and agriculture."*

Michael could not wait to work on the books I purchased in Spain and immediately began setting these up, starting with the works of Seneca. He also found time to send out copies of the Bunkillarny Reader. Reginald's and Boston's propaganda campaign had corralled many people—something he wanted to counter. In the Reader, he covered the torrent of events surrounding the reclamation of the throne and refuted Boston's claims regarding Prince John, Nealland, the battle, etc.

Fortunately, neither Boston nor Hugh had discovered my prized manuscripts at the bottom of the crate, the books from Caxton, the first to be printed in the English language, along with the original Gutenberg Bible. I still planned to take these back to the 21st century, where they would be worth tens of millions.

Even though Gwendolyn and I had lived together at the shop and in the cave, we had never really dated—something that did not seem to matter much these days. People did not waste much time dating or on long engagements. Overseen by a guardian, you saw each other a few times over maybe a month and got hitched. Come to think of it, that's how it was until the 1950s and 60s when my grandparents were married. I guess because of the depression and wars, many of my friend's grandparents did the same—dated a few times and got married. When life is precious, as it was after the Great Depression and World War II, you don't waste time before repopulating the species. *

While riding our horses, Gwendolyn showed me an obscure path off the main road that led down to a broad, white sandy beach I did not know existed. The relatively flat approach, with its tall grasses and sandy inlets, would make a wonderful links golf course someday. Taking our shoes off, we held hands, kissed, and walked along the seemingly endless beach, dipping our toes in the water, warmed by the sun's rays penetrating the white sand. When I hiked up my pants and went in up to my knees, I realized I did not want to swim in the cold bay. Feeling all was right with the world, we laid down on the beach and cuddled.

Induced by the sun's restoring rays, I soon fell into a delicious beach nap. Upon waking, I looked out to the sea that had been but a dozen feet away, which had vanished and was now 150 feet out, where I saw Gwendolyn with that previously unexplained bucket she had tied to her horse, now searching for cockles. As dusk approached, the sky illuminated the striated clouds in iridescent purples, violets and brilliant reds, the bright orange orb slowly retreating behind the hills and mountains on the opposite shore to its rest. As the sun slowly ducked behind the sea, we witnessed the spectacular, fabled green flash—amazing! Gwendolyn said, "The saints be blessin' us, they are."

In the twilight, I gathered up driftwood, made a fire, and boiled the cockles over an open flame. Gwendolyn had some bread and butter and garlic that, after we drained most of the liquid, we added to the bucket. It was delicious.

The beach, where we rarely saw another soul, became our special place. On warmer days, we would bring books and lay on the beach reading to ourselves or to each other. I would sculpt out a curvaceous loveseat in the sand for us to be more comfortable.

I knew that some couples did not discuss basic things such as how many children they wanted, something I promised myself not to let go by. She said, "I would like as many bern as God intended us to have. But, I would like to name our first son Michael."

"I would hope to have four or possibly five children," I said.

"I know nothing of your family. How many children did your parents have?"

I considered avoiding such questions by using my standard amnesia excuse, but since we would be sharing our lives together, I wanted to be honest, "I have two older brothers and two older sisters."

"So, you're the youngest too."

"Yes"

We talked about where we would live once we were married, and she said, "There is a delightful cottage just off the main road in town. Poor Mrs. Murphy died recently, and I heard it will be for sale. Since you are his partner now, I expect me da will lend us the money to buy it. It's the prettiest cottage in town, with a kitchen and a beautiful yard with a large willow tree overlooking the river. I know you enjoy reading by the river, so we can build a bench above the stream to read together.

Ryan can build us a slough to bring water to the house for an inhouse and the kitchen sink, as you invented fer me da's house. This will save me walking to the river to fetch it. It has two bedrooms—one for us, one for the girls, and the boys can sleep above in the attic. There's a barn for Chester and space for a surrey, in which we can transport all of our bern."

"Rand, I am going to be the best wife ever. I be cookin' and a cleenin' and raisin' our bern. I'll keep the homefire a burnin' whilst you be a working, and ye can come home to a tasty meal every eve. Just you wait and see."

I was a bit shocked by this last statement. Gwendolyn, with her feisty temper, her critical contributions at the shop and her teaching, seemed like a modern woman to me, not to mention her sword-wielding ferocity. I realized that in this time, women were tied to the home. In my time, there were options. Sure, some ladies stayed home to care for the kids, which is great but not required by society. Still, without modern appliances, taking care of kids and a home these days was a 60-hour-a-week job.

I was amazed at all Daisy did. Stoves would not be invented for centuries, so the apprentices would bring in the wood to stoke the fire in the kitchen's hearth, where Daisy would cook over an open flame using a variety of hooks, utensils and big cast iron kettles that John fashioned. Breakfast always had porridge, brown bread and sometimes bacon, eggs, or sausages, but there would be no potatoes until after Columbus returned from the Americas.

Since there were no refrigerators or supermarkets and only the wealthy lords had ovens, she would have to visit the baker, grosser, fruit vendor and the butcher or fishmonger nearly every day to obtain our provisions. All the roads were made of dirt that became muddy and ended up in the house, therefore without vacuum cleaners, dusting and cleaning the floors took hours. Monday was laundry day when she would spend the entire day rubbing clothes against rocks in the river. And of course there were no dishwashers, so she would have to wash all the pots and pans and dishes by hand. With all the work she had to do, it is no wonder that she appreciated not carrying a couple of buckets to the river to fetch water, for I had invented a way to bring it to the kitchen.

Since there were no refrigerators or supermarkets and only the wealthy lords had ovens, Daisy would spend her mornings gathering fresh foods. She visited the baker, the grocer, the fruit vendor and the butcher or fishmonger every day except Sunday. All the roads were made of dirt that became muddy and accumulated inside; therefore, without a vacuum cleaner, dusting and sweeping the floors took a substantial amount of time. Mondays were the laundry day when she would spend the entire day rubbing clothes against rocks in the river. And, of course, there were no dishwashers, so she would have to wash all the pots, pans and dishes by hand. Since I had devised a way to bring water into the house, with all the work she had to do, it is no wonder Daisy appreciated not not having to carry all that water every day.

I didn't mind Gwendolyn working at home, but there was so much work to do these days. Coming home to a warm homecooked meal would be nice, but I was afraid she would become unhappy and unfulfilled, cooped up in a small bungalow all day. It also bothered me that women were such an untapped resource these days. After all, that is what drove the economy of the late 20th century when women finally were able to obtain more education and entered the workforce in record numbers, nearly doubling our productivity.

I had to pursue it further, "Gwen, would you want to give up all you do for the shop—the accounting, the editing and the teaching? Your sister, Megan, works there sometimes creating our artwork. Would you want to, too?"

"Well, I ha' ner thought about that because I always envisioned meself at me home once I married. Sure, a few women like Mrs. McNab work at the pub or shop, but she only has the twins. Most women ha' six to ten bern that survives and are constantly pregnant."

"If that is what you want to do, that is fine with me."

"Ye know, I have spent so much time building our busness, I would like to keep a doing it. And there be no one else who can keep the books. Da certainly can't. But Megan had permission from her husband to work. Would you grant me such permission, Rand?"

"Certainly, we could hire a part-time maid. Daisy has a younger sister who might fill the role."

"Thank ye, Rand." Then, she wrapped her arms around me and gave me a big kiss. "You are such a good man. I'll still be a makin' your dinners, though."

She asked, "Tell me more about your family and where you come from. I know you remember now."

This was a question I had been avoiding. I knew I had to tell her I came from the 21st century, San Francisco and America, and what I did there, but I did not know how to approach the subject—my developing apps. An app, how could she possibly understand something so esoteric that exists in an imaginary cloud? How could she believe me? Like when she first cared for me, would she think I was crazy and cut off the engagement? To be honest, I had to tell her before the wedding. It would not be right not to tell her. I began searching my mind for a way to explain it to her when, from behind us, I heard our names called out. Turning, we saw the thin, fit, pretty McNab twins, Shannon and Sharon, dancing along the beach as if they were at the bar Irish dancing. They had no idea, but thankfully, they saved me—at least for now.*

Sir Southam asked me to help him gather accounting evidence against Boston, something Lady Catherine suggested. With the help of a disgruntled senior bookkeeper, who did not condone Boston's schemes, we found that he and Reginald had skimmed hundreds of pounds from the shire's coffers—amounting to a large fortune.

The trial commenced as planned in the large, packed main hall. Thinking that the royals would be seen as biased to those who still supported Reginald, Sir Southam would preside as the judge. Since he had gathered evidence, this would probably not be allowed in a 21st-century courtroom, but the Irish justice system was still evolving. Lady Catherine hired Stanforth to handle the case. Reginald acquired an equally renowned Dublin lawyer to defend them.

One by one, Lord Southam read off the charges:

1. Instigating an unjustified war between Neilland and Donegal.

2. Treason for attacking Prince John at the Battle of Neilland.

3. Illegally appropriating over 2,000 pounds from the crown.

4. Poisoning of King Patrick.

5. Attempted rape of Queen Catherine and attacking King Patrick.

6. Pursuing and attacking King Patrick and Queen Catherine at the port as they tried to escape and murdering the royal guards.

7. Conspiring the assassination of Prince John, King Patrick and Queen Catherine in London.

8. Bombing of the Neilland guard post and killing four loyal

Bunkillarny soldiers.

In exchange for leniency for her testimony against Reginald, the woman scorned, Brehana produced the poison potion that Reginald acquired from her and administered to King Patrick. She said, "I did no ken who the poison was intended for and thought it would be used only to make that person sick." In return for her testimony, she would be granted safe passage to Scotland, where, using her well-honed, feminine wiles and perhaps a love potion, she would likely attach herself to some wealthy lord there.

During the trial, the ordinarily confident Reginald looked grim and sweated profusely, emitting a foul odor. Accustomed to their luxurious quarters, he and Boston did not enjoy their time in jail. As the trial played out over three days, they heard progressively more boos when they entered the hall. While waiting for the trial, Reginald wrote a note to King Rory of Donegal asking him to intercede on his behalf, which he gave to a loyal guard to deliver to the king immediately. King Rory responded in no uncertain terms that he considered him a disloyal cur and would have nothing to do with him.

Towards the end of the trial, Stanforth called a surprise witness. Boston, hoping for consideration, mimicking repentance and ignorance, told the jury composed of twelve peer council members and nobles that he had been present when King Edward died. Instead of helping his King, who had been thrown off his horse, Reginald gave the king his hand, then withdrew it, causing the beloved King to fall to his death. The regicide alone was enough to sentence Reginald to drawing and quartering.

It took the jurors less than two hours to convict Reginald on all nine counts and sentence him to multiple death sentences. The trial's large audience did not want to wait for the execution but rather threatened to grab him and tear him limb from limb. Sir Southwick said that he would transmit Reginald to London, where he would be tried for the attempted regicide, the drawing and quartering, and execution to be fulfilled there. The royals did not protest this, for they feared a possible counter-uprising from those still loyal to him, and having him out of the country would allow the shire to heal.

Instead of being drawn and quartered, in exchange for his testimony, Boston would be exiled from the British Isles—a more merciful sentence. Hugh, the knight, was sentenced to five years.

Michael published a daily account of the trials in the Reader. The council members sensed that attitudes towards Reginald had dramatically shifted from that of a hero and noble leader to that of a conniving traitor, the people wondering why they ever supported him.

Afterward, life in Bunkillarny settled back to peaceful normality. The brothel and troublesome bars were closed. It was as if a devastating storm had passed by the sun was shining, and everyone seemed even more joyous and friendly than before. When the second press arrived from Germany, all of us at the print shop celebrated its arrival.

Seamus was fired and left for Dublin, where he threatened to build a print shop. By taking away the major market in Ireland, he would crush us. Michael did not fear this because Seamus did not possess the education, patience, language or business skills required to lead such a venture to success, plus he would find it difficult to acquire financial backers.

To increase our throughput with the second press, Michael hired three more apprentices and promoted the two we already had, including Tommy to journeyman. One of the advantages of the reading classes was that Gwendolyn could assess those who would be promising apprentices. One such standout was Sean, John's youngest son, an intelligent young man with superior language and mechanical abilities. We all spent a substantial amount of time training the new lads, which took us away from our regular duties and reduced our productivity for a while—the way it always is.

Soon, Michael and I dove into the Spanish treasures; he did most of the layout and translations to English while I did the type setting. I fired up my iPhone and looked up each of the prized works from Salamanca. I was stunned to see that one, in particular, was not listed in Wikipedia—a book by Plato similar to his Republic, which he evidently wrote afterward. I read this 2,000-year-old manuscript and was amazed at the philosophical insights it revealed and the wisdom it contained, for it was a bridge between the thinking of Socrates and Aristotle that would have inspired Alexander to conquer the known world.

Plato's grand work included texts on how to organize, seize, and rule lands, like Machiavelli's Prince 2,000 years later. It would add to the world's understanding of Greek philosophy, to be studied by students throughout the ages, and was a work that would still be relevant in the 21st century. I was proud that I had recovered this important work, which would have been lost to mankind. However, I was not sure if we should print it for fear it might alter history. Perhaps I should take it back with me, and release it in the 21st century when it would not alter the future.

Encouraged by this remarkable finding, I examined the remaining treasures, including several plays by the fifth-century BC Greek tragedian Euripides. In Wikipedia, I read that only eighteen of his ninety-plus plays had survived intact, while for his others, there were only fragments. The copy of the papyrus scroll I held in my hand contained a collection of his plays, including four that had been lost forever, with every word clearly visible, and three that had never been seen in the future.

I remember studying one of his most famous plays in college—Media. As I recall the plot:

The hero, Jason of Jason and the Argonauts, had taken Princess Medea as his wife. They lived happily in Corinth for twenty years and had two sons until Jason decided to marry a younger Princess. Medea sought revenge, and after a dreadful mental struggle, she decided to punish her husband by murdering the princess and her sons, thereby leaving him to grow old with neither wife nor child.

I also found three out of the over sixty lost plays of Aeschylus, the father of Greek tragedy. Other manuscripts were not listed in Wikipedia that also would have been lost to mankind but were not monumental enough to have the potential to alter history.

I hid the scroll under a board under my bed that might contain a fifth gospel of Christ. I promised not to disclose the existence of this until I had permission from Father Dominic, and if he told me to do so, I would tragically have to burn it. Of all the remarkable works I had discovered, this was the most remarkable. To think it contained unknown stories and words of Christ. I wish I could read it, but I could not understand ancient Aramaic.

While Gwendolyn taught reading, I began teaching the arithmetic classes, I enjoyed, especially since some of the brighter students would soon be ready for more advanced math.

While Michael and I were working on a particularly tough layout for the Moorish algebra book, he mentioned, "Partner, something we should consider is to visit Rome to acquire the Roman Empire's works as you have so successfully done in Spain. Italy is, after all, the center of the literacy revolution—even more so than Germany or Paris and far beyond London. It is a renaissance of the Romans' art, literature, and science 1,000 -1,500 years ago, building on that legacy and stretching into the future."

Michael continued, "This would be a continuation of the work that John commenced here in Ireland, then in London and Spain. Once we have built up our completed titles, you could travel to London to bring the books to Colleen and deliver the promised books to the Queen Mother. Then you could travel to Spain, and Granada to deliver Queen Isabella's books. And then, travel to Rome to acquire their literary treasures, for us to print in English for the first time."

"Michael, that is a wonderful idea. Gwendolyn and I had planned a honeymoon in London, and I would like to take her to Spain, too, to meet the Alvarezes, especially Sophia, who would be like a sister to her. Traveling to Rome would be an added pleasure." I thought that traveling to Italy, the focus of the Renaissance, would be much safer than traveling through Spain, where I had to face all those banditos. And Granada was near the coast, so I would not have to spend weeks traveling through central Spain.

"We will have to think more about this because it will be a large expense, and without the two of you here for such a long time, we will not be able to produce as many books. Since she, more than my other daughters, enjoyed my stories about sailing the seas so much, I know Gwendolyn would relish such an adventure. It could be your dowry."

"That sounds wonderful, Michael!"*

After the trial, Patrick announced his abdication so his brother could assume the throne—an act that the royals and council had feared might cause consternation. The abdication was surprisingly well-received thanks to Michael's series of articles in the Reader on Prince John.

Most subjects thought Patrick was too young, that Reginald betrayed John, and that as the eldest son, John was the legitimate heir anyway. In this case, the pen was indeed mightier than the sword.

I wondered how these changes would have transpired throughout the shire without the Reader. As far as I knew, it was the first circulated newsletter in European history. Without the Reader, some subjects may still have favored Reginald. Others may have resisted John's ascension to the throne, while for many, the pace of change would have seemed too rapid and confusing. Still, only a tiny portion of the populace could read, but even the serfs would hear a more accurate story from those who could. Putting something down on paper avoided the constant, telephone-like mis-telling of the facts.

Plans for the coronation proceeded at a rapid pace. John insisted that Captain Black, Carlos and Francisco stay for the ceremony because he wanted to honor them for risking their lives for himself and his family. Our wedding would be scheduled for late spring/early summer. I asked Francisco to be my best man. He replied, "I shall bring my beautiful wife and perhaps even my children. You are, after all, beloved members of our family."

"Please bring any of the Alvarez Clan that would like to make the Journey, especially Carlos's brother Jose, father, Diego, and their mother. They are all invited. I hope our hospitality matches theirs." Carlos promised he would be there with his brother Juan, and although they had never been out of Spain, he expected his parents to join them. Captain Black said he would not miss his goddaughter's wedding and, as a present, would provide free passage in his best cabin to London for the wedding couple. He would soon travel to London with Lord Southam, the royal guards and Reginald in chains.

The days passed effortlessly as if I was fated to be a 15th-century printer—a thought that initially bothered me until I realized how similar printing was to Web page layout. To break up the monotony of type-setting, I periodically pulled the devil's tail to obtain a workout—one as good as going to the gym, except that rather than just working my muscles, I was simultaneously producing something of value—book pages. The apprentices did not mind a break from the tiring devil's tail.

As these fantastic books were bound, I would look at the growing stacks with a sense of pride, thinking that we would soon distribute these throughout Ireland, the British Isles, and Spain, as well as the other Latin versions throughout Europe. Unlike 21st-century paperbacks or hardbound books, these were built to last for decades and possibly survive the centuries to come. People in the 21st century regularly discard their paperbacks, which were not designed to last, and many would only read the electronic versions. In contrast, their owners treasured these leatherbound hardbacks meant to be passed down to their children and grandchildren. They would populate shelves of learned families and prominent libraries and universities throughout Europe: at Cambridge, Oxford, Salamanca, Barcelona, the Sorbonne, Heidelberg, etc. The ideas they contained would help to enhance the world and fuel the Renaissance, thereby influencing generations to come.

In the back of my mind, I wondered how I would explain my origins to Gwendolyn. I enjoyed my life in Bunkillarny, its people, and printing these fantastic books, but periodically, I terribly missed my own place and time. I thought about the prospect of taking Gwendolyn back there. She had felt the tingling in the cave, too, so I assumed she could join me. She was a remarkable and beautiful woman, who all my family and friends (Paul, Betty, Jenny, Wes, Mike) would adore, but I was not sure if she would enjoy 21st-century San Francisco with all those people, noise, and congestion. It would be an attack on her senses. On the other hand, compared to northern Ireland, the weather was marvelous; there were all those modern conveniences and innumerable books to read.

If she did not like the city, we could always move to a more remote area, such as Carmel or Santa Rosa, where I could work remotely. Of course, if I could take the treasured texts back with us, we would be set for life and could acquire a house on a California beach. I knew I needed to talk to her about all this before we wed, but somehow kept putting it off. Would she think I was insane? Would she call off the wedding? If she did believe me, would she want to stay here? Would I lose her? After all I had been through, this was a prospect I could not endure.

Rob's literary journey began by writing scores of proposals, presentations and business reports, which led to authoring books that successfully predicted the future of the Web and the course of the U.S. economy. Based on his father's Olympic Diary and scrapbook, he delved into the golden decade of sports when his dad was a world class athlete in football and track winning the first US medal at the Chariots of Fire Olympics. Fascinated by how history predicts the future, he began writing fictional works regarding time travel and the similarities between the current digital revolution and the transformative printing revolution of the 15th/16th century that gave birth to the Renaissance and Enlightenment.

Rob possesses a BS in systems analysis and operations research from Miami University, along with an MBA in Policy and Organizational Behavior from Case Western Reserve University. In addition to being a leader in four national/international associations, Rob has been a guest columnist for the Cleveland Plain Dealer. He has conducted numerous presentations for dozens of universities and management groups on various leading-edge topics. As a management consultant, he served as the regional practice manager for Towers Watson, where he wrote the white paper and business plan to found its successful quarter-billion-dollar systems line of business (2025 dollars).

Earlier, he served as a hospital CIO and project manager for TRW, which launched the first satellite to leave Earth's orbit, designed the fastest chip and search engine and operated the first worldwide satellite network. TRW also built the rocket engines that flew man to the moon and owned Atari, where Steve Jobs first worked. While at TRW, Rob constructed its financial models and managed its largest corporate project. He designed and implemented over 60 human resource, healthcare, and financial systems and has consulted on behalf of dozens of *S&P 500* companies, including Kraft, Sherwin Williams, Verizon, GE, Toyota, Goodyear, BP, Bank America, JP Morgan Chase, Callaway Golf, Qualcomm, Northrop Grumman, Parker Hannifin, Eaton, Scripps Clinic and the Cleveland Clinic. Always on the bleeding edge of technology, Rob learned a couple dozen languages on numerous platforms.

Also by Robert D. Oberst

In addition to numerous articles on various technical and non-technical topics, Rob Oberst has published five other books thus far, all of which travel backward or forward in time and are based on history.

Time Traveler 1491: Transported Back to 15th-Century Ireland, Rand Joins the Global Revolution.

When venture capitalists steal his lucrative app, Rand seeks solace on a backpacking expedition to the bottom of the Grand Canyon, where he slips and is swept into the turbulent rapids. Nearly drowned, battered, and bruised, he seeks refuge in a hidden cave, where a mysterious galvanic force overcomes him. Barely able to move, he wakes in the bed of a beautiful maiden who nurses him back to health. While recovering, her father, Ireland's first printer, teaches him the revolutionary profession that, similar to the Web five centuries later, is transforming the world. Becoming embroiled in castle politics but unskilled in their weapons, Rand has one advantage—a downloaded copy of Wikipedia on his iPhone, which he must access judiciously before its battery dies.

2020 Web Vision: How the Internet Will Revolutionize Future Homes, Business, and Society,

This book appears in over two dozen countries and at universities on five continents, including Harvard. It accurately predicts how virtual technology transforms our world and empowers us, especially during the devastating pandemic. Published over 20 years ago, *2020 Web Vision* was remarkably prescient in predicting what transpired over those two decades, including working at home through virtual technologies, online shopping, grocery delivery, robotic assistants such as Siri and Alexa, the decline of malls, the vacating of corporate offices, AI and the changing migration patterns towards more desirable locations. According to its prophecies, we are in phase one of the Web's evolution, with much more to follow.

The Financial Time Machine: Predicting Our Economic Future

Based on the generations' economic behavior, generational economics forecast the Great Recession and the stagnant course of the U.S. and major world economies for over a decade, including the dangers facing us in the 2020s, such as inflation, ultra-low unemployment, stagflation, and a growing mountain of debt. This book analyzes the various generations, their economic behavior, and the cycle that has shaped our economy back to the Civil War and will continue to play a key role in our future.

Olympian, All-American & National Football Champion—Gene 'Kentuck' Oberst: Rockne Protégé

Gene grew up crippled in a Twain-like Ohio River town, then overcame his handicap to become a national championship Notre Dame football player and an All-American who won the first medal for the U.S. in the *Chariots of Fire,* Paris Olympics—the only American javelin medal in the Olympics' first fifty years.

Renaissance Olympian: Mentored by Rockne, Gene Oberst becomes a Renowned Coach, Professor & Artist

The story picks up after Oberst wins the first U.S. medal at the Paris Olympics, the first time the American flag flew over an Olympic Stadium, and travels to Louisiana to be St. Johns College's founding four-sport coach, athletic director, trainer, and janitor. As portrayed in fifty letters between Gene and his mentor, Knute Rockne (America's winningest football coach), Gene faces numerous challenges, but Rockne is always there to help. Indeed, he may not have married his wife, Catherine, if not for Rock.